# FLYING
# CROOKED

ISBN: 978-1-946886-53-8

Cover design by Rachel Kelli

Published by
Middle River Press
Oakland Park, Florida
middleriverpress.com

First Printing
Printed in the USA

# FLYING CROOKED

A NOVEL

## STEVE BORGESS

MIDDLE
RIVER
PRESS

*For my father,*

*Joseph S. Borgess*

*Gear up, July 20, 1924—Gear down, May 24, 2022*

*A daring pilot in extremity;*
*Pleas'd with the danger, when the waves went*
*high*
*He sought the storms; but for a calm unfit,*
*Would steer to nigh the sands, to boast his wit.*
*Great wits are sure to madness near alli'd,*
*And thin partitions do their bounds divide.*

—John Dryden

*Absalom and Achitophel*

# PROLOGUE

*Miami International Airport, April 6, 1979*

Captain Jacob Kegan was Air Logistics' chief pilot, currently an executive in a gray tailored suit but a man better suited to his uniform. He was tall, brush-cut, and barrel-chested, with the flinty gaze of a battle-hardened general. His hazel eyes were framed by deep crow's feet, and his brow was permanently knit from decades scanning the sky for trouble: towering squall lines, gray ice-laden clouds, Messerschmitt fighters bearing down on him, guns blazing yellow.

Today the trouble was with the FAA. As he climbed the three-story block and steel stairwell to his office, he was fuming. With the release of the NTSB aircraft accident report he was holding in his hand, the Feds at the Miami Flight Standards District Office had informed him they'd be conducting a safety audit of his airline. Although Kegan's company had no connection with the airplane or airline involved in the crash, the accident had caught the Feds with their head up their ass—and now they were going to stick it up everyone else's.

What a shitstorm the FAA was brewing. There'd be new operating procedures, more crew training, more maintenance inspections, more paperwork, more operating manual revisions—more of the whole damn lot of it. Not only would the FAA and his company headquarters have Kegan tied down for months to come, but this mess would shred his wife's social calendar as well.

He carried the accident report rolled like a club in his right hand, swearing under his breath as he reached the top landing and entered the antechamber to his office. When he passed his secretary's desk, he growled, "Hold my calls," without so as much as a glance at his venerable aide.

She nodded and fixed her gaze on the blue-jacketed booklet in his hand.

She'd heard the rumors, bore the scandal: the flight crew's incompetence, the damning violations of standard maintenance and safety procedures that the NTSB had uncovered and named as contributing causes to the crash. She knew the crew. Her estranged husband was a captain for that airline.

Kegan tramped into his office and closed the door behind him. Tossing the report on his desk, he went to the window behind it. The mid-afternoon sun was blazing, and he squinted against the glare as he pulled the blinds shut.

He turned, pulled back his chair, and sat down at his desk. Donning his glasses, he reached for the report. Dust motes swirled in the striated sunlight, and a fan gyrated lazily above his head. The tick of a wall clock was the only sound in the room.

Kegan studied the cover of the report like a Celt regarding an insult by the enemy of his clan.

NATIONAL TRANSPORTATION SAFETY BOARD
AIRCRAFT ACCIDENT REPORT
CONTROLLED FLIGHT INTO TERRAIN
JETSTREAM INTERNATIONAL AIRLINES FLIGHT 1023
DOUGLAS DC-8-21, N804PA
KATUNAYAKE INTERNATIONAL AIRPORT
COLOMBO, SRI LANKA
OCTOBER 26, 1978

Controlled flight into terrain meant the pilots had flown a functioning airplane into the ground. It was a scathing indictment of their skill and professionalism. But Kegan had known one of the men involved personally since they'd flown Lockheed Constellations together for Malayan Airways back in the '50s.

He rocked back in his chair and tossed the report on his blotter. Removing his readers, he turned and studied the collection of photos and model aircraft on the bookshelves across from his desk, artifacts he'd collected over his decades flying for non-scheduled airlines. The non-scheds took the toughest and most dangerous jobs in the industry, and Kegan had always been proud of his role with them. The queens of the industry—American, Pan Am, TWA, United, and the rest—could keep their glamour. Kegan had always preferred it right where he was, doing the work that required the greatest skill airline flying demanded.

But, from the FAA's and NTSB's perspective, there was no distinction among airlines. The Feds expected the same level of regulation compliance from them all, whether the airline carried pampered American tourists on vacation to Europe, provincial Mali pilgrims on the hajj to Mecca, delivered businessmen to a junket in Las Vegas, or brought food and critical medical supplies to a war-ravaged people in Sudan.

It took the type of people willing to break rules to get those tougher jobs done, the type of pilots who wouldn't scruple over exceeding a crosswind limit on an icy runway in Ypsilanti or balk at landing amidst the clatter of small arms fire during a brutal civil war. It took the type of flight attendants who didn't become unhinged when a humble pilgrim attempted to make a cooking fire in the aisle or urinated in a seat pocket. Men and women who knew when the rules were out and the mission was in, and the world needed them.

*Just ask the US State Department … or the DoD … or the goddamn CIA for crissakes*, Kegan mused. *Ask them who they keep in their Rolodex for jobs like those. It damn sure isn't United, Delta, or Pan Am, is it?*

He rocked forward and sneered as he reached for the report. Putting on his glasses, he sat back and perused it. He'd seen many of these in the course of his career, the pages upon pages of excruciating detail, every nut, every bolt, every procedure examined, and yet, as Kegan so often suspected, the most important detail of all was always missing. Because in an accident like this—an accident where the cause was buried in the hearts and minds of the pilots rather than in the aircraft or the processes—you had to know those men as Kegan did, and the FAA and the NTSB did not. And there was only one place to look to prove that:

Appendix D – Cockpit Voice Recorder transcript..........page 75.

He turned to the transcript and began to read.

The Cockpit Voice Recorder recorded the crew's voices and cockpit sounds during the flight's last thirty minutes on a continuous loop. Although CVR transcripts are colorless and sanitized (hash marks and asterisks in place of the men's unintelligible words and expletives), Kegan imagined the scene: the black of night, lightning flashing through turgid clouds, the weary visages of the crew. And then, there it was. The evidence he was certain he'd find. He circled the entry at 2341:30.3 and continued reading.

When he finished, he closed the booklet and put it on his desk. Taking off his readers, he looked toward the bookshelf in his office and cleared his throat as his eyes welled with tears.

• • •

INTRA-COCKPIT DIALOG AND SOUNDS

CAM (Cockpit Area Mic); CAM 1 (Captain); CAM 3 (Flt. Engineer).

| TIME&<br>SOURCE | CONTENT |
|---|---|
| 2339:40.4<br>CAM | [sound similar to that of heavy rain] |

2341:23.2
CAM 3                        more ahead…see it?…*radar

2341:26.8
CAM 1                        yeah…uh…okay, want to break it off…go-around?

2341:30.3
CAM 3                        your call…*…your call #

2341:32.4
CAM 1                        okay…uh…but, how is he?

2341:35.1
CAM 3                        …*… not good

2341:37.5
CAM 1                        okay…okay…continue…uh…okay…then…uh…flaps ten

2341:38.2
CAM                          [sound similar to that of flap lever actuation]

2341:45.7
CAM                          [sound similar to that of stabilizer trim actuation]

2345:42.2
CAM 3                        here it comes…glide slope, keep it coming.

2346:38.8
CAM 3                        uh…okay…gear down…uh…flaps twenty-five

2346:45.2
CAM                          [sound similar to that of landing gear extension]

2347:29.6
CAM 1                        flaps full

2347:50.3
CAM                    [sound similar to that of flap lever activation]

2348:05.7
CAM 3                  gear lights?

2348:10.7
CAM 1                  three green

2348:17.4
CAM                    [sound similar to that of engine power increase]

2350:08.8
CAM 3                  flaps…wing slots?

2350:55.3
CAM 1                  light out

2353:30.9
CAM 3                  seven dme, late, late, faster…now…now…go now…

2353:35.7
CAM 1                  crossing altitude was, uh…okay…I'll keep it coming

2353:54.2
CAM 3                  hydraulic system…checked

2353:58.1
CAM 1                  okay…sink two thousand…here it comes…

2354:09.6
CAM                    [sound similar to that of heavy rain]

2354:18.3
CAM 3                  final checks completed…cleared to land…* ready for a cold #

2354:28.7
CAM 1                   ah…okay…okay…crossing altitude was…ah

2354:33.8
CAM 3                   more on the other side there…* radar…see it? see it?

2355:25.7
CAM 3                   hey…what the #…what's that? [loudly]

2355:28.8
CAM 1                   oh my god [loudly] that's…oh # [loudly]

2355:30.2
CAM 3                   pull up…oh# # [loudly]

2355:34.6
CAM                     [sound of impact – end of tape]

*Part One*

# CLIMB

# ONE

I t was 2:00 a.m. on a Friday and their fourth night of flying that week. As the vintage DC-3 crossed over Groton, Connecticut, the sky was clear, the air calm, and the airplane's Pratt and Whitney engines resonated with a baritone growl. Inside the cockpit, the instruments were lit with a warm, candle-like glow and Captain Jack Dolan, age twenty-six, gazed blearily at the scene ahead: the lights of Long Island in the distance, the black void of the Sound cleaving luminous shores, and a waning moon low on the western horizon.

He looked down and massaged his eyes.

Ed, his copilot, was looking at him and chuckled. "You look like shit," he said.

Jack shifted his gaze east and flipped him the bird.

Ed smiled and scanned his instruments. Ed was flying the leg from Boston to Philadelphia. The airplane was loaded with Flight 508's usual mix of priority freight: machine parts, hazardous chemicals, two pallets of lab rats, and the miscellaneous boxes they'd loaded at Logan International. Their route that night had begun in Philly at 9:00 p.m. and proceeded to Newark, New Jersey. From there they went to Boston and were now returning to Philly. If everything went as planned, they'd fly a turnaround to Washington, D.C., and be back in Philly by 8:00 a.m. to finish the night. But the schedule was often laid waste by weather, mechanical, or freight delays. The previous night it had been all three, and they didn't get home until 10:00 a.m. on Thursday. By the end of a week like that, the cumulative fatigue was crushing and their sleep deficit was severe.

Keystone Airways didn't have autopilots installed in their airplanes, which meant all flying had to be done manually. With his hand on the yoke and his feet on the rudder pedals, Ed made a small correction to the airplane's altitude. As he eased the airplane into a descent, the radio crackled. "Keystone Five-Oh-Eight, New York Center now on one-three-two-point-five."

Jack unclipped his mic from its holder and raised it to his mouth. "New York now on one-three-two-point-five, Keystone Five-Oh-Eight," he replied. After tuning the new frequency, he said, "Good morning, New York. Keystone Five-Oh-Eight with you, level at six."

"Roger, Keystone Five-Oh-Eight, good morning, sir, radar contact. Maintain six thousand feet. Heading two-four-zero and cleared direct Robbinsville when able."

Jack answered by repeating the clearance and then reached for the navigation radios. He tuned them to the Robbinsville, New Jersey, VOR station and confirmed its Morse code identification.

Ed leaned forward to adjust his VOR for the inbound course and sat back. "DME's been showing a twenty-knot headwind up here. What about lower?"

Jack eyed the three-digit odometer slowly rolling down the miles. "Yeah, I noticed that too."

"What about giving four a try?"

Shifting his gaze outside, Jack stared into the night sky as if he could divine its secrets. "Maybe," he said. "But at least it's smooth up here, and after that ass-kicking we got last night, why don't we just stay put?"

Ed shrugged. "I'm just ready to be there."

Jack nodded. "Yeah, me too," he said through a yawn.

With no intercom in the cockpit, they had to speak loudly to be heard above the noise of the airplane and their heavy David-Clark headsets. Anything more than a few words at a time was exhausting, so most pilots avoided it. But Ed was an exception; he seemed impervious to the strain and continued the chat as he trimmed the props. "I got a few hours sleep after we got home this morning," he said. "But I have to be up for the kids when they get home from school at three. Eileen doesn't get home from work until five."

Jack gazed at him blearily through bloodshot eyes and nodded. At thirty-five, Ed was jowly, prematurely bald, and married with three kids. He was a former parochial school teacher and only now beginning a new career as a pilot. Jack grimaced at the thought of a house full of screaming kids and remarked, "I don't know how you do it."

Ed gazed at his instruments and said, "I don't either. It's not just the hours but the kids, Eileen's job, and the money—which sucks, of course."

Jack nodded and doubled down on his effort to end the chitchat by shifting his gaze east.

"Anyway," Ed persisted, "it beats the hell out of a room full of seventh graders. And hey—the money wasn't much there either; you know what I mean?"

It was hopeless. Jack looked at him wearily and said, "Yeah, figured that. Did I ever tell you I went to Catholic school?"

"No. But with that mouth of yours, I already knew," Ed gibed.

"Mom thought it would improve my morals. Little did she know about those working-class girls in short plaid skirts."

Ed laughed. "True enough. The girls in my classes had ten years on the boys."

Jack turned to look east along I-95 six thousand feet below him. Emergency lights were flashing, brake lights solid for miles and miles, a highway parking lot at 2:30 a.m.

"Plans for the weekend?" Ed asked the back of Jack's head.

Jack pretended he didn't hear.

"The *weekend*," Ed said more loudly. "Any plans?"

Jack turned, pursed his lips, and shook his head.

"Nothing with Amanda, huh?"

"No. It's over. We had a fight last weekend. I'm done."

Jack had met her at the bank's drive-through: Amanda the petite porcelain blond with the cover girl looks behind the window, Jack the swarthy handsome guy driving the ugliest rust bucket she'd ever seen. They'd started casually dating, but Amanda had never let it go beyond that and Jack had become increasingly frustrated. The weekend before they had been at an old taphouse where she liked to hang out on Saturdays with her clique, her friends from Brandywine, Delaware, the same people she'd been around all her life. Amanda was flitting about as usual and Jack standing at the end of the bar alone when a girl he'd never seen before came over to him and said hello. "Debra," she'd said with a smile and extended hand. She was pretty but in a tomboyish way, and clearly in the midst of a weekend project. She wore no makeup and had her mahogany hair up in a bun, a smudge of paint on her cheek. If there was a figure beneath her speckled shirt and baggy jeans, Jack saw no hint of it.

"I'm with Boeing," she'd announced, her gaze at him even, her hand soft but firm. "I'm an aerospace engineer at the Ridley Park plant. I did my master's thesis on the DC-3, and Kerry told me you fly them for Keystone in Philly."

They laughed and talked about the airplane's quirks, and Jack ordered two beers for them. Debra was touching his arm from time to time, and Jack was getting turned on. She wasn't as pretty as Amanda, but there was something much more to her. On the spur of the moment, he suggested she come along with him some night in the jumpseat to experience the airplane at work. He never expected her to take him up on it, but she'd seemed genuinely enthused. Jack was in the middle of writing down his phone number on a napkin for her when Amanda came over, unhinged, screaming at Jack and causing a scene. Jack had seen strains of that before—her childish jealousy any time he had any conversation with another girl—and rather than get into it, he'd apologized to Debra, handed her the napkin, then turned and walked out with Amanda on his heels in a rage.

"Ugh. Sorry to hear that," Ed said as he trimmed the throttles.

Jack shrugged. "Hey, she's twenty-two going on fifteen. I've known that all along. I should have ended it sooner."

"You've told me she can be like that."

"She's dumb as a box of rocks, Ed, and there's never been anything more than petting. I've had enough of that bullshit too. It was time."

"*Really?* You've been going with her for months, right?"

"Since last spring."

"Huh … So, you got something else lined up?"

Jack sighed. "Doing *this* for a living, Ed? Hard meeting girls when you live like a bat and come home smelling like avgas and wet boxes."

"You got a point. But what about the Gooney-Bird girl? You think she'll take you up on it? Come to work with us some night?"

"Only if she's fuckin' nuts, right? What kind of chick would want to do *that?*"

"Is she hot?"

Jack gave him a look.

"I mean it … so, is she?"

"She's smart, Ed. She speaks in full sentences and she's into more than movie stars and *Cosmo*, so yeah, that's pretty hot to me. As for the rest, we'll see. Anyway, she's probably just into the airplane. It'll be over the minute she sees my car."

Ed pursed his lips. "You're right," he said. "I wouldn't want to be seen in your car either."

The radio crackled. "Keystone Five-Oh-Eight, say heading."

Jack picked up his mic and glanced at the directional gyro. "Keystone Five-Oh-Eight, heading two-four-zero, direct Robbinsville."

"Roger, sir, come left, heading one-nine-zero for traffic departing Kennedy. I'll have direct Robbinsville once he's past you."

Jack replied to the change in clearance as Ed banked the airplane to the right.

They continued in silence for the next fifteen minutes, Jack battling to stay awake, Ed flying and admiring the spectral blue glow of New York City coming into view. A few minutes later, Ed checked his watch and said, "Got about an hour to go."

Jack was staring vacantly out the left side windshield.

"*JACK!*" Ed yelled.

Jack blinked and turned to look at him.

Ed pointed to the fuel tank selector switch. "The mains," he said. "It's time to switch. The aux tanks are probably done."

"Right … right," Jack said absently.

"Are you okay? You really seem out of it. Sure you don't want a little shut-eye?"

"No, no, I'm okay," Jack insisted. He reached for the boost pump switches on the overhead panel and flipped them on. "Go ahead," he said.

Ed moved the fuel selector valves to MAIN, and the engines continued to roar without a hiccup. Satisfied that the fuel flow was reliable, Jack reached up and shut off the pumps.

"We've still got time," Ed said sheepishly. "You really should get some rest."

The truth was, with any other copilot Jack would have already taken a nap. But though Ed was a great guy to work with and a competent pilot *most* of the time, every now and then he could drop the ball, like he did the previous February. They were flying this same leg from Boston to Philly, and lab rats were always on the manifest. During winter, the pallets of rats were loaded first to be near the cockpit's heat. But on that night—while Jack was inside the office and on the phone to the dispatcher—Ed had forgotten to load them until last. So, rather than unload and reload the airplane, Ed loaded them at the rear of the cargo area opposite the drafty door with only a tarp to protect them. The temperature that night was in the teens, and those rats were just a load of furry ice pops by the time they got to Philly, their bemused expressions, their little snouts and paws frozen to the mesh. Keystone had to pay for the damage, and Jack got an ass chewing by the chief pilot. From that night forward, he vowed never to trust Ed completely again. Jack would only nap when the airplane was parked on the ramp and they were waiting for freight. He looked at Ed and said, "I will when we get to Philly."

Ed shrugged but knew why Jack was hesitant. "Sure … whatever," he said, looking crestfallen.

The radio crackled. "Keystone Five-Oh-Eight, right turn now direct Robbinsville and contact New York Center now on one-two-eight-point-four," said the controller.

Jack replied and Ed adjusted his VOR for the inbound radial. When it was set, he banked the airplane further to the right to fly direct to the station.

Jack clipped his mic and turned his gaze east. The airport beacon at West Hampton Beach blinked its lonely vigil, and his eyes became fixated on it. As his consciousness ebbed, his eyes began to flicker … and flicker … and flicker before his head dropped sharply, and then jerked up with a start. He tried to shake it off and rubbed his burning eyes.

Ed clucked his tongue and said, "You're going to hurt yourself if you keep doing that."

Jack continued rubbing his eyes and said, "You're right. Maybe I'd better take you up on that offer."

"Your call, sir."

Jack yawned and scanned the engine instruments. He pointed at the right engine cylinder head temperature gauge and said, "That's been running a little hot all night. Looks okay now, but let's keep an eye on it, okay?"

Ed stifled a yawn and said, "Yeah, I noticed that too. You want me to open the cowl flaps?"

Jack's eyes narrowed and he studied him closely. "No, not now," he said. "Only if it goes any higher—but look, Ed—are you sure you're all right?"

"Of course," Ed replied. "You're just contagious. I'll be fine."

Jack had doubts, but he had no choice. He needed to close his eyes and get some rest. "Alright, then," he said as he took off his flight jacket and loosened his belt. "You've got it. I'm out for a bit. Wake me before we begin to descend."

"Sure, but with this headwind, you got an hour or more, so relax."

Jack reached for the volume control on his headphones. He started to turn it down but had second thoughts. Air traffic at that time of night was nearly non-existent, so the radio would be quiet, and no matter who he was flying with, he never liked being too disconnected. He left the volume where it was, rolled his flight jacket into a pillow, and hunkered down in the DC-3's small rigid seat. With his knees bent and body curled, he was out in an instant.

# TWO

*The sky over the North Atlantic, September 1, 1978*

He was walking through a misty field, tall grass brushing his thighs. A girl was calling out to him, her pleas faint but urgent. Jack tried running to her, but his legs wouldn't move. He struggled and pulled, but felt like he was mired in tar until a voice exploded in his ears and startled him awake: "… KEYSTONE Five-Oh-Eight … KEYSTONE Five-Oh-Eight … DO YOU *READ* … DO YOU READ?" she bellowed.

Jack bolted upright, his heart pounding. The view ahead was black as pitch. The engines howled and the wind shrieked. Jack felt weightless, only his seatbelt restraining him. His eyes shot to the horizon indicator. The airplane was in a hard left bank and steep dive. The airspeed needle was winding up and up—170, 180, 190 knots—and the altimeter needles were winding down, down at the speed of a stopwatch.

They were pitching out of the sky and diving headlong into a black abyss as Jack grabbed the controls, forced his feet onto the rudders, and thrust his right hand onto the throttles. With his eyes on the horizon indicator—the white line nearly vertical and at the far side of the instrument—he rolled in full right aileron and pulled the power to idle. His right foot pressed hard against the rudder, and his leg quivered under the strain as the airplane rolled heavily to the right. When the bank angle came to zero, Jack neutralized the ailerons and rudder and began pulling on the yoke. As the nose began to rise and the g-force came on strong, the blood rushed from his head. He clenched his gut to slow it. The airplane's hundred-foot wings flexed under the stress, and the ancient airframe groaned under the sudden strain of lift. As the nose came up, the airspeed came down, and the altimeter needles stopped their wild unwinding. The wind noise returned to normal; and the engine roar the same.

"Keystone Five-Oh-Eight, New York, I see you are level now at 3,700 feet, is that correct?"

Jack ignored her, his breath coming quick and his pulse still racing. Through the periphery of his vision, he caught a glimpse of Ed in the dark, his body limp and his arms hanging by his sides. But first things first, he had to ensure the airplane was back under control. He pushed up the throttles to maintain speed and cautiously tested the controls: up and down, left and right. Everything was working properly, with no adverse feel or response, and Jack blew out his cheeks. "Sweet Jesus," he muttered as he scanned the other instruments. They were twenty-three hundred feet below their assigned altitude and one hundred eighty degrees off their assigned heading. Jack turned and looked to the left. The lights along the south coast of Long Island were twinkling in the distance. They were far over the Atlantic Ocean.

"*Shit*," he muttered, then snapped around and looked at Ed. He was slumped in his seat, his chin on his chest and his head canted against the side windshield. His eyes were closed, his mouth partially open.

*Dead!* Jack thought. *He's dead!* A wave of nausea rose in him, the same feeling he'd had seeing his first combat casualty in Vietnam.

"Keystone Five-Oh-Eight! Keystone Five-Oh-Eight, if you read, squawk ident!"

Jack grabbed his mic and snarled, "Stand by, New York, stand by. Keystone Five-Oh-Eight's got a situation here; I'll call you back. Stand by!"

The female controller answered with a tone of relief. "Roger, sir, roger … New York standing by."

Jack reached for Ed's left wrist and felt for a pulse. He let his wrist go and grabbed his flashlight. He directed the beam at Ed's chest. It was gently rising and falling in an even cadence. He sent the beam to Ed's face, and his eyelids twitched.

Seized by rage, Jack dropped his flashlight and grabbed Ed roughly by his arm. "HEY!" Jack yelled, yanking and shoving him while he tried to maintain control of the airplane. "HEY GODDAMNIT! WAKE UP … WAKE THE *FUCK* UP, ED," he bellowed.

Ed twitched again, and his eyes opened.

Jack shoved him. "GODDAMN IT, ED … WAKE UP!"

Ed shot upright and glanced about with a bovine cast. "Oh … oh," he muttered. He wiped the spittle from his mouth, and stupidly fumbled for the controls.

Jack pushed him away. "*NO!*" he shouted. "*NO … NO,* you don't! Do you have any idea what you've done, Ed? Do you have any idea what you've done? You've ruined my career!" he snarled. "You've *ruined* my fucking *career!*"

"Keystone Five-Oh-Eight, New York, you're leaving my airspace, sir. Are you declaring an emergency? Can you come right heading two-seven-en-zero?"

"Take the airplane!" Jack commanded. "Do what she says. Bring us around to two-seven-zero and maintain altitude—if you can *manage* it!" He gave Ed a final shove.

Ed sat up and took the controls. "I'm so sorry," he said. "I'm so sorry. I don't know how—"

Jack pointed his finger at him like a gun. "Yeah, well—too late for *that*," he snapped. Grabbing his mic, he said, "Roger, ma'am, Keystone Five-Oh-Eight is coming right to two-seven-zero, negative emergency, stand by, please."

"Roger, Keystone Five-Oh-Eight, New York, copy negative emergency, is that correct?"

"Roger, ma'am, but stand by please, stand by."

"Roger, sir, New York standing by, over."

He needed a moment to think. They'd deviated far off their assigned course and altitude without clearance, and no matter that Ed was at fault, Jack was the captain and he'd go down for it too. It was a serious violation of the Federal Aviation Regulations and may have put other flights around them in jeopardy of a mid-air collision. Jack would have to answer for that. Declaring an emergency would get them off the hook for now, but the lies he'd have to tell the FAA in their investigation could sink more than just his career. On the other hand, confessing and telling the truth was not an option either. There was no provision for pilots sleeping on the job. An FAA violation on his license would be inescapable and any hope of a career with a reputable airline over unless Jack could somehow talk his way out of this disaster, right *now*, before it went any further.

He lifted his mic and said, "New York, Keystone Five-Oh-Eight, negative emergency, ma'am, but we do have a situation here. We're heading two-seven-zero and level at 3,700."

"Keystone Five-Oh-Eight, New York, roger, sir, I've been trying to call you for the last five minutes. Understand negative emergency."

"Yes, ma'am, negative emergency. I thought it might be, but we've got the problem straightened out. I couldn't call you back until now."

"Roger, sir, your clearance was to maintain six thousand feet and fly direct Robbinsville on heading two-four-zero. But when you leveled off, I showed you heading zero-seven-zero and level at 3,700 feet, is that correct?"

Silence.

"Keystone Five-Oh-Eight, if you're having trouble transmitting, squawk ident, please."

And then a thought occurred to him, and he said, "Ah, roger, ma'am, the radios are fine, but stand by please; we do have an issue."

"Keystone Five-Oh-Eight, say again? Are you declaring an emergency?"

"Stand by, ma'am, please."

Jack turned and looked into the cabin. Then, looking at Ed with his thumb pointed over his shoulder, he said, "That eighteen-hundred-pound pallet of auto parts—you're certain you secured it, right?"

"Of course," Ed said, his brow knit. "We both did, remember? Everything strapped down tight like we always do."

Pointing at his face, Jack growled, "*Wrong* answer." Lifting his mic, he said, "Roger, New York, sorry for the delay, ma'am. The problem was ... well—the problem was we've been having some issues with the freight onboard. The freight shifted and offset the airplane's CG. We had to scramble to correct it and, well—in correcting the problem, we got off heading and altitude."

Ed looked astonished. Suddenly beaming, he gave Jack a big thumbs-up.

Jack glowered at him.

The radio was silent. Jack fingered his mic nervously as he awaited a response. He conjured an image of the controller at her radar unit in the darkly lit Air Traffic Control Center at Islip, New York, lit by the ghostly glow of her radar screen, and by now, after all that had happened, her supervisor summoned and standing by her side.

"Keystone Five-Oh-Eight, say your intentions," came a deep, gravelly voice. "Are you able to proceed to Philadelphia, sir?"

Shit! The supervisor! Jack's heart sank. He tensed and cleared his throat. "Ah, well, sir," he said, hoping to dodge the issue, "I, ah ... I'm not sure."

"Keystone Five-Oh-Eight. Roger, sir, are you declaring an emergency, or do you want to proceed on course to Philadelphia?" the supervisor demanded irritably.

"Actually, sir," Jack said, "it now seems we've got the problem corrected. If you'd like, we can climb back to six thousand feet and go direct Robbinsville now."

"Roger, Captain. Stand by," the supervisor replied.

Jack closed his eyes and toyed nervously with the mic as he waited for an answer. Everything he'd worked for and dreamed about for years was hanging in the balance.

Ed started to say something, but Jack put up his hand to silence him.

Shortly after, the female controller replied, "Keystone Five-Oh-Eight, New York."

She was back! The supervisor was gone! Jack brightened and sat up. "Keystone Five-Oh-Eight, yes ma'am, go ahead," he said cheerfully.

"Roger, sir, Keystone Five-Oh-Eight's cleared present position direct Robbinsville, climb and maintain six thousand feet. When you're ready, sir, I've got a phone number for my supervisor. He needs to speak to you when you get to Philadelphia. Advise when you're ready to copy, over."

Jack fell back in his seat feeling like he'd just been punched. *Game over*, he thought. He'd have to answer for what happened after all.

"Keystone Five-Oh-Eight, New York, do you read?"

He stared out the windshield glumly in silence.

"Keystone Five-Oh-Eight, New York."

Jack pulled a pen from his pocket, looking like a man sentenced to the gallows. "Roger, ma'am," he moaned. "Keystone Five-Oh-Eight, ready to copy."

# THREE

*The sky over New Jersey, September 1, 1978*

T hey continued the flight in silence, Ed flying the airplane while Jack stared out the windshield and stewed.

As the lights of Philly came into view, he rehearsed what he'd say to the supervisor. He'd press the case he'd made to the controller—the shifting of freight—and hope the supervisor found it credible. If he didn't, there'd be no escaping an FAA investigation into their deviation. The supervisor would file a report with the Flight Standards District Office in New York, and not only would they hit Jack with the clearance deviation, but they'd also hit him with the FAA's catch-all violation in cases like this: FAR 91.13, the careless and reckless operation of an aircraft. No respectable airline in the world would touch him with that on his record, and Jack would spend the rest of his career flying derelict airplanes, for derelict airlines, with derelicts just like himself.

• • •

After landing in Philly and shutting down the engines at the Cargo City ramp, they completed the checklist and Jack bolted from the plane.

Passing up the use of the phone in Keystone's dispatch office for fear of being overheard, Jack went to the pay phone outside the building. He pulled open the grimy glass doors and pushed some quarters into the slot of the phone. His fingers quivered as he dialed the number. As it began to ring, he leaned back against the side of the booth and looked down, his stomach in knots, his heart racing.

The supervisor answered. "New York Center, Williams," he growled.

Jack stood erect, cleared his throat, and said, "Yes, sir. Good morning, this is Jack Dolan, the captain of Keystone Five-Oh-Eight."

"Yes, Captain, I've pulled the tapes of your clearance violation, and I've been reviewing them. What happened back there?"

"Well, sir, as I told your controller, we had a problem with the freight. Although we had it secured in Boston, somehow it had come loose and shifted. I had to leave my seat to secure it, and when the copilot got out of his seat to throw me some more tie-down straps, he let the airplane drift off course and altitude. He's kind of a new guy and I should have been more attentive to him, but the weather was good and I figured it would be better for me to handle the problem with the freight and let him continue flying. It was my mistake, sir. I should have been more careful."

Silence.

"Sir? Mr. Williams?"

"Stand by, Captain."

Jack heard mumbling as if the supervisor had his hand cupped over the mouthpiece.

As he waited for Williams, Jack stared at his boots and clenched and ran his fingers through his hair. The floor was filthy with mud, grime, and cigarette butts.

Suddenly, "Okay," said Williams. "Look, Captain, uh ... stand by one ..."

Jack closed his eyes and prayed like he did during a rocket attack in Vietnam.

"I'm sorry about that," said Williams. "So, look, Captain, I appreciate the call, but I've got another issue going on here. I've got the information I need for your company. Keystone Airways in Philadelphia, is that correct?"

"Yes, sir, that's correct," Jack said, his eyes narrowing. Something was up. He sensed it was good.

"All right. Anyway, look, if I need anything more, we'll be in touch."

"In touch?" Jack said. He desperately wanted this resolved in his favor, and didn't want to push but felt the pressing need. "I see, Mr. Williams, but sir ... can you tell me—"

"I've got to go," Williams said, his tone clipped and firm. "We're good, Captain. You get it straight with your copilot, and I'll do the same with my controller."

Dare he feel relieved? "I'm sorry, sir," Jack pushed. "Did you say—"

"I said we're *good*, Captain. Keep an eye on that copilot of yours. Now, I've got to go."

"Yes, sir! Yes, *sir*, I will, and thank—"

Click.

Jack looked at the receiver in awe, then clapped it on the hook and fell back against the glass. He couldn't believe his luck.

*Never again*, he vowed as he returned to the airplane. "Never, never … never again."

. . .

When they returned to Philly that Friday morning, their workweek was over.

As they left the company's terminal, Jack shoved open the door and let it slam in Ed's face. But then, at the bottom of the stairs, he paused and turned around. With his flight jacket slung over his shoulder, he looked up at Ed standing at the top of the stairs, his hands in his pockets, crestfallen.

"I'm sorry," said Jack. "I'm sorry for being such a shit."

Ed looked puzzled and started to speak, but Jack held up his hand. "We were *both* whipped last night, and I should have called Ernie yesterday to tell him we needed a break. He would have understood."

"But we never want to put another guy out," said Ed. "Someone who's got the night off."

"But that's what we do here, Ed. We cover for one another, and we trust one another. We know that when the call comes in, we've got to go. That's what I should have done. Period. End of story."

Ed nodded and looked down. "Yeah, me too."

"No, *not* you, Ed … *me*," Jack said, a thumb pointed at his chest. "I

35

get the big bucks, remember? It was my call and my responsibility, and I'm the one who screwed up. So, I'm sorry I was such an asshole. Let's put it behind us and never let anything like this happen again. Fair enough?"

Ed smiled self-consciously with that single-hearted humility Jack had seen in him so often before. "Fair enough," he said.

Jack threw him a wave and rounded toward his car.

"Jack!" Ed shouted.

Jack turned around wearily.

"You're a great captain—the best."

"You, too, Ed. Have a nice weekend."

. . .

Driving south on I-95 with the morning sun glinting through the windshield of his '69 Valiant, Jack decided it was time to move on.

Although Keystone had treated him well and he really liked all the guys he worked with—especially his chief pilot, Ernie—at twenty-six, Jack's clock was ticking loudly. Thirty was the age limit for major airline hiring, and if Jack didn't start making more notable progress toward his goal soon, any hope of success would be dashed.

Beyond that, he'd logged over a thousand hours as a captain in the DC-3 and achieved the objective he'd set when he took the job: pilot-in-command experience in a large, multi-engine, crewed airplane. There was nothing more to accomplish with Keystone in terms of advancing his career and—given last night's experience and others like it—continuing to fly for Keystone was only putting his career goals at further risk. So, it was time to move on, but the question was to where? The traditional way of advancement to the major airlines for Jack had faltered, and he needed another plan.

Jack walked into his apartment and noted the empty pizza box and Pabst Blue Ribbon cans his housemate, Frank, had left on the coffee table. Like Jack, Frank was in his mid-twenties. He was an accountant for the city of Wilmington, Delaware, and, also like Jack, had a hard time meeting any women. But, unlike Jack, Frank's problem wasn't that he worked nights and came home smelling like avgas and wet boxes; Frank's problem was that he subscribed to *Hustler*, wore polyester leisure suits, and left his trash on the furniture and floor.

In his bedroom, Jack pulled off his epaulets and shirt, kicked off his boots, and stripped off his trousers. After a steaming hot shower, he dried himself and went to the bedroom window to pull down the shades. With his hair still damp, he collapsed face first on his bed and was unconscious in an instant.

Three hours later, he woke to the howl of lawnmowers and the arguing of a landscaping crew outside his first-floor window. Sunlight blazed around the shades and pierced his eyelids like needles. Staring blearily at the ceiling as the mower roared by, Jack blinked and rolled over to try and get more sleep.

Two hours later he woke again, this time to loud hammering in the apartment above him. Throwing off the covers, he climbed out of bed and teetered toward the kitchen. The pantry-size galley held its usual clutter of dirty dishes, Chinese food cartons, and more of Frank's beer cans that hadn't yet made it to the floor. After pushing some of the trash aside, Jack grabbed the coffee pot on the stove and dumped Frank's morning grinds into the overstuffed trash bin. He washed the percolator, filled it with water, shook a pile of Maxwell House into the basket, and put the burner on high.

As he waited for it to perk, he mused about Keystone and the night before.

Although flying freight for a small airline wasn't much of a career aspiration, the job still meant a lot to Jack. For the first time since he began his professional flying career, he was making a respectable salary—$16,000 per year—though every spare dollar Jack made he devoted to paying down the debt he'd accumulated during his flight training and the low-paying jobs he'd had to take to build experience. It felt good to return the money to his mom and dad. It felt good to feel like a man again and not a mendicant.

But beyond the pay, Jack greatly valued his position as a captain—and not only a captain, but a captain in command of a DC-3: a 25,000 pound, radial-engine beast of an airplane that took far more skill to fly than the little De Havilland Twin Otters and Beech 99 Commuters his friends were flying as copilots at other airlines.

And that skill was put to the test on a nightly basis because, like all freight airlines, Keystone operated on a very tight budget: there were no autopilots, intercoms, or, most importantly, no weather radar installed in any of Keystone's airplanes.

During summer, that meant Jack would have to find a safe path through fast-moving squall lines and thunderstorms depending entirely on his instincts and wits. Even the smallest misjudgment could put them in the midst of the most violent turbulence, tearing the old airplane apart and sending it to earth as a pile of flaming junk.

And winter was no relief from danger or the demands on his skill. Frequently, the same weather system covered the whole of the Northeast and they'd have to fly five or six approaches to minimums on any given night with fog, freezing drizzle, or snow blanketing their entire route. Further complicating this was the arrangement of the DC-3's instruments. All three of the company's airplanes were WWII vintage, and every airplane had its instruments arranged differently. Scanning the scattershot, mismatched layouts effectively while keeping the airplane on track through a descent in clouds and turbulence demanded extraordinary skill. In addition to that, there were the frequent ice encounters, chunks of it riding up and down on the de-icing boots like frosty gremlins mocking Jack in the beam of his flashlight, the engines and wind roaring as he inspected the leading edge through the open cockpit window. Jack would have the throttles balls-to-the-wall pushing the run-out engines for all they were worth to keep the airplane flying. As the pungent scent of alcohol wafted through the cockpit, slabs of slushy ice would be slung from the prop blades, crashing into the fuselage with loud thuds, rattling their nerves.

Adding to those threats and the demands on Jack's skill was the company's scrimping on maintenance. The airplanes were never really repaired but just patched up enough to fly again. In the thousand hours Jack had logged as a captain in the DC-3, he'd also logged more than a dozen engine failures, one engine fire, several brake and hydraulic failures, and one hazardous cargo spill that burned a hole through the side of the fuselage. And those were just the routine problems. The episode with Ed was in a class by itself.

The coffee was perking furiously, and the aroma roused Jack from his reverie. He filled a cup, added some milk, took a sip, and grimaced. Making coffee was a dark art that Jack hadn't mastered. Jack's version had enough caffeine to light Philadelphia; and enough oily scum to fill city hall. He dared another sip and ambled into the living room as he considered his options for moving on.

Despite all that he'd achieved at Keystone, Jack faced three huge hurdles to advancement in his career: first, the American economy stuck in the rut of stagflation and the meager airline hiring that came with it; second, his lack of heavy jet experience; and third, his lack of a four-year college degree. Beyond that, because of the thousands of ex-military pilots who had all the education and experience requirements the airlines were seeking, competition for the few jobs that came up from time to time was fierce. If anything was going to change the odds against Jack for the better—given the huge holes in his resume—then Jack would have to be the agent of that change.

Passing the desk against the wall in the dining area, Jack paused and brushed through the mail stacked on top. Pushing aside the electric bill, some junk ads, and a *Playboy* for Frank, Jack found the latest edition of *Aviation Week* magazine at the bottom. He picked it up, took another sip of coffee, and went to the couch and sat down. Putting his coffee cup on the table next to one of Frank's *Hustler* centerfolds—a gynecological perspective, a pizza crust covering her face—Jack sat back and opened his *Aviation Week*.

In the contents section, he found an article that caught his eye. It was about Air Logistics International, a US supplemental airline (or "non-sched" as they were commonly known). The airline was based in Miami and had purchased some DC-8s from Delta. Air Logistics would soon be adding them to their fleet and hiring pilots. Jack's interest piqued, and he turned to the page. After reading the article, he put the magazine down, picked up his coffee cup, and went back to the kitchen for breakfast.

He loaded two slices of bread in the toaster, scrambled two eggs, and gave further thought to Air Logistics.

Jack remembered applying to them and updating his resume in the past but couldn't remember how long it had been. Supplemental airlines were typically not high on Jack's list of coveted careers, particularly a charter freight outfit like Air Logistics where he'd spend his life on call and flying mostly at night. Jack had had more than enough of that. Also, the pay and working conditions were not as good at the non-scheds as they were at the scheduled airlines. But the one huge advantage non-scheds did have for pilots like Jack with holes in their resumes was that they were a lot more accessible for an interview.

Unlike the scheduled airlines that used an impartial send-us-an-application-and-wait-until-you're-called, multi-day, multi-department, physical and psychological rectal exam to select their pilots, the non-scheds were notoriously subjective. In the end, it all came down to the airline's chief pilot: if he liked you, you were in; it was just that simple. And not. Because to get to the chief pilot, you first had to get past the most implacable, bloodless, and intimidating force in all of aviation: the chief pilot's secretary, his blue-haired barbarian at the gate. Traditional methods of applying and waiting were a breeze by comparison.

As Jack scooped up the last scrap of egg from the pan with a piece of toast, he thought of his friend, Gary Lednum. Gary was a ham-fisted pilot—and eventually gave up flying professionally—but he was a world-class salesman, a talent he was finally putting to highly paid use. In fact, Gary was so good at selling *any*thing, he even managed to sell himself as an experienced pilot for an interview with Capitol International Airlines. Although Gary had nothing close to the DC-8 experience they required, he succeeded with sales techniques he'd learned from his dad. He started cold-calling the chief pilot's secretary and schmoozing her with cards, candy, and flowers. And then one day, pow! She calls and tells him the company is starting to hire. She says if he wants to stop by—the company's headquarters was nearby in Wilmington, Delaware—maybe he can snatch a few minutes with the chief pilot, and he did! Although he ultimately got the boot because he didn't know when to quit schmoozing, at least he'd had a shot at the job, which was a lot more than anything Jack had achieved by doing things the conventional way.

And then Jack frowned. Jack was no Gary. In fact, when it came to salesmanship, Jack couldn't even sell light bulbs to his neighbors for his Cub Scout troop. His mother had to buy them all to clear out his obligation. Salesmanship was clearly neither Jack's forte nor his style, particularly the Gary method of sales, which Jack considered cheesy and importuning. As he washed the dishes and wiped down the counter, Jack decided against it—and then had second thoughts.

*Desperate times, desperate measures*, he decided.

He folded the dish towel, tossed it on the counter, and went to his closet for his file on Air Logistics.

# FOUR

J ack put the file on the bed. Sitting in his threadbare jockeys, he opened it and looked it over. Beyond an additional four hundred hours of flight time, there was nothing new to add. He closed the folder and set it aside.

After mulling it over a bit more, he decided that he had everything to gain—and only one non-sched freight airline to lose—by giving the Gary-method a go. If worst came to worst, they'd tell Jack to piss off and he'd be back where he started. On the other hand—if it did work—at least he'd be out of the minor leagues and into the majors: heavy jets, great pay, and a professional career, if not the most prestigious one.

He got up, sifted through his box of files, and found the *Aviation Week Industry Directory* buried at the bottom. He turned to the contents and found the listing for Air Logistics International Airlines and the phone number of the chief pilot's office along with his name, Captain Jacob Kegan, and the name of his secretary, Claire Desmarais.

Back in the kitchen and with the receiver wedged between his cheek and his shoulder, Jack dialed the number. But as it started to ring, he suddenly began to feel anxious. Another ring and his throat tightened, another and a hot flash swept through him. What if this was the only decent airline he ever had a shot at? What if he totally blew it because of this stunt? What a stupid, stupid thing to do! He panicked and started to hang up when he heard a woman with a disarming French accent, answer. "Good afternoon," she said pleasantly. "Captain Kegan's office, this is Claire, may I help you?"

Jack froze.

"*Allo?*" she said.

He felt like a man caught stealing. It was fight or flight, and he impulsively chose fight. He cleared his throat. "Oh, uh … yes!" he said.

"Pardon me? May I help you?"

"Ah, yes, ma'am … I … uh … I'm calling about a job," he blubbered.

"Job?" she said quizzically. "What job are you speaking about? This is Captain Kegan's office. Perhaps you have the wrong number?"

Jack cleared his throat. "Maybe I should start over," he said. "My name is Jack Dolan, and I've sent a pilot application and I was—"

"Do you have recent DC-8 *expérience*?" she interrupted.

Pause.

"*DC-8* experience?" he asked. "Ah, well … no, ma'am, I don't, but—"

"Then you will not be considered at this time. In the future, please make any further inquiries only by mail. We do not accept any application requests or updates by phone."

"Ah, no, ma'am. I mean, to say, yes, ma'am! I mean, I understand. But I have been flying—"

"Only by *mail!*" she insisted.

"But I do have pilot-in-command experience in a large Douglas airplane, and—"

Click.

He stared at the receiver like a door closed in his face, Jack on the porch with a box full of light bulbs. He hung up the receiver with the dial tone buzzing.

He turned away, ran his fingers through his hair, and sighed. Sales was not his strength.

Suddenly, there was a loud thumping on the apartment door. He staggered toward it, still thinking about the call, and without thinking further he turned the knob and opened it.

The building superintendent was standing in the hall in his scruffy beard and blue coveralls.

"Can I help you?" said Jack, bleary-eyed and teetering in his jockeys.

The big swarthy guy recoiled and gave him a once-over. Then catching a glimpse of the centerfold spreadeagled on the table, he looked at Jack's jockeys and grimaced.

Jack followed his gaze and groaned, "Ugh … yeah, so *what* is it?"

The super pointed his thumb toward the parking lot. "You own that green Valiant?" he grumbled.

"Yeah, that's mine … So what?"

"You got to move it, pal. They're sealing the parking lot today, and your car's in the way."

Jack nodded and slammed the door in his face.

As he walked to the kitchen, he picked up the *Hustler* and threw it against the wall. From the cabinet below the sink, he pulled out the phone book and found an FTD florist.

"Yes, please," he said to the florist. "Those daisies sound just right. The small bouquet, and when you're ready, I've got the address in Miami. Oh, and I also want to include a note."

> Thank you for your time and patience,
> Jack Dolan.

Desperate times, desperate measures, he reminded himself. Whatever the outcome, it felt good to be taking control.

# FIVE

It was Friday morning, and Jacob Kegan was standing at his office window gazing absently at the broad view of the airline's ramp and hangars below. He was looking forward to the weekend ahead. He had plans to play golf with his wife and another couple on Saturday, and on Sunday he would preview pilot applications while sitting by the pool at his home in Coral Gables. He thought of the interviews that would soon begin.

Air Logistics was adding some new jets to its fleet, DC-8-61 series airplanes that had been purchased from Delta Airlines. The new airplanes were the first 60-series, or "stretched eights" that Air Logistics would be operating. They were much more expensive to buy than the 30-series airplanes the company currently operated but more cost-effective because they carried a larger payload over longer distances. Also, the three new stretched eights had been converted to a quick-change capability, meaning they could be reconfigured from freight to passenger work as the mission required. That flexibility would be needed in the changing market for airline service following the deregulation of the industry earlier that year.

It was a bold move and a big gamble for privately owned Air Logistics International, an airline known for its scrupulous control of costs and aversion to debt.

Kegan was fifty-eight years old, near retirement, and thrilled by the company's decision to buy the bigger airplanes. The new jets meant he'd be leaving his career at a high point: new pilots coming on line and higher pay for his other pilots who hadn't seen a significant pay raise despite a decade of rising inflation.

There was a knock on the door, and he turned. His secretary, Claire, was walking in with some folders in the crook of her arm.

"Here are a few of the applications you asked for," she said with a heavy French accent. "I'll put together some more, but these are the best I've seen so far."

"Oh, great. Thank you, Claire," Kegan said, glancing over his shoulder. "Put them on the desk. I'll bring them home and give them a look during the weekend."

She nodded and set them down.

"They've all got recent DC-8 experience?"

"But of course. It's the company's new policy, *non?*"

"Yes … how do they look so far?"

"Impressive," Claire said, raising a brow.

"We're hiring five to start, and given your track record, they'll probably be the first five I pull from that pile." He smiled.

Claire smiled too, then turned for her desk and left.

New pilot hiring was Kegan's responsibility and a job he cherished. To be able to offer a career to a pilot with a first-class airline thrilled him, the pilot's excitement and enthusiasm palpable when he'd make that call telling them they had the job. Normally, an airline's director of operations would be in charge of that process. But at Air Logistics, the DO was a nepotistic hire and suit-conscious fop. He was the brother-in-law of the company's president and a former Braniff captain fired for stealing liquor minis from the airplanes, among other imbecilities.

Fortunately for Kegan, the president kept the dolt locked up downtown in his titular position and oak-paneled office. But every now and then the DO would have a brainstorm and become a pain in Kegan's ass. His latest—a notion he'd gleaned from some of Air Logistics' competitors—was requiring recent DC-8 experience for all new pilots. He argued it would substantially reduce training costs.

Kegan argued the cost advantage would be minimal and limiting his choice to those pilots with prior experience in the DC-8 was shortsighted. A pilot's skill, devotion, temperament, and character were far more important in the long run. But the pointy-heads in the accounting department agreed with the DO, and Kegan lost.

But for Kegan, that didn't mean the fight was over.

# SIX

*Brandywine, Delaware, September 8, 1978*

On Friday, September 8, Jack called again. This time he'd thoroughly rehearsed what he would say. When the barbarian with the sexy accent answered, Jack remained calm and told her he was calling to include some Boeing 707 flight time he'd logged in a simulator at the Pan Am flight training center in New York. He told her he'd read that Air Logistics would be hiring soon and he wanted it included in his application immediately, if possible.

Claire had been reviewing dictation when the phone rang. She vaguely remembered the voice and patiently waited for the first opportunity to cut him off. But suddenly, surprisingly, he politely brought the call to an end by thanking her for her time before she'd even had an opportunity to speak.

After Jack hung up, he called the florist and ordered carnations.

On Wednesday, September 13, he called for the third time.

Claire had broken a nail, and when she picked up the receiver, she frowned as she examined the damage. "Good morning," she answered. "Captain Kegan's office."

Jack was poised. He figured he'd already blown it by now and had nothing to lose. "Good morning, Mrs. Desmarais," he said. "This is Jack Dolan. Sorry to trouble you, but I have a phone number change for my application. Since the company is selecting pilots for the three new airplanes it recently acquired, I thought I'd better give you an update as soon as possible."

She rolled her eyes, the receiver wedged between her ear and shoulder as she continued to study her broken nail. "Mr. Dolan, as I've told you before, we do not accept updates to applications over the phone. This must be your last call or I will remove your application from our files and *dispose* of it."

"I'm sorry to be a bother," Jack said politely. "But Air Logistics is my *first* choice of airlines to fly for, and I'm very concerned I might miss the call if I don't get it updated in time. It would kill me if I lost the chance, Mrs. Desmarais."

"By *mail*, Mr. Dolan. By mail. Do *not* call again."

Jack apologized, thanked her for her patience, and ordered a half dozen petite yellow roses.

# SEVEN

It was 9:15 p.m. on a drizzly Tuesday, and the night's work at Keystone Airways had just begun. Trucks were backed up to the loading dock of the company's terminal at Cargo City, and forklifts scurried about with pallets of freight. The clang and clatter of machinery and the clamor of men echoed through the cavernous four-story steel and concrete warehouse. On the airport side of the terminal, a fleet of three DC-3s and four SC.7 Skyvans awaited their cargo. Inside the terminal, the mobile construction trailer used as a dispatch office was lit by bright fluorescent lights and a cloud of cigarette smoke hung in the air. The clatter of teletype machines, the peal of telephones, and the loud conversation and laughter of dispatchers and pilots filled the room. A long plywood counter with a clear plexiglass top separated the dispatchers and pilots as they briefed and conversed across the top of it. Aircraft logbooks, load manifests, flight plans, and weather forecasts were laid out in order of their aircraft type and flight number.

Jack was at the far end of the counter studying the teletype sheets with the METARS, AIRMETS, TAFS, and area forecasts for their scheduled route. It was the easiest trip Keystone had: just four legs.

A slow-moving warm front was affecting weather across the region. Low ceilings and visibility were at every station. To make matters worse, pilot reports indicated areas of light to moderate rime ice over the Alleghenies between four thousand and eight thousand feet, the altitudes normally planned for Keystone's flights.

Abruptly, the loud conversations and laughter stopped. The room was silent but for the clatter of teletypes as everyone turned to look at the woman who'd just entered the trailer.

Jack was oblivious to the change, his eyes and mind on the weather reports and his jump seat passenger who was accompanying them that night. He wanted the trip to come off smoothly, but the uncooperative weather made him feel anxious about that prospect.

Phil Benson, Jack's copilot, was leaning casually against the counter looking toward the entrance to the trailer. "Show time," he announced. "I thought you said she's no looker."

"Huh?" Jack said without looking up. He was highlighting a sequence report.

"Your girl," said Phil, jutting his jaw toward the crowd of men at the entrance.

Jack put the paperwork on the counter and looked up. The only things he could see were the backs of other pilots. A moment later they parted, and he saw through the opening a young woman he didn't recognize standing on her toes, waving at him and beaming.

"Holy shit-ski," he muttered. "That might be her."

"Well, you never know," Phil deadpanned. "This place is such a chick magnet, could be anybody, right?"

"Jack!" she shouted and waved.

He returned her wave, looking dumbstruck.

• • •

She'd called him the previous Sunday. Jack had just come in from running errands and was putting away the groceries. Frank was prone on the couch in his AC/DC t-shirt and jeans, vacantly gazing at a Phillies game on TV.

When the phone rang, Jack turned and reached for it. "Hello?" he said, cradling the receiver between his head and shoulder, a quart of milk in his other hand.

"Hi, uh … is this Jack?"

"Um … yes," he said, his brow furrowed as he tried to place her voice.

"This is Debbie Moretti. We met a couple of weeks ago at Paul's Place in Chester."

"Oh … ah, *Deborah?*"

"Debbie, yes," she giggled. "I hope I'm not catching you at a bad time, but you had offered the opportunity to fly with you some night—see the DC-3 at work—and if the offer's still good, I'd like to take you up on that."

"Oh, ah … *sure!*" said Jack, surprised. He put the milk on the counter, leaned back against the wall, and ran his fingers through his hair. "Okay, sure, sure … so, ah … when are you thinking you'd like to go?"

"Would sometime this week be okay? I mean, if it's too short notice, then another day—"

"Oh, no, no … that's fine. But I'm off tomorrow," Jack said. "My first night back will be Tuesday. And then any night through Friday. But hey, we really should check the weather first. You'll enjoy it more if the weather's good."

"Oh … okay," she said hesitantly. "But that might make it hard to arrange my time off. I kind of need to plan ahead for my job, you know, to be off the following day."

Frank had suddenly appeared at the kitchen's entrance. "*Deborah?* Deborah who?"

Jack waved him off.

Frank stuck his tongue between two fingers, grabbed his crotch, and began thrusting his pelvis.

Jack gave him a sharp look and swung around, turning his back to him.

"Ah … okay, sure, anytime," Jack said. "But if we can plan around the weather, I mean—if that works for you?"

"Actually, Tuesday's great!" said Debbie. "I've got some vacation days, and Wednesdays are good days to take off. So, is Tuesday okay? I figured it might be too much to go straight to work after flying all night."

"Oh, absolutely," Jack said. "After flying all night, we'll go straight to bed … er, I mean—"

She laughed. "It's okay. I understand. So, what time should I meet you and where?"

Jack gave her the info and hung up the phone. He felt excited. This would be fun, something different. He remembered how she looked, how she was dressed but suddenly didn't care. She was the first girl he'd met who showed any interest in his work, and she was knowledgeable about the airplane. Any friend of the DC-3 was a friend of Jack's. Who gave a damn if she's plain?

· · ·

But now here she was, and hot as could be. Her mahogany shoulder-length hair was styled and full-bodied but pulled back in a way as if she knew she'd be wearing a headset. Her form-fitting khaki slacks, hiking boots, scarf, and light blue blouse topped by a brown pilot-style leather jacket were perfect for the occasion. Her attire neither hid her shapely figure nor amplified it.

As she came through the cluster of men, they turned, their eyes following her as she walked straight toward Jack. She approached him and greeted him with that disarmingly confident smile and handshake she'd offered him before.

"Welcome to Keystone," Jack said awkwardly and immediately regretted it. He was trying to recover from his surprise at her appearance.

"Thanks! I'm really, *really* excited!" she said, scrunching her shoulders and glancing around the room.

Following her gaze, Jack said, "As you can see, the décor is Bunker Revival." He gestured toward a heavy-set grumpy looking guy staring at them from behind the counter. "That's Charlie. He's not only our chief dispatcher but brilliant at creating battlefield ambiance. The hanging of weather charts, sectionals, and hazmat regs is his real genius. The cigarette smoke he imports for atmosphere."

Debbie chuckled and continued looking around. "I see," she said.

"Very impressive." She turned to Jack, her olive complexion, brown eyes, and bright smile sparkling in the lights. "So, this is where you do all your flight planning?"

"Yeah, the weather, the load, inspecting the aircraft logbook to see its recent maintenance history and such. From here, we'll go out to the airplane and you can watch as I do the preflight inspection and preparation of the cockpit—"

"Or come with me," Phil interjected, "and watch as I bust my butt loading freight while our captain here drags his feet pretending he's got something more important to do. Oh … and hi." Phil smiled, extending his hand to Debbie. "I'm your copilot, Phil Benson."

"Oh, sorry," Jack apologized with a self-conscious grin. "I didn't mean to ignore you."

Phil cocked his head toward him. "We're still working on manners," he told Debbie. "It was only last week he learned to eat with a fork."

Debbie laughed and smiled.

Jack couldn't take his eyes off her.

# EIGHT

An hour later, Phil was flying and they were en route to Baltimore. The ride was smooth in stratus clouds at four thousand feet. Light rain streaked across the windshield in tiny beads and dripped onto the pilots' legs through the windshield's weary seams. Outside, the red anticollision beacon reflected against the mist. Inside the cockpit, it felt as close and isolated from the world as a diving bell at the bottom of the sea.

The airplane's engines bellowed. Jack turned to Debbie, who was seated on the jump seat that folded down between the captain and copilot. "This first leg's the easiest," Jack said loudly. "The entire load is FedEx stuff. We do a contract for them between Philly, Baltimore, and Pittsburgh. After that, it gets back to our normal mix of things, airplane parts for the Piper factory at Lock Haven and UPS freight. Anyway, for these first two legs, the freight is clean, light, and easy. Nothing but those air boxes and bags of envelopes." His thumb pointed back toward the cabin. "No nuclear waste, diseased lab animals, cyanide gas, or any of the other fun stuff too dangerous or important to carry by truck or train."

Debbie's face fell.

"Only kidding … about the nuclear waste."

She pursed her lips. "You're so funny," she said, giving his shoulder a little push. Changing the subject, she pointed to the instrument panel. "I can tell by some of the placards and configuration that this is a C-47 and not a DC-3. Are all three of your airplanes ex-military?"

"No," said Jack over his shoulder. "Two C-47s and one DC-3, a former Eastern Airlines airplane. The C-47s the company bought as surplus. But all three are old school and demanding to fly. Not only are the instruments in a non-standard arrangement but they're arranged differently on every airplane. Like these black-on-black artificial horizons." Jack pointed to the instrument. "And, worse, those damn drum DGs and fixed card ADFs."

"I see that." Debbie's eyes narrowed as she studied the instrument.

"It means that during NDB approaches while you're bouncing around in the goo, you're doing all this math in your head to figure out how to stay on course: magnetic heading plus relative bearing equals magnetic bearing, and so forth. We don't do many NDBs, but there's a few and it's a bitch, er … it's tough."

"It sounds like a bitch." She smiled.

"Don't let him fool you," said Phil. "He makes it look easy."

Debbie shifted her gaze to the back of Jack's head and held it there. "I bet," she said with an approving grin. Phil caught this and smiled discreetly.

"Phil's a former Army pilot and West Point grad," said Jack. "His wife's an Army physician assigned to the Navy base downtown. Oh, and don't believe his BS. Phil's a better pilot than I'll ever be, and he'll be out of here and flying for the majors long before I will."

Phil made a face and waved him off.

"Only reason I'm sitting here, and he's there," Jack said, pointing at him, "is because I'd already passed my ATP written and had a thousand hours more fixed-wing multi-engine time than Phil did. When one of our guys got hired by Flying Tigers last year, the company needed a new captain quickly and I got the nod."

"Plus, I'm better looking, better dressed, and a *lot* more mature," Phil gibed.

"Gee, I don't know," Debbie teased. "You guys are having such a love-fest, maybe I ought to bail out and go home!"

"Nah. Too late! You're one of us now," said Jack. "You're stuck."

"Yeah," Phil told her. "You're one of us now, a full-fledged freight dog … lucky you!"

• • •

Later that night in Pittsburg, Phil and Debbie waited in the cockpit for Jack, who was on his way back to the airplane from the flight planning office. It was 2:40 am and they were about to start the third leg of the night: Pittsburg to Williamsport, Pennsylvania. The weather had gotten worse as the night settled in, with low stratus and fog across the route, and moderate rime ice reported at four thousand feet. Jack had filed for eight thousand feet to get above the clouds and the ice.

In the close, drizzly conditions, the ramp lights were haloed by the mist and shadowy figures glided in and out of the gloom. Inside the airplane, the damp cardboard boxes gave off a fecal scent, and the air had a fetid chill.

Even though Debbie's hairstyle had gone flat, her spirit was still buoyant in spite of the hour and the weather. After getting up to let Jack pass by and slide into his seat, Debbie buckled into hers.

Jack began his briefing, turning to face them both. "So, here's the deal. Although we've got minimums for takeoff here, the weather in Williamsport is iffy. The ceiling is eight hundred feet overcast and visibility is three-quarters of a mile. Although that's legal for the approach, it's going to be tight because the glide slope is out of service and it'll be a localizer only approach for Runway 27. Harrisburg's got seven hundred over and three, so that'll work as a good alternate. But, in all, it's crappy weather everywhere, and we'll have to keep an eye on it—especially for icing, which is moderate or greater in some places. I filed for eight thousand feet and that should keep us above all of it."

Phil nodded, pulled on his heavy David-Clark headset, and picked up the Before Starting Engines Checklist.

"Parking brake?" he said.

"Set."

"Logbook?"

"On board."

"Fuel selectors?"

"Mains…"

. . .

Half an hour later they were climbing through 7,400 feet when the clouds began thinning. Suddenly the tops were scudding past above them, and a moment later they broke into clear sky and pale moonlight, stars twinkling brightly all around them.

"Oh my God, that's breathtaking," said Debbie, the tops of the clouds racing by just beneath them. "Quite a view from your office, guys. A lot better than mine!"

Jack and Phil looked about and nodded, too weary to notice.

Forty minutes later it was time to begin their descent. Phil asked the New York Air Traffic Control Center for a lower altitude, and they were cleared to descend to six thousand feet.

Jack was flying that leg and had already briefed Phil on the Localizer Runway 27 approach to Williamsport. As they began the descent, Phil ran the in-range checklist:

"Altimeters?"

"29.98, set, information Delta."

"Carb air?"

"Cold," said Jack, confirming the position of the levers.

"Fuel selectors?"

"Mains."

"Mixtures?"

"Auto rich …"

When the checklist was complete, Jack turned to Debbie and explained that because approach minimums were set by the horizontal visibility at the airport and not the height of the clouds above it, in cases like these where the clouds were lower than the minimum descent altitude for the approach, there was a possibility they might not be able to see the runway in time to land even if the visibility on the surface was good. If that happened, then they would do a go-around and either attempt another approach or divert to their alternate airport and wait for the weather to lift.

As they leveled at six thousand feet, a coating of rime ice started to build up on the cockpit window frame. It was a part of the windshield that was not kept clear by the isopropyl alcohol squirting onto the glass. Phil turned on the wing inspection lights and pulled back his sliding windshield for a clearer view of the wing. A blast of noise burst into the cockpit and cold air was drawn from the cabin when the window was opened.

Phil aimed his flashlight in that direction. "Shit!"

"What?" Jack shouted above the roar of the engines and wind.

Phil ignored him as he directed his flashlight at the center of the right engine. He slammed the windshield closed and turned in alarm. "We've got oil on the crankcase housing."

"*WHAT?*" Jack exclaimed. "Damn it. And ice? Is there ice on the wing?"

"Not enough for the boots yet, and it looks like we're through it anyway," Phil said, directing his flashlight beam at the edge of the front windshield. The ice there had not increased.

"At least the oil temp and pressure are good," said Jack, looking at the engine instruments. "I wonder how long it's been leaking."

"Shit, who knows? What do you want to do?"

"Take the airplane," he said to Phil.

Jack looked at Debbie. "So, we've got an oil leak on that right engine. But as you know, these engines carry a lot of oil, and depending on how severe the leak is, we could go a while before we'd need to shut it down. We'll know we're there when the oil temp begins to rise or the pressure needle begins wavering. Problem is, we don't know how much oil has been lost already or how much time we've got until it's all gone. Getting the engine shut down before we begin the approach avoids the problems created by shutting it down in the midst of the close maneuvering needed during the approach or, worse, during a go-around. Anyway, shutting it down now is a better option assuming we're likely to land."

She appeared concerned but not scared, which relieved Jack.

Turning back to Phil, Jack said, "Keep an eye on those engine gauges and stay with center. I'll call the tower and see if they've got anything more recent than what they've got on the ATIS."

Phil nodded.

Jack tuned the tower frequency at Williamsport and called them. When he was done, he clipped his mic. "No change. It's still eight hundred over and three-quarters of a mile, but tower visibility's a mile. What do you think, press on or divert?"

Phil shrugged. "Press on. But like you said, I'd shut her down now. With a mile visibility, we have an excellent chance of getting in, and we don't want to be in the middle of an engine shutdown if we have to do a go-around. One way or another, taking a shot at it makes more sense to me than attempting Harrisburg in icing conditions on one engine."

"Glad we agree," said Jack. He turned to Debbie. "Did you follow that?"

"Yes," she said. "We're between a rock and a hard place, and you're choosing the rock."

Jack smiled. "Trust me," he said over his shoulder. "This is more routine than you'd ever imagine, and we're pretty good at it." He looked at Phil and said, "I'll listen to center while you call the company at Williamsport and tell them what's going on. Remind them we'll need a tow off the runway, and I'll advise center we'll be delayed on the runway in case they've got anyone else inbound behind us."

Phil nodded and reached to tune the number two radio to the UNICOM frequency that the company monitored.

Jack picked up his mic. "New York Center, Keystone Six-Two-Five."

"Keystone Six-Two-Five, New York."

"Roger, sir, stand by one, please," Jack said. Looking at Phil, he asked, "You feel that?"

Phil's eyes narrowed and he gazed at the panel vacantly. "Yeah," he said. "Yeah, I do. *SHIT!*" He turned for his side window, yanked off the bungee that held it closed, and pulled the window open. With his flashlight focused on the engine, he paused. Slamming the window closed, he looked at Jack. "Not good! Fuckin' oil's pouring out now and covering the entire crankcase. Got to be a blown jug."

"Right," said Jack as he straightened in his seat and took the controls. "I've got the airplane. Give me the Engine Shutdown Checklist."

Phil pulled the emergency checklist from its storage slot on his side of the cockpit.

Jack picked up his mic. "New York, Keystone Six-Two-Five is declaring an emergency. One engine shutdown, two hours fuel, three souls on board, and we'll squawk seven-seven-zero-zero." He twisted the knobs for that number on the transponder. "Also, please advise tower we will not be able to taxi clear of the runway after landing. We'll require a tow."

"Roger, Keystone Six-Two-Five, understand declaring an emergency, sir. I see you're squawking code seven-seven-zero-zero. Understand engine shutdown, is that correct?"

"Affirmative, Six-Two-Five."

"Roger, Keystone Six-Two-Five, I'll advise tower. Come left heading zero-six-zero, descend and maintain four thousand feet. You're number one for the approach."

Jack repeated the clearance.

The controller said, "Keystone Six-Two-Five, contact Williamsport Approach now on one-one-nine-point-three. They're being advised of your situation."

"Keystone Six-Two-Five, roger, sir, we'll go to approach," said Jack. "Thanks for the help."

"Company's been advised, too," said Phil. "I'm standing by with the checklist."

"Yeah, go ahead," said Jack.

"Hydraulic pump selector?"

"Left engine," said Jack.

"Right throttle close?"

"Right throttle, closed."

The airplane yawed to the right as Jack pulled the throttle to idle, but he corrected by pressing the left rudder and adding rudder trim to keep the airplane aligned with the wind.

"Props?" said Phil.

"Right engine, low RPM."

"Mixtures?"

"Number two, cut off. Confirm?" Jack asked, his hand on the right mixture control.

"Confirmed."

To complete the checklist, Jack guarded the feather button for the left engine as Phil pushed the button for the right. The airplane shuddered as the right prop came to a stop, the blades aligned with the wind to reduce aerodynamic drag.

"Okay, contact approach now," said Jack, "and give me the Before Landing Checklist when you can."

"Williamsport Approach, Keystone Six-Two-Five descending to four with Delta," said Phil.

"Roger, Keystone Six-Two-Five, altimeter now two-nine-nine-seven. This will be vectors for a Localizer Runway Two-Seven approach, glide slope out of service. Heading zero-six-zero, maintain four."

"Roger, sir," said Phil. "Present heading zero-six-zero, maintain four." Clipping his mic, he picked up the checklist. "Altimeters?"

"Two-nine-nine-seven, check and crosschecked," Jack said.

"Two-nine-nine-seven," said Phil. "Cowl flaps?"

"Set."

"Landing Checklist complete to the gear," said Phil.

Cocking his head toward Debbie, Jack asked, "How you doing?"

"I'm excited!" she said, pasting on a smile.

Jack risked taking his eyes off his panel to look at her. She showed her teeth in an even more exaggerated smile.

He reached for her left knee and gave it a shake. "Trust me. We got this."

"Yes, I can see that." Debbie nodded, but her smile was gone.

"Keystone Six-Two-Five, left turn three-six-zero."

"Left three-six-zero, Keystone Six-Two-Five." Phil put down his mic and looked at Jack. "Okay, so the localizer's identified on your side and Williamsport VOR on mine. I've got the one-ninety-eight-radial on my side for the IAF. Cross the marker at thirty-seven hundred, the MDA is fifteen hundred, and the missed approach point is four minutes and twenty-three seconds, which I'll call on my clock."

"That's it," Jack said, reviewing his approach plate as Phil spoke. "We'll plan gear down at the marker. If we have to go around, there's high terrain to the north, so I'm climbing to a thousand feet and then turning twenty degrees right to two-nine-zero."

"Keystone Six-Two-Five, left turn three-zero-zero to intercept, maintain four thousand feet, you're cleared for the approach."

"Three-zero-zero to intercept, maintain four, cleared for the approach, Keystone Six-Two-Five."

"Roger, sir, contact tower now on one-one-nine-point-one."

Phil switched frequencies and called the tower. "Williamsport, Keystone Six-Two-Five, outside the marker at four."

"Roger, Keystone Six-Two-Five, you're cleared to land, sir, wind two-four-zero at eight, and airfield fire and rescue is standing by."

"Roger, cleared to land, Keystone Six-Two-Five," said Phil.

"Okay, checklist's complete, gear to go," said Jack, his eyes on his instruments as he adjusted the throttle and rudder trim.

"Localizer's alive," said Phil.

The needle on the navigation instrument began to center. Jack banked the airplane to the left to capture the inbound course.

"Okay, there's the IAF," said Phil. "Descend to three thousand seven hundred."

Jack pulled back the throttle slightly and began a slow descent. Two minutes later, they heard the sound of the outer marker, the monotone *dah-dah, dah-dah, dah-dah*, and saw the small blue light on the instrument panel flashing.

"Crossing altitude thirty-seven hundred," said Phil. "Right on the money. Descend to fifteen hundred, and I've hacked the clock."

"Gear down," Jack ordered, his right hand giving the signal.

Phil reached between Debbie's legs and moved the gear lever to the down position, checked that the down line and system pressure were equal, and then moved the safety latch to the secure position. "Down and green," he said, pointing to the light on the instrument panel.

The extended landing gear created a large increase in drag. With one engine shut down, once the gear was extended, the descent would have to be continued to a landing or the gear would have to be immediately retracted to permit the airplane to climb during a missed approach and go-around. The gear on the DC-3 was always slow to retract and often did not retract fully on the first attempt.

Jack's eyes darted about the instrument panel to get the information he needed to fly the airplane with precision. "Call out altitude, sink, airspeed, and course." The callouts ensured Jack didn't fixate on one instrument and one flight parameter at the expense of the others.

"Twenty-five hundred, sink six, on speed," said Phil. "On course, one thousand to go, two minutes to missed approach point."

The further they descended toward the ground, the faster Jack's eyes darted about the panel. Even a small lapse in his attention at that point could result in abandoning the approach—never an easy maneuver but far more dangerous and difficult with an engine shut down and high terrain close by.

"Gear's down and locked, green light. Landing check complete." Phil's scan shifted between the instrument panel and the view ahead as he searched anxiously for any sign of the runway or approach lights.

Turbulence from wind passing over the adjacent mountain rocked the airplane. Debbie watched closely as Jack controlled the airplane with small and smoothly executed adjustments.

The deeper they descended into the gloom, the more the wind buffeted the airplane.

"Five hundred feet, one minute to go—on course, on speed," said Phil, his hands and feet now lightly touching the controls to back Jack up.

"One hundred above MDA, thirty seconds to go," said Phil.

With only seconds left, Phil shifted his scan rapidly between the clock and the windshield.

Debbie gripped her knees and her heart raced as she looked for the runway and watched the clock. She knew well the DC-3's limited climb performance on one engine and only now felt scared.

Jack continued scanning the instruments alone and ignored everything outside.

"MDA! Level off," said Phil. "Fifteen seconds to go! Ten … nine … eight … seven …"

Jack gave a signal with his right hand indicating he was going lower. He was going to bust minimums, a risky and illegal maneuver but no more risk, he figured, than going around. He edged the airplane lower by another hundred feet.

"… six … five … four … three … two …"

Jack chanced a glimpse out the windshield, saw nothing, and shouted, "Okay, going around! Props full forward!"

"*WAIT!*" Phil shouted. "ONE O'CLOCK … ONE O'CLOCK … ONE O'CLOCK!" His left hand pointed at three sequenced lights flashing through the murk.

Jack shot a glance in that direction. "Got 'em," he said. "I'm out; you're in!"

Phil moved his scan entirely to the instruments, and Jack flew the airplane by reference to the approach lights alone.

"Okay, level and on speed," said Phil.

"Correcting right! Correcting right!" said Jack as he banked the airplane slightly to align it with the approach lights.

As soon as the lights were straight ahead, Jack continued a slow descent. An instant later, the clouds disappeared and the runway was in full view, the white lights on either side of the pavement spreading out before them.

"Lights?" said Phil, his left hand on the airplane's landing light switches.

"Yeah," said Jack, continuing his descent for the runway.

The runway's large white numbers 2 and 7 wavered in the airplane's landing lights, and moments later the touchdown marks passed beneath them.

The main gear tires slid on the pavement, and as the airplane decelerated, the tailwheel descended and made contact with the runway.

Debbie sank in her seat and let out a long silent sigh.

Jack began gently applying the brakes. Once the airplane came to a stop, he set the brake, cut the mixture on the left engine, and called for the Shutdown Checklist.

Flashing emergency lights from the airport fire truck appeared off the left side, and Jack stuck his arm out his sliding window to give the rescue crew an OK sign and thumbs-up. He pulled in his arm, looked back at Debbie, and smiled. "So, other than that, Miss Moretti, how'd you enjoy your flight tonight?"

# NINE

J ack was asleep, and Phil was the first awakened by the room phone's pealing.

Reaching toward the nightstand between the beds, Phil knocked the receiver off the hook and pulled it back from the floor by the wire. He cleared his throat and grumbled, "Hello?" There was a pause as he listened.

"No, it's Phil," he said, rubbing his eyes.

Pause.

"*What?*" Phil exclaimed. "What's *that?*"

Pause.

"Alright, sure … I'll let him know," he grumbled.

Pause.

"Wait! You mean *now?*"

Pause.

"Yeah, *damn it!* … I'll tell him!"

Pause.

"Yeah, I GOT it, Kurt … goodbye!"

Phil slammed the receiver onto the phone and rolled onto his back.

"What's up?" Jack yawned.

"The airplane's fixed. They want it back yesterday."

Jack glanced at the clock. "It's 9:50," he said groggily. "We landed at what, 4:30?"

"Yeah. We checked in here about 5:30."

Jack swung his feet to the floor and massaged the back of his neck. He stood up and staggered toward the window. As he pulled back the curtain, a sliver of sunlight came through, and he squinted as he looked outside.

"What's it doing?" asked Phil.

"Looks like it's lifting. Did they say what was wrong?" Jack turned to look at him. "They got it fixed too quick if it was a jug."

"I didn't ask," said Phil. "But whatever it was, you know all they've done is plug it with gasket seal and slap some duct tape over it. That's why they want the airplane back. To get it properly fixed for tonight."

Jack nodded, let go of the curtain, and shuffled toward the bathroom. "So, what's the plan?"

"I'm thinking we head out for breakfast," said Jack. "Then we'll hit the pool for a while, get in a nap, then cocktails in the bar this afternoon. Dinner and dancing with Debbie tonight."

Phil reached for the lamp and turned it on. "Who's showering first?"

"You," Jack said, plopping on the bed. "I'll give Debbie a call, give her a heads-up. Did you call Karen?"

"No, she had an early shift today, and I didn't want to wake her." Phil got up and weaved toward the bathroom, scratching his chest. "She knows the drill. If I don't come home, she listens to the news on the drive to the clinic. Unless there's something about an airplane crash, she just figures I'll be late."

Jack dialed Debbie's room. Keystone had paid for two rooms, and the guys doubled up so Debbie could have her own.

She cleared her throat as she answered. "Hello," she said, cheerfully.

"Hey Deb, it's Jack. Sorry to wake you, but the company called and said the airplane's ready. They want it back in Philly as soon as possible."

"Oh," she said. "Oh, okay … okay, I'll—"

"You're more than welcome to come along with us, but if you'd prefer, we could get you on a bus or maybe an Altair flight to Philly. Not that I'd want you to, but after last night I'd understand."

"What? No! *No*," she said. "Not at all. I'm okay. I'd like to go with you guys, I mean—if that's all right?"

"Of course it's all right. I just feel terrible about all this and—"

"No, no … I'm fine," she broke in. "I'd love to go along, and I'll be ready right away. When do you need me?"

"We're washing up now and will be ready in a bit. Just give us a knock on our door whenever you're ready to go."

Debbie hung up and went into the bathroom. When she turned on the light, she cringed as she squinted at the mirror. The lights hurt but not as much as what she was seeing. Her hair was a greasy mop. Bags like prunes were under her eyes, and she had neither toothpaste, a brush, nor much of a makeup kit.

She forced back tears as she pulled back the curtain for the shower.

• • •

At the airport, they stood beneath the airplane's right engine and looked up at the freshly cleaned Pratt and Whitney 1830.

"They said it was a pushrod seal," Jack said, reading from the logbook. "Said it's been repaired, cleaned, and topped off with AeroShell 100. They said they ran it up, and it all checks good." Closing the book, he turned to Phil. "You believe that?"

"Nope. But they cleaned it up nice, and if they topped it off with oil like they said, we might just have just enough to leak our way home if it's not too bad."

"Agreed," said Jack, staring at the engine. "But if it comes unglued like last night, we're fuc—er, screwed." He gave a sheepish glance at Debbie.

"Why would we be fucked?" she asked, looking up at the engine.

Jack stifled a smile; he liked this girl. "Because according to the regs, we'd have to land at the nearest suitable airport along the route and that could be Reading or Harrisburg. You sure you don't want to go home by the commuter or by bus?"

Debbie glanced at the sparkling Altair Beech 99 parked at the passenger terminal nearby. She shrugged. "Nah … I'm all in. I mean, how could it possibly get any worse?" She gave her hair a self-conscious toss.

"With you along, it can only get better," Phil said with a smile.

"Yeah," said Jack. "You're our good-luck charm and the prettiest freight dog we've ever seen."

She made a face. "Was that a compliment?" she asked Phil.

"Absolutely," Phil said. "But only on Planet Jack."

She laughed. "Let's get out of here."

. . .

After they parked the airplane in Philly, Jack and Debbie jumped to the ramp and waited for Phil as he gathered the control locks from the aft storage compartment.

A mechanic greeted Jack by the cargo door.

Jack handed him the logbook. "No problem on the return from Williamsport. But that leak last night was pretty severe, plus we felt a vibration. Seems like it would have been more than just a pushrod seal. I've had them before, but not this bad."

The mechanic pursed his lips and nodded. "It's a contract guy who does the work in Williamsport. I'll look it over and see what gives."

Jack said to Debbie, "I've got to stop by the chief's office and fill him in on what happened for his reports. I won't be long, but if you want to run, go ahead, I understand." He smiled.

"Oh, uh … no, I don't mind. I mean … I *could* wait," she said with a hopeful air.

"Sure, no problem. Let me finish up here and I'll catch up with you by the door. I won't be long."

'Oh … ah … all right," she said. "By the door to the parking lot?"

"Sure," said Jack.

Debbie left and Phil jumped out with the control locks. "Hand me the ailerons," Jack said, reaching for the aluminum braces dangling from Phil's hand.

Phil looked at Debbie as she walked toward the open bay of the terminal. "Where's she going?"

"She's heading out. Give me the locks, and I'll give you a hand."

"Are you nuts?" Phil looked at Jack with his eyes narrowed. "Go get that girl, you dufus. I'll take care of the airplane."

"Think so?"

"I do. Her eyes were on you all night. The really good ones are hard to find, Jack, and it looks to me like you just found one."

Jack turned to gaze at Debbie. "What would a girl like that want with me?" he said as if asking himself the question. "Must be a million engineers at Boeing after her too."

"Trust me. Go."

Jack looked at Phil and gave a shrug. "Okay. See you Thursday, then."

"Go. *NOW!*" said Phil.

Jack stopped by the chief pilot's office, briefed him on the engine shutdown and emergency landing, and then caught up with Debbie, who was outside the building sitting on the top step, her arms wrapped around her knees.

"Hey, sorry to keep you," Jack said from behind her.

She smiled and stood up. "No problem. Pretty morning, huh?"

"I wish it hadn't been such a bust," said Jack. "I was hoping for good weather and no problems. I really wanted you to have fun."

Debbie rolled her eyes. "Oh my God, Jack, are you kidding? It was thrilling! I mean, I can't say I wasn't nervous, but I really enjoyed it."

Jack smiled self-consciously. Women had been absent his entire adult life: the all-male schools, the military, and now a career choice that almost entirely excluded them. His lack of self-confidence with them took over. "You're a great jump seater," he said, awkwardly extending his hand. "You're welcome back anytime you're up for a good fright!"

She swallowed her disappointment and put on a little smile. "Yeah … well, okay," she said as they shook. She looked toward her car. "So … I guess I'll be going."

"Yeah, uh … me, too," Jack said, looking toward the lot.

"Mine's that one," she said, pointing toward a new beige VW Beetle close to the stairs.

*Ugh*, Jack thought. He didn't want her seeing his. "Mine's over there," he said, waving vaguely toward the opposite side of the lot.

She nodded blankly, gave him a little wave, and started down the stairs.

Jack watched her leave, knowing Phil would kill him if he let her go. He girded himself for the rejection he figured was coming, and called out her name.

She stopped, turned, and looked up at him expressionlessly, her right hand shading her eyes from the morning sun.

"You're not officially a freight dog yet."

She gave him a puzzled look. Freight dog was the last thing on her mind.

"For it to be official, you have to be able to function like a human after a night like that. It's the final exam."

"How so?"

"Have pizza and beer with me at a little place I know in Brandywine. The test is staying awake while you do."

She beamed and gave him a thumbs-up. "Keystone Six-Two-Five, cleared for the approach!"

# TEN

The Sunshine Bouquet Jack had ordered the previous day arrived on Friday morning.

Claire got up from her desk to receive it from the FTD deliveryman. She peeled back the tissue and relished the scent.

He gazed around the office, stalling for a tip. "This place reminds me of the Marines," he said. "Every time I come in here, I feel like I should salute."

Claire followed his gaze and shrugged. "Maybe you should," she quipped.

"Reminds me of my barracks in Korea. Everything concrete block and puke green paint. Even those pictures of airplanes." He laughed cynically as he pointed at them. "The only thing missing is bombs."

The flowers came as a quid pro quo, so Claire felt no need to tip. She pursed her lips and threw him a wave. "*Au revoir*," she said, and turned to her desk.

He walked out showing her the back of his hand. "Adios," he grumbled.

She paused and peeled the tissue back further. The arrangement of little sunflowers, snapdragons, and daisy poms was irresistible. Claire smiled and preened them like a mother combing the hair of a child.

Normally, she wouldn't have stopped to enjoy them. Kegan bristled at the gifts whenever he saw them. He knew where they came from and why, "pilots seeking a shortcut," he'd grouse. The gifts—all manner of things: flowers, chocolates, perfume, even lingerie, *mon Dieu*—offended his sense of military bearing. "This is an airline, not a goddamn bridal shower," he'd growl as Claire received them from the deliverymen.

But today Kegan was attending a meeting at FAA headquarters in Washington, D.C., and Claire was alone. With the office under her command, she made a command decision: the flowers would stay.

Placing the bouquet down on her desk, she left to borrow a vase from the girls in the maintenance office down the hall. They were allowed to have flowers.

When she returned, she spotted a small envelope on the floor by her desk and bent down to pick it up. It had an FTD stamp in the corner and her name in a feminine print across the middle. She frowned and dropped it in the wastebasket as she always had. She never bothered reading the notes. What was the point?

Once the bouquet was set in the vase, she placed it on her desk next to the photos of her family. She smiled at the images of her *mama* in her beloved garden in Léon and the photo of her father and brother in front of their small house, laughing. That picture had been taken a year before they were executed for resistance by the Waffen-SS. Two years later *Mama* died of a broken heart, leaving Claire alone.

After the war, she married a neighbor's son, a French Air Force pilot with whom she'd fallen in love. But then, desperate to continue flying after the war, he left for Indochina to fly for the Foreign Legion. He and Claire lived apart for those three years. When he returned to France at the end of his tour, he soon left in pursuit of another flying job, this time with a small airline in Miami named Pan Tropic. Claire joined him, hoping to repair their marriage, but it wasn't to be. Philippe accused her of infidelity while he was in Indochina. Although it was true, she'd never admitted it. They'd been estranged ever since. There were no children.

Her job was the most important part of her life, and other than the office's spartan décor and "military bearing," she relished her position with the airline. At forty-three, Claire was still as trim as a thirty-year-old but far more seasoned. Her experience in Nazi-occupied France had inured her to willful men, and whether fending off aggressive pilots angling for a job, stiff-necked FAA inspectors angling for information, or presumptuous executives angling for sex, Claire played them all with *savoir faire*.

After another glance at the flowers and a bit more preening, she sat down to do some typing.

The IBM clacked like a machine gun as Claire turned Kegan's dictation into a letter. But typing was a rote task for her and her mind wandered, this time to the note she'd dropped into the wastebasket. Keeping the bouquet and not reading the note that came with it was churlish and beneath her. When had she changed from being professionally detached to just vulgar?

Feeling a pang of guilt, she stopped and stood up to retrieve it from the trash.

Plucking the envelope from the wastebasket, she ripped it open briskly and summarily regarded the florist's feminine script:

*Thank you for your time and patience. Air Logistics is my first choice of airlines and I would be thrilled at the opportunity for an interview.*

*Sincerely, Jack Dolan*

Claire dropped her hand with the note to her side and gazed across the room to the middle distance. She recalled the tenor of his calls, hesitant, tenuous, never forward as most others had been, men accustomed to command, attempting to command Claire too.

She returned the note to the trash and, on an impulse, walked to the filing cabinets behind her desk and squatted to open a drawer at the bottom. It was where she kept her slush pile, applicants whom she'd screened and found qualified but lacking in the DC-8 experience the company now required. When she came to the file marked D, she sifted through it, found Jack's application, and pulled it out.

Claire sat down at her desk and put the application on the blotter. She reached for her bag and drew out a lighter and a pack of Kent cigarettes. Tapping one out, she lit it and swiveled aside in her chair. With Jack's application in her lap, she crossed her legs and flipped through the pages, casually reviewing his certifications, flight time, and current employer. Everything checked out. He was certainly qualified.

Flipping to the front of the application, she came to his personal information and her brows went up. He was only twenty-six, which was at least ten years younger than any pilot the company had hired since she'd been there. Claire had found what she was looking for, an explanation for the dissonance in his behavior, the callowness of the man on the phone versus the brazenness of the man attempting to bribe her with flowers.

She assumed a decadent influence, a reprobate uncle, a rogue mentor, a hirsute ape with a pilot's license in the family was pushing young Dolan to do what he otherwise wouldn't. And yet, as she thought of it, she admired his ambition, his willingness to go beyond himself when needed. Kegan would value that too.

She put down the application, rocked back in her chair, and took another drag on her cigarette.

DC-8 experience in this round of hiring wasn't hard to find. The soft economy—"stagflation" as it was called—had a severe impact on air-commerce and pilot careers. It had been a decade of furloughs and career stagnation, no progress up the seniority list for Air Logistics pilots, and no growth in any airline at all. Thousands of highly qualified pilots competed for the few jobs that came up from time to time.

Though they were plentiful, pilots with the DC-8 experience the company was demanding came at a price in terms of their age. Nearly all of the men Claire had recently selected would be retired by the FAA's age sixty rule before they had an opportunity to upgrade.

In sum, that meant the new policy limited the pool of qualified candidates to men who didn't care about upgrading, and that was hugely off-putting for Kegan. As far as he was concerned, any pilot who didn't care if he became a captain didn't belong at his airline. Air Logistics' varied missions and worldwide authority required pilots with a lot of ambition and drive, but pilots who managed their ambition well. Such men were not easy to find. Kegan believed prioritizing DC-8 experience over temperament, tenacity, character, and flying skill was folly, and Claire agreed. Though she wasn't a pilot, she was married to one, and her husband was a prime example of what Air Logistics didn't need: ambitious pilots who were equally ambitious jerks. Air Logistics valued teamwork. Philippe valued only himself.

Leaning forward, she crushed out her smoke and reached for Jack's file. Kegan depended on her to pick the best pilots to be interviewed. She'd never failed him, and wouldn't now.

She stood up with the file in hand and marched into Kegan's office. He'd planned to stop by on his way home from D.C. to pick up the files she'd assembled for the weekend. Claire slipped Jack's in with the others. "*Bonne chance, jeune homme*," she muttered.

She'd taken a stand against the flawed policy. Let Kegan decide for himself.

Pleased with her decision, she returned to her office and smiled as she eyed the elegant little bouquet.

# ELEVEN

*Miami International Airport, September 25, 1978*

Kegan entered the office on Monday morning and stopped at Claire's desk. Handing her the pilot applications he'd rejected over the weekend, he asked "Get to that garden show?"

"I did." She took the files from his hands and smiled. "How was golf?"

"Very nice. Old friends, and a beautiful day on the links."

"And these? Did they meet your expectations?"

"Yes, even those. All of them were excellent. I'll make a list of those I want called in and give you that this morning. We'll begin the interviews a week from now. Plan two per day for a total of ten: one in the morning and one in the afternoon as usual."

Claire smiled and gave a nod.

Kegan walked to his office, and Claire swiveled to her filing cabinets to return the rejected applications to her slush pile.

When she came to Jack's, she paused, made a little pout, then shrugged and slipped it into the file marked D.

· · ·

By Thursday, September 28, Claire had scheduled the ten pilots for interviews beginning the following Monday morning. She was typing FAA Ops-Specs revisions when her phone rang. She pressed the button for the line and picked up the receiver. Cradling it between her head and shoulder, she examined what she'd typed as she spoke. "Captain Kegan's office. This is Claire, may I help you?"

"Good morning, Mrs. Desmarais, this is Jack Dolan."

She pursed her lips. She'd expected his call and closed her eyes as she composed herself. Kegan delivered the good news; only Claire delivered the bad.

"Mrs. Desmarais?"

"One moment please." She pressed the hold button.

Claire had inherited her father's iron will and her mother's soft heart. Only rarely did the two align for a single purpose, but when they did, Claire was unstoppable. Following through on her earlier decision, she put the receiver to her ear.

"Mr. Dolan, yes. I'm sorry to inform you, but Captain Kegan has seen your application and you are not being considered at this time. I've returned your application to my files. As I told you, DC-8 experience is required and only those pilots meeting that requirement are presently being interviewed."

On the other end of the line, Jack flinched. The blunt truth and her perfunctory tone hit him like a wrecking ball. He was dumbstruck, his hope collapsing into rubble.

Sensing this, Claire sighed. "However … as it is," she said hesitantly. "As it is, Mr. Dolan, there is *one* more thing."

Jack was staring vacantly at his bare feet. "One more *thing*?"

"Yes," she replied. "Perhaps if you were to stop by at a convenient time, Captain Kegan may be able to give you a few moments. Not an interview, you understand, but a chance to meet. In the future, should the company's requirements change, meeting now could be an advantage. I've seen this before."

Jack looked up; his jaw dropped.

"Mr. Dolan?"

"Yes … yes, of course," he stammered. "A chance to meet? Absolutely! When?"

"Any day next week will be fine. Captain Kegan will begin interviews on Monday. He leaves the office for lunch promptly at twelve o'clock. If you're waiting here for him, he might have a moment to talk to you on the way out."

Jack coughed. "Monday? As in next week?"

"Monday will be fine," she said. "Or any other day next week. It really doesn't matter."

*Next* week? he thought. *Is she nuts? How the hell am I going to manage that?*

"Did you hear me, Mr. Dolan?"

"Yes … yes, ma'am," he said, running his fingers through his hair. "Any day next week."

"That is correct, Mr. Dolan. Now, good day."

Click.

Jack stared blankly at the receiver and then hung it on the hook. He turned around, stumbled into the living room, and plopped onto the couch.

Fly from Philly to Miami for a chance visit with this guy on his way to lunch? To what end? A handshake, hello, and goodbye, and that's it? Beyond that, how the hell would he arrange it with Ernie, his chief pilot? Getting a day off—much less the several days Jack would need to make this work—was impossible at Keystone. There were no reserve pilots to take his place. Ernie could juggle the schedule and make do as best he could when someone was sick or there was some family emergency, but never any more than that. The only sure way to get off was to quit, which was unthinkable. Although Jack had issues with the job, until he had something certain in the bag, walking out of Keystone was madness. There was no guarantee he'd find anything else, much less something better, given the horde of pilots looking for work. There were countless guys who'd kill for Jack's job. Quitting Keystone was not an option.

He stood up and began pacing the room as he distilled the possibilities. He settled on three: one, quitting Keystone, which he'd already rejected; two, lying to Ernie about needing the time off for some family emergency; or three, forgetting the Gary method and returning to the accepted means of seeking a job, which was getting Jack nowhere.

He walked to the bedroom, fell back on the bed, and stared up at the ceiling. He'd be back to flying that night and again on Friday. If he went to Miami, the best time to leave would be Sunday in order to be back on the job by Wednesday night. Jack would miss two nights of work. That might be doable. Less doable was the cost of this charade, which would be every dime Jack had salted away for a true contingency—a legitimate interview. Pissing it away now on a wild goose chase was not in the cards.

As he stared glumly at the ceiling, he rubbed his eyes. The four hours of sleep he'd gotten since walking in the door that morning had petered out, and Jack quietly dozed off.

He woke at 4:20 p.m., got up, and was stumbling toward the living room half-asleep when the answer came to him: the truth. Tell Ernie the simple, unvarnished truth. No bullshit, no lies … no weaseling. "Walk like a man," he muttered as he reached for the phone.

When Ernie answered, Jack told him he'd just been offered the best shot at a world-class airline he'd ever have and couldn't pass it up. He needed Monday through Wednesday off next week to go to Miami and meet the chief pilot. Ernie grumbled, but Jack reminded him that the late-season Bermuda high that was dominating the weather over the East Coast was forecast to continue, so the night's flying would be easy. Ernie groaned. Jack reminded him how many times he'd picked up work to cover for married guys who needed to be off for a family obligation, and it was only fair to return the favor. Ernie whined under his breath, but finally relented and allowed Jack to go.

"Monday and Tuesday only, Jack," he said sternly. "I need you back to fly Wednesday night. No later!"

Jack agreed and hung up the phone. He grabbed the Yellow Pages under the counter, found the number for Eastern Airlines reservations, and booked a seat to Miami on Sunday.

# TWELVE

It was a mild Saturday evening for his second date with Debbie, and Jack had chosen a little mom-and-pop place in Brandywine. Pat and Mara's Irish Kitchen had a warm, pub-like atmosphere; great food; a friendly, vivacious crowd; and no romantic ambiance whatsoever. It was the perfect venue, for now.

They took a booth across from the bar. When the middle-aged waitress with cat-eye glasses arrived, she greeted them with a toothy smile and handed them menus. As she cleared the table of excess dinnerware, she took their order for drinks.

"A pint of Harps, please," said Debbie, glancing at the taps behind the bar.

Jack smiled. "Make that two." When the waitress left, he said, "You know your beer! Pretty good coming from a girl named Moretti."

"Oh, I'm full of surprises." She smiled.

"Me, too. I'm *half*-Italian. My better half—my mom."

"Good for Mom!" Debbie gazed at him intently. "I figured there must be some Mediterranean in your blood. That swarthy complexion, brown hair and eyes. Not an Irish freckle in sight. And oh … that Roman nose. A dead giveaway," she said with a wry grin. "Which, by the way—"

Jack fingered the scar across his bridge. "Rugby," he said self-consciously. "I joined a neolithic league in D.C. to blow off steam after the war. The ball was somebody's head."

Debbie recoiled. "*Ugh!* Well, you're full of surprises too, aren't you?"

Jack smiled and waved her off. "One of my many youthful misadventures." Changing the subject, he picked up the menu. "Their shepherd's pie and Irish stew are fabulous, but you can't go wrong with anything here. My favorite is bangers and mash with onion gravy."

"Sounds wonderful." Debbie put her menu aside and leaned closer to him to be heard over the lively crowd. "So, tell me more about this thing you've been doing to get an interview. I've never heard anything like it."

"To be clear, it's not something I like. I'm not naturally a schmoozer. But I feel like I haven't much choice. I'm embarrassed to admit it, but I didn't finish college. I dropped out and never went back."

"Oh," she said, looking puzzled. "Does that matter? Do you need a degree to be a pilot for that airline you told me about?"

"Technically no, but to be competitive, yes. At the major airlines like United or American, there's no escaping the need for a degree. But at supplemental airlines like Air Logistics—the airline I'm schmoozing—the hiring process is a lot more personal. The chief pilot usually has full control over it, and if he likes you, you're in. Not to make it sound easy, because it's not. But if I can get in the door and get a chance to sell myself, I stand a chance. My age, flying experience, and military service are all excellent advantages. The four-year degree I'm lacking is my only disadvantage."

"Why not go back to school?"

"Because I don't have the time. I'll be twenty-seven next June, and even going back full-time would put me past thirty when I graduate. All the majors cap their hiring at age thirty, so the effort wouldn't be rewarded. All that considered, I decided my best bet is to continue investing all my time building my flying resume—hopefully acquire some heavy jet experience—and let my lack of college be my only weakness. Beyond that, it's nearly impossible to go to school and fly at the same time. Just look at my work schedule and you can see why. Anyway, that's why I'm giving the Gary method a shot."

"Is Gary your friend who importuned an interview?"

Jack smiled sheepishly. "Yeah, he taught me that you weasel your way in by schmoozing the chief pilot's secretary. Hopefully, you succeed and she either recommends you directly, or she takes pity on you and invites you in for a few minutes of her boss's time—enough to wow him and get invited back."

"You don't strike me as a schmoozer, Jack, and I mean that as a compliment."

"I'm not, but desperate times, desperate measures ... anyway, enough about me," he said, their gazes locked. "Why aerospace engineering? How'd you get interested in that?"

"My dad. I'm an only child and grew up with Dad's love of airplanes and the space missions. It was something he passed along. I was imprinted pretty early."

"Does he fly?"

"Oh ... no. I mean, he'd like to, but he owns a printing business—a big one, in fact. It's a family thing, three generations. But Dad's first love was always airplanes. He wanted to fly during WWII, but his poor vision kept him out of it. After the war, there was never any time for it as a hobby. But our house is full of models and photos—my poor mom surrendered to his obsession—and then our trips to airports, and airplane and helicopter rides, and all the rest. Added to that, Mom's a math teacher and math is my strongest subject. Putting it all together, *ta da* ... aeronautical engineer." She smiled, holding up her hands.

"Math? *Ugh*," Jack groaned. "Will you walk out if I tell you that was my worst subject? Math's the reason I dropped out of college."

"Why didn't you just switch majors?"

"I went to SUNY Maritime College, an all-male military school, and there were only two majors: marine engineering and marine transportation. Both required passing calculus in freshman year. I probably could have pulled a gentleman's C out of it if I truly applied myself. When it came to school, I did well in what I liked and didn't give a damn about anything else. Beyond that, after four years of all-male parochial high school, I'd had enough of the all-male thing. I wanted to get out into the world, go to work, live a little ... and figure it out from there. Unfortunately, Uncle Sam had other plans and my plans weren't part of them."

The waitress took their order and walked away.

"So, you were saying," said Debbie. "About Uncle Sam?"

"I had a draft deferment at Maritime because it was a Navy ROTC program. But once I dropped out, my deferment was gone, and my lottery number came up fifty-nine. Six months after leaving school, I was in the Army and on my way to Vietnam."

"Oh, Jack! Oh, my God." She sat back and covered her mouth. "I only know the war from television, but Oh my God. I'm so sorry—"

Jack waved her away. "More importantly, when I got back to the 'world,' as we called home, it was time to get serious. Dad's a Pan Am pilot, and ever since I was born, I've been around airplanes. I learned to walk on the dirt floor of a hangar in Manassas, Virginia, and cried whenever Dad brought us in for a landing in one of his little airplanes—I never wanted the flight to end. Some kids get pacifiers; I got wings. Anyway, putting all that together as you say, I decided flying would be my career. Problem is, I'd decided late. By the time I got around to it, most other guys wanting to fly had already finished college. So, here I am, coming up far from behind, and the clock's ticking."

"I don't get the connection between a maritime college and flying. Why not Embry-Riddle or my alma mater, Purdue?"

"The short answer is teenage-head-up-your-ass syndrome. Somehow, at that point in my life, I decided I wanted a life on the high seas and Maritime was the way to go for that. All in all, it wasn't the school that failed me; it was me who failed to think it through."

"Your dad's a Pan Am pilot?" Debbie asked, lifting her pint. "Isn't there some way he might be able to help you?"

"No, not really," said Jack. "Pan Am has had pilots on furlough for at least ten years, and I doubt they'll ever hire again. The airline's been on the rocks for as long as I remember, and most business analysts don't think it'll survive this deregulation thing that's coming. Besides that, he's in Berlin flying for Pan Am's Internal German Service. After my mom and dad split up, he moved there to upgrade to captain."

"Internal German Service?"

"Pan Am was tasked with setting up the IGS after WWII because the Allies wouldn't let Germany have their own airline. It's still Pan Am, but it operates as an affiliate of the airline at large."

"I'm sorry to hear that," said Debbie. "I mean about your mom and dad."

"They're both terrific people but just not good together. It was a peaceful breakup. How about your folks?"

"Married twenty-nine years and going strong. They live a quiet life, but they're happy and we're a close little family."

The waitress arrived with their meals, and they ordered another round of pints, the date going wonderfully.

. . .

When they returned to Debbie's brownstone in Chester that night, Jack walked her up the steps to her door. It was their second kiss since they'd met and the second time Jack felt a bolt.

"I'll drive you to the airport tomorrow if you'd like," she said. They were standing at the door holding hands.

"I would like that, very much!"

They kissed passionately again, and an awkward hesitation followed. Both wanted to go further.

"When you come home." She smiled, her finger to his lips.

. . .

The next morning, Sunday, October 1, they arrived at the terminal in her Beetle. Cars honked loudly around them, and a police whistle shrilled as they kissed.

"You'll call me, let me know how it's going?" Debbie said, her hand on his cheek.

"Yes, of course," he said. "I figure they'll give me ten seconds and kick me out. I'll be home by tomorrow night." He grinned cynically.

"They're not kicking you out, Jack," she said, her gaze even. "They're crazy if they don't hire you. I'm not a pilot, but I know good structure when I see it, and I'm seeing it now."

When they kissed again, a cop knocked on the glass.

"Wish me luck!" Jack smiled, his bags in hand as he spoke through the open passenger window.

She shook her head, her eyes welling. "You don't need it."

She drove through the airport, hitting the steering wheel with the palm of her hand. "I'm not going to cry, I'm not going to cry, I'm not going to cry …" she repeated.

But the moment she stopped at a light, she burst into tears.

She knew he wouldn't be coming back.

# THIRTEEN

*Miami International Airport, October 1, 1978*

Jack arrived in Miami late Sunday afternoon. Standing at a display of hotel ads in baggage claim, he skipped over Holiday Inn, Hyatt, Marriott, and the InterContinental, and found a budget hotel closer to the airport. He dialed the number on the ad and booked a room for two nights, figuring that would be more than enough.

When Jack stepped out of the terminal, it felt like he'd walked out of a refrigerator and into a steam bath. Standing at the curb, he took off his jacket, loosened his tie, and flagged down a cab.

The Miami Airliner Hotel was certainly close. After a five-minute ride, the cab pulled up to the lobby across the street from the chain link fence marking the airport's east perimeter. As Jack got out and paid the cabbie, a jet roared overhead, crushing out any conversation.

The cab left, and Jack gave the place a once-over. It was nothing like the sparkling stainless and lavender art deco design he'd seen in the ad. As another jet thundered overhead, Jack climbed the stairs to the entry door. The lobby and front desk were vacant. The glass on the bottom of the door was cracked and covered with duct tape. Jack gave the handle a tug, but found the door locked. Spotting a grimy doorbell on the right, he pressed it and heard a buzzer on the other side. There was no response. A moment later, he pressed it again.

From a side room, a heavyset guy with long, unkempt hair and a baseball cap appeared. He paused, gave Jack a studied look, and reached for something behind the desk. A buzzer sounded and the door bolt clicked. Jack opened it and walked in.

After paying for the room and getting his key, Jack rode a rattling elevator to the second floor. The hallway to his room was dingy and smelled of mildew and cigarettes. The floral wallpaper was lifting at the seams. Televisions blared and little dogs yelped as Jack trudged by with his briefcase and bag.

He opened the door and gave it a shove with his foot. When he turned on the light, he found the drapes drawn tight, the air close and musty.

Jack dropped his bags by the bed and went to the air conditioner. When he twisted the knobs to full cold and the fan to high, the machine sputtered to life, and cool air whiffled from its vents.

He took off his suit and hung it carefully for the following morning. After unpacking his few things, he pulled on a pair of old cutoffs, a polo, and a pair of sneakers, and checked his watch—5:40 p.m.

Jack was ready for dinner and a beer, but there was something else he needed to get out of the way first, and he dreaded it. His research for an interview with Air Logistics had been extensive, but there was one piece missing. It was something Jack had been putting off until he got here, fearing he'd balk at the attempt once he'd studied it: the bio of the chief pilot whose secretary he'd been schmoozing.

He opened his briefcase and took out a dog-eared copy of the *Aviation Week Airline Directory*. Sitting down at the desk, he flipped through the directory and blew out his cheeks when he got to the section on Air Logistics.

The airline's chief pilot, Captain Jacob Kegan, was raised on his family's dairy farm in Ohio. He went to Ohio State, was captain of both its football and basketball teams, and then joined the Army Air Corps after graduating cum laude in 1940. Kegan advanced quickly in military service. At the age of twenty-three, he became the squadron commander of a B-24 unit that led an attack—code-named Operation Tidal Wave—against the Axis oil fields in Ploesti, Romania. It was the most dangerous and costly bombing mission of the entire war. Kegan was awarded the Silver Star and Distinguished Flying Cross for his valor during the operation. Following his military service, Kegan returned to his family's dairy farm, but after his father and mother were killed in a car accident, he sold the farm and returned to flying. He had been a pilot for Flying Tiger Lines and, later, Malayan Airways. He was hired by Air Logistics in 1954. Kegan was promoted from check airman to the company's chief pilot in 1972. He was fifty-eight years old and had been married to his wife, Beth, for thirty-three years. They had one child, a son.

Jack closed the directory, put it back in his briefcase, and rubbed his eyes as a wave of shame and doubt swept through him. Air Logistics wasn't a flight school, some air taxi, or a commuter outfit; he was walking into a titan in the industry, a highly respected international airline whose flight department was run by a man named Jacob Kegan, an athlete, honor student, squadron commander, and winner of the Silver Star and Distinguished Flying Cross. Beyond his military achievements, Kegan was a man with a history of success in a highly competitive civilian career. Jack couldn't imagine Captain Jacob Kegan—however desperate he might be—ever stooping to a stunt like Jack was attempting to pull off. His spirits sank.

He got up and began pacing the room, his head down, his eyes on the seamy carpet. He ran his fingers through his hair and fought an overwhelming urge to pack his bag and go home, catching a red-eye that night. He should have studied Kegan before buying an airline ticket, not after it. He shouldn't have been so goddamn impulsive.

He ambled toward the window, parted the drapes, and stared vacantly west toward the airport, squinting against the late afternoon sun. A 707 roared overhead for a landing on Runway 27. Jack's gaze locked on it instinctively as the jet descended to touchdown. A puff of smoke flew up as the tires touched the pavement.

Debbie somehow came to mind, her confidence in him, what she'd said to him about structure. He paused, looking aside as he considered it.

He let go of the drapes and returned to pacing the room. Jack wasn't a quitter. College was one thing, true, but this was more important. He hadn't quit college anyway, merely attempted some time off to consider his options. Jack had been impulsive at times, yes—but he'd never been a quitter.

He stopped pacing.

"Fuck Kegan," he muttered. "Who gives a damn about Kegan?" Jack had come here swinging for the stands, to strike out cold or hit a homer. Either way, he was giving it his all. The greater shame was in quitting, not failing.

He turned and grabbed his wallet and room key. He left the hotel in search of a diner, a deli … anything—so long as it was cheap and served beer.

# FOURTEEN

When the alarm went off at 7:00 a.m. on Monday morning, Jack was already awake. Reaching toward the nightstand, he punched the button on the clock and rolled onto his back. The roar of jets and the noise of other residents had been on and off all night. Between the intermittent racket and his anxiety over what lay ahead, he hadn't slept much at all.

He got up, showered, shaved, and put on his suit. He returned to the diner where he'd eaten the night before, the La Rosa Grille two blocks south. He ordered the breakfast special: eggs, bacon, and an English muffin. The food was good, but the coffee was spectacular; Jack had never tasted anything like it. When the waitress arrived to refill his cup with two steaming pots—one with the rich dark brew and the other with scalded sweet milk—Jack asked her what it was as she poured them simultaneously into his cup. She looked at him like he was nuts. "*Café con leche.*"

Jack drank three more cups of the sumptuous blend like a parched man at an oasis.

Back in his room, he called a cab, grabbed his briefcase, and headed out the door. A little after 9:00 a.m. the cab pulled up to the Air Logistics offices at the airport, Jack buzzing with anticipation, anxiety, and all that high-test coffee.

As the cab pulled away, he stood on the sidewalk staring up at the building and feeling let down. The white block structure was three stories high and had three horizontal lines of aluminum windows spanning its length. Only a small black and white sign, as austere as everything else about the building gave witness to its purpose:

AIR LOGISTICS INTERNATIONAL AIRLINES, INC.

1846 NW 36th St.

Miami, Florida

Only the animal disease laboratory Jack had seen on Block Island was slightly less inviting.

There were two glass doors at the entrance. He opened one and entered an empty vestibule. He found a directory at the base of the stairs, an aluminum and glass box with white plastic letters attached to a black felt background. Kegan's office was listed on the third floor.

Suddenly, the door swung open behind him, and a heavyset middle-aged woman entered. She passed Jack briskly and bounded up the stairway, her footfalls echoing through the hall. Jack glanced about to see if anyone else was coming or going, but the stairwell was devoid of life and sound, its stillness its most notable aspect.

He trudged up the stairs.

At the top of the third landing he saw three oak doors: one to the right, one to the left, and one in the middle with a unisex bathroom sign. The door to his left had a brass plaque:

CAPTAIN JACOB KEGAN

Chief Pilot

AIR LOGISTICS INTERNATIONAL AIRLINES, INC.

The voices of two men and the sound of their footsteps echoed up the stairwell, and Jack glanced down. They weren't in view yet, but if they were headed here, he wanted to beat them in. He put down his briefcase, smoothed his jacket, straightened his tie, grabbed his briefcase, and reached for the door. Pausing for an instant, he cleared his throat, and opened the door.

The door closed behind him, and he was greeted with a church-like silence and not a soul in sight. The walls of the office were the color of pea soup, the carpet a low pile and gray. To his left, he saw an L-shaped metal desk with a typewriter on the side. Further down the hall and to the left was a sitting area with two wing chairs and a coffee table. Beyond that, there was another heavy oak door with a brass plaque in its center. He figured that was Kegan's office.

Kegan's door opened. Jack caught his breath, thinking it might be him, but instead, a shapely woman emerged in a form-fitting, brown, knee-length skirt under her business suit. As she strode toward him, her head was down and her eyes were on a document in her hand.

Jack stood anxiously as she approached, his briefcase at his side.

As she drew near, she glanced up and startled. "Oh!" she said, her hand to her chest. And then with a puzzled look, she asked, "May I help you?"

"Mrs. Desmarais?" he said.

"Yes?"

"I'm Jack Dolan."

"Oh … oh," she said, a brow raised. "You … you're *here*." It was as much a question as a statement.

The young man standing in front of her gave her pause. He wasn't what she'd envisioned. Rather than the sweet, kind, quiet man she'd imagined from his calls and bouquets, he was a tall, broad-shouldered hunk with a cleft chin, an olive complexion, and dark brown hair and eyes—a dangerously handsome man and a type she knew well. She was married to one.

Jack looked worried. "I'm sorry," he stammered. "I … you did say Monday would be okay, is that correct?"

"Oh, Monday … Monday, yes." Then, catching herself staring at him, she averted her gaze to the room ahead of her and cleared her throat. "Yes, yes, of course, Mr. Dolan. Follow me, please."

Perfunctory and intimidating, she was even more striking than at first glance. She had aquamarine eyes, jet black hair, and a figure even a business suit wouldn't be able to hide. As she sashayed toward an unlit room Jack hadn't noticed before now, his eyes locked on her ass and he bit his lip. Pausing at the open door, she reached inside and flipped on the light. Florescent bulbs flickered to life from above, and the room filled with cold synthetic light.

"This is our conference room," she said, stepping aside for Jack to pass. "You're welcome to wait in here."

Jack gave her a nod and a smile as he passed to enter. The room was windowless and olive green like the rest of the office. There was a long mahogany table with eight ladder-back chairs in the middle of the floor and a matching sideboard against the back wall. Three black-and-white airplane photos and a fake plant in the corner were the only décor.

Jack laid his briefcase flat on the table and turned to look at her.

Claire said, "If you're still here at lunchtime, the only option is a coffee truck that stops in front at 12:15."

"Thank you," he said with a smile. "That'll be fine."

She gave him a nod and left.

*Coffee truck be damned*, he thought sardonically. *If I'm still in this cell in an hour, I'll hang myself with my tie.*

He pulled back a chair, unbuttoned his jacket, and sat down. Reaching for his briefcase, he snapped the latches quietly and removed a novel—Alex Haley's *Roots*.

At 9:45 a.m. the clattering of Claire's IBM stopped. A moment later he heard her say, "Good morning," pleasantly. "You must be Mr. Boyd?"

"Yes, ma'am," he said, with a distinct drawl. "Jeffery Boyd, pleased to meet you, ma'am."

"Nice to meet you too," said Claire, almost sincerely. A moment later he heard the click of a button. "Mr. Boyd is here. Shall I bring him in?"

Silence.

"Okay," she said. "I'll tell him."

Pause.

"Mr. Boyd, Captain Kegan will be with you shortly. In the meantime, you may have a seat over there if you'd like, and he'll be out soon."

"Thank you, ma'am, I will."

Jack stared vacantly at the paperback open in his hands. From the sound of it, he surmised what was going on. An interview. The first one of the week. Claire had told him interviews would be held this week. Jack's stomach was in knots. He glanced discreetly to his left to see Boyd as he walked past. He was average height, trim, forty-ish, brush-cut, wearing a navy blue suit and carrying a briefcase. Retired military, Jack figured, or furloughed from somewhere else, a DC-8 outfit no doubt, a guy with a ton of heavy-jet time.

At 11:35, Jack heard Kegan escorting Boyd back to the front office. "Well," said Kegan, "thanks for coming by, and you'll be hearing something from us soon."

Boyd said, "Thank you, sir. I appreciate the opportunity to come in." A moment later, Jack watched Boyd strut past the conference room door on his way to the stairwell. *I must be mad*, Jack thought. *I haven't got a chance.*

At 12:00 p.m., Jack caught his first glimpse of Kegan. He was a large man, tall, barrel-chested, brush-cut, and wearing a tropic weight gray suit. He passed the doorway without so much as a glance at Jack. Jack figured he'd wait a bit and then leave for the lunch truck, before deciding to pass on it entirely. He didn't want to risk losing an opportunity for Kegan to see him and greet him.

Kegan returned an hour later. He strode past the conference room door with his eyes straight ahead.

Jack thought, *So this is it.* This is what he should expect going forward. Claire had done all she could for him and needed to remain distant, and that was only fair. She'd warned Jack any meeting would be by chance and, even if it did happen, it would be brief. But Jack was already out of his comfort zone attempting this, and buttonholing Kegan on his way to or from his office was not in the offing. Jack sensed that would be suicide. Clearly, if he wanted to make good on this effort, he'd have to be patient. Everything would turn on time invested, chance, and good luck. He'd have to rethink how that might work. Until then, today would be for gathering intelligence. Tonight would be for planning the attack—or just packing up and going home.

At 1:20 p.m., Claire greeted another trim, forty-ish man with a high-and-tight haircut and wearing a dark blue suit, his briefcase in hand.

At 2:15 p.m., Jack's stomach was gurgling for food and he badly needed to pee.

He closed the book, stood up, and buttoned his jacket. He walked to the door, discreetly checked the office for Kegan, then cleared his throat.

Claire's head was down with work on her desk.

Jack cleared his throat again, and Claire looked up at him.

"I'm sorry to bother you, Mrs. Desmarais, but I was wondering if that bathroom at the top of the landing is for everyone?"

"Yes," she said flatly. Pointing with the top of her pen, she added, "Out the door and to your left."

She was chilly, distant; he understood that she had to be. "Thank you," he said, pasting on a smile.

Jack entered the bathroom and locked the door. As he stood in the stall, he closed his eyes, blew out his cheeks, and let loose an out-of-control stream. Piss speckled his pants. "Shit!" he exclaimed as he improved his aim.

He washed his hands and dried his slacks as best he could. He returned to the conference room, his stomach grumbling in outright revolt.

At 3:40 p.m., the afternoon interview ended the same as the morning one, with Kegan's same pleasant goodbye.

At 4:50 p.m., Kegan walked past the conference room with his briefcase in hand.

"See you in the morning," Jack heard him say to Claire.

"Good night," she replied.

Jack sighed. He was relieved the day was over. He was starving but waited patiently for another ten minutes to ensure Kegan had time to leave the building. How this chance meeting would occur if he didn't act to make it happen he hadn't figured out yet. But he'd put that off until later.

He gathered his things and went to the door. When Claire caught sight of him, he asked, "Shall I continue waiting?"

"No," she said impassively. "Of course not. Captain Kegan won't be back until morning."

"Goodnight," he said as cheerfully as he could as he passed her desk on the way out.

She gave him a glance and nodded.

Back at the hotel, he grabbed two bags of chips from a vending machine in the lobby and wolfed them down as he rode the elevator to his room. After taking off his suit, he pulled on the shorts, polo, and sneakers he'd brought—the only other clothing he'd packed in his small carry-on bag besides one change of socks and underwear—and left for the La Rosa.

Dinner was *frijoles y arroz* and a Red Stripe, double orders of each—and then another Red Stripe for dessert. What a feed!

Feeling satiated and mildly buzzed, Jack ambled back to the Airliner while assessing his meager assets and finalizing his plan: Claire had given him access to the sanctum, and Jack would make use of it to lay siege. His presence would be his weapon, his determination and perseverance his ammunition. He wouldn't quit. He'd stick with it until Kegan either relented and saw him or Jack had made it to Friday. Either one of those he'd chalk up as a success.

Back in his room, Jack called Ernie and told him he wouldn't be back until next week. Ernie blew a gasket, but Jack was firm and Ernie let him stay without threatening Jack's job. Ernie was a hell of a guy, a pilot's pilot, and a damn good friend. Jack owed him—big.

Later that evening while lying in bed, he watched TV and laughed at a rerun of *All in the Family*. From time to time he glanced at the phone and thought of calling Debbie but decided against it. He'd wait until he had something positive to report or he was on his way home. He'd wait until he'd succeeded, one way or another. He knew she'd understand.

# FIFTEEN

*Miami International Airport, October 6, 1978*

Friday morning, Jack's eyes opened with a start. The television in the room next door was suddenly blaring, and a dog began to bark. A man shouted, "*Cierra la puta boca*, goddamn it!"

Jack blinked, rolled over, and looked at the clock. It was 6:30, too early to get ready for the office, but too late to go back to sleep—even if he could. He threw off the sheets, rolled out of bed, and rubbed his eyes as he sat in his recycled underwear. The dog barked again, the man cursed again, and then a jet thundered overhead.

Jack stood up and stumbled to the bathroom bleary-eyed. He let the water run in the sink and stared in the mirror as he prepared to shave.

He'd made it. His siege had been a success even if by his lowest measure of success: Jack had stuck it out. He hadn't conquered Kegan, but Jack had conquered himself. He'd defeated his indignation, his humiliation, and his shame. He'd defeated his impulse to leave sooner. He'd take whatever little victory he could find.

And now he had only ten more hours to endure in that room, ensconced in his rumpled, sweaty, roach-coach-stained shirt and suit and his recycled underwear. But then, his appearance didn't matter and hadn't from the start. No one besides Claire had taken note of Jack all week. Kegan always kept his eyes glued on the door he was entering or exiting. Not once had he glanced at Jack alone in that room.

When Jack checked out, he brought his duffle bag with him to the office.

When he entered with his briefcase and bag, he gave Claire a smile and a nod. But this time, instead of an inscrutable expression, she smiled, and it caught him off guard. He figured she was just happy it was Friday; and that she'd be rid of him soon.

He glanced at his watch before taking off his jacket. Nine hours and fifteen minutes until his freedom bird to Philly. It couldn't come fast enough.

Jack took off his jacket, pulled down his tie, and rolled up his sleeves. He sat down and took out his checkbook and a stack of receipts from his briefcase to assess the damage. Altogether, this boondoggle had cost him more than two weeks' salary and a credit card close to its limit. His wallet had $16.00 in cash, just enough to get home.

He grimaced, tossed the checkbook back in his case, and took out his copy of the *Miami Herald* that he'd been scrounging from the diner every morning. He pushed the chair back from the table, opened the paper, and crossed his legs. After the headlines, a story in the business section caught his eye, an article about an airline named Pan Tropic. The company was based in Miami, and though it had filed for bankruptcy—*again*—it had been acquired by a local lawyer and businessman named Hirsch. The article said that after a change in management and a large infusion of cash, the airline was back in the air and doing well. It had recently completed a contract in Pakistan and had more contracts on the books.

Jack had never heard of Pan Tropic Airlines, and curious, he put down the paper and reached for the *Airline Directory*. Opening it to the index, he found no entry for Pan Tropic. He shrugged and tossed the directory back into his case. Jack knew South Florida was home to an array of small airlines, many with shady purposes.

Returning to the paper, he picked through it and found an article about Hannah H. Gray. She was the first woman inaugurated as head of an American university. He thought of Debbie and how much he admired her. Women were really moving up in the world.

When he finished the article, he found nothing more of interest in the paper. He got up and put it in the trash. Back at the table, he sat down and took out his copy of *Roots*. The slave Kunta Kinte had been strapped to a post and was being whipped. Jack empathized. Misery loves company.

At 11:00 a.m., the pilot who'd come in for the morning interview left and Jack watched him as he passed the conference room door. He walked by trim and erect. It had been the shortest interview of the week. Jack figured the guy was toast—and hated himself for feeling good about it.

Kegan left for lunch an hour later.

Jack had been tidying himself up before following Kegan out for lunch, but this time he didn't bother. He left his tie loose, his collar unbuttoned, and his jacket on the table as he left the office. Outside at the picnic bench, he squinted against the sun and waited for the roach coach to arrive. The temperature had been getting warmer by the day, and by Friday it was unbearable. Any delight he'd felt about Florida's weather was gone. It reminded him of Vietnam, sweat beading on his forehead and running down his back.

At 12:40, Jack returned to the conference room, and Desmarais looked at him with a reproving gaze. He figured she was miffed by his appearance, but so what? Jack wasn't there to impress *her*. Apparently, she was as tight-assed as her boss. *Screw your military bearing*, Jack thought as he entered the room. "Here's your military bearing, ma'am," he muttered. "I stuck it out here—and you can stick it up your ass."

At 1:00 p.m. Kegan returned to his office. At 1:40, Jack got up to stretch. His exercise routine had been ambling in circles around the table. Jack wondered how many miles he'd covered since he'd arrived in his cell. He grinned sardonically. He should have scratched the hours into the wall like POWs do for the months and years. The Hanoi Hilton. The thought of it made him feel somber and ashamed for equating his pain.

Three circumnavigations later, he paused and looked toward the door. It occurred to him that no pilot had come in for an afternoon interview. Jack had seen Kegan coming back from lunch and that confirmed that he was there—or did it? Had Jack somehow missed him leaving again?

He scowled and resumed pacing. What if Kegan had slipped out for the weekend, passing the conference room while Jack had his nose in his book? His temper rose. He edged to the doorway and snuck a peek outside.

The office was vacant.

Sticking his head out further, he saw Kegan's door was closed.

The office had been silent ever since he'd heard Desmarais knock on Kegan's door. There was a muted conversation between them, the door closed, and then nothing since. *They're in there together*, he concluded. He hadn't seen anything like it all week. They were probably hiding and hoping he'd leave. And then a better thought occurred to him, and he chuckled. Claire was hot. Maybe Kegan thought so too. Jack paced the room and smiled as he plotted a clandestine revenge: a quick dash to Kegan's door, a hard knock at a timely moment, a quick dash back to the conference room to hide. Their afternoon delight ruined! Claire's hair and makeup mussed. Kegan's military bearing while pulling up his pants. HA!

Jack's smile continued as he paced. When he'd completed another circuit of the table, he stopped to study the photo of an Air Logistics DC-4 in Air Corps livery hanging on the wall. The plaque at the bottom read: *Templehof Airfield, Berlin Airlift, 1948*. The airplane was low on approach and in landing configuration. There was a bunch of kids standing and waving at it from a pile of bomb rubble. His smile vanished as he thought of those children … and those pilots.

Without the determination, grit, and courage of them all, the city would have starved. The Russians would have won and West Berlin handed over to them to rape and pillage as they pleased. The Russians had been counting on that. But what the Russians hadn't counted on was the grit of Berliners, and those freightdogs, GIs, ground pounders, boonie rats, and grunts of America who do the dirtiest, deadliest, and most important work a man can do keeping the country free. West Berlin wasn't saved by generals or diplomats or presidents or prime ministers; West Berlin was saved by a small contingent of freight dogs delivering food and medicine to a city under siege.

Jack blushed with pride as he considered his accomplishments. He had much to be proud of despite his lack of a college degree or flight time in a DC-8.

He looked down at his shoes, his hands in his pockets as he weighed the benefits of staying there any longer. He had nothing to offer Air Logistics beyond his skill as a pilot and his tenacity, gumption, and perseverance as a man. If that wasn't enough, then a couple more hours cooling his heels in that room wouldn't make any difference. Jack had come, Jack had tried, Jack had busted—and that was that.

On the other hand, if he left now—and found an earlier flight to Philly—he could be home in time for a late date with Debbie! There'd be pizza and beer, laughter at Jack's folly ... and then *SEX!* Debbie had promised him *sex!*

That clinched it.

Jack wheeled around to grab the Eastern Airlines timetable from his briefcase—and froze in his tracks when he saw her.

Desmarais was standing in the doorway looking at him, and she seemed pissed.

Jack was dumbstruck. What was this?

She regarded him, then clucked her tongue and rolled her eyes. Jack's hair was tousled, his necktie loose, and his cuffs rolled to his elbows. "Mr. Dolan ... *mon Dieu*," she grumbled. "Get yourself together ... Captain Kegan will see you now."

# SIXTEEN

*Miami International Airport, October 6, 1978*

N ow?" Jack said, shocked.

"Yes, now, Mr. Dolan … get dressed and follow me, please." She rounded for her desk.

Jack undid his belt, opened his pants, and gave his shirt a military tuck. He rolled down his sleeves, buttoned his collar, and put on his tie. He raced around the table for his jacket, pulled it on, straightened it, and smoothed his hair. He threw his copy of *Roots* into the briefcase, closed the lid, grabbed the handle, and took off. The contents dumped onto the floor with a crash. "Shit." He'd forgotten to latch the lid.

He approached Claire's desk with his jacket buttoned and his brief-case by his side. She was leaning back against her desk and studying her nails. As he came near, she looked at him and gave him a once-over. She pursed her lips and shook her head in exasperation. "All right. This way, please," she said.

As he followed her to Kegan's office, it occurred to Jack that Kegan had come out to greet all the other candidates halfway—but not him. Not good.

She gave Kegan's door a knock and opened it. "I have Mr. Dolan," she announced. Jack heard a muffled grumble from inside. Claire stepped back to let Jack pass. "Go ahead," she said, her right arm gesturing toward the office.

Jack gave her a smile as he passed.

Kegan was writing at his desk. He didn't look up as Jack walked in. Another not good.

Jack minced his way closer to the desk and glanced around the room. It was much larger than he'd expected. A wall-length span of windows was behind Kegan, the blinds drawn closed against the afternoon sun. Two brown leather chairs like those in the waiting area were positioned at angles in front of the desk.

Jack stopped between them. As he waited for Kegan's attention, he caught himself holding his briefcase in front of his groin. He looked like Adam hiding his junk from God after the Fall. He moved the briefcase to his side and stood at attention.

Kegan lifted his gaze and eyed Jack over his readers. Pointing with the top of his pen, he grumbled, "Have a seat."

Jack sat down in the chair to the left—the captain's side—and set his briefcase down beside him.

The room was silent except for the quiet whir of a ceiling fan gyrating slowly above them and Kegan's pen scratching on paper.

Jack looked around the office. The room was the same ugly color as the rest of the place and had the same Spartan décor. But Kegan's desk was an exception. It was a ponderous relic of oak pocked and scarred with age as if salvaged from an ancient railroad office. On top were a couple of framed photos, a small lamp to the right, and a stack of manila folders. Kegan was writing on a yellow legal pad atop his blotter.

On the left wall of the room were gray metal shelves that held binders and books, some airplane models, old black-and-white photos, and various framed certificates. On the wall to the right, a badly bent and scarred Hamilton Standard propeller was mounted with a small plaque engraved with Cyrillic beneath it. The raid at Ploesti, Jack figured. Behind Kegan, sunlight pierced gaps in the blinds, and dust motes drifted through the striated light.

"Claire told you we're hiring only pilots with DC-8 experience," Kegan said without looking up.

Jack cleared his throat. "Yes, sir. That's correct. She was clear about that."

Kegan put his pen down on the pad and looked at Jack with an inscrutable gaze. "But you came here anyway ... *Why?*"

Jack picked nervously at a callous on his hand. "I thought it important—"

"Important to impose yourself on this office?" Kegan barked.

Jack tensed. "No, sir. Important to have a moment with you. I wanted to let you know how much I would value a job with Air Logistics."

"Everyone I've seen this week would value a job with Air Logistics, Mr. Dolan. The difference is that they've got DC-8 experience and came here at my invitation. Unlike them, you *don't*, and you *didn't*."

"Yes, sir. I understand that. But I've got something more."

Kegan scoffed. "Oh, you *do*, do you? And what might that be, sir?"

"I want it more than they do."

Passion in a pilot was important to Kegan. Passion was what drove a pilot's performance. Kegan's eyes narrowed and, leaning toward Jack, he said, "And how is it you're privy to that, Mr. Dolan? Are you a mind reader?"

"They were committed for only a few hours, Captain Kegan. I've been committed to this all week."

Kegan was silent as he studied Jack, his angry visage unchanged.

Jack swallowed but held his gaze. Tiny beads of sweat formed at his hair line. He prayed they wouldn't trickle.

The fan above them whirred, and the electric clock quietly ticked.

Kegan rocked back in his chair. He steepled his hands and said, "So, you think by coming here uninvited, you've demonstrated that, is that it?"

"Yes, sir. I have."

Kegan leaned forward and, with his elbows on his desk and a finger pointed at Jack's face, he said, "And what *I* believe is that all you've done is demonstrate your ability to wheedle your way in here. In fact, all you've demonstrated to me is that you're looking for a shortcut by sucking up to my secretary. What you've demonstrated to me is that you're either unable or unwilling to get here the hard way—the way those other men did."

Jack's temper flared and his eyes blazed. He was in no mood for further humiliation. He looked down at his hands and held his tongue as he gathered his thoughts. Looking up and straight into Kegan's eyes, their gazes even, Jack said, "No one flying scheduled freight in DC-3s four or five nights a week, five or six legs a night across the northeast, would consider that a shortcut or doing things the easy way, Captain Kegan. And it's an insult to some of the best pilots—and men—I've ever had the pleasure of working with to make that remark. Beyond that, sitting in that conference room cooling my heels all week was no shortcut either ... all due respect ... sir."

Their eyes were locked, the air electrified.

But then Jack caught the faintest of smiles creasing Kegan's lips. There were three important qualities he sought in a pilot, and now Jack had scored on all three: temperance, passion, and persistence. Kegan rocked back and swiveled his chair. He crossed his legs, steepled his hands, and set his gaze across the room.

"I told Mrs. Desmarais that Air Logistics is my first choice of airlines," Jack ventured. "I admire its approach to business, its tight cost control." He cleared his throat. "Its military bearing, sir."

Kegan ignored this. "Besides your lack of DC-8 time, there's another huge hole in your resume—you quit college."

"I didn't quit, Captain Kegan. I made a tactical retreat. I left because I'd made a poor choice. Every degree path the school offered involved passing calculus in freshman year. I was unaware of that when I applied. On top of that, the freshman calculus class was a mix of guys like me, marine transportation majors, and marine or nuclear engineering types. The engineers had already taken calculus in high school, and I hadn't. Higher-level math is not one of my strengths in any case, but that math professor wasn't making allowances. If you couldn't keep up, well, as far as he was concerned—too bad. The point being, I *couldn't* keep up, sir, and since walking out was more bearable than flunking out, I left midway through the second semester."

Kegan shrugged. "Well, you're honest, I'll give you that. And I'll give you that your other grades were acceptable. Why didn't you get help with the math?"

"I could have but didn't, and that's the most honest answer too. A tutor certainly would have helped, but I felt I was too far behind and decided that leaving and attending another school made more sense."

"So, you dropped out rather than getting kicked out," said Kegan, "but made no effort beyond quitting and walking out."

"If that's how you see it, Captain Kegan, then yes. I screwed up. I screwed up, sir, and I've been paying for that mistake ever since. As I said, my plan was to transfer to another school in the fall—something better suited to my academic abilities—but once I dropped out, Uncle Sam had other plans."

"What'd you do in the meantime between school and the service?"

"I took a job as a mechanic at a motorcycle shop for the summer, something to tide me over until I got into another school."

"You're a good mechanic, then?"

"Decent, yes. But a better road racer. The shop hired me to do both."

Kegan raised a brow and gave Jack a sideways glance. "Road racing motorcycles? Is that what happened to your nose, or are you a boxer too?"

"No, neither," Jack said and smiled. "This is rugby," he said, fingering the scar. "I'm not very good at rugby."

"Rugby? Road racing?" Kegan said, eyes narrowed. "Do you have a death wish, Mr. Dolan?"

Jack laughed. "No, sir," he said. "I raced motorcycles because I was pretty good at it and that was useful to the shop in helping them sell their brand. I played rugby not because I was good at it but because I needed a way to blow off steam when I got back from Vietnam. I was assigned to Fort Myer in Arlington, Virginia, and there were rugby leagues that played on the D.C. Mall on weekends, so I joined."

"Still race? Still play rugby, do you? We need healthy, functioning pilots here, not invalids, Mr. Dolan."

"No, neither," Jack said. "After getting my face kicked in, I figured keeping it in one piece was more important than kicking in someone else's, so I stopped. As for racing, I quit after a bad high-side on the track at Bridgehampton on Long Island. I won't be going back to it."

"High-side?" Kegan asked. "What's a high-side?"

"Gas that Suzuki two-stroke I was racing too hard coming out of a turn, and the rear tire spins and loses traction. Precession forces the bike sideways on the track, and the instant traction returns, off you go like a rodeo rider thrown by a bull. Happens in a second. I hit the pavement with my shoulder first, and the bike was totaled."

Kegan pursed his lips and nodded. "Sounds like fun. I'll remember never to try it. As for rugby, I get the need to blow off steam after the war. I vented mine getting up at 3:00 a.m. every day and milking cows. And that brings us to the Army. How'd you wind up there?"

There was a lot more to that story than Jack was going to tell. Honesty was best served with a dollop of prudence. Jack's dalliance with his boss's young wife had him needing to get out of dodge—and fast—but Jack would keep that part to himself. He gave Kegan the sanitized version: "When I dropped out of college, I lost my draft deferment and my lottery number came up fifty-nine. Knowing I was going anyway, I enlisted."

"You like airplanes. Why not the Air Force?"

"The Army was a three-year hitch; the Air Force and Navy, four. Knowing I'd have to get back to college when I got out, the sooner I finished my service, the better for my career."

"But you never went back to school."

"No. Given the nature of flying, it's tough to do both—as most of us know."

Kegan gave a nod and swiveled his chair to look at Jack directly. "And Vietnam?" he asked. "How'd you wind up there? By the time you went, the war was winding down."

"When we got to Oakland Army Base for deployment to Vietnam, they sent nearly everyone back but me. One look at my MOS and they told me I'd be going. Anyway, my orders came through, and I got there in February 1972."

"What was your MOS?"

"05B20, Radio Operator, or 'RTO' as we were called. I was assigned to the  First Signal Brigade, 14th Signal Company in Da Nang. But the 14th was just a headquarters company. Most of their signalmen were farmed out to where they were needed. I was sent to a MACV unit operating in Hue. We assisted and advised the 1st ARVN Division in and around Quang Tri near the DMZ."

"I Corps in February of 1972? Then you've seen action?"

Jack was surprised by Kegan's knowledge of the war. "Yes, sir," he said, "at least through the spring of that year. The NVA was staging the Easter Offensive, and a concentration of their attack in I Corps was on the city of Quang Tri, just south of the DMZ. It was pretty rough March through June—nearly eight thousand ARVN were killed in action around Quang Tri alone. But after that, the North was defeated and the rest of my time was mostly garrison duty. At the end of America's combat mission, I was assigned to the Four Party Joint Military Commission to supervise the cease fire. I was with the final contingent of US forces that left Da Nang in March of 1973."

"Did you receive any decorations?"

"Yes, sir, the Combat Infantry Badge of course, and two Bronze Stars. One for valor and one for service."

"Tell me about the valor."

Jack shrugged and looked down at his hands. "It was nothing," he said, glancing at the prop on the wall. "Nothing like Ploesti from what I've read."

"Not true," said Kegan. "Tell me about it, please."

"The 1st ARVN Division was getting hit hard by NVA regulars in Quang Tri. There was a risk of being overrun and command wanted us exfiltrated, but we told them we'd stay. The ARVN needed the air support we were calling in, and we stood with them to provide it. All the other guys in the unit got awarded the Bronze Star, three got the Purple Heart, and one a Silver Star. Twenty were killed in action. I wasn't alone, sir. They were damn good soldiers and some of them close friends."

Reaching across his desk, Kegan grabbed a framed photo and turned it around. "That's my son, Dave," he said. Sitting back and looking proud, he told Jack, "Dave was with the 366th Tactical Fighter Wing—the 'Gunfighters.' He was in Da Nang in 1972, the same time you were there."

Jack leaned to study the photo. It was a black-and-white shot of a handsome young pilot in a flight suit standing on the boarding ladder of an F-4. Jack could see the resemblance. He sat back and smiled. "Yes, sir. The 366th were our guardian angels. It was the 366th who came in low and hot to save our asses time and time again. Please tell Dave I said thanks. There's a whole lot of boonie rats like me who wouldn't be around without him."

Kegan suddenly flushed, and his eyes glazed. Jack sensed a bad turn, and his gut tightened.

Kegan abruptly stood up and turned his back to Jack. He split the blinds with his finger as if looking outside.

Kegan coughed and covered his mouth. He cleared his throat.

"I'm sorry, sir," Jack offered. "If I said something wrong, I—"

Kegan raised a hand for him to stop.

Moments passed, Jack on edge, Kegan as if gathering something within.

He cleared his throat again and slowly turned around with his hands in his pockets. "I'd like to tell him that," Kegan said. "But Dave's been missing in action since April of that year."

Jack's face fell. "Oh … oh God, I'm sorry, sir."

Kegan shook his head. "What you've just told me means more than anything I've ever heard. His mother will be—" He looked down and cleared his throat again. With his voice cracking, he finished, "His mother will be very proud."

The intercom buzzed loudly and they jumped. Kegan picked up the phone and pressed the button. "Yes?" he said irritably.

Pause.

"No," Kegan said sharply. "Tell him I'm busy, damn it. Tell him I'll call him back."

Pause.

"Then tell him *again*," Kegan snapped. He slammed the receiver on the hook and moved to sit down. "That was Claire with our principal FAA inspector on the line."

Jack nodded. He sensed the meeting was coming to an end in any case. He knew his time was up, but then Kegan had given him more time than Jack had ever imagined he would, and Jack was pleased. He thought of Debbie and couldn't wait to boast to her about his success.

Kegan reached for a drawer in his desk, opened it, and took out a sheet of letterhead and an envelope. Placing them on his blotter, he pulled his pen from his pocket and began to write. When he finished, he scribbled something on the envelope, sealed it, and set it aside. Standing up, he rounded his desk and stopped in front of Jack. He leaned back against the edge with his hands in his pockets. As Jack looked up at him, Kegan said, "Look. Much as I respect your flying experience, your military service, and your gumption coming in here and sticking it out like you did—and let me tell you, while you're not the first to try it, you've certainly broken the record. Most only last a day or two."

Jack gave a wry grin.

Kegan frowned. "But all that said, I can't hire you without DC-8 experience—*Period.*"

Jack felt like he'd been punched. The wind had gone out of him. He nodded sullenly. "I understand."

"No, you don't," Kegan corrected him. "None of you guys do. What you don't understand is that pilots don't run airlines anymore: accountants, and lawyers, and, well, business types do. And some of those folks have it in their heads that pilots with prior DC-8 experience save us a lot of money in training costs. And the truth is they do, to a point. On top of that, add up all the DC-8 qualified applicants out there, and there's no need for us to look beyond that pool of candidates." Turning, he put his hand on top of the stack of manila folders on his desk. "See this?" he said.

Jack looked at the files.

"Right here, twenty-two guys, half of them rated as DC-8 captains, and all of them ready to come here tomorrow and begin as copilots. Twenty-two *DC-8-30* qualified pilots," he emphasized, "and I'll hire five, at most, during this round of hiring."

Jack nodded and averted his gaze.

"If it was up to me," Kegan said, "I'd give you a shot at it, because we need more in a pilot than just his skill with an airplane. We need men who don't throw up their hands at the first obstacle they run into or open their union contract and quote me chapter and verse whenever things don't go as planned. The characteristics we need in our pilots can't be taught; you've either got them or you don't—and I believe you do."

Jack was hearing him but wasn't listening, Kegan's voice droning in the background.

"I want to hire you, Jack."

Jack heard "hire you" and turned and looked up at him. "Sir?"

"I want to hire you ... but you'll need some DC-8 time in order to move this ahead. Once you've got that and you successfully pass our academic and personal evaluations and a simulator and medical exam, I believe you'll have a career here."

"DC-8 time? But how will I—"

"With this," said Kegan, reaching for the envelope on his desk. He handed it to Jack.

Jack took it and looked at it, puzzled. Looking up at Kegan, "Captain Gerhard Halder?" he said. "I'm sorry. I don't—"

"He's the chief pilot for, er ... er ... ah ... anyway," Kegan said with a desultory wave. "They've recently changed their name again. It's Miami charter outfit on the airfield. They've just picked up a contract to fly the hajj. Are you familiar with the northwest section of the airport?"

"I believe so," said Jack. Of course he knew it. Corrosion Corner was like a ship-breakers wharf at the seedy end of a waterfront, a haven for every low-rent outfit plying the charter trade from South America to the Caribbean.

"Turn left on NW Thirty-Sixth Street," Kegan droned. "It's two miles west of here. Follow the fence and look for a sign that says Hangar Four at the northeast corner of the last parking lot on your left. I spoke to Halder this morning. He told me he'd be there throughout the day. He's looking over an airplane they've leased. Find him, and tell him I sent you with that letter, understand?"

Jack was thoroughly perplexed. "The *hodge*, sir? I'm sorry—"

"Hajj," Kegan corrected him. "The Muslim pilgrimage to Mecca." He checked his watch. "It's 3:20. If you leave now, you'll have a good chance of catching him. Ask anyone down there to point him out. They'll know who he is."

"Pilgrimage, sir?"

"It's an annual event," Kegan said as he ambled toward the door. "A sacred duty for Muslims; big money for the airlines that fly them. This particular contract came up on short notice, and Halder may be short of crew. The company operates three 30-series DC-8s like ours, but all of them are down for maintenance and they let their people off for vacation. Anyway, this contract came up suddenly, and now they're scrambling to find replacement equipment and crew. One way or another, it's worth a shot."

Jack tucked the letter into his jacket pocket, reached for his briefcase, and stood up to follow him. "But won't they require DC-8 experience too?"

"Not if they're in a bind. Introduce yourself and give him that letter. I think it'll help. Halder and I go back a way. We met under, well—let's just say under *unusual* circumstances. We're not friends, but we've got a

114

good working relationship. Fact is, he's one of the best there is at his end of the business. If anyone can put that hajj deal together, he can."

"His end of the business?" said Jack. He didn't like the sound of it.

"The sort of things that pop up suddenly. They're very good at it, flying anything anywhere in the world," said Kegan. "Like this hajj deal."

"I see," said Jack.

"Anyway," said Kegan, guiding Jack toward the door, "give him that letter. I'm sure it'll help."

Jack nodded and passed him by.

"Oh, and one more thing," said Kegan from behind Jack.

Jack turned around.

"Halder's bite is worse than his bark. Turn tail and run, and you'll be mauled, understand?"

"Mauled," Jack said. "Of course. *Mauled?*"

"Just stand your ground," Kegan said as he continued toward the door.

They passed Claire's desk, and she looked up at Jack with a demure smile. He wondered vaguely what the hell that was about.

"Finish that contract," Kegan said. "Come back here with a few hundred hours in Halder's DC-8s, and I'll see to it your application is put at the top of the docket."

"I will," Jack said, feeling nothing but a pressing need to flee. That office was suddenly like a plastic bag around his head, and he needed to breathe.

Kegan opened the door for him, and Jack stepped out onto the landing.

"Fly safe," Kegan said with a stern look.

Jack turned around.

"You know what I'm talking about. Keep your head up."

Jack knew exactly what he was talking about.

"Call Claire when you get back. She'll let me know."

"I will," said Jack as he turned for the stairs.

Kegan smiled and closed the door. When it latched, he rounded to Claire and marched to her desk. Leaning down, his fists on her desktop, he said, "I've sent him to Halder. Ask Philippe to keep an eye on him, will you?"

"*Philippe?* Pffff," she snorted and averted his gaze.

Kegan's eyes were ablaze. "Even so," he growled. "I feel responsible— and so should you."

# SEVENTEEN

J ack hotfooted it down the stairs like he'd robbed a bank. There was little time to dither if he wanted to pursue what Kegan offered, and still make his flight. But he needed a moment to think. The opportunity Kegan had given him came with significant risks.

He paused beneath the portico and put down his bags. He pulled off his tie and jacket and gazed across the parking lot, heat shimmering off the asphalt and cars. Jack didn't need a suit for an interview in a junkyard.

A white Mercedes motored to the portico and stopped. Jack picked up his bags and shuffled to the side as a captain in an Air Logistics uniform, crisply starched and pressed, got out from the car. After pulling his kitbag and suitcase from the back seat, he placed them on the curb. Walking to the other side of the car, he leaned in and gave the woman driving a kiss. They chatted a moment, and she drove away. The captain skipped up the steps with his bags in hand, and Jack reached for the door to hold it open for him.

"Thank you, sir," the captain said with a cheerful smile as he passed.

Jack smiled back and watched him wistfully as he jogged up the stairs. Jack had seen a nametag above his wings and assumed he was a check airman on his way to a meeting with Kegan. He let the door close and returned his gaze across the lot.

If Jack wanted to be that captain someday—and he most certainly did—then bold effort and risk-taking were needed to overcome the deficiencies in his resume. It was madness that had gotten Jack to Air Logistics, and only madness would get him back. There was no other way.

And yet, how much risk was too much? Jack had come to Miami to put jobs that threatened his ambitions behind him, not dive headlong into another. Not only would he be flying for an operator at Corrosion Corner, but Jack would be flying as a copilot in an airplane far beyond his experience level, and flying in international operations, where he had no experience either. His career—indeed, his life—would be entirely dependent on the low standards of some scud-running airline and its scrubby captains. If he wasn't careful—and lucky—Corrosion Corner would become a House of the Rising Sun, a place he entered and was never able to leave.

He checked his watch and gave it more thought.

Subtracting the time needed to get to his flight, Jack still had an hour and a half to walk to Corrosion Corner, find Halder, and give him Kegan's letter. It seemed doable. Beyond that, any further decision Jack needed to make about the job, he could make the same way he did as a captain flying into dangerous weather: he'd take it one leg at a time. So long as Jack remained vigilant and was committed to doing a one-eighty and getting the hell out of there the moment things got too dicey, the risks would be manageable. With that settled, the only other risk was a failed effort—and that he'd manage as well.

Bingo. Decision made: Jack was going.

He grabbed his bags and launched down the steps.

At the exit to the parking lot, Jack paused to study the path ahead. The airport boundary was lined with a chain link fence to the left and NW Thirty-Sixth Street to the right. He'd be walking along the shoulder of the road with a mere eight-foot margin separating him from the speeding eastbound cars and trucks. He'd be going through in that blazing sun, and it would be a brutal hike.

At 4:15, Jack arrived at Hangar Four, dust and grime clinging to his sweaty face and clothes.

The building was a huge old-school design, with block sides and a traditional arched wood roof. To the left of the hangar, the washed-out, wingless carcass of a DC-4 was on its side against the fence. Its windshield frames were barren, and oil cans, rusting machinery, and other debris piled up against it like a trash-feathered nest. Adjacent to the DC-4, a C-46 squatted like a giant bullfrog on flattened struts and dry rotted tires, its cockpit windows opaque. One of its cowlings had been blackened by fire, and lines of bird shit streamed down its rudder. Beyond those two derelicts, Jack saw many more classic airliners now skeletal and decaying in the weeds. Cattle egrets foraged among them like little ghosts gliding through a graveyard.

There was one entrance to the hangar, a red door at the east corner of the building. Employees Only was hand painted on it in silver. The door had a hasp but appeared permanently ajar. Jack opened it and walked in.

The hangar was cavernous and wonderfully cool. A trace of avgas, oil, and grease suffused the air. Small birds chirped and darted about the rafters as if the hangar was an aviary. There was a pleasing sense of peace about the place, and Jack paused for a moment to cool off and take it in.

There were three airplanes inside: a Convair 440 on stands over his head, a Lockheed Electra across the bay from it, and a Beech 18 parked near the open doors. The aging airplanes Jack had anticipated, but the quiet sense of order he hadn't, and his interest in the job unexpectedly piqued. That was unsettling. Another rejection on the same day would be difficult to bear.

Suddenly the squeal and thudding of a pneumatic wrench shattered the quiet, and Jack searched for the source. Walking in the direction of the sound, he passed near the Convair's left nacelle, the cowling and engine removed. The exposed firewall looked like the stump of an amputated limb, fluids weeping from its severed lines.

The wrench squealed again, and Jack saw a technician with sound-suppressing earphones working on an APU on a stand nearby.

Jack approached him and yelled, "Hello!"

The technician looked up.

"I'm looking for Captain Halder," Jack said.

The technician nodded and pointed his wrench outside toward the ramp.

A Boeing Stratocruiser in an Ecuadorian livery was blocking the view of the tarmac. Jack gave the technician a wave and began walking toward the hangar's open doors. But halfway there, he saw a locker room to the right and made a dash for it to wash up.

Afterward, and feeling refreshed, Jack checked his watch: 4:35 p.m. He still had forty minutes to find Halder.

Outside on the ramp, Jack searched amid the dozen obsolete airplanes that were parked there, their oil blackening the pavement, their varied liveries and registries adding a sense of intrigue. Wandering a bit further along, he spotted a weathered DC-8 in Pan Am colors, the only jet on the tarmac. With its flattened nose strut and tail high in the air, it was poised like a cat about to pounce. Jack put down his bags and shaded his eyes against the glare of the sun as he looked for Halder. If he didn't find him at the DC-8, Jack's effort would be a bust.

But a moment later, he caught sight of a man rounding a power cart on the other side of the airplane. He was looking up at it as if doing a walkaround. He had a clipboard in one hand and a flashlight in the other. When he came to the right wheel, he aimed the flashlight up and stopped to inspect the gear. His hair was blond, and a set of noise-suppressing earphones were clamped about his head. In his white airline uniform shirt and khaki slacks, he was like a paleontologist studying the blackened bones of some ancient beast mounted above him.

Halder.

Girding himself, Jack strode forward. As he got closer, a Northeast Airlines 727 took position for takeoff on Runway 09 nearby. Suddenly its landing lights came on and black plumes of smoke billowed from its engines. The thunder of its jets shook the air, and Jack winced, put down his bags, and held his ears as the 727 roared past.

As the jet climbed to the north, Jack approached Halder, who was writing on his clipboard and didn't see him coming near. "Hello, sir," Jack yelled.

Halder was unmoved.

"Hello, sir, I'm looking for Captain Halder!"

Halder looked up, and upon seeing Jack, his eyes narrowed. He had a scar at the corner of his mouth that lifted it into a sort of permanent sneer. He gave Jack a once-over and frowned. "*Ja,*" he said with a thick German accent. "I am Halder … but I am not hiring pilots."

Jack put down his bags and pulled Kegan's letter from his back pocket. Offering it to Halder, he said, "Yes, sir, that's what I figured. But Captain Kegan at Air Logistics sent me to see you. He said to give you this."

Halder eyed the envelope like it was a steaming turd.

"Captain Kegan said you've got a new contract," Jack said. "He said you might need crew."

Halder slapped his clipboard and flashlight atop one of the DC-8's main gear tires and grabbed the envelope from Jack's hand. He tore it open roughly and pulled out the letter. As he studied it, his frown grew into an angry scowl.

"Captain Kegan said you've known one another a long time … He said you met under unusual circumstances."

Halder ignored him, folded the note, and stuffed it into his pocket. "We met over the Balkans," he said, "and if my guns had not jammed, we would not be having this conversation."

Jack let the remark hang. As he held his gaze on Halder, the hot breeze blustered through the gear well, rustling their shirts and tousling their hair.

"Captain Kegan is wrong, my friend. I have no need for pilots and, most of all, no need for pilots like *you!*" he said, pointing at Jack.

"Pilots like me, huh?"

"Pilots that need to be *trained!*" Halder clarified.

Jack nodded and looked aside. "Okay, then," he said. "Sorry for the bother. I'll give Captain Kegan your regards."

Halder exploded. "*Bother?*" he snarled. Pulling the letter from his pocket and shaking it at Jack, he continued, "Sorry for the bother, you say? Well, let me tell you, my friend, sticking me with this *bull-sheet* is more than just a bother, you see."

Jack's temper got the best of him, and he pointed back at Halder. "Well, let me tell you, *my friend,* what a bother this has been to *me!*" he snapped. "Kegan suggested I come here with that letter of introduction and give it to you."

"*Introduction?*" Halder snickered. "Is that what he told you it was?"

An Eastern L-1011 powered up for takeoff, its engines howling. Jack held his ears, and the two men paused and watched as the airplane roared past. The L-1011 was soon aloft and banking north, but Halder held his gaze on the distance as if lost in thought.

Jack waited patiently for another minute. He sensed something was up, something in the offing … something in that letter he wasn't aware of. A short while later and speaking to Halder's back, he said, "Captain Halder, I've got a flight to catch. If you've got nothing more for me, I'll be on my way."

Halder blinked, turned, and looked at Jack with an even gaze. "I have no need for pilots, Mr. Dolan … But I do have need for an assistant if you are interested."

"*Assistant?*" Jack said, puzzled. "What kind of assistant?"

"This contract came to us on short notice, and our airplanes are down for maintenance. To make it work, we have leased this one, and two more like it at Fort Lauderdale. All of them are in poor condition and will need much work to fly. We have very little time. I need an assistant to run errands, deliver paperwork, parts, people … all of that and more."

Jack scoffed. "*Errands?* You want me to be your errand boy … your go-fer? Jesus, are you kidding me?"

"*Gottverdammt!* Shut up and listen," Halder barked. "When you are done as my assistant, I will provide you three takeoffs and landings to prove your skill. If you prove to me you can fly and you prove to me you are a good fit with my people, you may stay on for the contract. If I decide no, then I will put you off wherever we are, and you will find your way home at your own expense."

Jack gave it a moment's thought. Passing on a chance to fly a DC-8 was unthinkable, and there was time to think the whole arrangement over if he agreed. Jack didn't need to be back in Philly until Monday night, and two more nights at the Airliner wouldn't kill him. "Okay," he said to Halder. "Fair enough. But how long would I be a go-fer and how much does it pay?"

"Two weeks, no more. We have to leave for the Middle East by then at the latest. How much do you make flying that DC-3 Kegan said you fly?"

"$1400 per month."

"I will match that as my assistant and pay you that until you are a qualified copilot. If you succeed and we keep you on, your pay will be $3,800 per month, plus incentive pay."

Jack raised a brow. "$3,800 per month? Are you *serious?*"

"I do not make jokes, Mr. Dolan."

Jack looked down. "Jesus," he muttered to himself. He hadn't considered the money. That was a lot of *money.* Then, looking at Halder, he asked, "And the takeoffs and landings? When will I get those?"

"Ferrying an empty airplane on the way to the hajj."

Jack recoiled. "That isn't legal," he blurted. "I'd be exposing myself to an FAA violation. I need to be fully qualified first."

Halder's eyes blazed. "Who the hell do you think we are?" he snarled, gesturing toward the other airplanes on the ramp. "These … these … *scheißvögel?* Of course you will be legal. You'll be flying under Part 91; the training you need is minimal, and you will get that. If you stay on, your training will continue until you are fully qualified for Part 121 service. Now I have no more time for this. Do you want the job or do you not?"

Halder's non-answer was all the answer Jack needed. They'd be exploiting a gray area in the regs, but if that's all there was to flying from Corrosion Corner, Jack could live with it. It was no different than at Keystone where he skirted the regs all the time. "Okay," Jack said to Halder. "I'll take it ... When would I start?"

Halder looked at Jack like he was nuts. "*When? Are you deaf? TODAY!*" he exclaimed. "I just told you we are pressed for time; did you not hear me?"

"*WHAT?*" Jack blurted. "*Today?* I live in Delaware ... I've got another job I have to give notice to ... I mean ... where will I live, how will I get around, and—"

"The Casa Dorado," Halder said.

"Casa Dorado?"

"That is the crew hotel in Miami. All your expenses are paid by the company, and I will provide you a van for your work and your other needs."

*Can't be any worse than the Airliner*, Jack thought. "Where is it?" he asked.

Halder sighed and said with an exasperated gesture, "Down the road from here." Pulling a business card from his shirt pocket, he offered it to Jack.

Jack reached for the card.

"Go to that address. I'll tell my secretary to wait for you. Her name is Maria. She won't wait past sunset, so go *now*, Mr. Dolan! There's a phone booth in the hangar and numbers for a cab. Maria will take care of your paperwork and make arrangements for you at the hotel. There is a briefing in the lobby bar on Sunday at seventeen hundred hours. Any other questions you have will be answered then."

"So this," Jack said, studying the card. "This Jet—"

"*NOW,* Mr. Dolan. Maria will not wait. Leave now!"

Jack nodded and looked sheepish as he slid the card into his pocket. "Okay, I will," he said. "But ... I mean ... it's kind of embarrassing and I hate to ask—"

Halder rolled his eyes and reached for his wallet. He pulled out a twenty-dollar bill and handed it to Jack. "That will get you to the office and hotel. You'll get more when I see you on Sunday. Now go, Mr. Dolan ... *Mach schnell!*"

# EIGHTEEN

*Miami International Airport, October 6, 1978*

Jack called a cab and waited by the curb. When the car arrived, he tossed his bags in the back and jumped in. The cabbie was an aging black man in a battered tweed derby. "Where to, *nonm?*" he asked with a heavy Creole accent.

"516 NW Eleventh Street," Jack replied.

The cabbie frowned but said nothing. He shifted the car into gear, and turned for the exit to the lot.

Jack caught a whiff of body odor and opened the window.

As the wind tousled his hair, Jack stared vacantly across the highway. The stakes couldn't have been higher for him at that moment, and he felt a conflicting mix of anxiety and eager anticipation.

His decision to accept Halder's offer meant that Jack was either suddenly launching his career forward or heading for disaster. There seemed to be no middle ground. Would Halder keep his promise? Could Jack prove himself in an airplane far beyond his experience level with nothing but on-the-job training? Was the airline he suddenly worked for on the straight and level?

In all, it was a hell of a gamble and Jack had good reason for feeling both the apprehension and thrill he felt at that moment.

The unmistakable hiss of AM radio broke his concentration. The driver was fiddling with the dial, trying to secure a signal on a scratchy Creole talk show. The cab weaved back and forth across the lane as he focused on the radio rather than driving.

Jack pursed his lips and drew Halder's business card from his shirt pocket. He ran his thumb across the embossed black lettering:

Captain Gerhard Halder, Director of Operations

Jetstream International Airlines, Inc.

516 NW 11th Street, Miami, FL 33136

He had no recollection of Jetstream International Airlines in his job search efforts—but then, the same could be said about Keystone. There were hundreds of little airlines around the world that no one had ever heard about: some good, some very good, and a lot of them bad. But so what? Keystone had been good to Jack, and small companies often had advantages, particularly when it came to promotion. All large airlines—Air Logistics included—were heavily unionized and promotion was tendered on a strict seniority system. Small airlines weren't, and that meant promotion was based strictly on merit. If Jetstream offered a faster path to captain, then chalk one up for Jack. At least there was that.

Jack looked ahead as they veered off the highway and onto an exit ramp. The car turned left and motored slowly through an area of garish pawn shops, auto repair joints, scuzzy bars, and vacant lots. Scrub vegetation peppered the sandy ground between the buildings, and telephone and electric lines crisscrossed the streets. Graffiti was everywhere.

A mile later, the cabbie made an abrupt U-turn before coming to a hard stop in front of a single-story block building. He looked over his shoulder and said, "$6.75."

Jack craned his neck to look up at the washed-out sign above the building's doors:

PAN TROPIC AIRLINES, INC.

516 NW 11th Street, Miami, Florida.

He recoiled and snorted. "Oh, *shit!*" It was the name of the bankrupt airline Jack had read about in the *Miami Herald*. "Something's wrong," he said. "This can't be right!"

"516 Northwest Eleventh, *nonm!* Now whatchu want to do?" the cabbie snarled.

Jack looked up and down the street. There wasn't a phone booth in sight.

The cabbie threw up his hands in anger.

"All right, all right," Jack said. "Forget it. We're here." He handed the cabbie a five and two ones and told him, "Keep the change."

Jack grabbed his bags and got out at the curb. The driver dropped the car into gear and sped off, leaving Jack in a cloud of fumes.

"Asshole," Jack grumbled.

Inside the building, he found a small lobby. It was deathly quiet except for the buzz of fluorescent bulbs in the ceiling, the bottom of the fixtures speckled with dead flies. The floor was black-and-white vinyl tile in a checkerboard pattern, the walls a cheesy blond paneling.

Across the lobby, there was a door with a bright brass plaque: HIRSCH ENTERPRISES, INC. Another door to Jack's right also had a plaque, but this one was engraved in plastic: JETSTREAM INTERNATIONAL AIRLINES, INC.

He let out a sigh, dropped his bags, and reached for the knob. The door was locked. He twisted the knob and shook it violently. "*Shit!*" he exclaimed, and a bolt of panic shot through him. "God *damn* it!" he yelled. She'd already left! How the hell would he get out of there?

The peephole blackened, and then a lock rattled. The door suddenly swung open, and a plump Hispanic woman in a floral dress and a beaming smile was standing on the other side. "*Hola!*" she exclaimed with a heavy Spanish accent. "You must be Jack!" She frowned and waved a finger at him. "I heard what you said."

"Yes, ma'am. Sorry. I'm Jack Dolan," he said, relieved. Pointing his thumb over his shoulder, he added, "I'm sorry, that sign? *Pan Tropic?*"

She rolled her eyes and said, "*Si, si,* that old sign, *señor* … Don't worry, that is nothing. You're in the right place." She gestured for Jack to come in. "*Mira, mira*, come, come," she said. "We have much to do."

"So, we're Jetstream too?"

She shrugged. "*Si*, we are both, I think."

Maria led him to a sitting area with two winged chairs and a scarred coffee table. "Sit, please. I will get the folder. I have it ready," she said.

Jack sat down and put his briefcase by his side. Maria grabbed the folder from her desk and asked, "Do you need a pen?"

"Yes, please."

She handed Jack the folder and pen, and Jack examined the cover. Something called Aerolínea Caribe had been whited out with thin long strokes and Jetstream International Airlines typed over the top of it. He pursed his lips and flipped through the pages to see what was in store. But it was just a boilerplate pilot application, the same thing he'd filled out so often before. When he came to the page for breaking down his flight time by all the varied categories: single engine, multi-engine, instrument, PIC, SIC, and so on, he held it up to Maria and said, "Do you *really* want me to do all this? I mean … I will if I have to, but we'll be here for hours if I do."

Maria's face fell. "Oh, no, no, no, *Señor* Dolan! Captain Halder did not say, but we do not do that."

"Okay. Good," Jack said, "because I hate doing these things, and besides, it doesn't matter. Captain Halder has already told me I'm not qualified."

Maria smiled kindly and said, "Oh, I know. So just fill out the important things. All those pilot things? No. They are not important."

"Not important," Jack repeated. He made a face and said, "So, tell me, Maria. When was the last time a pilot filled out an application here?"

She shrugged. "Everybody here is always here, even before Pan Tropic too." She smiled and said, "You are the first!"

Jack raised a brow. "Lucky me."

"Please, please, *señor*. We must do this and go."

Jack set to work on the application and whipped through it quickly. He stood up and handed Maria the forms along with his pilot's license, medical certificate, passport, and driver's license. "Usually they want these too," he said.

Maria made copies of his documents and handed them back to Jack. "Now I will call the hotel, get your room, and call you a cab. Wait inside. He'll honk when he's here."

. . .

The cab arrived at the hotel lobby, and a doorman in uniform greeted Jack as he got out. "Good afternoon, sir," he said. "Welcome to Casa Dorado. Do you have bags?"

Jack had been gawking at the hotel's façade. He looked at him and hoisted his shabby duffle and briefcase. "Only these," he said. "But Alfred will be along with my Louis Vuitton shortly."

The doorman wasn't amused.

Jack smiled. "Only kidding. I'm good, thanks."

He entered the coralline lobby openmouthed and paused to take it all in. The atrium was three stories high and decorated with tropical accents. Elevator music softly filled the air, and a few gray-haired guests milled about or lounged on the tufted leather chairs. As Jack passed the concierge in uniform standing by his podium, he smiled and gave Jack a nod.

Standing at the front desk, Jack noticed a brass plaque on the wall:

This property owned and operated by:
HIRSCH ENTERPRISES, INC.

A pretty young clerk handed him his key and smiled as she answered his question: "Yes, sir, all expenses are covered. Just sign the check to the room."

"*Bar*, too?" Jack asked, astonished.

"Yes, and on Sunday evening, our lounge is reserved exclusively for your group." She giggled and scrunched her shoulders. "They're so much fun!"

Jack pictured Halder's malicious sneer and looked at her like she was nuts. He pointed across the lobby at the neon sign above two teak doors: sun-SACIÓN. "There?" he asked.

She smiled. "Yes, sir, that's it! Have a wonderful stay!"

He glanced at the lounge, picked up his bags, and walked toward the elevators.

The hall to his room was whisper quiet. Polished brass sconces adorned yellow orchid walls, and the carpeting was a deep coral sand. As he entered his room, the late afternoon sun gave it an autumnal glow. Heavy drapes framed the window sheer and a stunning view of downtown Miami. Jack dropped his bags and fell back on the bed's plush white comforter. He spread his arms, made a snow angel, and laughed. "Oh my *God*," he chuckled. "Mr. Go-fer, here I come."

# NINETEEN

*Miami, October 7, 1978*

Saturday, Jack slept late, the drapes drawn tight, the room like an icebox. He hadn't slept so soundly in years.

He ate breakfast in the hotel café and mulled over his decision to stay on as a go-fer. The dissonance between the company's dumpy office and this luxurious hotel was puzzling, but Jack figured it was explained by the article he'd read in the *Miami Herald*. The paper had said Pan Tropic was under new management and there'd been a large infusion of cash. He remembered the name Hirsch mentioned in the article, the same name he'd seen on plaques in the office and behind the front desk on the wall. Obviously, Hirsch was a big-money guy and the source of the cash. If the new Pan Tropic—aka Jetstream—was moving beyond the fly-by-night it had been at Corrosion Corner, then Jack wanted in. If his "crew" digs at the Casa Dorado were any indication, so far, so good, and he'd stay the course.

After dropping off his suit to be cleaned and pressed, Jack used the hotel's courtesy van to take him to a mall. He'd need some clothing for the job, another pair of slacks, jeans, and a couple more sport shirts at a minimum. A pair of swim trunks for the pool would be nice to have too.

Back at the Casa Dorado, he put his new clothing in a drawer and went for a long walk. When he returned to the room, he sat down at the desk and stared at the phone. During his walk, he'd decided there was no more putting it off. He had three important calls to make, the first two difficult, the last one routine.

He reached for the phone and dialed the operator to place the call.

Debbie's housemate answered.

"Hey, Crystal … it's Jack Dolan," he said cheerfully. "How are you?"

"Oh … oh my God … I'm, I'm fine, but Debbie's out, Jack. She's at her parents' house, and I know she's been dying to hear from you. Do you have their number?"

"Oh, ah … no, I don't, Crystal. But listen, please tell her I called and I'll try again tomorrow. Please tell her everything's been up in the air and I've been waiting until I had something more certain to report before I called."

"Okay, I will … Are you home?"

"Oh … ah … no, no, Crystal, I'm still in Miami; things are still a bit uncertain. But please tell her I'll know more tomorrow night and I'll call her back then."

They hung up, Jack feeling sheepish that he'd been spared talking to Debbie. He should have called her long before now.

The next call was to Ernie at Keystone, and Jack tensed at the sound of the ringer. When Ernie answered, Jack wasted no time. He told his boss he wasn't coming back and why. There was a pause, and Jack grimaced as he waited for Ernie's response. But instead of anger and reproach as Jack expected, Ernie just sighed and said, "Yeah … okay, Jack. I'd figured that was what you were up to, and I've been planning for it. It's not my first go-around with one of our guys leaving, and with this deregulation thing coming, things will be changing everywhere, and soon."

Jack said, "I'm sorry for the short notice, Ernie. Keystone's been good to me. You're a great chief pilot, and I'm sorry for putting you and the company out."

"Right, well … what can you do?" said Ernie. "I understand why you're taking the opportunity and moving on. You're a good stick, Jack, easy to get along with, and you've always pulled more than your weight around here when we've needed you, so best of luck with the new outfit. If you ever need to come back and we've got a spot for you, you'd be welcome."

That came as a huge relief. Jack thanked him and hung up.

Jack's last call was to his roommate, Frank. Jack filled him in on what was going on and told him he'd send him a check for the rent to cover whatever time he'd be gone and said he would stay in touch as best he could.

After hanging up, Jack went to the hotel restaurant for dinner and then ended the evening with some television and another deep and restful sleep.

. . .

On Sunday morning he finished breakfast and lingered in the restaurant with a *Miami Herald*. But instead of reading it, he used it as cover for a surveillance mission. Halder had said the Casa Dorado was the "crew hotel" for anyone not residing in the Miami area, but apparently, all of them did. After more than an hour of sipping coffee and glancing over the top of the paper, Jack hadn't seen anyone who looked like a pilot, only fat, bald old men and fat, bejeweled old ladies.

He signed the breakfast check, wiped his mouth, and tossed the napkin on the table. With nothing more to do until the meeting at 5:00 p.m., he bought a paperback in the gift shop—*Eye of the Needle* by Ken Follet—and lounged by the pool. Later, he took a long walk and decided to try Debbie again when he got back.

She picked up on the third ring. "Hey!" he said. "It's me—"

"*JACK!* I'm so sorry I missed your call. Are you home? Do you need a ride? Do you need me to pick you up?" she gushed.

"Oh, no … not yet, Deb. Actually, I'm still in Miami. But first, I'm so sorry for not calling sooner. It's been a crazy week—really *crazy*—and even now, believe it or not, I'm still not sure I've got anything to report."

"You mean you're still there hoping for an interview?"

"Oh, no. Actually … I got an interview and a job, but not the one I came here for, if that makes sense."

There was a pause.

"Debbie?"

"A job?" she asked. "Not the one you went there for?"

"I'll know more soon. There's a meeting here in the hotel bar at five, and I'll know more when it's over. But for now, they've hired me to be an assistant and promised me I'll be able to fly if the assistant job works out."

"A meeting? An assistant? Fly for who, Jack?"

"Jetstream International Airlines, I think. But it could be Pan Tropic … I'm not sure."

There was another pause.

"Anyway," Jack continued. "It's crazy, but bear with me, Deb, and I'll call when the meeting's over. I'm sure it'll be brief. The guy running this thing is brusque, and that's putting it politely. I doubt it'll go over an hour, and I'll call as soon as I'm back in the room."

"You said you're meeting in a bar? Our engineering meetings are in windowless rooms, Jack. What hotel are you staying in? Don't they have a conference room or something like that?"

"The Casa Dorado in Miami."

"Casa who? And who's Jetstream and that other one, Pan-something-or-other? I've never heard of them."

"Me neither. But then I figured who's ever heard of Keystone, right?"

Silence.

"Look, Deb, the other thing is—I had to quit Keystone. They needed to know what I'm doing, and I didn't have any more vacation time to cover my time away. They've been good to me, and I couldn't hold off any longer."

"So, what you're really *saying,* Jack, is you've got another job and you're not coming home. Is that it?"

"It could be. At least not right away. But I'll know more tonight."

Her tone sharpened. "You should have called me sooner. You said you would."

"I know. But truthfully? I felt embarrassed, Debbie. The entire effort was a failure until Friday, and even now, I don't know what I've got. I'm calling only because I promised I would, and I know I waited too long."

"No," she said firmly. "The truth is, Jack, that you're staying in Miami and not coming home. I just wish you had told me that the moment you knew. I know it wouldn't have made any difference—and I don't blame you for following your star—but as a courtesy, you should have let me know. I feel taken for granted."

He closed his eyes and pinched the bridge of his nose. "I would never take you for granted, Debbie, and you're right," he admitted. "I should have called sooner."

"Anyway, look," she said. "I've got to go."

"I'll call you. I promise."

Pause.

She sighed. "Sure. Whatever."

"Bye Deb."

"Bye Jack."

Click.

He hung up feeling like a heel, but he had to shake it off. It was 4:40 p.m. and time to go.

He dressed in his freshly pressed suit slacks and shirt, cuffed his sleeves, and walked out the door.

# TWENTY

*Miami, October 8, 1978*

The elevator dinged, and the door opened. Jack stepped out—and froze.

The lobby was throbbing with rhythm and blues, the hip-swaying beat of Stevie Wonder's "I Wish." Jack turned to face the lounge, and his jaw dropped. The barroom was the source. A bolt of panic shot through him. Did he get it wrong, the wrong time and place? He turned and looked to the front desk. The girl who had checked him in was on duty. He pointed with his thumb over his shoulder as if to ask, "*There?*"

She smiled and nodded.

He was dumbstruck as he edged closer and read the sandwich board posted outside the doors:

Private Affair

Guests Only

Suddenly, the two teak doors burst open, and Jack looked up. Two gorgeous women in skin-tight miniskirts burst out, their long legs strutting to the beat, their heads thrown back in raucous laughter, their big hair bouncing.

Jack gawked at them as they passed and then made his way mincingly toward the double doors. Pushing open the one to the right, he peeked inside. The room was dimly lit by the liquor racks behind the bar and a mirrored ball circulating from the ceiling. The room was packed. *Packed!* Women danced to the arousing R&B, and loud conversation, laughter, the clink of glasses, and tobacco smoke filled the air. It was a party well underway.

Jack opened the door further, slipping inside, and the door closed behind him. As his eyes adjusted to the light, he tried to make sense of what he was seeing. Most of the people present were women—*women*—and every one of them was as seductive as the two he'd seen in the lobby. They appeared older than Jack—thirty-something or maybe forty—and all held a drink in one hand and a cigarette in the other. They chatted or danced, but oddly, only with other women. Not one of them was paired with a man.

As for the men, there appeared to be half as many as women, and rather than dancing, nearly all of them were piled up at the bar, their backs to him, many with hands raised and clamoring for drinks. The few elsewhere were scattered in small groups of two or three. All had closely cropped hair, and most were balding and paunchy. The youngest appeared to be in their forties and the older ones in their fifties or sixties. And unlike the women, who were dressed to kill, the men wore common casual attire, plain cotton slacks or jeans with a polo or short-sleeve shirt, but a few were in mechanic's overalls too.

And then it hit him. Pilots! Of course! Pilots and flight engineers and those in overalls: mechanics. Which would make the women *flight attendants!* It hadn't occurred to Jack—the freight dog—that flight attendants would be part of this. They'd be flying the hajj, flying passengers. Flight attendants would be part of the crew.

He was still gawking slack-jawed when a silky female drawl came from behind. "No one will care if you stay, baby-doll … but I would not try getting *served*."

Jack turned to look at her.

She was wearing a slinky white skirt and a saucy smile. Her long auburn hair was styled to one side and cascaded over her shoulder. She had eye-catching cleavage and was holding a drink in her right hand, her elbow cocked on her hip in a come-hither pose. "Are you okay?" she asked, her brow knit. "You look vexed, sugar."

"*Vexed?*" Jack repeated. He glanced at the bar and then back at her. "Vexed," he said. "Oh, uh … no, no. I'm here to meet someone."

A shapely brunette in a halter top and bellbottoms cruised up to the auburn's side. She had a wineglass in her hand and gave Jack a look up and down as if he were a figure in a wax museum. She looked at the auburn with a puzzled expression. "What's *this?*" she asked.

Ignoring the brunette, the auburn asked, "Who might that be, darlin'?"

"Captain Halder," Jack said. "He's with Jetstream International Airlines. I was told to meet him here."

She looked astonished, shot a sideways glance at the brunette, and then looked back at Jack. "Oh, *well,*" she said. "That's us, sugar … But who are *you?*"

Jack smiled and said, "I'm new. I'm Jack, Jack Dolan. I've been hired. I'm with you guys."

"*Hired,* are you? And for what might that be for, sugar?"

Jack balked. There wasn't a chance he'd say go-fer. "Pilot," he said confidently. "I'm a copilot."

The brunette let out a snort and laughed. She covered her mouth and turned away.

The auburn gave her a sharp look and said, "Well, okay, Mr. Peter Pilot, if you say so. But baby-doll, you would not be the first man to intrude on one of our briefings, and Mr. Ramón takes intruders very *seriously.*"

"Who?"

"Ramón. He's our barman here and boss-hoss here. Tell him Eddie sent you, and maybe he won't run your head through those big ol' wooden doors."

The brunette thought this was hugely funny and couldn't stop giggling. Jack's gaze darted between them until he decided he'd had enough. "I'll let him know," he said, then wheeled around and set off for the bar.

As Jack edged through the crowd, the skeptical stares and studied looks he got from the partiers made him feel like a prep school kid crashing a beat party in the Village. He was way out of his league.

When he reached the bar, he slid between a narrow opening and bellied up to the side as he was pushed and shoved by other patrons. Leaning across the bar, he saw three harried Hispanic men. The closest was a silver-haired guy with a Cuban flag and crossed rifles tattooed on his forearm. Jack caught his eye, the barman nodded, and then he gave Jack a second look and frowned. A moment later the barman came over, wiping his hands with a towel. But just as he began to speak, a woman thrust her arm in front of Jack's face, an empty wineglass in her hand. "Pinot noir!" she shouted. The barman took it, scowled at Jack, and left.

She was a petite blonde with a page boy cut and cover girl looks. She was in a black tank top and miniskirt that clung to every curve. She ignored Jack's gaze as she swayed to "Stayin' Alive."

Jack smiled and said, "Beat me to it."

She looked at him with the inscrutable gaze of a cat sizing up a dog across the street, her green eyes glistening in the bar lights.

"No problem though," Jack said sheepishly. "I've heard a man can live a week without beer."

She clucked her tongue and rolled her eyes. With a heavy Germanic accent she said, "You should leave."

"I will if you come with me."

She made a face and looked away. Her hips had never stopped swaying.

The barman returned with her wine and passed it to her. Straddling the bar with his arms, he leaned toward Jack and, with a menacing gaze, said, "Out, *cabrito!* This is a private party." With a nod toward the doors, he added, "Go now and there won't be trouble."

Jack met his gaze and said, "No. I'm here to see Captain Halder. He told me to be here at 5:00 p.m."

The barman raised a bushy eyebrow and looked at the blonde for confirmation.

She was watching them both with interest. She glanced at Jack and said, "Don't ask me … I've never seen him before." Looking at the barman with an impish smile, she said, "Throw him out, Ramón. He's trouble."

Ramón scowled. "Stay here," he ordered, a fat digit aimed at Jack's face. Jack watched him as he turned to walk down the bar.

"Get ready to get your ass kicked," she said with delight and then took a sip of wine.

Jack ignored her and continued watching the barman, who'd stopped in front of a patron Jack couldn't see. As he spoke, he gestured in Jack's direction, and Jack figured it was Halder who he was talking to. And then it occurred to him the blonde may be some relation. Halder's daughter? She was the right age, right accent, right looks, and had the same nasty attitude. Halder's hot little clone from hell, Jack figured, and just Jack's luck.

A moment later the barman returned, and this time he smiled. "*Capitán* Laney is coming," he said.

"*Who?*" Jack said. "Captain *who?*"

The barman nodded to the right, and Jack turned to see Marlboro Man working his way through the crowd. He was tall, deeply tanned, and square-jawed with a salt-and-pepper crew cut. But his most impressive feature was his eyes, the sclera so purely white it was unworldly, and his gaze held Jack transfixed. "Hi," he said cheerfully as he came near. Extending his hand, he announced, "I'm Sam Laney. I'm the company's chief pilot and check airman. You must be Jack!"

Surprised to find that he was known to anyone else besides Halder, Jack stammered, "Oh, I … yes, sir. Jack Dolan, yes, sir," as they shook hands. "Did you say, chief pilot? I thought Captain Halder was—"

"Gerhard's the DO," said Laney. "They're running late, but they'll be along soon."

"*They*, sir?" he said. "I'm sorry—"

"Gerhard and the others," said Laney. "Manny and Jimmy. That's why we have these things, gives everyone a chance to know what's going on at one time."

"Ah, I see," said Jack. "Are they captains too?"

Laney chuckled as if Jack had said something funny. "No," he said, shaking his head. "Manny and Jimmy are the company's new manage-ment." Laney looked at the barman who'd been watching them and said, "It's okay, Ramón, he's with us."

The barman gave Laney a nod and regarded Jack. "What can I get you, *señor*?"

"A beer, please," said Jack. "Anything on draft would be fine."

"And you, *Capitán* Laney?"

"Sure. Make that two."

As Ramón left, Laney said to Jack, "So, Big Jake gave me a call last night. Seems you wowed him on an interview."

"*Big Jake*, sir? You mean Captain Kegan?"

"Yeah, Big Jake, or *Shaky* Jake as he's also known around these parts. You see that prop on the wall in his office?" Laney asked. "Man, is that a story. Damn thing hit with flak and wouldn't feather. That's where the *shaky* comes from, Jake finessing that shot-up Liberator all the way home, the airplane shaking itself to pieces. Saved his crew, his whole squadron, really. But hey, look," he said. "Call me Sam. None of that sir shit here. We're not much on formality. Everyone goes by their first name."

"Sam it is!" Jack smiled.

"Anyway, Jake and I were in the Air Corps together. We did our primary training on PT-22s, those little bastards as deadly as they are beautiful. Anyway, we survived and we've been close friends ever since. He gave me a call last night and said he'd like to see you get some time in the airplane, asked if I'd give you a hand."

"So you'll be my check airman?"

Sam smiled and said, "That'll be me."

The blonde had been standing by their side and watching all this as she sipped her wine. Looking at Jack closely, she blurted, "So, he's no bullshit?" She looked at Sam and said, "He's a pilot? My *Gott* … That's terrifying."

"This is Anna Van Blerk, one of our flight attendants," Sam said with a testy tone.

Jack smiled at her and said, "Nice to meet you again, Anna."

"How old are you?" she asked.

Sam looked miffed and said, "Philippe's been looking for you, Anna. Why don't you run along and see what he wants."

She scowled at him, gave him an insolent shrug, then rounded and sashayed into the crowd.

Jack's eyes were on her bottom as she disappeared.

Sam chuckled. "Looks like you're even," he said.

"I hope she's no relation to Captain Halder."

"To *Gerhard?* No, not at all," Sam said. "Gerhard's daughters, well … no," he said. "Anyway, Anna's not German; she's an Afrikaner."

"Ah. Anna Van-something-or-other. So that's a Dutch accent?"

"Van Blerk, and yes, of sorts," Sam said. "But look, forget that. You'll get used to it. We're mostly like a family here but sometimes a frat house. There's a lot of hazing. It doesn't mean anything."

Jack smiled. "Hey, I give as good as I get."

"I'm sure." Sam laughed. "You wouldn't have gotten past Gerhard if you couldn't."

Jack eyed the two women dancing near them and asked, "So, they're all flight attendants?"

"Mostly," Sam said. "Those two—Donna and Kathy—are ours, but some of the guys brought their wives too. Most of them flew for us at one time or another. Altogether, there are twenty-four cockpit and forty-five cabin crew. We always take more girls than we need on these contracts because a few of them won't last. The new ones they hire have no idea what they're in for—even though we make it pretty clear."

"Why's that?" Jack asked. "I mean, what is it they're in for?"

"The work. Especially for the girls. Long days and lousy living conditions—West Africa especially. Anyone not accustomed to it has a tough time adjusting. Throw in an airplane full of provincial people who don't speak English and have never been in an airplane before, and, well … it takes a special type to make it. Many do, but some don't, and some won't even finish the contract, though the pay is great if they do."

"Is that where we'll be flying from, West Africa?"

Sam looked puzzled. "*We?*" he said. "Gerhard said you'd only be flying the ferry flight over."

Jack looked glum and said, "Captain Kegan told me to come back with a few hundred hours, Sam, not just a few takeoffs and landings. I was hoping to achieve all of that not only for Air Logistics but to have the experience for this or another jet airline if Air Logistics doesn't pan out too."

Sam looked aside and gave it a thought. Looking at Jack, he said, "Alright. But let's not get ahead of ourselves. For now, we'll focus on getting you some time in the airplane and discuss any other options as we move along. Fair enough?"

Jack smiled. "Fair enough," he said.

"Now the next question: are you married?"

Jack laughed. "*Me?* No, no," he said. "Hell, I can hardly keep a girl-friend in this line of work."

"That's good," Sam said and then hastened to add, "I mean, good that you're not married because if you do stay on, you'll be away for at least six weeks. Wherever we're headed, this much is certain: it's a hajj contract and that's how long they usually endure. It's tough on any marriage but particularly hard for a young one."

"Nope, no marriage, not even close," Jack assured him.

Ramón was passing by, and Sam raised his fingers in the victory sign. "Hey," he shouted. "*Dos cervezas, por favor!*"

Ramón gave him a nod and kept walking.

Looking at Jack, Sam said, "Sometimes he forgets. This bunch keeps those guys hopping."

"I've noticed."

A loud burst of laughter erupted down the bar, and the two of them looked in that direction.

Sam smiled and said, "You'd think these knuckleheads hadn't seen each other for months." He looked back at Jack. "So, Jake told me you're a Vietnam vet. He said you were there the same time Dave went MIA, is that right?"

"Yes, and I was sorry to hear about that. There were more than six thousandsorties flown in I Corps that spring. I guess Dave's was one of them."

Sam nodded and shifted his gaze across the room. "Dave was an only child. Jake and Adel took it really hard."

"I can only imagine."

Looking around the room, Sam said, "Most of us here are vets, World War Two and Korean guys mostly. In fact," he said, pointing at two men on the other side of the lounge, "Freddie over there's a Korean F-86 ace, and Dan Peterson was a Tuskegee airman."

Jack was impressed. "No kidding," he said. "An ace and a Tuskegee guy, huh?"

"That's right."

Jack shrugged. "That's amazing. I never imagined—"

"Anyone like that at Corrosion Corner?" Sam asked, smiling.

Jack's face fell. "Oh, no, Sam … I didn't mean it that way."

"Hey, don't worry about it. Most of what you've heard is true, and a lot isn't. You'll see as we move along. Anyway, point is, for a small company, we've got a hell of a crew here. A couple of Vietnam guys, too, but they were there long before you were."

"I figured there'd be a few," Jack said, glancing around the room for anyone who looked his age.

"Philippe Desmarais and Gerhard, actually. They were there in the early '50s with the Foreign Legion, back when the Frogs were screwing up the place. Long before we got dragged into it."

"Desmarais? Isn't that Captain Kegan's secretary's name?"

"Claire, yes," Sam said. "She's his wife."

Ramón arrived with two foaming mugs of beer and placed them on the bar. Sam grabbed his and Jack did the same. As Ramón wiped his hands on his apron, he looked at Jack and said, "I am sorry. If I knew you knew *Capitán* Laney, I would have never questioned you."

Jack smiled and said, "Nah, don't worry about it."

Ramón looked at Sam and raised a brow. "So," he said, "did you tell him about our time in Cuba?"

Sam made a face and shook his head. "No, Ramón; not here; not now."

Ramón frowned.

"Cuba?" Jack said. "Now *that*, I would like to hear."

"You see, you see," said Ramón, a finger waving at Sam. "Now tell him, tell *him!*" he demanded.

Sam sighed, put down the mug, and looked at Jack. "Long story," he said. "But to keep it short, Ramón and I were wrapped up in that Bay of Pigs fiasco and that's it. The end."

Ramón winced. "And?" he said. "*And—*"

Sam gave him an exasperated look.

Ramón leaned across the bar and pointed to Jack's face. "You make him tell you!" he said. "You make him tell you this because he will not unless you make *him!* This man," he said, flailing his finger at Sam, "this man is a great *capitán*, a *piloto* of great courage and skill! There are many Cubans who owe their lives to him—*Many!*" he exclaimed. "And he is too much a good man to tell you. But you make him tell you, *mi amigo*, and you will learn much about great courage and skill."

A glass crashed on the floor, and gales of laughter followed. Sam turned to look and Jack followed his gaze. Ramón grimaced, rounded to one of the other barmen, snapped his fingers, and shouted something in Spanish. The man grabbed a bucket and mop and raced toward the commotion.

Continuing their conversation, Jack said, "Well, I'm intrigued. I was only nine when the Bay of Pigs occurred and never understood what that was all about, only that it was an embarrassing failure for the US and Kennedy."

"Not to mention the CIA," Sam said. "Anyway, Ramón was with the FRD and I was flying C-46s for Southern Air Transport at the time. We'd met loading guns and supplies in Nicaragua. That was the high point. After that, it went downhill fast. We got out of there one step ahead of Fidel's firing squads. But SAT did a lot of flying to Cuba before the revolution, and we left many more friends behind than we got out—most of whom were executed or imprisoned. Point being, never mind Ramón. There was nothing glorious about it."

Jack's brow was knit. "*SAT?*" he said. "Weren't they a CIA outfit like Air America?"

Sam's eyes narrowed, and he said, "That's right. But I started with the civilian version before the CIA bought them out. So, tell me, how does a young guy like you know about SAT?"

"Vietnam," Jack said. "I had a chance to talk to an Air America pilot. He told me about their history, SAT and such. I've always had a thing for the C-46 and Air America's mission. If I had the chance, I would have loved to have flown for them."

"That'll pass," Sam said. "Trust me."

Jack shrugged. "Maybe," he said. "But I'd still like to hear the *whole* story. I'm betting it's a rip."

Sam gave him a look. "Yeah, a rip," he said. He put his half-empty beer on the bar and his hand on Jack's shoulder. With a nod toward the crowd, he said, "C'mon, let's make the rounds and I'll introduce you to some of the other guys in the crew."

# TWENTY-ONE

*Miami, October 8, 1978*

Sam made his way through the crowd with Jack trailing him. He was leading him toward a group of men gathered at the other side of the lounge. "Boogie Oogie Oogie" was on the box, the party in full swing. But Sam and Jack hadn't gone far before a man's hand came out of the crowd and gripped Sam's arm. Sam stopped and wheeled around. "Charlie!" he said with a broad smile.

"Hey, Skipper! We missed you on that last one! Nice to see you back," Charlie exclaimed, shaking Sam's hand.

"Yeah, I missed you guys too! Hey, where's Cheryl?" Sam asked. "Did she come with you tonight?"

"She ran out to call the babysitter. I'll tell her you're here. She'll want to say hi!"

"Yeah, me too!"

"So, rumor has it this one's your last? You're hanging up your kit bag?"

"Yeah, it's time. Peggy doesn't even want me doing this one."

"She'll change her mind after she's had you home a few months," Charlie said. "Last time I skipped a contract, Cheryl had my bags packed and my uniform pressed two weeks before we were scheduled to go out on the next one."

"I'm sure you're right. But the Feds aren't asking them, are they? So, age sixty it is, and adios."

Charlie clapped him on the arm and said, "Yup. Another year and my time's up too."

"Speaking of getting old, look here," Sam said and, reaching for Jack, added, "I have someone I want you to meet. Charlie, this is Jack Dolan. Jack's been hired to give Gerhard a hand and do some flying with us."

"Oh, yeah?" said Charlie, looking pleased and offering Jack his hand. "Nice to meet you, son, welcome aboard!"

"Yes, sir, thank you," Jack said as he shook his hand.

"Charlie's one of our captains," Sam said to Jack. "He was a B-29 aircraft commander in the Pacific and flew DC-6s for JAL back in the '50s when they were using American crews."

Looking at Charlie, Jack added, "I've read about that. The Japanese hired you guys on contract?"

Charlie smiled, shrugged, and averred, "Had to take what we could find. Slim pickings for pilots after the war. Got to do what you got to do, right? Anyway, good to see a fresh young face around here." He looked at Sam. "God knows, we need it!" He laughed.

"Tell Cheryl I'll catch up with you guys later," Sam said.

"I will," said Charlie, and looking at Jack, "Nice meeting you. I look forward to flying with you."

The same scene was repeated continually as Sam and Jack crossed the room. The two of them never got more than a few feet before someone happy to see him stopped Sam and greeted him. It was quickly evident that Sam Laney was not only an essential man in this company but highly regarded too.

They were a few steps further into the crowd when the sultry auburn Jack had met when he first entered the bar intercepted them. Slipping through the crowd like a rail through reeds, she put her hands on Sam's chest and looked up at him saucily. She lifted herself on her tiptoes and gave him a peck on his cheek. Then, slipping her arm around his waist, she rounded and studied Jack with that lickerish gaze.

Sam said, "Jack, this is Eddie Duval. Eddie's one of our lead flight attendants."

Jack smiled and uttered, "Hello again, Eddie."

Sam looked at her and asked, "You've met?"

She smiled and nodded without taking her eyes off Jack.

Jack felt self-conscious and averted his gaze.

Sam slipped her arm off his waist, and reaching for Jack, he said, "C'mon."

As they moved further across the room, Sam looked back at him and warned, "Don't let all that baby-girl crap fool you. I've seen Eddie take down a pair of drunk Gunnies on the way home from Vietnam. They were spitting out 'yes, ma'ams' and 'no, ma'ams' faster than a clip from their M-16s."

Jack laughed. "I believe it!"

A few steps further in, Jack caught a glimpse of a fiery redhead coming at them like a rugby forward making for the goal. Pushing aside a heavy-set guy in mechanic's coveralls, she collided with Sam from behind and threw her arms around his waist. "Ha! Gotcha, there ol' fella!" she yelled in a thick brogue.

"Maggie!" Sam said, turning around, smiling broadly, and grabbing her by her shoulders. "Where have you been, love? Peg's been calling you every day. She's getting worried—"

"Ah, Jaysus," Maggie swore in a deep and nicotine-gnarled voice. "Where the hell have I been, da? The question is where the fook have you been? A bloody whore's melt that was, that fookin' eejit in charge o' things. Do you know what I mean like?"

"Ah, now, c'mon," said Sam with a self-conscious glance at Jack. "Let's give him a break—"

"A break, would ya?" she exclaimed. "Jaysus, a hundred and eighty-five of them manky gowls groping us from takeoff to landin', and all the while that cunt telling us to take care? C'mere 'til I tell you, da! There's not a soul here wouldn't a boxed the be-jayzus out of the bastard."

"Okay, enough, enough," Sam said. "I get it."

"Aye, I hope you do!" Maggie declared. "We can't be doing that again."

"Right. You're right; now look," he said, changing the subject. "I've got someone I want you to meet. This is Jack Dolan. Jack's helping Gerhard out, and then he's going to be flying with us."

She gave Jack an incredulous look and then turned it on Sam as if he had to be joking.

"Jack, this is Maggie Dunn, our chief flight attendant."

Jack extended his hand, smiled, and said, "Nice to meet you, Maggie."

"Aye," she said, shifting her gaze to him and giving his hand a listless shake.

She was thirty-something, short, stout, and braless, her ample breasts beneath a rumpled and carelessly fitted baby-doll dress. A mop of red hair covered her brow and tumbled onto her shoulders in long and unruly tresses, and her complexion was freckled and pallid. She reminded Jack of the Dublin urchins he'd met as a boy. Maggie was as unkempt, irreverent, and profane as any of those girls, but a type he found wildly attractive as adults.

"Maggie's talking about the contract they just completed," Sam said to Jack. "They were shuttling laborers from Karachi to Kuwait and back. I stayed behind on that one, so one of our other captains managed things in my absence." He shot a reproving look at Maggie and said, "Unfortunately, Miss Dunn and Captain Stone don't always agree."

She snapped at him like a terrier. "Bollocks!"

"Alright," Sam ordered, holding up his hand. "Enough."

"Bollocks," she grumbled, looking down and rummaging for something in her handbag.

"Where in Ireland are you from, Maggie?" Jack asked.

"Dublin," she muttered without looking up.

Jack's brows went up. "No kidding?" he said and smiled. "I was there a few times as a kid. The last time was when I was fourteen. My grandparents lived in Kimmage. Do you know that area?"

She looked up at him with a piercing gaze. "I do," she said. "Me ma's place is on Devenish."

"I don't remember that one," said Jack. "My grandparents' was on Durrow," he said, recalling the small, brick, two-story row house with an unheated privy in the back. It was on a cul-de-sac, and a man with a horse-cart delivered turf and coal for the fire. A neighbor named Francie had a pigeon coop, and he and Jack would smoke Players and watch the birds as they darted among the chimney tops. It was February on that last visit, the sky cold, gray, and drizzly, the earthy scent of turf burning in the fires.

Maggie pulled a pack of Chesterfields and a Zippo from her bag. Giving the pack a shake, she drew out a cigarette with her lips and dropped the pack in her bag. With a single deft flip of her wrist, she opened the lighter, ignited her smoke, and closed the lighter with a snap.

Jack hadn't seen that since Vietnam. He'd thought it was a soldier's thing. Odd seeing it done by anyone else, especially a woman.

She exhaled to the side, her cigarette between two nicotine-stained fingers. "Left in '59 and never been back," she said, plucking a bit of tobacco from her tongue.

Jack said, "The time I was there was in '65."

Maggie looked up at Sam and changed the subject. "You missed a good one, *da*, but the next time you're stayin' home, I'll be stayin' too, mind ya."

"Well, this one's my charm, love, so one way or another, you'll have to make it work with him going forward. Gerhard's settled on it. Brad's taking my place."

"CAP'N SAM!" a man bellowed, and they all turned.

"Ah, Jaysus, 'ere we go," said Maggie to no one. "The other fookin' eejit in this outfit."

He was a big man, nearly as tall as Sam, and coming at them like a runaway barge, people parting in his path like flotsam in a bow wave. He was sixtyish with a cringeworthy combover, and when he got to Sam, he took his hand and shook it with gusto. "Well, I'll be goddamned, you ol' cuss," he yelled in a low-country drawl. "You're back! Gerhard said y'all might retire!"

"Retired? Not yet, Bobby." Sam scowled. "But I will be tonight on a busted medical if you don't let up on that hand!"

"Oh ... oh, right," said Bobby, letting go. "So hey, word is you're doing this hajj with us, is that true?"

"That's the plan," said Sam. "One more and I'm done."

"Well, hot damn, and thank you, thank you, *Jesus*," he said, his hands steepled and his eyes on the ceiling. "I mean, I got to tell you, Sam, that Karachi thing? That son-of-a-bitch Stone? What a fuckin' goat-rope that was, skipper—"

Sam cut him off with a sharp look and a raised hand. "Yeah, yeah, got it!" he snapped. "Maggie's already filled me in."

Bobby looked at her and said, "Oh? She did? Good girl!" He winked.

"God bless us," she muttered, rolling her eyes and taking a drag on her smoke.

"Right, well—never mind all that," Sam said. "Now look here, I've got someone I want you to meet. This is Jack Dolan. Jack's a copilot helping Gerhard get this thing together. After that, he'll be staying on to do some flying for us. Jack, this is Bob Mumford, our chief flight engineer."

Jack smiled and extended his hand. "Pleased to meet you, sir."

Mumford recoiled. "*What?*" he said to Sam. "*Flying* with us? Are you serious?"

"Yeah, damn it, I'm serious."

"Wait! Wait! You've got another copilot when I can't have any more engineers? You got to be shittin' me, Sam! Since when?"

"Since Friday."

"Friday?" said Mumford, looking astonished. He pointed a finger at the floor. "You're tellin' me it was *this* Friday?"

"That's right."

"Christ a'mighty, Sam! I told Gerhard that I needed to bring Tommy Esposito back, and he told me no way! He said we already had a full crew and we're not taking on anyone else! How the hell is it you guys get a new copilot—of all things—when I can't have any more mechanics and engineers?"

"Because that's the way it is, now let it go," Sam snarled.

"But Sam!"

"But, *what?*" said Sam, his ire now reaching a boil.

Bobby frowned and turned to Maggie for support. But Maggie had averted her gaze and affected disinterest.

Bobby sighed and turned to Jack. "Bobby Mumford," he said and extended a hand the size of a cinderblock. "And you're who?"

"Jack Dolan, sir. Pleased to meet you."

"Yeah, sure … sure," said Bobby, letting go. "So who you been flying for, kid?"

"Keystone Airways in Philadelphia. Freight in DC-3s."

"Gooney Birds, huh?"

"Yes, sir."

Mumford jutted his lip and nodded. "Okay, so where'd you get your DC-8 time?"

Sam jumped in. "Point is, Jack doesn't have any," he said. "Which means he's going to need some ground school. Bobby, I need one of your engineers to cover it."

"*What?* One of my engineers?" Mumford huffed. "Holy shit, Sam, so not only do I get screwed out of anymore engineers, but now you're going to take what little I got for this?" he said, pointing at Jack. "Hell, all my guys are already being run ragged trying to get this thing together, and now you want me to do ground school too? Bullshit!" he exclaimed, "I can't spare anyone for that!"

Sam fixed his jaw and glowered.

"God*damn*, Sam!"

"Just get it done! Am I clear?"

"Yeah, yeah, sure. But goddamn to hell," Bobby grumbled.

"Ah, take the piss out of ya," Maggie snorted. Dropping her smoke to the floor, she crushed it out with her foot.

Bobby looked at her and beamed. Throwing his arms wide, he smiled as if all that had just happened hadn't. "I love it when you talk like that," he said. "Now where's my Irish kiss, you hunk-ah, hunk-ah gorgeous?"

She gave him a thorny gaze. "*Kiss?* Kiss me arse, ya 'fookin' culchie."

With a mischievous glint in his eyes, Bobby said, "Well, yes, ma'am. I believe I will!" He reached out, grabbed her, spun her around, and pulled her toward him. With his arms locked around her waist and holding her from behind, he jiggled her, her breasts flopping.

"Loose me or I'll kick the be-jaysus out of you, you cheeky bastard!" she shouted.

"Bah!" he said, letting her go.

Rounding on him with her finger aimed at his face, Maggie growled, "Next time you put a hand down on me like that, Bobby Mumford—"

"Aw, c'mere," he uttered, drawing her back.

She rolled her eyes and submitted. As he embraced her, he rocked her gently, her head turned and her body limp. Then he whispered something in her ear, causing her to straighten and shove him away forcefully. "Go way out of that," she hissed. "Where's your fookin' manners, eh?"

Jack felt embarrassed by their behavior and needed a break anyway. He looked at Sam, smiled, and asked, "Where's the head?"

"Out the doors and to the left," Sam said.

Jack nodded and started for the exit.

. . .

Bobby looked at Sam and said, "Did you get the word about these airplanes they've leased?"

Sam said, "Yeah. I've heard they're pretty rough. But you're the first guy I've spoken to who's actually seen them."

"They're 21-series airplanes, retired Pan Am stock. The leasing company's had them since Pan Am let them go, and it looks like they've been ridden hard and put away wet."

"Yeah, figures," said Sam. "But beggars can't be choosers, and it's all Gerhard could find on short notice. But, look, on this other matter, I want to make sure we're clear about this kid."

"Who?"

"*Who?* Jack!" Sam said. "The young guy who was just here."

"So, what about it?"

Sam looked miffed. "About getting him some training, Bobby. Gerhard hired him to be an errand boy, and that's fine. But he'll be flying with us too. I want him trained. I want him legal … at least for the ferry, understand?"

"Yeah, sure, skip. But what's the deal? I don't get why we're doing this. What's the point?"

"It's a favor to Jake. I spoke to him last night. He wants to hire the kid but can't unless he's got some DC-8 time. Jake's cut a deal with Gerhard, parts for the airplanes he's got in stock in exchange for payment and some flight time for the kid. Problem is, if I know Gerhard, he's gaming the deal and will let the kid go on some excuse the moment he's done with him as an errand boy."

"So what? Who gives a shit? The kid took the job; the kid takes his chances. Just like we all do."

"I *do*, that's who! I give a shit, Bobby, so get it done! Clear?"

"Alright, alright, I got it, skip. But like I told you, it's going to be tough finding someone to do it. The airplanes need a lot of work, and all my guys are tied up with that. Besides, if he's going to be a go-fer, how's he going to find time for ground school?"

"Let me worry about that."

Bobby shrugged. "Sure, whatever … I'll call Joe Bartolini, get him down here. Joey's the best for that sort of thing anyway."

"Joe? Perfect!" Sam said. "Why isn't he here already?"

"Mama won't give him up until she has to. That New York, Italian family, Catholic bullshit, you know what I'm talking about."

"Right, well, I hate to put him out—"

"I wouldn't worry about it. I need him anyway. I'll get his ass down here pronto."

"Alright, fine. Now on to the airplanes. You say they're rough?"

"Yeah, one of them is here in Miami and the other two in Fort Lauderdale. All of them are missing equipment, especially the overwater stuff: the rafts, the signal gear, and the HF radios. The worst of them is here in Miami. It needs all of that plus Loran and both Dopplers. The panel's been stripped."

"Jake's got all that stuff. Anything that's still current, he'll have in stock."

"Hope so. And let's hope he has parts for those old JT4s. If not, I'll have to go to Tucson for those."

"Sounds like a plan," Sam said. Looking at Maggie, he asked, "Have you seen the cabins?"

"Aye, they're the filthiest things I've ever seen," she said. "Carpets frayed to the matting; seat covers faded, stained, and torn; and the galleys and lavs smell like a bloody sewer. We'll have to do something about that. No one can work in them the way they are now."

"They won't spend money fixing up interiors on leased airplanes for a hajj, Maggie. But we'll certainly get them cleaned."

# TWENTY-TWO

*Miami, October 8, 1978*

Jack re-entered the bar, "I Heard It Through the Grapevine" rocking the room.

He craned his neck in search for Sam, but given Sam's height, it didn't take long to find him. He was among the group of pilots he had been leading Jack toward earlier. Jack began working his way in that direction.

As he came near, Sam caught sight of him and put an arm around his shoulder. "Hey! Hey! Listen up! Listen up!" he shouted. "Here's the new member of our crew I've been waiting to introduce."

The men became quiet and turned to give them their attention.

"Gentlemen, this is Jack Dolan," Sam announced. "Jack's been flying Gooney Birds as a captain for a freight outfit in Philly, so he knows how to keep the blue side up through long nights, busted airplanes, and grimy weather. Jack will assist Gerhard getting this thing together, and when he's done, he'll be joining us as a copilot for the ferry flight over. Please give him a warm welcome."

The men clapped and cheered, and Jack smiled and waved.

Sam began the introductions by pointing to the furthest man on the left and working right. When he came to the distinguished-looking Tuskegee pilot he had pointed out earlier, he said, "That's Dan Peterson. He was a P-51 pilot with the Red Tails. Dan's got a Distinguished Flying Cross and a hell of a story to go with it."

Jack waved, and Dan smiled and lifted his glass in a toast.

When Sam finished—about a dozen men introduced in total—a man Jack hadn't met took Sam by the arm and guided him to the side. They became engaged in conversation, their voices muted, Sam bending an ear to hear. From their behavior, Jack could see the conversation was private, so he took the opportunity to slip away, search for Halder, and get another beer.

With his empty bottle in hand, Jack was cutting a path toward the other side of the room when suddenly the music was turned down, and the lights turned up. Some of the women booed, but then everyone's attention shifted toward the entrance to the lounge. Three men were spotlighted and standing by the doors. Halder was in the middle in khakis and a white uniform shirt. Two middle-aged men in dark, sharply tailored suits were standing on either side of him.

Halder began working his way alone to the center of the dance floor, and the crowd parted to make an opening.

"Welcome," he said, smiling with his hands raised beneath the lights. "Welcome, my friends, and thank you all for coming tonight. It looks like nearly everyone has joined us, and that is good." Gesturing toward the doors, he added, "As you can see, Mr. Manny Hirsch and Mr. Jimmy Caffaretti have joined us as well."

A round of applause went up with cheers and whistles. Halder continued smiling and looking around the room, then tamped down his hands to bring it to an end. He cleared his throat and said, "So, although many problems remain, the points of greatest interest to you regarding the hajj are now final—"

"That's a laugh," a man yelled. "For the next ten minutes, maybe."

"*Ja*, well," Halder said cheerfully. "But that is the nature of our business, Hank, is it not?"

Hank threw him a wave, and Halder waved in return.

Chatter began among some of the men, but the women silenced it. "*Shush!*" they ordered. "*Shush!* Let him speak!"

Gerhard gave them a little bow. "Thank you, ladies, thank you," he said. "Now, please, everyone, I must tell you there is good news, but there is also bad news about this next operation."

Loud groans went up, and a man shouted, "Give us the bad news first, Gerhard."

"*Ja*, well, Ben, the bad news is that our airplanes are still down for overhaul and the replacements we have found are in *very* poor condition. To be honest, it will take all of our best work to make this happen. I wish it would be better, but—*it is what it is*—as I often hear you say."

The mumble of conversation overtook the room.

"But please, *please*," Halder said, waving his hands to stop the chatter. "As I said, there is good news too, and that news is *very* good. As it turned out, we will not be flying from West Africa as planned but from Indonesia. That means you will be based in Colombo, Sri Lanka, the midpoint between Indonesia and Saudi Arabia, and the living and working conditions will be much better."

There was applause, but it was restrained. "Never been to there," a man shouted. One of the women said, "Tell us more, Gerhard."

"*Ja*, well, make no mistake, my friends, this is a very big improvement, you see. Now listen, and I will explain. To begin, we plan on two flights departing from Colombo for Indonesia every morning—one to Jakarta, and one to Medan—then both flights returning to Colombo in the afternoon. Back at Colombo, those same two flights will refuel, do a crew change, and then depart for Jeddah and return to Colombo late that night. One airplane will remain in Colombo every day for maintenance and as a reserve. As always with the hajj, you will deadhead empty on one leg and fly passengers on the next. The work schedule will be one day on and one day off throughout the flying phases of the contract. For crew quarters, we have arranged a hotel on the ocean in Colombo—a classic resort from colonial days, I must tell you, and one highly favored by Europeans for vacation. Mr. Caffaretti will have more details for you in that regard, but altogether, this will make a much nicer operation for everyone, particularly our ladies. Indonesia is a modern country, so nobody cooking in the aisles, pissing in the seat pockets, or shitting in the sinks—and much less malaria too!" he hastened to add.

A round of applause erupted. The women were cheering the loudest, whistling and clapping.

Halder waved for silence.

As the cheering ended, he gestured toward the entrance and said, "Now, please give your attention to Mr. Hirsch, who would like to say a few words before Mr. Caffaretti fills you in on more details regarding the accommodations."

Manny Hirsch stepped into the spotlight to wild applause. He was a short, balding, heavyset man in his fifties with a diamond ring that sparkled on his left pinky. Standing at the center of the floor, he beamed and waved as he looked around the room. Jack sensed no pretense or imperious mien about the man; in fact, he appeared to be enjoying his new business adventure like a kid with a new toy.

As the applause trailed off, Manny began. "Thank you all ... Thank you all so very much," he said in a thick New York nasality. "Now ladies and gentlemen, I'm here tonight not only to enjoy this celebration with you but to thank you all for the fantastic job you did on our last contract. Needless to say, your dedication and professional effort under demanding circumstances has paid off for us all *very* well."

Cheers and applause followed, and Manny clearly enjoyed their accolade. As it trailed off, he said with a brow raised, "But now, this latest surprise. As you know, our friends at ONA not only filed for bankruptcy last week but went straight into liquidation! Ka-*boom*." He threw up his arms. "All of their commitments were suddenly up for grabs, and among those contracts were some for the hajj that were quite lucrative. In fact, the first one we snagged out of Kano was outstanding. But *then*," he boasted with a finger raised, "but then we did one even better! By working our magic, we hoodwinked Capitol Airlines into taking the Kano contract off our hands and then grabbed this Indonesian deal right from under their noses!"

Everyone laughed and clapped. Manny shrugged and held out his arms, feigning innocence.

As the applause ended, Manny continued, "Now, of course, the only problem is this came up on very short notice, which is why we've asked you back and postponed a long overdue vacation. Although we regret the inconvenience of that, I promise the bonus you will receive for providing this extra lift to Merpati Airlines in Indonesia will more than make up for your loss!"

Cheers, whistles, and applause followed. As they trailed off, Manny continued. "Now Gerhard tells me the only real challenge is the substitute airplanes we've found, but as I have told him, no one in the *world* could make this happen better than the men—and the very beautiful ladies—we have gathered here tonight!" There were more whistles and cheers, and speaking above them, Manny said, "Well, that's all I have, and I won't detain us from our celebration any longer. But Mr. Caffaretti has a few things you'll be interested in hearing about our departure plan and accommodations in Sri Lanka, so please give him a warm welcome."

Manny turned around and clapped as Caffaretti took the floor.

He was also fifty-something but heavily built and wearing a black sharkskin suit that traced broad shoulders and large biceps. His snow-white hair was pulled tight to his skull and finished in a Samurai's chonmage, a fashion statement with no uncertain message. The crowd went silent as he began to speak, his Brooklyn accent a muted baritone.

Jack cocked an ear to listen, but from behind him came a man's hillbilly twang: "A guinea, a Jew … and a *Nazi*, too," he rhymed.

Jack winced and turned to look at him.

He was wizened and thin but with a distinct pot belly that hung over a silver belt buckle the size of Texas. He smiled at Jack and aimed his Miller tall boy at Caffaretti. "Our management team," he said by way of an explanation. "The honchos who run this outfit. What a collection, huh?"

"I'm sorry?"

"Buddy Reid," he said, offering his hand. "I'm one of the flight engineers."

"Jack … Jack Dolan."

"Yeah, I know," Buddy said as they shook. "But, hey, look, don't take that personal. It's a joke around here. Hell, no one gives a shit who they are—no one gives a shit who *anybody* is—you could be a fuckin' pigmy for all we care. The only thing that matters is you're good at what you do and get along with everyone."

"*Nazi?*" Jack said. "I thought Göring was the only Nazi in the Luftwaffe."

Buddy gave him a look and snorted. "Hey, when they're shootin' at ya, kid, they're all fuckin' Nazis."

Jack had a wry grin. "You have a point," he admitted.

A woman standing next to them hissed, "*Shush!*" With her eyes on Buddy, she put her finger to her lips.

Buddy made a kissy face. "Marry me, Dianne."

"How about I poison you instead, Buddy," she retorted.

Buddy laughed, looked at Jack, and whispered, "Wait 'til he's done. He won't be long ... Jimmy ain't much of a talker."

Caffaretti concluded with details about the Mount Lavinia hotel in Colombo, and then the lights dimmed and the music resumed.

"So, were you Air Corps?" Jack asked.

"Yeah, engineer on B-17s, the 457th at Glatton."

"How many missions?"

"Too many," he mumbled.

Jack decided to change the subject. "So, our management team," he said. "They're good at it?"

Buddy brightened. "Oh, hell yeah," he said. "Best we've ever seen. Manny's a *business*man, not some fuckin' Cessna pilot who thinks he's an airline guy. Manny's into everything down here: got his own lawyer firm, construction company, car dealerships, hotels, clubs, limo outfits, you name it—all kinds of things—and all kinds of contacts too. Anyway, he knows business, and he and Jimmy run the airline that way, not like some rich brat's travel club."

"That's what it was like at Pan Tropic?"

"Yeah, pretty much," Buddy said, lifting his beer to take a swig.

"Who owned the company before?"

"A real estate asshole and his drug addict kid—all the profits going up his nose—and they weren't the first. There were a lot of others before them. But now, with Manny's head for business, Jimmy running the back office tight, and Gerhard's genius for flight ops? I mean, put it all together and we're golden. These days, the contracts keep coming, our airplanes are being well maintained, and the crew is solid: no dickheads in the cockpit; no drunk bitches raising hell in the cabin. Gerhard and Jimmy got rid of 'em all."

Jack looked across the dance floor at Caffaretti. "I bet," he said somberly.

Buddy eyed the two women dancing next to them. "I hate this disco shit," he grumbled. "Why don't they ever play any Marty Robbins?"

Jack choked back a laugh. He thought of his dad's Marty Robbins LP. "Gee … I can't imagine," he said with a chuckle.

"They plan these things," Buddy groused. "Manny's girls."

"What's a Manny's girl?"

"Girls who work for him in his businesses. Jimmy posts the openings, and he and Maggie and Eddie do the interviews. They get their emergency training at Eastern, and Maggie and Eddie take care of the rest. That girl there?" he said, leering and pointing his bottle at the woman who'd shushed him. "That's Dianne. She came over from his hotel operation." Buddy looked at Jack with a lascivious grin. "She's somethin', ain't she?"

Dianne was a fortyish, tall, and shapely copper-blond with a neck-length cut and short, tight skirt. Jack sensed a divorcée on a new adventure. He looked at Buddy and remarked, "They're all pretty hot, actually."

"Damn right," Buddy affirmed. "Manny don't hire no hags. Hell, you ought to see the gals he's got working his Porsche dealership in Palm Beach. *Woo-eee.*"

Jack laughed. "Maybe they'll take my Valiant in trade." He chuckled. "I'll have to drive in and let them check it out."

"Yeah, sure," said Buddy. "But look—in case you haven't heard—don't be getting any ideas," he warned. "Once we're on the road, there's rules— no messin' around."

"Rules?" Jack asked. "Whose rules?"

"Jimmy's and Gerhard's. It's one of the first things they changed when they took over 'cause of all the people problems we had at Pan Tropic. Got enough on our plate just running the flight op. It's that old thing, don't shit where you eat, right? Causes too many flare-ups in a small outfit like this, so no messin' around on the road, that's the rule now."

"Huh."

"But that's about the only rule," Buddy added. "Other than that, the rule is: if it works, it rules."

"I got that impression."

Buddy smiled and raised his bottle in a toast. "To the Prophet's pilots," he said.

Jack clinked his bottle and, looking puzzled, said, "Who?"

"Us," Buddy said as if it was obvious. "We are! The Prophet's pilots. The hajj."

"What prophet?"

"Mohammed or whatever. The guy those people worship. Like Jesus or Moses or Buddha or somebody. A desk clerk in Mali told me that. He told me we were the 'Prophet's pilots' and were blessed because we flew the hajis."

"*Blessed?*"

Buddy laughed. "Yeah, can you believe it? This pack of shysters, sluts, and stick-jockeys? Blessed, my ass. But hey, like I told him, I'll take any blessings I can get, hoss."

"I don't know much about it," Jack said. "I never heard of the hajj

164

until this past week. Is that true what Captain Halder said about flying out of West Africa?"

"Oh, yeah. They're some of the poorest countries on the planet. Most of those folks hardly been in a car never mind an airplane. They come onboard terrified; you can see it in their faces. It'd be like putting you or me in a UFO."

"I can imagine."

Buddy lifted his bottle, examined it, and gave it a swirl. "Anyway, I'm ready for another. How about you?"

"I'd like to, but I've really got to find Captain Halder. He told me he'd catch up with me here, and I haven't spoken to him yet."

Buddy gave him a smile and said, "Well, good luck. Nice talking to you, Jack, and welcome aboard!"

. . .

After searching the room and failing to find Halder, Jack stopped at the bar to order a beer. The barman brought it over, and as Jack took the bottle from his hand, he felt a firm grasp on his elbow. He turned around and was surprised to see Halder. "Put it down," Halder ordered.

Jack put the bottle on the bar. Halder leaned toward him and spoke into his ear. "There is a white Econoline van in the parking lot," he said. Taking Jack's hand, he pressed a set of keys into his palm. "Be at Hangar Four at 0700 tomorrow. You will pick up two mechanics and bring them to Fort Lauderdale. There's a map of Miami in the glove box if you need it."

"Hangar Four? 0700? I'll be there."

Halder pulled a roll of greenbacks from his pants and stuffed it in Jack's other hand. "Buy whatever you need, but I want receipts!" he said. "Call the office when you get to Fort Lauderdale. I will have further instructions for you then."

Jack nodded and stuffed the cash and the keys in his pockets.

"If you have any questions, call the office. Maria will know where to find me—"

"Gerhard!" a man shouted.

Jack and Halder turned to look at him, and Halder grimaced.

He was fortyish, average height, and trim but with a receding hairline and a heavy five o'clock shadow. As he pushed through the crowd and closed in on them, his dark eyes were ablaze with indignation. Stepping up to Halder, he pointed at his chest and said, "Philippe told me what's going on. This is bullshit, and you know it!"

Halder said, "I tried calling you, Brad. Things changed, and I had no choice."

Brad shifted his gaze to Jack and sneered as he gave him a once-over. "So, this is the new guy," he grumbled. "The one Kegan sent over?"

Halder looked at Jack and said, "This is Captain Bradley Stone. He will take over as chief pilot when Sam retires after the hajj."

Jack cleared his throat and offered his hand. "Jack Dolan," he said. "Pleased to meet you, Captain Stone."

Stone ignored Jack's hand, looked at Halder, and said, "What do you mean no choice? We had an understanding, Gerhard. We agreed! No more of this bullshit!"

"*Ja* ... well," said Halder. "Things changed, and now is not the time for this, Brad. We will take it up in the office tomorrow. Not here; not now!" He turned about and started for the doors.

Stone grabbed his arm.

Halder pulled free and kept going.

Suddenly Sam broke into the scene, put his face in Stone's, and drove his finger into his chest. "Let it go, Brad," he ordered. "Let it *fucking* go!"

Stone knocked it away and snarled, "Let it go, my ass. First Larry, and now *THIS!*" he yelled and pointed angrily at Jack. "Fuck you, Laney ... *FUCK* you!"

Sam glowered, and his arm shot out and he gave Stone a shove.

Stone came back at him with a swing, but Sam dodged it and seized his arm.

Suddenly Halder was back. He threw himself between them and shoved them apart. "KNOCK IT OFF!" he yelled. "*GOTTVERDAMNT* ... KNOCK IT OFF!"

Bobby Mumford grabbed Sam from behind, lifted him off the floor, and drove him toward the doors.

"TOMORROW!" Halder yelled at their backs. "My office, 9:00 a.m.!" Turning to Stone and pointing his finger, he added, "0900! *Verstehst?*"

Stone smoothed his shirt and scowled. "Yeah, sure," he said. "0900. *Verstehst!*"

Halder spun around and went after Sam.

Stone cut to the right and pushed his way toward an exit by the bar.

Jack watched it all go down, dumbstruck, and was still standing there when he felt a punch in his arm. He swung around and saw the blond he'd met at the bar earlier, the girl named Anna. She pouted and waved her empty wineglass in his face. "I'm out of fuel, Mr. Pilot," she moaned enticingly. "Fill me up or I'll crash."

"Did you see *that?*" Jack asked. "Did you see what just happened?"

"See what? You look like you saw a ghost."

Jack looked toward the exit and ran his fingers through his hair. "I think I did," he muttered. "My own."

She made a face. "So, are you getting me my wine or not?" she huffed.

"Can I take a raincheck, Anna? I've got an early go tomorrow. Maybe next time, okay?" He turned and made for the doors before she'd given him an answer.

Anna watched him disappear, and with a coy smile, she muttered, "Count on it."

# TWENTY-THREE

*Islamorada, Florida Keys, October 9, 1978*

It was 6:00 a.m. and the meeting with Halder and Stone was in three hours. From his Keys wardrobe, Sam had selected the least blood-stained khakis and polo he owned and slipped his bare feet into a pair of salt-encrusted Topsiders. An ancient blue blazer he'd dug out from the back of the closet would complete the ensemble. He hadn't been so well dressed since his daughter's graduation.

Sam stumbled onto the porch and plopped wearily into a deck chair. The predawn hours at his home were his favorite time of day, Venus twinkling in the sky, the palms in the yard rustling quietly in the nightly breeze. Alongside the dock, his '73 Merritt tugged gently on its lines, its white topsides glistening in the lights.

Peggy came to his side and handed him a steaming cup of coffee. He glanced up and smiled at her as he received it. She was a year younger than Sam and fair-skinned but radiant. They'd started dating in high school, and he thought her as gorgeous now as she'd ever been. They'd been married for thirty-four years, hitched as soon as he came home from the war. Peggy was a nurse at a local clinic and loved the outdoors and the Keys as much as Sam did—though his passion for fishing she could take or leave.

He'd come home from the meeting the night before too late to talk about it. Peggy was already asleep, and that was just as well. But this morning, as she put her cup down on the table and pulled back a chair with a look of concern, she asked, "So, what's going on? Why are you going back?"

Sam was staring into his cup and not smiling at his boat. It was her first signal something big had gone wrong.

"There was a dustup at the meeting," he replied. "Brad and I got into it. Gerhard wants us back this morning to straighten it out."

"*Dustup?*" she asked with a wary gaze at him over her cup. "Got into *it?*" Her eyes narrowed. Peggy was long accustomed to Sam's euphemisms: *dirty weather* for a hurricane; feeling *iffy* when he had appendicitis. "What's a *dustup?*" she demanded.

Sam gave her a shrug. "I pushed him … he pushed back."

Her face fell and she put her cup on the table. "Oh, Sam … please."

Still staring into his cup, he explained, "He doesn't want Larry upgraded to captain, and he's got his nuts in a knot over that young guy Gerhard hired, the one Jake called me about the other night. Brad doesn't want him flying with us, says he doesn't have the experience and that *bullshit's* got to stop."

There was a pause.

"Have you considered he may be right, Sam? If Jake can't take him, why should you? And *Larry* upgrading? *Really?* What more is there to say?"

Sam averted his gaze and said nothing.

A stronger gust rustled the palms, and the boat's lines went taut.

She reached across the table and touched his arm. "You can't save the world, Sam," she said sweetly. "God knows I love you for trying … but you can't. So please stop, Sam—just stop. For me, for our girls."

He looked at her with a wan smile and said, "I told Jake I'd help the kid, and I want to, Peg. As for Larry? We've been through it all, and let's not rehash it. I need to get this done, and you know why."

She frowned and sat back.

Sam put his half-full cup on the table and stood up. He grabbed his blazer, circled the table, leaned over, and gave her a kiss.

"Take some coffee with you!" she said, her hand on his cheek.

He smiled. "I'll stop on the way."

"What time will you be home?" she asked as he left.

"In plenty of time for cocktails," he said, his blazer slung over his shoulder.

169

. . .

At the intersection of US 1, Sam turned left and drove east. The ocean air blustered through the open window of his pickup, his thoughts wandering to the end of his career, a bittersweet occasion in his life, and Peggy's plea for him to let go—his certainty that he never could.

Halfway across Islamorada Bridge, he glanced to the right. The breeze was quickly freshening, the sea covered with whitecaps and long streaks of foam. "You can't save the world," she'd said. But that wouldn't make it go away.

In 1937, Sam was seventeen, with the Depression grinding on. Two years earlier the Keys had been devastated by a hurricane, and hundreds of people had lost their lives, including several of his friends. Sam's family had avoided the tragedy only because their father, a commercial fisherman, had moved them to the mainland so he could take a temporary job as a mate on an offshore boat out of Tampa. But when the job ended and the Laneys returned to Islamorada, they had no reason to stay: their home had been washed away by the storm. When Sam's mother landed a job as a cook in a Key West hotel, they moved there to keep the family solvent and the kids in school. Months later—with Sam's father still out of work and his mother worried about keeping the family together—she reluctantly agreed to use the little cash she'd saved to buy his dad a boat. It would enable her husband to get back to fishing and, above all else, keep him from leaving to find work as so many other husbands and fathers had been forced to do.

The boat he bought was a thirty-two-foot cedar on oak sharpie that was configured as a smack. It was a good choice for the Keys since it could be worked both as a fishing boat and a transport for the coastal trade delivering freight and dry goods to the isolated islands. She was flat-bottomed like a dory, with a square stern and some dead-rise aft for good sea-keeping ability. A small cuddy-cabin was forward, and two fish boxes had been mounted on either side of the centerboard trunk. The masts, sails, and rigging had been hauled off, and a cantankerous bitch of a jump-spark engine was installed in their place. Although the motor was useful for steaming through the tight channels and tidal passages that abound in the Keys, sails were a more reliable form of propulsion.

It was early September of that year, and the children were returning to school. But there was also a strong run of snapper reported along the patch reefs off Big Pine Key, and Sam's dad decided to keep him out of school to help with the fishing. Sam's mom was angered by the decision. She'd seen Sam transfixed by the Pan Am Clippers that landed and took off from Key West harbor and wanted that for him, his dreams come true. But Sam's father prevailed in the end, the family's hard times overcoming her objections.

Once the decision was made, Sam asked his father if his friend Tommy O'Connor could come along with them. Since the fishing would be with hand lines rather than nets, another angler on board ensured a larger catch, and Sam's father agreed to the plan. Tommy was thrilled and his mother agreed. With five hungry children and her husband long gone in search of work, the extra income would help the O'Connors too. Three days later, the trio motored to Big Pine Key and took up residence in the fishmonger's shanty on the east side of Pine Channel.

It was hot and hazy that first week of the trip, and they'd leave the wharf in the cool air before dawn. Motoring south past Little Munson Island, they continued outbound until the reef dropped away and the water turned from turquoise to indigo blue. After the anchor line came taut in the current, they began chumming with a mixture of fish oil and oats. It was never long before the yellowtails began to bite, and the action was fast.

Midway through the afternoon of their fifth day, towering white clouds began forming an unbroken line to the west over the Gulf. The breeze, which had been light and fickle all day, suddenly became blustery. Cat's paws danced across the glassy surface of the sea, rippling it like the hide of a skittish horse. Lightning licked at the water, and thunder rumbled in the distance. A fish tugged on Sam's line, but he ignored it and looked at his father, whose haggard gaze was on the sky to the west.

"Right!" his dad said, quickly winding in his line. "We've done right good, lads, but time to head in." Tossing his tackle in the boat, he pointed to Tommy and said, "Jump fo'ard, son, and start drawing down on that anchor line." Pointing at Sam he said, "Prime the motor, and I'll secure the catch. Set to it now, boys, *now!*"

Sam pulled in his line and dropped it into the bilge in a heap. Tommy sprang to the bow as the sky quickly darkened and wispy gray clouds went scudding by low overhead.

There was a flash of lightning and a loud rumble of thunder, and as Tommy's foot landed on the foredeck, a wicked blast of cold wind slammed into the boat and threw it on its beam end. With his bare feet covered in fish slime and chum oil, Tommy's foot flew out from beneath him, and his hands flailed in the air as his head hit the Sampson post with a sickening crack. Sam watched in shock as Tommy slid over the side, his body lithe as an eel.

Lightning flashed, thunder boomed, and a wave of roiling black and green clouds raced over them. Sam ripped off his shirt as his father leapt for him and screamed, "NO, SAM, NO!"

But too late. Sam was already plunging headfirst into the sea.

Down, down, down, he kicked and pulled himself into the dark billows of Tommy's blood. Kicking, pulling, clawing at the sea, Sam followed the trail of blood, his ears splitting from the pain, his lungs burning for air, until his right hand found Tommy. Clasping him tightly, Sam turned and lunged for the surface.

He burst above the waves and sucked desperately for air, but it was full spray. Coughing and choking, he swirled round and round in search of the boat. But in the moments since he'd plunged into the sea, the ocean had gone from calm to high breaking seas. The sky was black but for the flashes of lightning. There was a horrific howl of wind, and the rain and sea were lashing at his face.

A moment later, Sam was at the crest of a wave with Tommy tightly in his grasp when he saw the boat and his dad in the trough below them.

"LET HIM GO, BOY," his father screamed at Sam. "SWIM TO ME, SAM, SWIM!!" he yelled as he pushed and pulled furiously on the engine's start lever. But the wicked bitch refused to fire, and Sam, equally stubborn, refused to let Tommy go.

At the top of the next crest, the boat was nowhere in sight and Sam was certain the sea had taken it. A deep melancholy overcame him, and his swimming slowed. Waves towered above them in the following trough, and Sam noted the eerie silence at the bottom, the fury of the storm masked by the huge seas ahead and behind them, and a strange sense of detachment set in, an extraordinary sense of peace. It was as if everything that was happening was happening to someone else, and Sam was only an observer.

The next wave crashed over them, plunging them beneath the surface, drowning them in salt water, the warm ocean filling his lungs. There was a flash of lightning, and Tommy's face was lit like a ghost. He was smiling, his hand waving to Sam in the tumult, beckoning Sam to follow … follow … the warm sea embracing Sam like a womb, and then sleep coming down … gentle sleep … Tommy smiling, nodding … Sam gently, gently letting go …

SLAM!

Sam was seized by an implacable force! His shoulder was pierced with searing pain, and he was wrenched back to life. In the next moment, he felt himself pulled like a crab pot, his chest crushed against the boat's wooden gunnel, his father's powerful grip yanking him over the side. Sam fell on his hands and knees in the bilge, coughing and retching violently, the boat awash in blood, dead fish, and tackle, the storm still raging all around them.

• • •

Sam's father steered them home, his jaw set, his flinty gaze fixed on Little Munson Island. The fury had passed, and a saffron sky had settled in its place. The little smack rolled and yawed in the lingering seas, and gulls cawed and careened playfully above their wake. The steady cadence of the motor was the only other sound.

Sam lay listlessly on a thwart and stared vacantly at the gulls, tears streaming from his eyes.

Tommy was gone.

# TWENTY-FOUR

*Miami, October 9, 1978*

I t was 6:15 a.m. on Monday as Jack finished breakfast in the hotel café. He scribbled his initials and room number on the check, took a final sip of coffee, and then got up and left.

The final events at the briefing the night before had weighed heavily on him, and sleep had come in fits and starts. Stone's acerbic greeting and the altercation between him and Laney had Jack unsettled. Back in the room, Jack wasn't in the mood to admit it to anyone—much less Debbie—so once again he'd broken his promise to call her. He'd give it another day, see what transpired, and call her that night with a clearer head.

As he stepped outside the hotel, a bellman was standing next to a baggage cart. "Morning, sir!" he said cheerfully. Glancing up at the sky, he added, "Looks like some weather coming later."

Jack paused and looked up. "Looks like it," he said indifferently.

"Can I get you a cab?" the bellman asked.

"Nah, I'm good," Jack answered, scanning the parking lot. "I've got wheels out there somewhere. A white Econoline." Looking at the bellman, he asked, "Have you seen one?"

"There's a white van that belongs to Hirsch on the back lot," the bellman said. "That's the only one I've seen."

Jack smiled. "I'm sure that's it." He circled the hotel and found it parked in back, black and gold lettering on its side:

HIRSCH MOTORCARS, INC.

Mercedes-Benz, Bentley, Porsche & Audi

Jack put the key in the lock, and the door opened. In the back, he saw a set of nose gear tires, some toolboxes with assorted parts, and a drum of Aero-Jet oil strapped to the right-side wall.

He buckled in, and at the intersection of LeJeune Road, he turned left and headed toward the airport. When Jack drove up to Hangar Four, he saw two men standing outside by the curb. They were each holding a white Styrofoam cup in one hand and a cigarette in the other. They were unshaven and wearing dark blue shirts and jeans with work boots.

Jack stopped in front of them and asked, "You guys with Jetstream?"

They pursed their lips and shook their heads.

"I'm here to pick up two mechanics headed to Fort Lauderdale to work on a couple of DC-8s. Any idea where they might be?"

The guy to the left gave a shrug and said, "Right here. That's us." He flicked his cigarette to the curb and rounded the van to the passenger door.

The other mechanic walked behind the van to enter it from the back. "Sorry about the seating," Jack said over his shoulder as he climbed in.

The mechanic sat down on one of the boxes. "This'll be fine," he said.

Turning to the mechanic in the passenger seat, Jack said, "You know where we're going? I'm new in the area, so I may need some help."

He pointed to the exit and said, "Sure. Turn right leaving the lot. I'll direct you from there."

Jack nodded and put the van in gear.

As they motored east on NW Thirty-Sixth Street, Jack gave him a sideways glance and said, "So, you're not with Jetstream, huh?"

"No. We're with Consolidated Air Services. We do contract work for everyone down here. Who'd you say that airline was?"

"Jetstream International," Jack replied.

He looked back at his buddy. "You ever hear of a *GIZ*-stream International?" he joked.

"*Jet*stream, you dickhead," the guy corrected him.

The mechanic in front hammered his fist in his lap and said, "Oh, yeah? Well, here's your *dick*head, Mitchie … come get it!"

Mitch laughed. "Sure, Pete. Let me get my tweezers and I will."

Jack looked in the rearview mirror. "So, you've heard of them, Jet-stream?"

"Yeah," Mitch said. "I've heard of them. They've been around a while. But they were something else before, Pan-something-or-other, I think."

"Pan Tropic," Jack replied.

Pete said, "Yeah, that's it. Now I remember. So, you work for them or for Hirsch?"

"Both. He owns the airline and the van."

Pete snorted. "Hell, yeah. Hirsch owns half of Miami, so why not?"

"That's what I heard."

"I'll tell you what though, those clubs of his?" Pete said with his brows raised. "Unbelievable, man. You ever been?"

"Me? No … no," Jack answered. "Like I said, I'm new here."

"Well, if he gives you any kind of employee discount, you ought to go. Ain't that right, Mitch?"

"Yeah, they're top-shelf if you can afford them," Mitch replied. "The girls are un-*fuckin'*-believable."

"So they're strip bars?" Jack asked.

"Yeah, but classy," Mitch said. "Not the usual trailer trash you see in those other joints, biker chicks lookin' at you like you're Daddy raping them again or something."

Jack grimaced.

Pete pointed to the sign ahead and said, "Get in the right lane and follow that to I-95 – Fort Lauderdale."

Jack checked the traffic, put on the turn signal, and switched lanes for the exit northbound.

# TWENTY-FIVE

*Miami, October 9, 1978*

S am parked at the company's office in Wynwood. He glanced at his watch. He was fifteen minutes late, but insolence was his only play after losing his temper with Stone the night before, and Sam would play it for all it was worth.

As he got out of his truck, he caught sight of Brad's silver Porsche Carrera in the lot, the morning sun casting highlights on its paint. Sam smirked at the study in contrast. Brad Stone was no more in harmony with the sensuous curves of his car than he was with his airline, the angular and sharp-edged prick that he was.

"*Buenos dias*," he said warmly as he greeted Maria.

"Ah … *buenos dias! Capitán* Laney!" Maria beamed as she got up and did a little dance as she circled her desk. She threw her arms around Sam and gave him a hug.

"So, how is Juan doing?" he asked.

Maria stood back. "Oh, *Capitan* Laney," she said, "thank you for asking, and please, *please* thank Peggy for the beautiful card and flowers and the *very* generous gift. But *si, si*, Juan is doing much, much better every day. He can no longer do construction, but *Señor* Hirsch offered him a job as a *driver* of his limos and, *gracias a Dios*," she said, crossing herself in the Catholic way. "It will be so much safer! *Señor* Hirsch is *such* a good man. We are so grateful to you and Peggy and everyone who has been so, *so* generous. Every time I think of it … *Dios mio*," she said. "Everyone here is such kind people!"

"Well, I'm glad to hear that, and please give Juan my warmest regards. Tell him Peg is keeping him in her prayers."

"*Si, si,* and thank you, thank you, *Capitan* Laney, I will tell him. Now please, please," she said. "I know *Capitan* Halder is waiting. He will be mad if I keep you any longer." She smiled.

Sam patted her arm and said, "It'll be fine. Now sit. I'll let myself in."

Maria returned to her desk. Sam gave a knock on Halder's door and opened it. "Morning," he said brightly as he entered the office.

Halder was seated at his desk. He looked up at Sam and scowled. *"Ja,* good morning," he said. "So glad you found the time to join us. I hope we have not put you to any trouble."

Sam shrugged. "Just a little," he said sarcastically. He circled the vacant seat in front of Halder's desk and sat down adjacent to Stone. "Morning, Brad," he chirped with a patronizing grin.

Stone raised an eyebrow. "Morning," he said grudgingly.

Halder and Stone were in suits, Halder's clip-on tie tossed carelessly across the outbox on his desk. Stone was wearing an impeccably tailored navy pinstripe with a red tie. He had his right leg crossed over his left, and his black brogues were polished to a high gloss.

Sam sat down and stretched out in a relaxed pose, his sockless Topsiders crossed at his ankles.

Stone glanced at his Rolex. "My meeting with the FAA is at 10:00," he said. "We need to get started."

Halder gave Stone a look and rocked back in his chair. Reaching for a cigarette case in his jacket pocket, he took it out and removed a smoke. He lit it with a Zippo, slapped the lighter closed, and tossed it on his desk. "So," he said to Sam, "the engineers tell me the airplane here in Miami is ready to fly."

Sam gave him an indifferent shrug.

"You are out of landing currency, *ja?*"

"Yes," Sam muttered.

Halder leaned forward, pushed around some papers on his desk, and found his calendar. He took a drag on his smoke and studied the dates. Then, sitting back, he said, *"Ja,* so, what we have is a perfect opportunity. I'm thinking next Monday or Tuesday if it can be arranged."

"Arranged for what?" Sam asked with a wary gaze.

"You need landing currency, the airplane needs a test flight, and the FAA needs to do an observation of Brad conducting a check ride so he can complete his certification for check airman."

Sam's eyebrows went up. "So, that's it? You want me to be Brad's check ride dummy? That's my penance for last night?"

"*ACH!*" Halder said, reaching for the ashtray and crushing out his cigarette. Scowling at Sam, he said, "Knock it off! What I am doing is getting as much done in as little time and for as little money as possible. That's all. Your cooperation is expected."

They stared at one another and sparred with their eyes.

Stone leaned toward Sam and touched his arm. "Relax, I'm sure you'll pass," he said with a condescending smirk.

Sam looked over at him and said, "I know you're just trying to be nice, Brad, but nice doesn't become you. Better stick with being an asshole."

"*Ach! Gottverdamnt! Die nase voll haben!* Enough!" Halder exclaimed. He got up and rounded his desk toward the office door. He grabbed the knob, opened it, and turned to Stone. "You have a meeting to attend," he said.

Stone rose from his chair and buttoned his jacket. Sam got up as well.

"Not you," Halder said, pointing at him. "Sit down … please."

Sam rolled his eyes and sat down.

Stone walked to the door and extended his hand. "Thank you, Gerhard," he said with a smile. "I'll call you when I'm done."

Halder shook his hand and said as he ushered him out, "Maria has a letter for the Feds. I have to sign it, and you must bring it to them."

The door closed, and Sam sat in silence and stared at his hands in his lap, the creping and liver spots, the scars from a lifetime of bait knives and fishhooks he'd embedded in his flesh. He had a wan smile. Soon they'd be the only threat to his well-being, his days passing quietly until life's next big thing. Why wasn't he happier?

The door opened, and Sam looked back as Halder walked in.

He sat down, took out another smoke, and lit it. He tossed the lighter on his desk, rocked back in his chair, and crossed his legs. "Everything is changing, Sam," he said, "but maybe for the better, *ja?* You and I will not be here to see it all the way through, but we can help."

Sam averted his gaze and looked across the room vacantly. "Better for what?" he asked as if to himself.

"For everyone, Sam," Halder replied. "So, why? Why are you doing this? Why are you making it difficult for me?"

Sam met his gaze and said, "Because there are better choices than Brad, Gerhard. Why not Philippe for instance, or Brian, Mick … or *Dan?* Why not Dan, for crissakes? Because he's black?" The remark hadn't left his mouth before he regretted it.

Halder was crimson. With his cigarette pinched between his thumb and forefinger, he aimed it at Sam. "Fuck you, Laney," he growled. "You do not think I have enough to live down in this *Gottverdamnt* world without shit like that from you?"

Sam stared at his hands. "I'm sorry," he muttered. Shifting his gaze to Halder, "That was bullshit. It was way out of line."

"*Ja!* Out of line, Sam! What has got into you? Last night and now *this?*"

"Peggy tells me I should let go … Maybe I'm not ready."

Halder sat back, and took a drag. As he exhaled, "No, you are not," he said. "But who is? What I will tell you is that I *did* ask Dan and Dan said, 'Screw that.'"

Sam rolled his eyes.

"*Ja*, well, you know Daniel, Sam, always straight to the point. But he also said his wife's career on Broadway is taking off, and he's not leaving Manhattan. He said he is happy to pick up what trips he wants and leave it at that. So, after Dan, I asked Mick, but Mick told me to piss off, too. He wants nothing to do with any more FAA scrutiny. He told me he went through enough of that already. And as for Brian? I disagree. We all like Brian, but Brian is too—what to say—too much wanting to be liked to do the job. You cannot give a man a down on a flight check and stay his friend. You know that better than anyone, Sam. But *somehow*, you do it! You stay friends with everyone you supervise. That's very unusual. You should know that, *ja?*"

Sam looked down at his hands. "So, that leaves only Brad," he said, sullenly.

"*Ja!* Brad! Who else? *Philippe?* You must be joking! Philippe is too busy fucking all the women. So, no … no," he said, reaching and crushing out his smoke. "It must be Brad because he has a clean record, excellent flying skills, he can call the shots, as you say, and—very important to Manny and Jimmy—he is young enough to be around here for a long time. All the rest of us will gone in a few more years at most. Brad is our youngest captain and the best choice all around, so that is the decision. It is final."

"But he's also got the temperament of a badger, Gerhard, and though he's got excellent skill with the airplane and he knows the book better than anyone, his people skills are nonexistent. How's that going to work out on the line? Have you thought about that? Have you spoken to anyone about how he handled things on that Karachi contract?"

Halder gave a flip of his hand and said, "*Ja,* well … we take what we have and we work on the rest. But what you can do, Sam, is help us by giving Brad the help he needs. Tell the others about the company's plans for a cleaner future, maybe some schedules, *ja?* No more months from home flying the hajj, no more living in Bamako! That is something everyone could be happy for."

Sam was still staring at his hands.

"We are depending on you, Sam … all of us. So, what is it you need, tell me? What must we do to get you to work with us on this?"

Sam looked up and said, "I want to finish Larry Schaff. I want to see him through the upgrade."

There was a pause, their gazes even.

Breaking the silence, Halder said, "*Ja,* well, of course. But what troubles me is what troubles Brad. We think that accident is what is making your decision. It wasn't your fault. Why do you let it bother you?"

"A sense of responsibility?"

"*Responsibility?* Do you not think there are things I want to redo if I could? Do you have any idea of my regrets, Sam—my family, Algeria and Indochina, the Foreign Legion—do you know how many times I have begged the devil to take me? But then I learned everything is forward, Sam, we can only go forward. I cannot redo the past, and regrets don't help make the future better. Regrets can only hold you in the past."

Halder's wife and two young daughters were killed in Dresden during the Allied firebombing of that ancient and beautiful city. He'd sent them there in the belief that Dresden was a low-value military target and wouldn't be attacked. But it was near the end of the war, the Allies owned the air, and the bombing mission was rated as a low-risk means of breaking the will of the German people to continue the fight. Countless civilians had been consumed by the inferno—the attacks were controversial to this day—and Gerhard's wife and young daughters were among them.

Sam knew this. "Yes. Only forward, Gerhard. And that is what I want to do for Larry—move forward."

"But Brad does not believe Larry should upgrade. You disagree. Have you considered that Brad may be right?"

"No. He's not."

"All I am saying is maybe Brad has a point, *ja?* Have you considered that, Sam? Maybe Stone's judgment of Schaff's abilities is correct?"

"He did a fine job on his rating ride in the simulator, and I'll be looking at him hard during his Line Operating Experience. He deserves another shot at it."

Halder sighed. "I have doubts about Schaff myself. I have flown with him, you know. I think you might be allowing him, *ach*—what to say—too much room to wiggle. Maybe because of his problems, his wife, his son; maybe you see too much of that, Sam. Maybe that is *all* you see."

"I don't agree. I believe that once he's out from under scrutiny, he'll be fine. I know him; I've trained him; I've tested him … you and Brad haven't."

"I trust you, Sam, but I also want Brad's point of view. I want you to have Brad fly with him during some of his Line Operating Experience. When Larry is finished, then the three of us will talk about it and I will make a final decision. That is the best I can do."

Sam nodded. "Okay," he said. "Fair enough."

Halder smiled. "Good. That is all I ask. Now look," he said, sitting back and steepling his hands. "I haven't told anyone about this, but it is not a secret. We are putting a lot of money into our own airplanes during the refit in St. Louis. Manny believes that there will be a great opportunity under this airline deregulation business. If he is right, these hajj and war zone contracts we fly will become much less. We will be like the big boys, *ja?* No more monkey tricks just to survive."

Sam had a wry grin. "Business … monkey *business*," he said.

Halder flipped his hand. "*Ach!* You know what I mean, Sam. No more crazy risks. And if that is true, then we need someone who can take the lead doing that, and that man is Brad. You understand what I am saying, of course."

"To a point, maybe."

"Our business will be changing soon, and we will need to add crew. We need captains and copilots we can upgrade. Larry Schaff? We'll see. But there are no others behind him. I need pilots who not only know the rules but *want* to play by them. The time of running this airline like a combat mission or flying club is coming to an end, Sam. Pilots like you and me and Dan and Philippe … *ach!*" he said, throwing up his hand. "We are over too. From what I am reading about the future, the next generation of airplanes will need computer technicians, not pilots. You and me? We will soon be *kaputt.*"

The phone rang in Maria's office, and she answered the call. A moment later she knocked on Halder's door and opened it. "*Capitan* Halder," she said, "can I interrupt?"

Halder nodded.

"That young man you hired is on the phone. He say he is at Consolidated in Fort Lauderdale. He say he dropped off the mechanics and wants to know what to do."

"Thank you, Maria. Get his number and tell him to wait by the phone. Tell him I'll call back soon."

Maria nodded and closed the door.

"So, when do you plan on doing this flight test you're talking about?" Sam asked.

"As soon as we can schedule it with the FAA," Halder said. He leaned forward and consulted his calendar. "I think maybe the sixteenth or seventeenth?" He sat back. "We will see. I will call you as soon as I know."

"Okay … so, meeting adjourned?"

"*Ja* … get out."

Sam stood up and smiled at him.

"Go!"

"Sure. But one more thing."

Halder scowled.

"That flight check would be a good opportunity for Jack to get some stick time too. Maybe a few bounces out at Dade County. I assume that's where we're headed."

"What? *Nein* … NO!" Halder snarled. "With the FAA onboard and the airplane in the condition it is in, who knows? We are not going to risk trouble or airplane damage just to train some copilot for Kegan." Leaning on his desk and pointing his finger at Sam, he added, "And you are not to take risks with him when you're on the road, understand? Not at any time! Let him jerk the gear, talk on the radio, and fly during cruise. No takeoffs, no landings, and send him home after he has sat through three, am I clear?"

"Jake expects him to finish the contract, Gerhard. That was the deal for the parts he sold us."

"Don't push me, Sam."

Sam gave a shrug. "Okay," he said. "It's your call. But he'll need some ground school and a least one sim period before putting him in the airplane with me, even for a ferry flight. He's not doing this without at least a semblance of legality, and that's my bottom line. You want to tell Jake, or should I?"

Halder glowered at him.

"So, what's it going to be?"

Halder threw up his hand. "*Ach!* Some ground school and one sim period! But not this week! This week I need him for what I hired him to do. Now get the hell out!"

Sam turned toward the door and threw him a backward wave.

"Tell Maria to get Dolan on the phone."

Sam gave him a nod and kept walking.

# TWENTY-SIX

*Miami, October 9, 1978*

It was 8:20 p.m. on Monday when Jack parked the van and finished his final errands for the day. He entered the hotel and went straight to his room to place the call. Since it was a work night, Debbie was certain to be home. Throughout the day he'd struggled with what to say to her but had decided to just wing it.

"Hello, Crystal, it's Jack Dolan," he said pleasantly. "Is Debbie in?"

His greeting was met with a frosty silence and then Crystal's hand cupping the receiver. A moment later Jack heard a clunk as though it had been dropped on a table.

A short while later, it was picked up again. "Yes," Debbie said dryly.

"Debbie! It's Jack."

"I know."

Her tone said it all, and Jack hesitated. "Look, Deb," he said ruefully. "I'm sorry I didn't call you back on Sunday night like I said would, but the meeting ran longer than I expected and some of it left me unsettled about what to do. I needed more time to gather my thoughts."

"I understand things change, Jack. But this is the second time you've promised a call and didn't follow through. Even a brief call just to say you can't talk now but will later would have been fine. But not finding a moment to follow through on a promise is something I can't abide. As I told you before, I feel taken for granted."

"Yes. You're right. I should have called in any case."

"So, what did you learn at that meeting that you haven't already told me?"

Jack cleared his throat. "The airline has a contract to fly the hajj, Deb. It's the Muslim pilgrimage to Mecca. They told me that if I helped them as an errand boy, they'd give me a shot at flying for them as a copilot. I know it sounds like a crazy scheme, but if it works out, it would give me the jet time I need to be competitive at Air Logistics and all the other airlines that I've applied to."

"The hajj? They fly Muslim pilgrims from *Miami?*"

Jack laughed. "No, Indonesia, actually."

"For how long?"

"About two months. First, we take the pilgrims to Mecca, and after their rituals, we bring them home. A lot of people go, so they can't all be moved at once."

"How big an airline is this?"

"They have three DC-8s and about two dozen cockpit crew—pilots and flight engineers—and about twice as many flight attendants," he added blithely.

There was a pause. "Wait," she said. "Flight attendants? Women?"

Jack closed his eyes. "Uh ... yes, I guess."

"You guess?"

"I mean yes, of course. Women."

"And these women—these twice as many flight attendants as pilots—they just fly off for months at a time, no boyfriends, no husbands, no families, nobody at home they're responsible to?"

"Uh ... well, I'm not sure," he mumbled, and then a thought came to him and he brightened. "But look, it's not like you think," he added. "First of all there's these rules, see? And, besides that, everyone here is really old. I'm the youngest guy they've ever hired."

"*Rules?* Rules for what?"

"Rules against ... *um* ... you know, fraternizing. Getting together after work."

"You're serious."

"Oh, yeah. They really make a point of it!"

"They need rules to prevent old men from fraternizing with old women, Jack? Exactly how *old* are these old women flying the hajj?"

"Oh, um, I don't know." He paused as if to consider it. "Thirties at least," he answered. "Even *forties!*" he added as if that sealed it.

Silence.

"Deb … Deb, are you there?"

"Rules," she muttered as if amazed. "Like the Ten Commandments?"

Jack lowered his head and closed his eyes. Why did he have to mention *flight attendants?* "Look, Debbie," he said, "I know this sounds weird—"

"Weird? No. Not weird, Jack. But not workable either. The kind of life you're describing isn't for me. Men—*women*—taking off and galivanting around the world together for months at a time? Nope. Not me, sir. You must have me confused with one of them. I'm pretty much a nine-to-five kind of girl, weekends with family and friends. A bit of travel is nice, but I like my home and I want a relationship with someone who feels the same way. From what you're telling me, we're headed in very different directions."

"But it's not certain and I may be home sooner, Debbie. Besides that, I *really* like you a lot, and even if this thing pans out, it's only for one contract. Once I have the heavy jet time I need, I'll be back."

"Boeing has offered me a position in Seattle, Jack. I've been keeping them on hold for a while—mostly because I didn't want to break it to my parents—but I've since told my mom and dad and they've been very supportive. I've decided to take it. And what you're telling me now makes me even more certain."

"Seattle?"

"Yes."

"How soon would you leave?"

"Soon. Crystal has a friend to take my place in the apartment, and then it's just a matter of packing my things and driving out there."

"Can I call you when all this settles? I mean, when I'm back home?"

She sighed and said, "I don't know. I guess. Crystal will know my number. Call here. I'll tell her to let you have it."

Jack laughed. "I get the sense she'd like that," he joked. "I get the sense letting me have it with a frying pan would be just fine."

Debbie didn't laugh and Jack was hesitant to say any more, but he sensed the conversation was about to end, and it just came out. "If somehow we can find a way to make it work, I have to see you again—I *have* to," he blurted.

There was a pause and then, "Me too," she said sadly, softly. "Take care of yourself, Jack. I wish you well." Her voice cracked. "I have to go …"

She hung up suddenly.

Jack sat back, ran his fingers through his hair, and stared at the floor. Why did every woman in his life blow up like the Hindenburg?

# TWENTY-SEVEN

*Miami International Airport, October 15, 1978*

It was Sunday morning and a week since Jack had started work as a go-fer. Throughout that time, he'd been shuttling people, parts, and paperwork between Miami and Fort Lauderdale at least sixteen hours per day. He'd been so occupied with the work—and actually enjoying it—that it had been easy to forget that he had no certain future with Jetstream at all.

But on Friday afternoon, that suddenly changed. Maria told him that *Capitan* Laney had arranged ground school for Jack. She told him to be at the airplane in Miami on Sunday and that one of the flight engineers would be there to provide Jack's training.

This was a huge development. It meant Halder was taking him off the go-fer trail and putting some time, money, and effort into preparing Jack to fly. How much training Halder had arranged remained to be seen, but anything at all was significant from Jack's perspective. Over the previous week, the thought of a career with Jetstream had become ever more intriguing. Neither the seedy reputation of Corrosion Corner, nor the company's past, nor its tawdry office, nor the dustup between Laney and Stone had tempered Jack's enthusiasm for what he'd found here. There was an energy about the airline, a strong sense of fraternity and adventure, and a swashbuckling attitude he found alluring. Whatever the risks ahead, he'd deal with them. But for now, at least, Jack felt on top of the world as he arrived at Hangar Four to begin his training.

The airplane was parked in the same greasy spot it had been when Jack first met Halder. Over the course of the week, Jack had seen it surrounded by vehicles, equipment, and mechanics. This morning a gaggle of them were assembled in a circle around the left main landing gear, looking at it as if perplexed. The flaps were extended to the full down position and two of the four engine cowlings were open. Halder had said the airplanes were in poor condition, and from what Jack had observed over the week, that was no exaggeration. But his thrill was undiminished, and by the time he reached the mobile stairs attached to the forward entry door, Jack was moving at a full gallop.

He bounded to the top landing and paused to look back across the massive jet. As the wind tousled his hair, he surveyed the airplane's immense wing and fuselage, the tail towering above the ramp. But although the jet was huge and exotic compared to the ancient DC-3, it was nearly as weathered and neglected. The Pan Am livery was sun-bleached and thinly whitewashed, bare aluminum on the wings and engines was dulled and dirty, and there were oil streaks from the leading edge to the flaps. A prominent puddle of fuel glistened under the left inboard engine.

Jack turned and entered the cabin. It was his first time in any of the three jets, and he was immediately struck by the odor, a noxious effluvium of sour milk, excrement, urine, and mildew in air so close it felt like a crypt. Whoever had used the airplane last had parked it here, closed its doors, and left it to fester like a cesspool in the sun.

Beyond the stink, the next most striking thing about the interior was its shabbiness. The Pan Am blue carpet and upholsteries were stained and threadbare, and the white overhead linings were coated with a sallow film of nicotine that was sticky to his touch. Two rows of economy seats extended from the forward galley to the aft. A first-class section was non-existent.

Jack grimaced and turned to have a look at the cockpit.

The smell followed him as he stepped inside, and he saw the same evidence of neglect and hard use he'd seen outside and in the cabin, but no matter. The moment Jack entered, his heart leapt and he felt a thrill. Like an adolescent boy with a harlot stretched out seductively before him, Jack ogled her charms, the cockpit's vast array of gauges, switches, levers, and exotic controls.

The DC-8 was his first jet. What did it matter where she'd been?

He edged between the flight engineer's seat and sat sidesaddle on the forward jump seat to take in the cockpit more fully. The most impressive thing beyond its complexity was the DC-8's industrial composition, everything about it drab and purposeful. Beneath the amber wash of nicotine, three colors predominated: battleship gray for the seat upholstery, fairings, moldings, and metal surfaces; black for the glareshield, radio panels, and control yokes; white for the needles and nomenclature on the instruments and panels. The few other colors were as sparse as jokes in a Puritan's sermon. There was a small patch of blue on the horizontal deviation indicator, a bit of red on the engine-fire shutoff levers, and a few thin green, yellow, or red lines to mark an operating range or limitation on a lever or a gauge—and that was it.

Across from him was the flight engineer's station, a 3x4 foot gray metal panel packed with sixty-three gauges, eighteen levers, and dozens of switches, warning lights, and placards. Jack studied it in awe. The panel schematics alone were an indecipherable maze. It would take months of study and years of experience to master the airplane's intricacies.

Looking up and left above the pilots' stations, Jack surveyed the overhead panel, with its dozens more switches, levers, lights, buttons, and gauges.

Looking down and between the two pilot's seats, he studied the pedestal panel. It contained the throttles, engine shutoff levers, and, further aft, the radios and navigation equipment. Some of those nav components he recognized, but others he didn't. Those intended for oceanic flight were a mystery, and Jack was further intrigued, but then came a twinge of anxiety.

He returned his gaze to the engineer's panel, and for the first time in Jack's flying career, he felt daunted. Though he'd been hired as a copilot, knowledge of all the airplane's systems was a requirement for all three crewmembers, not just the engineer. Until that moment, he'd never truly considered how far above his head he was tilting. Whatever training Jack was about to get would be minimal given the cost of it and the time constraints they were facing. But that wouldn't relieve him of having to master all the airplane's systems before he'd be allowed to fly. And then it occurred to him that this was Halder's out and might have been his plan all along: throw Jack into the arena, and when he invariably fails, send him back to Kegan with his tail between his legs. Problem solved.

The heady sense he'd felt as he'd approached the airplane from the hangar had vanished, and a gloominess overcame him. So close, and yet so far. The task before him was impossible.

A manila folder was projecting from the captain's seatback, and Jack pulled it out and opened it. It was a coffee-stained and rumpled meteorological file dated 6 de Mayo, 1978. The route depicted on the chart was from Santiago, Chile, to Miami. Jack sifted through the pages, looked at them vacantly, and then closed the folder and stuffed it back in the seat pocket.

His despair deepened.

A gust of wind blustered into the cockpit and sent a little whirlwind of dust, petrified food crumbs, and pencil shavings on the floor into a circle, a silver gum wrapper sparkling like a jewel in the middle. Jack looked at it blankly as a cockroach sprang from a corner and skittered into a gap in the bulkhead.

There was suddenly a commotion outside, and Jack looked up. He heard a man swearing loudly, his heavy footfalls on the mobile stairs.

Jack got up and looked out the entry door.

A short, stocky guy, fiftyish, was trudging up the stairs with a lazy man's load of thick blue binders. They were clasped beneath his arms, and his monk's tonsure was covered in sweat. The tail of his green paisley sport shirt fluttered like a pennant above his blue Bermuda shorts, and an untied lace on his black oxfords menaced every step.

Jack stood back as he staggered into the entryway and dumped the binders in a pile on the floor. The heavy books hit with a thud and splayed open. The pages rustled loosely in the breeze.

He sighed, pulled a handkerchief from his back pocket, and gave Jack a look up and down. "Sunshine State, my ass," he grumbled as he wiped the sweat from his brow. "You from down here?" he asked in a thick Brooklyn accent.

"No, uh … I'm from New York too, actually."

He looked at Jack like he was lying. "Oh, yeah?" he said with an incredulous gaze. "From wheres? Upstate? You sound like you're from upstate."

"Long Island," Jack said matter-of-factly.

The man smiled and held out his hand. "That ain't New York, kiddo … Long Island's the fuckin' boondocks. Joe Bartolini," he said, his grip strong and heavily callused. "You're Jack, right?"

Jack looked at him, puzzled. "Yes, sir," he answered. "Jack Dolan."

Joe nodded and moved him aside to have a peek in the cockpit. "I'm one of the flight engineers," he offered without looking back. "Bobby asked me to do your ground school."

"Oh?"

Joe made a face and looked back at him. "Hey, don't worry," he said as if insulted. "I'm a lot smarter than I sound."

"I wouldn't have thought otherwise," Jack lied.

Joe turned around, edged past him, and walked back toward the cabin. "Jesus," he snorted, stopping at the galley and staring into the dark with his hands on his hips. "This thing smells like a fuckin' garbage truck." He waved for Jack to follow him. "C'mon," he said with a backwards glance. "We'll open her up and blow some of this stink out of here."

He spoke over his shoulder as he led Jack down the aisle, "Lesson number one, how to operate the doors," he said. "Once we do, I'll show you how to open the windows in the cockpit, and that'll get air moving through even faster."

"Are you a mechanic too?" Jack asked to his back.

"Yeah, engineer and mechanic. In an outfit like this, every flight engineer is a licensed Airframe and Powerplant mechanic too," Joe explained. "We got to be for this kind of work. Never know where we'll wind up, know what I'm sayin'? Sometimes we're out there ... I mean *really* fuckin' out there. Got to be self-reliant."

"Makes sense."

Joe stopped, turned around, and put his finger on Jack's chest. "Oh, and hey," he stated. "Plan on getting some grease on your hands now and then. No prima donna pilots in this outfit anymore. I mean, we had a few, but they all got shitcanned when these new guys took over. Hell, even the girls help out these days."

"The girls work on the airplanes?"

"Oh, yeah," he snickered with a lascivious grin. "You think they look snazzy in their uniforms? Wait 'til you see them in their underpants pulling a spare bogie wheel out of the baggage compartment in 120° desert heat. Whoo-eee!" he said, fanning his face. "Now that ain't somethin' you'll ever forget."

Jack stifled a laugh. "*Underpants?*" he said. He could only imagine.

Joe started back down the aisle, his hands slapping the headrests as he passed. "A hundred and eighty seats in these ass-haulers," he said. "Perfect for the hajj. Guess you never done one of these before, huh?" he said over his shoulder.

"Me? No. I was flying freight out of Philly."

"Oh, yeah? Who you been flyin' for?"

"Keystone Airways."

Joe shrugged. "Never heard of 'em."

"You're not alone."

"So, Bobby says you got no jet time, that right?"

"No. None."

Joe gave another shrug and kept walking. "No matter ... We'll get you fixed up."

When they reached the aft galley, Joe showed Jack how to open the passenger doors. Once they returned to the cockpit, he explained how to open the captain's and copilot's sliding windows. With the windows and doors open, the easterly breeze rushed through the airplane.

"Good! Now c'mon," Joe said, pulling Jack from the captain's seat and back to the engineer's. As Jack stood beside it, Joe explained how to operate the levers that controlled the seat's position forward, aft, and sideways. The seat moved so the engineer could access the throttles and overhead panel on the front end of the cockpit, the engineer's panel on the right side, and the circuit breaker panels on the aft bulkhead.

As Jack sat in the seat, Joe hitched up his shorts and sat down on the aft jumpseat. With his arms on his knees, he leaned toward Jack and said, "Okay, so that's the end of the easy part, kiddo. From here on in, the real fun begins and it starts right there." Joe pointed to the engineer's electrical panel.

Jack looked at the fifteen gauges and a dozen or more switches, lights, and controls, and sighed.

Joe waved him off and said, "Meh, don't worry about it. I'll get you through. But look," he added with a more somber tone. "Before we get any further, there's some things Sam wants me to explain to you, see?"

Jack sensed a shoe about to drop and swiveled the seat to face Joe.

"Okay, so look, I'm going to give it to you straight, no bullshit. What Sam wants you to know is that the FAR Part 121 training program for new pilots and engineers on the DC-8 is six weeks long, including four weeks of ground school and two weeks of flight training and testing. And let me tell you, there ain't a spare minute in any of it, see? You get behind, you're finished … *capeesh?*"

Jack nodded and his brows were knit.

"But even if Sam and Gerhard wanted to do all that, we don't have the time."

"No … we don't," Jack said.

"Right. So, instead, what you're going to get is the old Pan Tropic version of things, which means a little bit of schooling and a whole lot of pencil whipping, know what I'm sayin'? I mean, you'll be more or less legal for the ferry flights over there—but that's it, kiddo, nothin' else."

"But that wasn't the deal I'd made with Captain Halder."

"I'm just telling you what Sam said. Anything more? *Eh* … you gotta take it up with them."

"So, Sam's saying there's no chance I'll fly the hajj, is that it?"

"What he's sayin' is you'll get the takeoffs and landings you were promised, but once we get to where we're going, you'll either be going home because, well … you ain't got the chops for this. Or—if you do stay—you'll have to continue your FAR 121 training OJT. But that ain't kosher for the Feds, see?"

"But you're saying it's possible, in other words, if I have the chops?"

"What Sam's sayin' is that if you do stay on, the only way you'll stay on is to finish your training on the job, and that ain't straight up by the book. At Pan Tropic, we called it flyin' a little crooked. But that's just the way it has to be to get the job done, see? Point being, if you're thinking, fuck that, I'm gone, well—now would be a good time to *di di mòa*, know what I'm sayin'?"

Jack smiled at the prospect of staying on and Joe's GI jargon. "You were in Vietnam?" he asked incredulously.

"Nah. Just in and out with the Air Guard now and then. I picked up the lingo from the grunts in the base clubs." He smiled. "Makes me sound like I really was there, right?"

Jack grinned. "Sure … But look, Joe, tell Sam I get it. Tell him thanks for the heads-up, but I'm staying on if I can. Flying freight required a little flying crooked too," he said, "and I'm a lot better off here."

Joe stood up and clapped Jack on the shoulder. "You're okay, kiddo," he assured him. "You're going to fit in here just fine. I'll let 'em know."

Jack looked up at him and said, "I take it that was my final interview for Jetstream."

Joe rolled his eyes. "You got it, kiddo. Now c'mon," he declared. "Let's take a break, let this thing air out a little more while we grab a Coke or somethin' in the hangar. Meantime, while we're in there, I'll arrange for an electric cart, juice this old dog back to life, and let you see all the bells and whistles while we train."

Jack stood up.

"Oh, one more thing," Joe said. "When we come back, this'll be coming at you like a firehose, and it ain't going to stop until they take this thing for a test hop next Wednesday. Until then, we'll do hands-on training during the day, and you can hit the books at night, see?"

"So four weeks of ground school in four days, is that it?"

"You got it, pal. But don't forget that for a Part 91 ferry flight—no paying passengers or freight—all you need to be is familiar with the airplane. It's not like you have to pass a check ride or an oral or somethin'. Point is, even though I'll be giving you everything you'd need to pass an oral, there ain't no oral, so just remember as much of it as you can."

"That's not how I do things, Joe. I'll be doing my best to remember it all."

Joe smiled, grabbed him by the arm, and gave it a shake. "Yeah, I already figured that," he said. "But don't worry. I know this airplane better than my little missus knows her recipe for marinara. You give me all you got, and I'll give you everything else, trust me. Now c'mon," he said, starting for the door. "Let's get out of here before this stink makes me puke."

# TWENTY-EIGHT

*Miami International Airport, October 15, 1978*

As they crossed the ramp, a Convair 580 was doing a runup, the roar of its props and the whistle of its turbines deafening and the pungent odor of jet fumes in the air. Jack looked over at Joe and shouted, "So, how long have you been with the company?"

"Since I retired from the Guard eight years ago," Joe replied. "I put in my twenty and figured I was done with the flying thing, but then this damn inflation, see? It was eating up my retirement check so fast I told my wife if we don't do somethin' we're going to be broke. I says to her some of the guys are moving to Florida, where it's so much cheaper, and maybe we ought to go there too. But the little missus looks at me and says, 'Fuck *that!* You *go!* I ain't goin' nowheres!'"

Jack raised a brow.

"Wait 'til we get inside," Joe yelled. "Can't hear shit out here."

Once they were inside the hangar, Jack continued the chat. "So, the little missus would rather be in Brooklyn, huh?"

Joe shrugged. "*Meh.* Family, friends, and church, she's got a point. But then some of the other guys were talking about civilian gigs they'd found, and Pan Tropic was one of them. I figured if me and her could live in Brooklyn and I could come down just to fly, then why not, right?"

"Seems like a plan. So were you a pilot in the Guard?"

"*Me?* Nah. My pop had no money for college, and besides, I was happier in my uncle's garage. Big family business. Figured someday I'd take it over. I joined the Guard to stay with the business and keep my ass out of a trench in Korea, which was comin' on hot and heavy in '51."

"What unit were you in?"

"The KC-97 outfit at Floyd Bennett."

They walked up to the Coke machine in the hangar, and Joe reached into his pocket for change. As he sifted through it for quarters, Jack saw a woman coming toward them, someone he vaguely recognized. "Is that *Maggie?*" he asked, puzzled.

Joe looked up, smiled, and waved. "Yeah," he answered. Looking at Jack, "You've met?"

Jack barely recognized her. She was nothing like the wild thing in the baby doll he'd met at the bar, her free-range breasts and tangled mop of hair; instead, Maggie was prim and put together in a white tank top, khaki shorts, and white sneakers. Her hair was pulled back and bound in a ponytail, and she was wearing makeup. "We met at the briefing," Jack said. "Come to think of it, I don't remember seeing you there."

Joe waved him off. "Bah. I never go to those things," he said bluntly. "I only come down when it's time to go or when Bobby needs me—like this time."

Maggie walked straight up to Joe, and he threw his arms wide and beamed. "Hey sweetie! Gimme a hug!" he greeted her.

She stopped, gave him a look up and down, and cringed. "God bless us, Joseph," she said with a sigh. "Does your mother still dress ya?"

Joe laughed and looked down at himself. "What?" he joked. "I don't match?"

She bit her lip and shook her head.

"C'mere," he said, waving her toward him.

She smiled warmly, and they embraced. When he let her go, she said, "Gerhard said you fellas would be out here training. But I need to inventory the cabins to see what's missing. Will I be in the way?"

"No. Not at all. We'll be in the cockpit all day," Joe replied. Turning and reaching for Jack, he added, "Hey, Jack says you've met."

She glanced at Jack and smiled politely, and he smiled in return.

"Have you been in the airplane?" Joe asked her.

"Only for a moment," she said, looking stern. "Bloody piss-pot, isn't it? I think I can smell it from here."

"We're trying to blow some of that out of it right now. Stick around a little. I'll buy you a Coke or somethin'. Give it a few more minutes to clear out."

Maggie frowned. "I can't, love," she said. "I need to get up to Fort Lauderdale and inspect those too. Gerhard wants a full inventory by this afternoon."

"Sam told me they're all in bad shape," Joe said. "But they're even worse than I thought."

"Aye, and speaking of Sam ... did you hear about the other night, Joe?"

Joe narrowed his eyes. "No," he said. "What?"

"Sam and Brad ... a bit of a row."

"Ah, Jesus. *Again?*"

"Worse," Maggie said. "Sam grabbed him, and Brad took a swing."

Joe winced. "Did Sam say anything about it to you?"

Maggie shook her head. "No. I tried to get to him, but he'd already left the hotel. I called Peggy the next morning, and she told me it was about Larry. She said it's best to stay out of it."

"Peggy's right. We all should stay out of it. They'll have to work that out themselves."

"I know," Maggie agreed. "But I feel so bad for Sam. It's so unfair. Stone's such a cunt. If you could have seen how he carried on during the Karachi trip, do you know what I mean, like? It's why he got fired from Pan Am, and now Gerhard's promoting him to chief pilot? Jaysus, how can that make any bloody sense?"

"I know what you're sayin', Maggs, but Peggy's right. They got to work it out themselves. Stay away from it."

"Aye ... I know." She sighed.

There was a pause, and Maggie looked out at the airplane. "Well, anyway," she said, "I'd better be off." Putting on a smile and looking at them, she said, "I'll see you guys out there," and then turned and started toward the ramp.

"Hold your nose!" Joe warned.

Maggie threw him a backward wave.

The moment she turned around, Jack caught sight of the horrific scar on her right shoulder blade under her tank-top strap. Purple tentacles radiated from a white, plastic-like core, and her shoulder was visibly deformed. He recognized it as a battle wound and then recalled her hand trick with her Zippo whenever she lit a smoke, which was often.

Joe followed his gaze and said, "Vietnam. She usually hides it under her clothes."

Jack looked at him, puzzled. "She grew up in Ireland. How the hell did she wind up in *Vietnam?*" he asked.

"Her mom died suddenly, and the stepdad was a drunk and a fuckin' pervert. Maggie stowed away on a steamer to Canada to get away from him when she was sixteen. From there, she made her way to family here in the US. They took her in until she finished high school, then told her to take a hike. She joined the Army to get the GI Bill for college and become a nurse, but then Vietnam. She was a medic there in '68 when the shit hit the fan. She volunteered to stay past her DEROS because of all those troops comin' in all shot up. A few weeks later, a rocket attack hits the compound, and she took that hit. They gave her a Bronze Star and a Purple Heart and sent her to Clark in the Philippines to recover. She was there for months."

"Tough break," Jack said. "So, how'd she wind up here?"

"She came over with Sam."

Jack looked at him, confused. "With *Sam?*"

"Yeah. They met on her flight to Travis after she finished her first rehab at Clark. Like Sam always did on those flights, he went back to talk to the vets. He met Maggie, saw how fucked up and depressed she was, and his heart melted. He starts telling her all his crazy stories about life in the Keys to cheer her up, and Sam bein' Sam, even Maggie—who's really standoffish with men—warms right up to him. When he finds out she's got no one to go home to, he insists she come home with him! I mean, it's not like it seems. Peggy and Sam run that house of theirs like a fuckin' dog pound and bring in any asshole who needs a little TLC. Well, next thing you know, *bada bing bada boom*, she's on her way home with him. I mean, she was living with them and their two daughters for more than a year as she got better. So now she's like a third daughter. Just another member of the family."

"So that's why she calls him *Da?*"

"You got it, champ. They're tight as two peas in a pod. Maggie *adores* him."

"And that was a Pan Tropic charter Sam was flying?"

"*Pan Tropic?* No. Hell no. Sam was still with Trans Meridian Airlines back then."

"Wait! *TMA?* Sam was a captain with *TMA?* I don't understand. What's he doing here?"

Joe shrugged. "He got fired," he said flatly.

Jack was dumbstruck. He'd just learned that Stone had been fired from Pan Am, and now Sam had been fired from TMA, an airline as highly regarded as Air Logistics. What the hell kind of outfit was he getting himself into here?

Joe noticed the look on his face and pushed a quarter into the machine. "Pick your poison," he said. "It's a long story, but I'll keep it short."

"7-Up," Jack said.

A bottle tumbled down the chute, and Jack reached for it. Joe put another quarter in the slot and pressed the button for Coke. As he grabbed the bottle, he explained, "Sam got fired because of the accident."

Jack recoiled. "*Accident?*" he blurted. "What accident?"

"The Trans Meridian crash at Calverton, Long Island."

"Oh! Right! I remember that," Jack said. "I was just a kid at the time, but my dad flies for Pan Am and I remember him talking about it. Pan Am did some of their training at Calverton too. And you're telling me that was *Sam?* He was flying?"

"Yes and no," Joe said. "It's complicated, but listen and I'll explain. Like all the New York-based airlines, TMA had an agreement with Grumman to use their airfield at the Calverton plant for training and transition. And the thing is, it wasn't the only accident like that back then. I mean, back in them days, there were a lot of training accidents. The crazy stuff we had to do in the airplane before simulators came along! Hell, not long before Trans Meridian's accident, American lost a 707 off Montauk practicing Dutch roll recovery. We used to do that here too. We'd turn off the yaw dampers, the check airman would induce a roll with the rudder trim, and holy Christ, hang on! What a fuckin' ride sometimes. Hairy stuff, know what I'm sayin'? Anyways, there was a bunch of training accidents back then. Trans Meridian wasn't alone."

"Okay, but back to Sam. How was he involved?"

"He was a check airman supervising a *new* check airman who was conducting Larry's rating ride. That's how TMA does things, check, double-check, and fuckin' triple-check, know what I'm sayin'? What a pack of Nazis those bastards are. Anyways, the new check airman was in the right seat, Larry in the left, and Sam in the forward jump seat observing."

"Larry's the guy Maggie mentioned, the guy Sam and Brad are fighting over."

"Yeah, Larry Schaff."

"So, Sam wasn't at the controls?"

"No."

"What happened? What did the NTSB determine was the cause?"

"Truth is, they never really figured it out. The last maneuver was a two-engine approach, with engines one and two at idle thrust to simulate shutdowns. As they got close to Decision Height, the airplane suddenly yaws hard right and drops out from under them like the wings came off.

Next thing they know, they're plowing through the approach lights and break up in a fireball along the right side of the runway. Sam and Larry survived somehow, but the other two guys were killed on impact. The NTSB found what they thought was some bird damage to the number three and four engines—which could have been the cause, of course—but they didn't find enough to be conclusive. Anyways, like they always do when they can't find the answer, they just put the whole thing off on pilot error, and that was that."

"So why was Sam implicated in the crash if he wasn't flying? Why did he get fired?"

"Well, that's a whole 'nother story, champ, and a raw deal if there ever was one. The way it was, the vice president of flight who selected Sam to be a check airman retired just before the accident occurred. The guy who took his place was this prick who had it in for Sam ever since their days flying C-46s in the war. Sam was the unit's flight standards guy, and he gave this jerk a down on a check ride. Well, this guy's one of those pricks who never forgets a grudge, see? So, he fires both Larry *and* Sam, and since Sam was a check airman and considered management, there wasn't nothin' the Air Line Pilots Association could do for him. As for Larry? Well—ain't nothin' they could do for him either bein' he was flying the airplane and the check airman was dead. Long story short—Sam and Larry both got the ax."

"And Brad disagrees with Larry upgrading to captain?"

"You got it. Major pissing contest between them two over Larry. Sad thing is, even though Sam's the greatest pilot I've ever flown with, Stone's a damn good stick too. They should be close buddies and not at each other's throats. And maybe Stone has a point about Larry. I mean, much as I like Sam—we *all* do—a lot of us think Brad's got a point about Larry. He's got some issues. But the trouble with Stone is that even when he's right, he doesn't know how to handle things. Maybe if he'd calm down a little, take some personality lessons—you know, get some of that 'charm school' shit they give those astronaut knuckleheads before putting them out in public—Brad would be better liked around here. Until then, though, Brad's the Duty Asshole in this unit and no one really gives a shit what he thinks."

"Okay, but back to Sam," Jack said. "How did Sam wind up here?"

"A year after the accident and after months and months of rehab, Sam got his medical back. That's when he took the job with Pan Tropic. I mean, what else could he do, right? By that time he was too old to get hired anywhere else and Pan Tropic was right here in Miami, close to home. Once Sam was on, he helped get Larry on too because—you know, Sam bein' Sam—it was the right thing to do."

"Even though Larry was at the controls when they crashed?"

"Right, because there's more to the story, see? Like I told you, TMA's a pack of Nazis and they had this up-or-out policy. What that means is, you have to take the upgrade to captain when your seniority number comes up for it, and you have to make it through the program or you get shitcanned, no going back to the right seat. It's a lot of pressure for some guys, and Larry's one of them. And then, on top of that, when Larry's number came up, his wife was dying of breast cancer. But that asshole VP of flight didn't give a shit. He made Larry go through the entire program anyway. Then, in the middle of Larry's training, his son gets in this huge car wreck and the kid's paralyzed from the waist down. All the TMA training guys—Sam first among them—knew this and tried to put a stop to it. They said Larry ought to be put on leave or somethin' so he could take care of his family, delay his upgrade 'til he could get his head fully in the game. But that prick VP turned it down, said they had too much already invested in him to stop. Anyways, like Maggie told me, Sam's always felt bad for Larry, knew he got fucked over bad, and wanted to help make it right. Larry needed the job, and that's why Sam got Halder to take him on here as a copilot."

"Jesus. What a story. That's sad. But what about Stone? Why was he fired from Pan Am?"

"I only heard the rumors, something to do his final probation board. There was a stack of bad reports about him. But then I also heard there's more to that story, somethin' about Brad catching a senior captain doing somethin' bad in the Dominican Republic. But who knows? Thing is, Stone—who was on probation—reported the guy to the company, the company wanted it buried, and Stone went down with his morals. Anyways, Maggie's right. Brad's an asshole, and most of us just wish he'd leave. He should get a job with TMA, where he'd fit right in."

"Huh," Jack muttered. "I see."

"Nope. You ain't seen the half of it yet, kiddo. We all got our reasons for being here, champ, you included. But the biggest reason of all is that we're one big happy family of type-A mission hackers, the best I've ever known, and I've known some great ones in the Guard. Once we get going, you'll see it for yourself. You either fit in with that or you don't—and Brad don't." He looked at his watch. "Alright, enough of that," he grumbled. "We're wasting valuable time. Let's get that power cart ordered and get started on what we're here for. You ready for this?" he asked, looking at Jack with a brow raised.

"Born ready, Joe."

Joe nodded and gave him a pat on the back. "Attaboy," he said. "Let's do it."

# TWENTY-NINE

*Miami International Airport, October 15, 1978*

The midday sun was blazing, and the morning breeze had freshened. Towering clouds billowed over the Everglades, and distant lightning licked at the ground.

Jack was seated at the engineer's panel in the jet. The DC-8-21 Flight Operations Manual, Volume 1, was in front of him on the engineer's tiny desk. Joe was standing beside him to his right. Outside the airplane, the generator they'd ordered was hooked up and running, the roar of its diesel through the open windows forcing them to speak loudly.

After showing Jack how to check the generator's frequency and voltage, Joe reached for the switch on the electrical panel and connected the generator to the airplane. The toil-worn jet was jolted awake. Warning horns blared, lights flashed, and instrument needles flickered with the sudden shock of electricity. Joe's practiced hands flew about and silenced the warnings quickly, and the cockpit buzzed quietly with life.

Frowning as he looked at a gauge on the electrical panel that hadn't budged, Joe gave it a hard rap with his knuckle, and its needle suddenly sprang erect. He smiled at the gauge and said, "Wake up, sunshine. Vacation's over."

Reaching down in front of Jack, Joe flipped the flight manual's tabs to the one labeled LIMITATIONS. Pointing at a page packed with boxed numbers, lists, warnings, and conditions, he said, "I don't need to tell you these are your responsibility," he said. "Get *everything* on these ten pages into your memory as soon as you can. That's job one, and I can't help you with that."

Jack surveyed the page. "Yes. Of course," he said.

Joe flipped to the tab labeled EMERGENCY and tapped his finger on the manila cover. "And everything in here marked with an asterisk," he added. "Those are the checklist items you have to do from memory."

Jack nodded. "Got it," he replied. It was the same for every airplane. There were things a pilot needed to know immediately and without reference to a manual.

"Good," Joe said. Then pointing at the fuel panel—with its fourteen gauges, ten levers, eight warning lights, and nineteen switches and selectors—he continued, "We'll start here and work clockwise around the engineer's station. Pointing out each system as he went, Joe said, "After fuel, we'll cover the air conditioning and pressurization controls, and then the electrical system and the engines. After the engineer's panel, we'll jump to the pedestal panel between the pilots' seats for the autopilot, navigation, radios, throttles, start levers, spoilers, flaps, trim, alternate ejector controls, and radar. From the pedestal, we'll move to the overhead for the engine fire and shutdown levers, doppler navigation, lighting, and anti-icing, and from there, we'll do a quick review of the upper panel for the emergency brake, KIFIS system, master warnings, and pitot cutoff. After that, we'll move down to the pilots' panels for the landing gear, flight controls, and instruments, though you'll cover those in greater detail during flight training. When that's all done, we'll spend some time with the performance manual and calculations, and then go back to the cabin for galleys, lavs, emergency equipment, and evacuation procedures. Last of all, we'll do the walkaround, and once that's done—*bada bing bada boom*—we're finished!" He smiled. "Piece of cake, kiddo."

Jack gave him a look and blew out his cheeks. "Four weeks of training in four days?" He sighed. "Piece of cake, my ass, Joe. Even DC-3 ground school was a week, and that was tight."

Joe grabbed his shoulder and gave it a shake. "Hey, don't worry. For a Part 91 ferry flight, you only got to be familiar, champ. That's all we're aiming for here. It's not like you're getting ready for an FAA oral or somethin', so relax. Just pick up as much as you can with me during the day and as much as you can out of the books at night. That's all Sam expects. Truthfully, even four weeks isn't enough to get a guy fully qualified on this beast. So, just do your best, see?"

"Sure."

"Trust me," Joe assured him. "Now enough of that, and off we go—"

He reached in front of Jack, and as he traced his finger along the white lines of the fuel panel schematic, Joe explained how the lines represented the pipes that connected the crossfeed and refueling manifolds, the aft auxiliary and forward auxiliary tanks, the number one and four main tanks, the number two and three main tanks, the number one and four alternate tanks, and the number two and three alternate tanks. He showed Jack how each tank could be isolated from the others and how every tank and manifold could be connected to feed any of the airplane's four engines independently. He had Jack position the levers and turn or flick the switches to get a feel for their operation.

When they finished that, Joe reached for Volume 2 of the airplane's Flight Operations Manual. He plunked it on the engineer's desk, opened it to the tab marked FUEL, and pointed out the location of the static and climb vents as well as the vent manifold and anti-siphon line on a schematic of the wing. He had Jack operate the fuel pumps, including the boost and reservoir pumps, and then discussed the pressure and relief valve settings and the limitations that applied. Moving to the fuel quantity gauges, he explained the maximum and minimum fuel quantities allowed. He pointed out the fuel pressure gauges, the tank selectors, the crossfeed selectors, the auxiliary tank selectors, and the fill valve control switches. When he finished that, he covered the fourteen pages of normal, abnormal, and emergency operating procedures, including the limitations on fuel temperature and pressure, as well as the procedures for the use of the fire/fuel shutoff valves and the fuel dump system in the EMERGENCY section of the manual.

Finally, to wrap up his briefing of the fuel system, Joe returned to the fuel quantity selector valve, and pointing at it, he gave Jack a stern warning: "Whatever else you do," he cautioned, "before using this thing, don't *ever* forget to get the backlash out of it first, see? Because if you don't leave at least one thousand pounds of vent space in the inboard main tanks when you do—regardless of fuel density—we got *BIG* trouble, champ, especially if we're really out there somewheres, like—I don't know—El-Obeid or somethin'."

Jack stared at the selector switch like it was staring back at him with a rictus grin. He looked up at Joe, puzzled. "El-*who*?" he asked. "Where's that? Never heard of it, and why would I be messing with the fuel quantity selector switch in the first place?"

"El-Obeid's in Sudan, you putz. But under *NO* circumstances are you going to be messing with it *anywheres*, got it? I'm not teaching you how to *operate* the selector valve, kiddo; I'm teaching you to keep your greasy little copilot mitts off the fuckin' thing, *capeesh?*"

Jack rolled his eyes. "Sure. My pleasure," he said. "Especially in El-whatever."

"Yeah, well—fuhgeddaboudit. Just remember what I told you, and leave it alone. Now look," he continued, shifting his finger to the fuel dump controls. "This is another thing you're never going to touch, but you have to know why, see? Because if you fuck it up, you'll empty the tanks at 5,500 pounds per minute, and that's enough to do some serious damage to the flight plan unless you're lookin' at a runway straight in front of you, know what I'm sayin'?"

"Sure. Hands off the dump valves. No problem."

Joe smiled. "That's it," he said, clapping him on the shoulder. "You're gettin' it, kiddo, you're doing good. But look, here's another very important thing to remember about fuel dumping, especially as a copilot: when dumping's complete, a total of 13,700 pounds will remain in the mains, about 1,200 pounds in the alternates, and another 8,600 pounds in the aux tanks. You'll need to know that for calculating a landing weight and

Vref following an engine fire, compressor stalls, or some other disaster on takeoff. Trust me, when it happens, it'll be comin' on fast, with the captain up to his neck flying the airplane and briefing the girls for an emergency landing, the engineer dumpin' fuel and runnin' a million checklists, and you on the horn to ATC declaring an emergency and setting up everything on both sides for the approach. There'll be no time for screwin' around and looking up those numbers in the book. So, have them branded in your brain. Got it?"

"Got it."

Joe looked at his watch. "Okay," he announced. "We're on schedule, moving right along … Any questions so far?"

Jack snorted and put his finger to his head like a gun. "Nope," he said with a laugh. "Got it all locked up right here … know what I'm sayin'?"

Joe made a face and said, "Okay, smart ass, have it your way. But just remember what goes around, comes around in this outfit, and sooner or later it'll be your turn."

Jack laughed again. "Yeah. Sam warned me about that. I'm ready."

Joe reached for the operating manual and flipped to the HYDRAU-LICS tab. "Alright," he said. "Enough with Mr. Funnyman already. Let's keep goin' …"

At 11:40 a.m., Joe was halfway through his briefing of the hydraulic system when Maggie came forward and asked if he could give her a hand. She led him back to the aft galley, and Jack was alone in the cockpit.

His head was down and studying the hydraulic schematic when suddenly he heard people coming up the stairs and entering the airplane. Jack looked up and saw Brad Stone looking sharp in olive slacks and a white polo. Standing next to him was an attractive woman in business attire, a gray, knee-length skirt and pink blouse. Her hair was dirty blonde, and her brow knit as she held her hand to her face. The fresh air had done little to lessen the stink, particularly near the forward lavatory where they were standing.

Brad entered the cockpit, paused a moment to look it over, and then shifted his gaze to Jack. "Gerhard told me you'd be out here. How's it coming along?" he inquired.

Jack put on a smile. "It's going well," he said. "Joe's a terrific instructor."

Brad nodded, offered a manicured hand, and said, "We met the other night. Brad Stone, I'm one of the company's check airmen—or soon to be."

Jack reached up to shake. "Yes, sir, Jack Dolan," he replied. "I uh … I remember."

"I understand this is your first jet?"

"Yes, sir. Prior to this I was flying as a DC-3 captain."

"That's what I heard. Captain Halder tells me you came here under special circumstances."

Jack cleared his throat and replied, "I was hired as a go-fer in exchange for an opportunity to fly and build some experience with the DC-8. I thought it a fair trade."

Brad raised a brow. "Actually," he corrected him, "you were hired in exchange for parts that Kegan had promised us but then reneged on unless you were part of the deal. It would be more accurate to say you were hired as a quid pro quo."

The insult stung, but Jack kept his composure. "I don't know anything about a quid pro quo," he answered. "My agreement with Captain Halder was precisely what I told you it was, and if there was anything more, I had nothing to do with it."

Brad grinned. "Nevertheless, the outcome was the same, and now you're here." He shifted his attention to the captain's oxygen mask hanging from a quick release near the seat. He slid behind Jack and reached forward. He pulled down the mask and examined it, running his finger around the seal. "This thing's filthy," he remarked as he replaced the mask on its hanger. Returning to the back of the cockpit and changing the subject, he said, "May I ask you something else?"

Jack looked up and studied the gaunt little man with the five o'clock shadow, receding hairline, and dark piercing eyes. "Go ahead," he said, bracing himself for whatever was coming next.

"Turn around and face the copilot's control column."

Jack pivoted in the seat and looked at the copilot's yoke.

Pointing toward it, Brad said, "There on the left side, that narrow tube mounted vertically on the column … Do you see it?"

"Yes."

"Do you know what that is?"

Jack shook his head, looked back at him, and said, "No, not yet. We haven't gotten that far. We're covering the engineer's panel first. The pilots' panels and controls will come later."

"It's the indicator for the pitch trim compensator," Brad told him. "Inside that tube is a rod that moves up and down, the tip coming into view as the PTC becomes active. It's like a dog's prick moving in and out of its sheath, so we call it the dog's prick. It indicates impending Mach tuck. The further the rod protrudes from the tube, the closer the airplane's condition is becoming to that danger. My question, Mr. Dolan, is this: what is Mach tuck, and what control force changes might you expect in that condition?"

Jack didn't hesitate. "Mach tuck wasn't an issue in the DC-3 or anything else I've ever flown," he said, stating the obvious. "The best I can do is an informed guess."

"Feel free."

"Given that it's related to Mach effect, I'd say it's due to a transonic condition over the top of the wing. How the control forces would be changed, I don't know. But I'm sure Joe will cover that as we proceed with my training."

"I'm sure he will," Brad said flippantly. "So, I'm going to call that an incomplete, but I'll toss you a few points for trying."

"Thanks for the points," Jack retorted. "And now—if I may—I'd like to ask you a question, Captain Stone."

Brad gave him a shrug and said, "Sure, go ahead."

"Where did you first learn about Mach tuck?"

"Pan Am," Brad answered bluntly, setting Jack back with his candor. "Their training is renowned throughout the industry," he boasted. "If we had their resources or could afford to send our new hires to Pan Am for training, we would. But we have neither the resources nor the money, and the learning curve for pilots first transitioning to jets is very steep. Those—like you—coming straight at it without extensive simulator or flight training first are most at risk of an accident. To avoid that outcome, we prefer to hire only pilots with substantial experience in these aircraft. Bringing on anyone as inexperienced and untrained as you is a material risk to everyone who depends on this company for a living. I'm sure you understand that, and to be clear, that was the point of my inquiry, Mr. Dolan—not to humiliate you. Now what was the point of yours?"

"My point was that my agreement for pilot employment here was with Captain Halder, sir. Perhaps you should discuss your disagreement about me with him."

"I already have," Stone admitted. "But we need those parts, so you're still here, and we need to find a way to make this work. And that leads to my next question, Mr. Dolan: are you a reader, a book learner?"

"My name is Jack, and yes … I'm both."

"Jack, of course. Please call me Brad. So, what are you reading now, Jack?"

"The DC-8 operating manual … *Brad*."

Brad smiled. "*Touché*, sir. Good answer," he replied. "But I see you have a lot of answers, Jack, and I'll be prepared for that in the future." Reaching for his wallet, he withdrew a business card from a fold and a Mount Blanc from the placket of his shirt. Using his palm for support, he scribbled something on the back of the card, capped his pen, and handed the card to Jack. "Take this," he said. "It will help you become better prepared too."

Jack took the card and looked at both sides. On the front was Brad's name and position as a captain with Jetstream International Airlines, and on the back:

*"Aerodynamics for Naval Aviators,"*
*Currents Bookstore, Moody La., Flagler Beach, FL.*

"That's a terrific little shop," Brad said. "They've got a good selection of nautical and aviation subjects and an even better selection of fine fiction. I go there often. Stop in while you're running errands for Gerhard, and buy yourself a copy of that. Expense it to the company, and review the section on high-altitude and high-speed flight thoroughly before we fly together, understand?"

Jack slipped the card into his shirt pocket and looked up at him. "I will," he said, and through a forced smile, he lied, "I look forward to flying with you."

Brad gave him a wry grin, clipped his pen in his placket, and said, "Somehow I doubt that. But good luck with your studies, and I'll be seeing you again soon." He turned abruptly and walked out.

Joe was standing in the forward entryway waiting for them to finish, and Brad slipped past him without a word. At the bottom of the stairs, he met the woman who'd accompanied him onto the airplane and they walked hand in hand toward the hangar.

Joe's brow was furrowed as he watched them leave. "What'd he want?" he grumbled.

"My head on a platter."

Joe scoffed. "Fuck him," he snarled. "Sam calls the shots around here—not that asshole." Turning to Jack, he said, "C'mon. I'm starved." He pointed at the flight manual and added, "Grab that and bring it with you. We'll jump in the van, find a place for lunch, and finish up hydraulics over a burger and fries."

"Is Maggie coming too?" Jack asked. "There's only two seats in the van."

"Nah, she's going straight from here to Fort Lauderdale."

As they walked toward the hangar, Jack said, "I told Stone you're a great instructor, Joe. I appreciate all your help, I really do. I hope I can keep up."

Joe waved him off. "Fuhgeddaboudit," he said. "Thank me when we're done. With that asshole stickin' his nose in this, it ain't going to be over 'til it's over ... know what I'm sayin'?"

Jack sighed. "Yeah. I've got that feeling too."

# THIRTY

*Miami International Airport, October 20, 1978*

It was 7:15 a.m. on Friday, and Jack was sitting in the hotel café finishing breakfast and reviewing his flashcards and notes. It had been six days since he began ground school with Joe.

Over the course of the week, Jack had been putting in eighteen hours a day, most of that time in the cockpit with Joe, and the remainder alone in his room with the DC-8's flight manuals. Repairs on the airplane had taken longer than planned, and the extra time was a godsend for Jack. Although his knowledge was still far less than he'd need to pass an FAA oral exam, he was confident he'd meet the standards of Part 91 for a ferry flight as a copilot. Following Jack's review with Sam, the airplane was scheduled for a maintenance flight to ensure it was ready to depart for the hajj. Jack secretly hoped Sam would give him an opportunity to fly the DC-8, maybe even make a takeoff and landing! He was thrilled by that prospect and feeling upbeat about the day ahead. He didn't see Joe looking glum and walking toward his table.

Joe yanked back a chair. "Change of plans," he declared gruffly.

Jack looked up at him. "What? Another delay?"

"No. Sam called me last night and said Stone will be doing your oral today, not him."

The news hit Jack like a wrecking ball. He looked stunned and dropped back in his chair.

"There's more," Joe added.

"You're joking."

"No. The FAA will be observing."

Jack felt the sting of betrayal, and a bolt of anger shot through him. He slapped his flashcards on the table. "No. No way," he said, shaking his head. "I fold. I'm out. Fuck this!"

Joe made a face and waved him off. "Calm down," he counseled. "Don't get your Irish up. You'll be fine."

Jack looked at him like he was nuts. "*Fine?*" he blurted. "I've worked my ass off preparing for this thing, but I'm nowhere near ready for an FAA oral, Joe, and you know that. You told me all I needed under Part 91 was to be 'familiar' with the airplane, and I am. But an oral's a whole different animal, and with the FAA observing? Bullshit! No way! This isn't going to be a legitimate exam; it's intended to be a lynching! And now, in retrospect, I can see that this was Halder and Stone's plan all along, a way to run me out of here while keeping their parts deal with Kegan. And fuck that!" he bellowed. "Fuck *that!*" He pounded his fist on the table. The flatware flew up and crashed down.

The elderly couple seated next to them looked over at Jack in alarm.

Joe smiled at them sheepishly and said, "My son. Sorry. He gets it from the little missus ... know what I'm sayin'?"

The couple gave each other a look, then got up and left.

Jack felt chagrined. "Sorry," he said to Joe. "Didn't mean to make a scene."

Joe glared at him. "Are you done?"

"Yeah. I'm done. I'm fucking overdone," Jack muttered sullenly.

"Good. Now shut up and listen."

Jack met his gaze.

"Sam told me Gerhard's fighting to keep this contract on track because time and money are running out fast. The airplanes were in much worse shape than he expected, and it's blowing the budget for this deal big time, see? If we're going to pull this hajj thing off, then we need to get going and going now. No more delays."

Jack shrugged insolently and looked aside.

"Listen to me," Joe continued. "Sam says four things need to happen today: first, the airplane needs to fly to sort out any remaining issues. Second, Sam needs landing currency 'cause he's expired and can't fly anywheres until he's current. Third, Stone needs to get observed by the Feds doing an oral and flight check so he can be a check airman during the hajj; and fourth, you need to be legit for the flight across the pond. Now that's it, you putz, and it all makes perfect sense, so quit your bellyaching. You're not going to be lynched. That's not how it works around here, ever! We're a tight group and no one's out to fuck you over—maybe not even Stone. Although him? *Meh* … I'm not so sure. Anyways, it doesn't matter because Sam will be around to keep him in line. So easy does it, champ. Keep your cool and you'll be alright."

"I don't trust Stone. You told me he went down for his principles at Pan Am, and if he did it there, he'd do it here. I don't deserve that. I was lied to. No one told me I'd be expected to pass an FAA oral after only a week of training on a transport jet."

Joe shook his head. "You're wrong," he said. "No one's fucking you over, and no one lied. Sam won't allow it. Besides that, you're wrong about Gerhard wanting you out of here. From what Bobby tells me, he's real happy with all the work you've been doing both as a go-fer and in ground school. Besides that, the FAA guy who's observing has been a friend of Sam's since they were cadets in the Air Corps together, and he'll let Sam make the final call. And, besides all that, Stone wants this check airman gig *bad*. He won't risk screwing that up by being his usual shithead self, see? Especially if there's some secret deal for parts that includes you. If Stone screws the pooch on that, Halder will rip his head off, and he knows it." He reached across the table and patted Jack's arm. "Calm down. It's going to work out, kiddo. You know your stuff, and this ain't no rating ride. It's just a company checkout that the Feds need to observe to certify Stone, not you, see?"

"You weren't with him in the cockpit last Sunday, and I was, Joe. I could feel his contempt."

Joe waved him off. "*Bah* … Everybody feels it," he said. "Now get your shit together and get out to the airplane early. Take a little time to relax, get comfortable in the seat, work that panel like you own it, and you'll water their eyes. Trust me."

. . .

As Jack approached the DC-8, preparations for the day's events were already underway. The generator and the air conditioning cart were running, the forward entry door was open, and a man in blue overalls was standing beside a fuel truck with a hose connected to the airplane's wing.

Jack climbed the stairs and stepped inside. Back in the cabin, the sunshades had been raised and the space was bright and cheerful. Instead of the stink of feces, urine, mildew, and sour milk, the spoor of cleaning fluids wafted through the air. Jack stepped further aft and touched a seat cushion. It was slightly damp. He looked up and around and touched the cabin's surfaces. The sallow nicotine and stickiness were gone. Everything was spotless, though the years of wear were still visible on the threadbare fabrics and carpet.

The cockpit was also spotless, the filth and grime washed away by an unseen cleaning crew. From the lingering scent, Jack assumed the job had been done the night before, and the venerable DC-8 was reborn, at least its interior.

Jack hung up his suit jacket, pulled back the engineer's seat to sit down, and found a brown leather attaché case already on top of it. He reached for the case, and saw BWS engraved on the brass plate beneath the handle.

Bradley Stone.

Jack had come out early as Joe suggested but not as early as he'd thought. Stone was already here and somewhere in the area.

Jack put the attaché on the aft jumpseat and sat down at the panel. He glanced at his watch: 8:05 a.m. He had an hour to go until his oral. He'd spend the time reviewing the systems and recalling what he'd learned.

At 8:55 a.m., he heard men's voices. Jack closed the flight manual he'd brought with him, stood up, and stowed the engineer's seat. He straightened his tie and smoothed his slacks.

Stone entered the airplane first wearing a smartly tailored tan suit. The man accompanying him wore a Glen plaid, light gray. He was slim, silver-haired, and distinguished-looking but with a friendly face and cheerful air. He carried a gray attaché case, and the white badge on his coat pocket had the FAA emblem with his name engraved in black letters: Bill Jensen.

"Good morning," Stone said flatly.

"Good morning," Jack replied. Turning to the FAA man, Jack held out his hand, smiled, and said, "Good morning, sir. Jack Dolan, pleased to meet you."

"Bill Jensen," he said brightly, his grip firm and warm. "Pleasure to meet you, too, Jack. Brad tells me you've been flying Gooney Birds, is that right?"

"Yes, sir, my last job. I was based in Philly."

"I've got a little time in them. But most of my taildragger time is in B-17s."

"Europe?" Jack asked. "I met one of our engineers who was a B-17 engineer in Europe. Maybe you know him? His name—"

"Buddy Reid!" Jensen interjected. He laughed and said, "Yes, Buddy. Quite a character, isn't he? Always a ladies' man. Both of us were with the Mighty Eighth in England. Buddy was with the 457th bomb group and I was with the 384th. But look, back to you, Jack. Brad tells me you've been talking to Big Jake. He says you've got a shot at Air Logistics, is that right?"

"Oh, uh … yes, sir, I believe so. Captain Kegan said I needed some DC-8 experience before they would consider me further. He sent me to Captain Halder in case he needed crew for the hajj."

"Well," Jensen said with a smile, "from what Sam tells me, it looks like you've got that covered."

Stone made a face and averted his gaze.

Jensen cleared his throat. "Yes, yes, of course," he said. Looking at Jack, he added, "Now, I realize this is not your first oral, Jack, and though you've likely heard this before, it's worth repeating: we always assume every candidate has been well trained and the exam is merely to confirm that. In fact, today I'll be less interested in you than in Brad, since he'll be administering the exam and responsible for upholding the standards we're looking for. He's being given a great public trust, and it's my job to ensure he's properly prepared for that."

"Yes, sir. I understand," Jack said.

Jensen smiled. "Good. So, with that, if you have your license and medical handy, I'll take them and we'll get underway!"

Jack reached for his wallet. "Yes, sir, right here," he said.

Jensen received the certificates, put them in his shirt pocket, and said, "Now, while Brad and I get the paperwork going and cover a few other things particular to Brad's job today, you're welcome to stand by or head into the hangar for coffee. What we have to do will take about twenty to thirty minutes." He glanced at his watch. "If you'll be back here by, say, 9:30 … we'll get started."

"Yes, sir, I'll do that."

"Great. See you then!"

Jack wandered toward the hangar and skipped the coffee. More caffeine was the last thing he needed. He spent the twenty minutes slowly pacing the floor, checking his watch, and rehearsing the numbers, lists, and limitations he'd been memorizing. When the time was up, he returned to the airplane and found Stone and Jensen waiting for him in the cockpit. Stone was seated sidesaddle on the forward jump seat, and Jensen was standing in the cockpit doorway.

Stone gave Jack a thin smile and gestured toward the engineer's seat. "Ready when you are," he said.

Jack pulled it back and sat down. Jensen hiked up his slacks and settled on the aft jumpseat.

Stone began the exam by explaining its standards and goals. He said it was a test of the applicant's systems knowledge, including numbers and limitations, normal operating procedures, and other information the pilot needed to know without reference to the manual.

Jack answered with a nod.

"Okay, then," Stone continued. "Let's start with some random questions from limitations: what are the two engine VMCs and what are they based on?"

"They're based on go-around EPR and with boost on," Jack answered, "flaps ten or more, 164 knots; flaps zero, 210 knots. With boost off, flaps ten or more, 200 knots, flaps zero, 215."

"Correct. And what procedure is used for the normal use of the PTC?"

"At or above 18,000 feet, operative and on; below 18,000 feet, override and indicator retracted."

"Correct. What restrictions apply with Overspeed Warning inoperative?"

"Point seven-eight Mach above 23,200 feet, and 340 knots below 23,200."

"Correct. How is maneuvering speed defined?"

"The speed at which maximum use of flight controls is permissible, and that's 235 knots at sea level."

"Correct. And if one ejector fails to retract, what additional drag and what percent should be added to the flight plan?"

"Three point five percent drag, and four percent to the flight plan."

And so it went for the next ten minutes. When Stone was satisfied with Jack's knowledge of the airplane's general limitations, he directed him to the electrical system and asked, "What will cause the illumination of the generator drive warning lights?"

"Generator oil pressure of 200 psi or less, or generator oil quantity of half gallon or less."

"Correct. How do you simultaneously disconnect the generators from the A/C bus tie?"

"Actuation of the guarded A/C isolation switch. It opens all A/C bus tie relays simultaneously."

"Correct. Now explain how the preferential circuit operates."

"It places one generator on at a time on the A/C bus tie in the order of number two, then three, then one, and then four."

"Must it be operational for flight?"

"Yes."

"And the Generator Overload light. What does that indicate?"

"That any generator has exceeded one point zero load on the ground or one point three seven in flight."

. . .

For the next hour and thirty minutes, Stone moved from one system to another, peppering Jack with random questions without a break. At an hour and forty minutes into the exam, Jensen quietly got up from the jump seat, stretched in the forward entryway, and ambled into the cabin.

Jack took note of his departure and considered it a good sign. If Jensen was concerned about Jack's performance, he wouldn't have left. Although Jack had missed a few questions outright and had stumbled on a couple of others, nearly all the questions he'd missed dealt with emergency procedures that a pilot was not supposed to rely on memory to complete. Jack's knowledge of the correct procedure to use and where to find it in the operating manual should have been sufficient.

But it wasn't sufficient for Stone. Because the moment Jensen was out of earshot, he returned to the emergency procedures. "Let's go back to hydraulics for a moment," he said. "You missed a few questions there, so let's dig a little deeper. Tell me this: what are the first seven items in the hydraulic failure checklist?"

Jack looked at him and said, "Unless I'm mistaken, those are not memory items."

There was a pause, and Stone sharpened his gaze. "No," he said tersely. "Strictly speaking, they are not. But your knowledge of why they are done in the order they are done allows me to assess the depth of your knowledge. If you can answer that question, then I'm less concerned about the others you missed. If you don't know the answer, then let's try it another way: following a hydraulic failure, why should extension of the ejectors by the alternate air system be avoided?"

Jack looked at the ejector switches with grim desperation. He had no idea what the answer was. He couldn't recall seeing it in the manual or Joe mentioning it, though he probably had.

"Nothing?" Stone asked. "Not even an informed guess?"

Jack felt like a wounded gazelle with a lion padding patiently behind and driving him to ground. Fear and despair washed over him. This was it. He was finished. There was no way out.

He heard Stone retract his pointer pen and rise from the jumpseat. He heard the click of the latches on Stone's attaché.

As Jack stared sullenly out the window and awaited the coup de grace, he heard Jensen bellow, "Well, hey there you ol' geezer!" Jack looked over his right shoulder and saw Jensen standing in the forward entryway, his arms raised as if giving a benediction.

"Geezer, my ass!" came Sam's reply, his footfalls rapid as he charged up the stairs. Loud guffaws and backslapping followed as the old two friends greeted one another warmly.

"Hey, heard you're a *grand*daddy!" Jensen said.

Sam laughed. "Yeah," he replied. "Elizabeth had a six-pound, two-ounce little boy last March. Peg and I are thrilled!"

"That's great news, Sam. And how *are* the girls?"

"Everyone's fantastic, Bill. And how about you? How's Eddy? Last I heard he was in test pilot school out at Edwards."

"Yeah, he went through in an Air Force slot. Finished up three months ago. He's at Pax River now. Navy guy, formally trained and qualified—not like you and me, ol' buddy," he howled.

Sam gave a sideways glance at Jack and smiled. Then he turned, took Jensen by the arm, and guided him toward the galley. They spoke in hushed tones, and a moment later, Sam gave Jensen a pat on the arm and walked quickly toward the cockpit. "How're you guys coming along?" he boomed as he burst through the doorway.

Stone was holding a file in his hands. "We're finished here," he said without looking at Sam.

"Good, that's good," Sam said. "You've been at it, what? An hour and a half?"

Stone shrugged. "Only long enough to establish his competence," he said. "Or lack of it."

"Jack's a copilot qualifying for a Part 91 ferry flight with a check airman and check engineer in the other seats, Brad. He's not here for a DC-8 rating. Besides that, Gerhard wants this show on the road." Sam turned to Jensen, who was standing behind him. "How about you, Bill? Anything more you need to see?"

"Oh, well—that would be up to Brad, of course," Jensen said. "But as for me? I thought it was an impressive job by both of them."

Sam looked at Stone. "Your call, Brad. But if Bill's satisfied, I know Gerhard will be too."

Stone glowered at him. "Well, then," he said without averting his gaze. "Congratulations, Jack … It seems you've passed."

*Part Two*

# CRUISE

# THIRTY-ONE

*Miami International Airport, October 20, 1978*

S am stepped out onto the stairs, put his fingers to his mouth, and let loose an earsplitting whistle. He waved his arms, and the ground crew started for the airplane. In the meantime, Brad had taken the copilot's seat and was preparing the cockpit for the flight. Jensen was seated in the forward jumpseat and setting up his audio panel and oxygen mask. Jack had quietly left the cockpit and ambled into the cabin to stay out of the way as preparations were organized and settled. Sam hadn't mentioned if Jack was welcome to come along on the flight or not, and he figured he'd take a seat in the back and wait until asked.

He took a window seat in an emergency exit row. He closed his eyes, put his head back, and sank into the seat warmed by the sun. Jack would take a few moments alone to let the success of the oral sink in and consider what he'd just achieved.

It had been nearly two weeks since Halder had hired him, two weeks of tumult, uncertainty, and long days either stuck in traffic on I-95, or waiting in parking areas for people or parts, or struggling to retain everything he'd learned about the airplane. But throughout, it had been a period of transformation, Jack's interest in Jetstream evolving from wary suspicion, to a medial antipathy, to a budding passion. At first he'd assumed the solidarity of these men was due to their relegation to the periphery of their profession, this bunch of freebooters who made their own rules and didn't give a tinker's damn for anyone else's. But Jack had come to realize he was wrong about that. These men weren't bound by their status as outliers but by a sort of reverse professional snobbery, a cynical pride. And while others may consider them at the bottom of the profession, these men considered themselves at the very top of it. So although Jetstream—formerly Pan Topic, formerly *whatever*—was a little no-name in the industry at large, it was swashbuckling and irreverent, and Jack found those qualities irresistible. The company had all the camaraderie and mission-hacking fervor of his MACV unit in Vietnam but without the dirt, the drudgery, and the dying. Jack wanted in, and he wanted in bad.

Bobby Mumford had just completed his walkaround inspection of the airplane and was trudging up the stairs. He held his kit bag in one hand and a flashlight in the other.

"All set?" Sam asked.

"Much as it's going to be," Bobby groused. When he got to the top of the stairs, he turned and looked down warily at the wet spot under the number two engine. "What'd they find for the fuel leak on that one?" he asked.

"A loose coupling in the heat exchanger," Sam replied. "They tightened it, ran it up, and said it's fixed."

Bobby scoffed. "Bullshit," he huffed. "Too much of a leak for just that. They should have pulled and replaced the entire unit."

"Maybe. But we'll find out today, won't we? Now c'mon, let's get going. We're not going to prove anything standing here."

Bobby dropped his kit bag in the forward baggage compartment and turned right to check the aft galleys and doors. "Back in a bit," he told Sam, speaking over his shoulder as Sam took his own kit bag and entered the cockpit.

As Bobby walked aft, he spotted Jack leaning against a galley counter. His arms were folded and he was staring at his feet. Bobby stopped and, with an incredulous look, asked, "What are you doing back here?"

Jack gave him a thin smile, shrugged, and said, "Staying out of the way. Not sure if I'm supposed to come along or not."

Bobby looked toward the cockpit. Sam was already in the captain's seat, so he reached for the flight attendants' interphone receiver and pushed the chime button. Sam picked up the receiver at the base of the pedestal panel. "Speak," he said.

"What do you want Jack to do?" Bobby asked. "Come with us or not?"

"*What?* Hell no! Tell him to get up here. I want him along to observe."

Bobby hung up the receiver and said, "Sam says get up there. He wants you along to observe."

Jack's smile broadened, and he gave Bobby a thumbs-up. As he turned and started toward the cockpit, Bobby reached out and grabbed him by the arm. "Hey," he said. "Joe told me you're doing a bang-up job, and I know Gerhard's happy about that too. Look, I'm sorry we got off to a rough start. How 'bout we have a do-over?" He let Jack go and offered his hand. "Bob Mumford," he said with a broad grin, "but everyone calls me Bobby except my exes, who only call their lawyers." He guffawed.

Jack laughed as they shook. "Thanks, Bobby. I appreciate the welcome."

Bobby tightened his grip and pulled Jack closer. "Stone rake you over the coals?" he asked, his eyes narrowed.

"It was an oral. I did my best with the time I had, but—"

Bobby let go. "Fuck him," he growled. "Stone's on a mission. Don't worry about him. We'll get you what you need. Big Jake and I flew connies together for a time during the '50s. He's a good man. You'll like Air Logistics. It's a great outfit."

"I appreciate that, Bobby, I appreciate the support."

"Good. Now go on up there and get buckled in. You're a part of the crew now, and we take care of each other. All of us except him, at least."

• • •

As Jack buckled into the aft jumpseat, he saw Stone looking up at the overhead panel, his fingers dancing across the switches as he configured the systems for flight. Sam was setting up the radios and his instrument panel for the departure. Bobby closed the forward entry door and armed the evacuation slide. "Cabin's secured and the door's armed," he announced as he entered the cockpit. He dropped heavily into his seat and buckled in, and then his hands flew around his panel as he prepared it for engine start.

Stone turned around and looked back. "Alright," he said. "When everyone's ready, I'll give my briefing."

A man's tinny voice crackled over the loudspeaker above Sam's head. "Ground crew to cockpit!" he said. "Brakes parked, you're cleared to start, Captain."

Sam lifted his mic and replied, "Roger, sir, stand by one." He glanced at Stone and gave him a nod.

Stone said, "To be clear, although Sam's in the left seat, I'll be in command of the airplane today. If we have to abort the takeoff, the decision is mine and will be executed by me. Sam, if I call abort, I'll take the throttles and you'll extend the spoilers and guard the handle until we stop. Bob, note our speed and stand by with the appropriate emergency checklist. After V1, any problem that occurs, we'll take into the air. Whoever is flying will continue to fly, and the other two guys will run the checklist. Unless conditions require something else, we'll plan on a return to Miami and land on Runway 09. We'll be under max landing weight, so no need to dump fuel, Bobby. Any questions?"

Sam shook his head.

Bobby said, "No."

Stone looked at Jensen and said, "Bill, you're another set of eyes for us today, so if anything doesn't look right, please call it out."

Jensen gave him a thumbs-up.

Sam leaned forward to make a final adjustment to his rudder pedals and said, "before starting engines checklist."

Bobby picked up the plasticized checklist on his desk and began reading aloud. "Logbook, Forms, and Flight Plan?" he said.

"On board and reviewed," Sam responded.

"Mask and oxygen?"

"Checked, ON, 100%." Sam said. Stone and Bobby checked their panels and replied the same.

"Gear pins? Three on board," Bobby asked and answered, and then he

234

continued with the next twenty-three items on the checklist. When the checklist was complete, Sam picked up his mic and told the groundman, "Turning number three."

Bobby announced, "Pressure's good."

Sam reached for the start buttons on the overhead panel and pushed the third from the left.

"Valve open," Bobby said, and a moment later, "Rotation."

The JT4A's turbine began to whine as it picked up speed.

"Oil pressure … and there's fifteen percent," Bobby said.

Stone moved the engine's fuel cutoff lever to the idle position and the rapid *tick, tick, tick* of the engine's igniters could be heard through the loudspeaker. An instant later, there was a throaty *womph* as the fuel ignited. The whine of the jet turned into a whistle as it reached idle speed.

"Valve closed," Bobby announced loudly.

"Turning number four," Sam said.

When all four engines were running, Sam said, "after start check."

Bobby's hands flew across the engineer's panel as he engaged the electrical and hydraulic systems, performed checks on their functions, and prepared the airplane to taxi. Jack's eyes were glued to Bobby's actions.

Sam glanced at the electrical panel and told the groundman, "Cleared to disconnect."

"Roger, Captain. Stand by. I'll signal when ready."

Shortly after the ground equipment was cleared, the groundman stood in front of the airplane with his hands raised, two red wands held vertically above his head.

Stone picked up his mic. "Miami, Douglas Eight-Oh-Four-Papa-Alpha at Consolidated for taxi," he said. "We have information Charlie."

"Roger, Four-Papa-Alpha, information Delta is now current, altimeter 30.02. Follow the Eastern DC-8 on Lima, and taxi Runway 9. By the way, sir, I don't see a clearance for you. Do you have one on file?"

"Ah, no, sir. We're local today," Stone said. "VFR to Tango November

Tango and return." He was referring to the Dade-Collier Training and Transition Airport. The long, isolated, swamp-locked runway was thirty-nine miles west of Miami. It was the first of six runways planned for the Everglades Jetport, intended to be the largest airport in the world, but the entire plan was scrapped due to environmental concerns. The single runway that was constructed remained in use for flight training.

"Okay, sir, I'll pass that along," the controller said. "Follow the Eastern, and call tower now on 118.3."

"Four-Papa-Alpha, follow the Eastern on Lima and cleared to taxi Runway 9," Stone replied. "Over to tower now, and thanks for your help, sir. We'll see you later."

Sam flashed the taxi light on the nosewheel, glanced out the left side windshield and said, "Clear left."

Stone glanced out his side windshield. "Clear right," he said.

The groundman signaled the airplane forward, and Sam advanced the throttles. But although the power came up and the engines whistled loudly, the airplane refused to budge. Sam pushed the throttles up further and then the brakes, frozen with rust, suddenly released and the airplane surged forward.

The groundman signaled Sam to begin a right turn, and Stone looked out the right side to ensure they were clear. "Flaps?" he asked.

"Fifteen," Sam said.

As the airplane continued to accelerate, Sam applied the brakes to slow it down. The left main gear shuddered loudly, and Sam grimaced and shot Bobby a look.

"Got it," Bobby said. He jotted a note about brake chatter on his squawk sheet.

Jack watched as the gleaming Eastern DC-8 passed ahead of them. Sam joined the taxiway and followed behind it.

As Sam continued the taxi, Jack shifted his gaze to Bobby, who was working his panel and preparing the airplane for flight. But when he came to the fuel controls, he balked, and Jack could see why. The fuel pressure warning light for engine number four was glowing bright yellow. It had extinguished as it should have after the engine was started, but now it was back on. Jack remembered that if it was illuminated after engine start, it indicated a first-stage failure of the engine-driven fuel pump. If the fuel pump's second stage also failed, the engine would shut down immediately, and for that reason, it was a "no-go" item in the airplane's Minimum Equipment List. By law, the pump had to be repaired before flight. Bobby pressed the light cap several times to ensure it wasn't stuck in the test position. Then, after glancing over his shoulder to ensure Jensen wasn't watching, Bobby deftly removed the yellow light cap, took out the hot bulb, and slipped it into the cup holder on his desk. With the socket empty and the light cap returned to its position, the light appeared to be out and the pump working properly.

Bobby looked back at Jack and gave him a wink.

Jack returned it with a thin smile and joined the deception. His only regret was doing it behind Bill Jensen's back, and for that he felt cheap. But beyond that remorse, Jack agreed with Bobby's decision. The point of the flight was to expose and correct as many problems with the airplane as possible before they departed for the hajj because they didn't have time to do it piecemeal; furthermore, the risks associated with a single engine failure during flight were small even if it occurred during takeoff. The airplane was lightly loaded, the runway long and dry, and there were no high obstacles to clear once they were airborne. Considering all these circumstances, Jack was certain that Sam—and even Stone—would agree with Bobby's decision. As for leaving Bill Jensen out of the loop? That was regrettable, but you've got to break eggs to make an omelet, and Jack was content to leave it at that. It had been no different at Keystone.

"Coming up on the runway," Sam said over his shoulder. "How's the checklist coming, Bobby?"

"She's a-comin', skip," he replied as he set the pressurization controls.

The Eastern DC-8 ahead of them had been cleared for takeoff. Its landing lights came on, its engines howled, and a black cloud of smoke was blasted behind it as it began to roll.

The radio crackled. "Four-Papa-Alpha, cleared into position and hold."

"Four-Papa-Alpha, position and hold," Stone replied.

"Before takeoff check," Sam ordered.

Bobby called out the final ten items on the checklist as Sam taxied the airplane onto the runway. Jack loosened his seatbelt and shoulder harness. He elevated himself to get a better view over Jensen's and Bobby's shoulders.

The DC-8 was positioned in the center of the runway, two miles of concrete stretched out ahead of them, and Jack buzzed with anticipation.

"Four-Papa-Alpha, fly runway heading, cleared for takeoff."

"Four-Papa-Alpha, runway heading, cleared for takeoff," Stone replied.

Sam turned on the landing lights, released the brakes, and advanced the throttles. He paused a moment for the four engines to stabilize, then pushed them up quickly.

The engines roared and Jack was thrown back into his seat as the airplane shot forward. He heard Sam say loudly, "Set max power, 2.06 EPR."

Bobby leaned forward to make the final adjustments to the throttles. "Okay, power's set," he yelled. "Ninety-eight percent."

Stone guarded the base of the throttles with his left hand and called out, "Eighty knots!" as the airplane quickly accelerated. The whine of the nosewheel tires was growing louder and louder. Suddenly, a shudder began from below and spread upward through the base of the cockpit. The faster the airplane accelerated, the more violent the shuddering became until it was so severe the instruments were a blur.

At 121 knots, Stone shouted, "V1!" with his right hand on the glare shield to try and dampen the violent shaking.

Sam gripped the yoke with both hands.

Bobby's eyes were locked on the engine gauges. If the faulty fuel pump failed now, it would be the worst time for that to happen.

"Rotate!" Stone shouted above the din and violent shaking.

Sam drew back on the yoke and the airplane's nose began to rise, but the shaking was so severe it felt like it would break into pieces. Up and up the nose came, the violence unabated, the main wheels still rumbling on the pavement.

"V-2" Stone shouted at 130 knots, and a moment later they were airborne. "Plus ten!" he yelled.

Sam gestured with his right hand and shouted, "Positive rate, gear up!"

Stone grabbed the gear handle and pulled it up. There was an explosive *whoosh* and the whining of hydraulic rams. A moment later the nosewheel slammed into its bed with a loud *thump*, and instantly the din and violent shaking ended. With only the whistling engines and the hiss of the wind filling the cockpit, the airplane climbed skyward steady and smooth.

Bill Jensen gave Mumford a nervous glance.

Bobby shrugged and said, "Nose tires squared off from sitting too long, or maybe the bearings shot … Who fuckin' knows? That's what we're here to figure out."

At 1,000 feet, Sam said, "Flaps up." Tapping the throttles, he added, "Climb power."

Bobby leaned forward and pulled the throttles back to climb EPR. The engines' roar subsided. Stone moved the flap lever to up, and the handle clicked into the slot. As the flaps retracted, Jack felt the change in the lift and drag in the seat of his pants.

Sam trimmed the stabilizer with the pickle switch on his yoke. "after take-off check," he said, the warning horn bleating as the stabilizer motor engaged.

Bobby picked up the checklist, reached for the ignition switches, and clicked them off. Jet engines didn't need ignition once they were running, but ignition was used as a backup source during critical phases of flight.

The radio crackled with the tower controller's voice. "Four-Papa-Alpha," he said, "left turn heading three-six-zero, and contact departure now on 119.6."

"Three-six-zero and 19.6," Stone said. "Adios."

Sam glanced to the left to check the sky for nearby aircraft, then rolled the massive jet smoothly into the climbing turn.

The venerable DC-8 had thrown off its torpor and soared aloft like a swift freed from a cage.

Behind the others and out of view, Jack beamed. Any thoughts or doubts he'd had about Corrosion Corner had been vanquished. He could barely contain his thrill.

# THIRTY-TWO

*The sky over the Everglades, October 20, 1978*

Only fifteen minutes elapsed before Sam was configuring the airplane for their first landing at Dade-Collier. But after just three more takeoffs and landings, Bobby had a list of eight squawks for the airplane's logbook, many of them required to be fixed before further flight: the brake chatter; the fuel pump failure; the nose strut vibration; a fuel feed pump that had failed; the anti-skid that had failed; the number two cabin compressor overheat light that came on and remained on despite efforts to correct it; the number three constant speed drive, which had failed and had to be disconnected; and the wing slot disagreement light that had illuminated but later cleared after they'd cycled the flaps up and down.

When the airplane returned to the ramp at Corrosion Corner and the final checklists were complete, Bobby got up and opened the forward entry door. Halder was at the bottom of the stairs, staring at a growing puddle of fuel beneath the number two engine. Bobby tramped down to brief him about the problems.

Stone remained seated and reviewed the logbook entries Bobby had made, while Sam and Bill Jensen got out of their seats. Jack had gone aft and ambled through the cabin.

As they stood on the landing at the top of the stairs, Jensen eyed the puddle of fuel and asked Sam, "When did you say you're leaving?"

"Saturday at the latest. Sooner if we can. We're already behind."

Jensen arched a brow.

Sam noticed and said, "We've managed worse. At least this time we've got Jake's parts and Manny's money. We'll make it work."

"What about the other two airplanes at Fort Lauderdale?"

"They're cleaner and were better maintained. Gerhard flew one of them last Friday and the other over the weekend. There were a few problems on each, but nothing as serious as this hangar queen."

Jensen nodded. "Well … good luck with it," he said with a smile.

"Hey, if anybody can pull it off, we can."

"Brad told me Jack was part of that parts deal."

Sam grinned. "Yeah, Big Jake had Gerhard by the balls, made him an offer he couldn't refuse. Gerhard wasn't happy about it, and especially not Brad—as you've just seen—but it'll be alright. I've got some sim time scheduled at Eastern tomorrow night, and between that and all the work he's done with Joe Bartolini, he'll be squared away for the ferry at least. If it turns out his flying is as strong as his study and work ethic, I'll send him home from Shannon with a recommendation that Jake take him straightaway. No need to carry it along any further than that. Jake can manage it from there."

Jensen smiled. "Sounds like a plan," he said. "He seems like a sharp young guy. I hope it works out for him."

"Me too." Grabbing Jensen's arm and giving it a shake, he added, "And, hey … we appreciate the help today, Bill. When I get home, it's time for you and me to get some fishing in. It's been too long!"

"Count on it!" Jensen exclaimed. "Sailfish will be tailing the reef by then. I'll bring Eddy along if I can get him away from Pax River for a few days."

"Absolutely, Bill. Plan on it!"

Stone stepped out of the airplane behind them and announced, "Ready when you are, Bill."

Jensen looked at him. "Sure," he said. "Let's debrief on the way in." Then, looking at Sam again, he said to him, "Give my best to Peg, and godspeed. See you when you get back."

• • •

Sam re-entered the airplane and found Jack near the forward galley. He was perusing an emergency evacuation card as Sam walked up and said, "Congratulations. Joe told me how hard you've been working."

Jack smiled, put the card down on the counter, and said, "Joe gets most of the credit. He knows the airplane like the back of his hand, and he's a hell of an instructor."

"Yes, he is," Sam agreed. "And look. About Brad. I'm sorry he got into it like he did, but he's been tasked with changing things around here, and he's jumping in with both feet. Don't take it personally."

Jack smiled. "I won't."

"Good. Now, what I also wanted to tell you is that I've arranged some simulator time for us at Eastern tomorrow night. It's a full motion sim, but it's the red-eye shift, unfortunately—the midnight to 4 a.m. slot. It's all they had available. Is that alright?"

"*Sim* time?" Jack said, surprised. "Oh, yes … *yes!*" he exclaimed. "That's fine! I wasn't expecting anything like that at all."

"Well, don't get too excited. It's only four hours in the box, but at least you'll get some feel for the airplane before actually flying it. We'll brief for a few hours beforehand, run through everything we're going to do, and then jump in. I'll position us on the runway, and you'll make the takeoff. Once we're cleaned up, I'll shoot us up to altitude, where we'll do some air work: steep turns, Dutch roll recovery, stall buffet, and such, and then an emergency descent. From there, I'll position us on downwind, and we'll finish out the period doing takeoffs and landings."

Jack was thrilled. "I'll look forward to it," he said. "And thanks for your intervention today, Sam. Without it, I was finished."

"No. That wasn't going to happen," Sam asserted. "You were well prepared for what you're qualifying to do. But look, regarding that, there's something else I want to discuss before we go any further. Joe made it clear that you'll only be legal for the ferry flight and nothing more, correct?"

"Yes. But as I explained to Joe—and previously to Captain Halder—Captain Kegan expects me to complete the contract. He said to come back with a few hundred hours in the DC-8, not just a few takeoffs and landings."

"I'm aware of that," Sam said. "But we haven't got the time to make you legal to fly passengers, and Jake was aware of that too."

"And so am I. But Joe also said if I stayed on, I could complete my training OJT. I know that's not kosher with the feds, but I don't care. I may be the youngest guy here, but I wasn't born yesterday, Sam. It wouldn't be the first time in my career I bent the FARs to get the job done."

Sam waved him off. "Yeah, no doubt," he said. "But you don't need to stay on for the hajj, Jack. I can talk to Jake; I can square it with him. Continuing past the ferry flight puts you—and the company—at risk of a violation of the FARs not only for the training you never accomplished legally but for other things we'll have to do as well. Remember, Jetstream isn't American, United, Pan Am, or even Air Logistics. We don't have the luxury of writing up a mechanical problem and leaving it for maintenance and flight scheduling to resolve. Given the condition of these airplanes, there'll likely be more compromises needed during this contract than usual. So why take that chance? Why not take the time you can get legally and leave it at that?"

"Because Air Logistics is not guaranteed with or without your help, Sam. The only thing Captain Kegan promised me was another interview; he didn't promise me a job. If Air Logistics doesn't pan out and I've left Jetstream, I'll be right back where I started: flying freight in run-out airplanes at night, taking even greater risks than I'd be taking here, while doing it for a fraction of the pay and job satisfaction. All things considered—including you and all the other guys I've met—for someone in my circumstances, Jetstream is a career opportunity. So, if I can stay on for the hajj, I want to stay on for the hajj. I'm willing to accept the risks because an even greater risk for me is giving up Jetstream without something equal or better in hand. I'm sure you understand."

Sam was looking aside as he listened and then nodded when Jack was done. Meeting his gaze, he said to him, "Alright, fair enough. So, we'll see how it goes and see how you handle the airplane, but the final decision will be up to Gerhard. That was your deal with him, correct? Three takeoffs and landings, and then he'd decide?"

"Yes. He said I'd have to prove myself in the airplane and prove I was a good fit with his crew. He said that decision would be his." Jack smiled. "But I assume he'll be basing that decision on yours."

"And Brad's," Sam reminded him sharply. "Don't forget Brad. Now, look, I've got some things I need to do before going home, and Gerhard needs you back in that van running errands. I'll meet you in the lobby at 2100 tomorrow night and we'll head over to Eastern from there. When we finish, you'll get a few hours of sleep, but then it's back to work as a go-fer. Get used to it. We do what we have to do to get the job done."

"That'll be fine," Jack said. "I'm used to that already."

Sam turned to leave, then stopped. "Oh, and another thing," he added. "If you're intent on staying, then you'll need a uniform and some equipment unless you brought them with you: a couple of shirts, slacks, epaulets, and a kit bag with an E6-B, flashlight, and plotter. Skip the hat and jacket; you won't need them for this gig. Your Jepp charts and binders will be provided by the company. Go to Bernie's Uniform and Aviation Supply in Hialeah for everything else. It's in the Yellow Pages. Stop in while you're running errands, and he'll have what you need. Bring your wallet. Those things are all on you."

"I will."

Sam threw him a wave, and as he turned toward the door, he said over his shoulder, "See you tomorrow night."

• • •

Over the succeeding five days, Jack continued his go-fer duties and completed his simulator training with Sam. He enjoyed his time in the box and did well, bolstering his confidence. He eagerly anticipated the airplane.

On Monday morning, October 23, one of the DC-8s at Fort Lauderdale departed with a cockpit crew and Maggie to complete arrangements at the airport and the Mount Lavinia Hotel for the crew in Colombo,

Sri Lanka.

By Wednesday evening, October 25, all crewmembers who lived beyond South Florida had checked into the hotel and were making final preparations for their departure the following day.

# THIRTY-THREE

*Islamorada, Florida Keys, October 26, 1978*

Six days had passed, and preparations for the hajj were complete. Mick Salyer—a Jetstream captain and one of Sam's lifelong friends—pulled his Wagoneer into Sam's driveway and tooted the horn.

Sam and Peg came to the door, and Peg threw Mick a wave. Sam gave her a peck on the cheek, and they spoke a few words. She was crying as he reached for his bags and wiped her eyes as she watched him walk toward the car.

The Jetstream crew wore civilian clothes when ferrying an airplane. Today, Sam was wearing a white cotton button-down, khakis, and Topsiders, while Mick was in a plaid western shirt, jeans, and cowboy boots.

Sam tossed his bags into the back of Mick's Jeep and took the passenger's seat. "Appreciate the ride, Michael," he said with a smile.

"Hey, no sweat," Mick said. "Betty's got plans for shopping with the girls next week. She'll bring the car home then. No point in Peg making the trip just to drop your skinny ass off."

"Please tell Betty I appreciate it. She's a keeper, isn't she?"

"Yeah. Wish I got it right the first time … or even the second," Mick said. "But at least I got it right eventually."

As they drove away, Mick tapped the horn and Sam threw Peg a kiss out the window.

"So what's the game plan?" Mick asked. "Did the launch crew get over there okay? I haven't heard a word since before they were supposed to leave."

"Yeah, they left from Fort Lauderdale on Monday. They'd planned to go nonstop to Shannon, overnighting there, and then continue to Colombo on Tuesday with a pit stop in Kuwait for fuel. Gerhard said they'd made it to Shannon okay but then diverted into Frankfurt with a hydraulic problem. They got it fixed, spent the night, and got to Colombo yesterday."

"Who was flying?"

"Reggie, Walt, and Phil. Maggie went along to help with the hotel arrangements too."

Mick stopped at the junction of Sam's neighborhood and the Overseas Highway and waited for passing traffic to clear. "So, how's Walt doing?" he asked. "Is he behaving himself, staying off the hooch?"

"So far," Sam said. "But Gerhard says this is his last chance. He's not paying to put anyone through a third round of rehab—much less a copilot."

"Can't blame him for that. Poor Walt. Nice guy, but whew, once he gets into the juice, man oh man—"

"Yeah … I know," Sam rued.

Mick pulled onto the highway and reached for a cigar in his shirt pocket. He pushed the lighter in on the dash, and Sam rolled open his window. "Do you really have to do that?" he complained.

Mick gave him a look. "Jesus," he said. "How's it you've lived in the Keys all your life and never learned the health benefits of smoking?"

Sam shook his head in disgust.

Mick relented and put the cigar back in his pocket. Sam rolled up the window and turned up the air conditioning.

Changing the subject, Mick said, "So, I heard we have a new copilot, a young guy we took on as a favor to Big Jake."

"Yeah, Jack Dolan. He's twenty-six and a DC-3 captain from Philly. Nice kid. I'll be flying with him and Bobby today."

"Why'd Gerhard do that? I thought we were done with that kind of shit. I heard Brad got wrapped around the axle about it."

"Yeah, he did, and I'm sure you heard about our little kerfuffle."

"Yes. And that too."

"Jake sent him to Gerhard as part of a parts deal he couldn't refuse. Jake's interested in hiring the kid, but he needs some DC-8 time to get past that dipshit DO of theirs. I told Jake I'd take care of it and smooth it over with Gerhard—but it didn't go over so well with Brad."

Mick gave him a sideways glance. "You're still a fuckin' Boy Scout, Samuel. Haven't you learned that no good deed goes unpunished?"

"You were a Boy Scout, too, as I recall."

"Only until I sold their candy and spent the money on cigarettes."

"There was *that*."

"Is he any good?" Mick asked. "Have you flown with him?"

"We did four hours in the sim. He's sharp: good hands and a quick study."

"How long will he be with us?"

"Jake told him to come back with a few hundred hours and the kid says that's what he wants too, but that's not going to happen. There's no need for him to stay on. I plan on sending him home from Shannon. Jake can fudge the flight time and experience any way he wants. No one would be the wiser."

"Why the hell does he want to stay on for a hajj if he's got Air Logistics in the bag?"

"Because he doesn't think he does have it until he has it, and he'd rather be flying DC-8s than DC-3s in the meantime."

Mick gave it a thought and then looked at Sam with a wry grin. "That might make sense to a clean-living man like you, ol' buddy. But to me it sounds like bullshit. From what I heard, he was at the briefing party and making the rounds. Word is, he caught a lot of eyes … mostly the girls'."

Sam looked puzzled. "So what?"

"So, a handsome, twenty-six-year-old, red-blooded freight dog shows up at one of our parties, sees all this hot-lookin' puss, and decides to stick around just to fly jets?" Mick guffawed.

"Not every pilot thinks with his dick, Mick."

"They would if they were better trained."

"And maybe if you'd show up at those things once in a while, you'd be able to judge for yourself instead of depending on me for everything."

Mick scoffed. "Nah," he said. "That's what friends are for."

Sam looked out the side window and shook his head. "I give up," he muttered.

A red Cadillac Eldorado was tailgating them as they approached the Jewish Creek Bridge. Mick had been eyeballing the guy in the rearview mirror for the last mile and took his foot off the gas. The Wagoneer slowed abruptly, and the guy in the Caddy braked hard, leaned on the horn, and then swerved across the double line to pass them. As he raced past, Mick stuck his head out the window and flipped him the bird. "Fuck you ... *ASSHOLE*!" he yelled into the wind.

"Look at that," he said to Sam. "Jersey plates ... figures."

"I'm sure he feels terribly insulted. Try to remember we need to arrive in Miami alive and not in jail, please."

Mick ignored the remark and changed the subject. "So, if this ... what's-his-name ... is any good, why not keep him ourselves? It's not like we've got a lot of captains coming up the pipe."

"His name's Jack Dolan, and no. Jake wants to hire him."

"Has anyone told this young man that he'll be sitting in the right seat at Air Logistics for the next twenty years of his life? Does he have any idea how slow the progression is there?"

Sam threw up his hands. "Out of my purview," he said. "I'll get him the DC-8 time he needs and send him back to Jake before he gets into trouble. The rest is up to him."

"Wish someone had done that for me," Mick said with a groan.

Like Sam, Mick was a Conch whose family's lineage in the Keys pre-dated Florida's statehood. Although his military service had been with the infantry through the Battle of the Bulge, his flying career was entirely civilian. In keeping with his family tradition, Mick had done a stint as a smuggler—forays flying to Cuba after Castro took over—but the Feds caught up with him, and he'd been with Pan Tropic ever since. He was tall, lean, and tanned to bronze. His scruffy beard and cowboy boots were his signature style—both in uniform and out of it.

"Well," Sam deadpanned, "maybe if you hadn't stolen the Cub Scouts' money, impregnated half the women in Key West, or got caught flying all those Cohibas into Sugarloaf in '63, someone would have done something nice for you."

Mick pulled the stogie from his shirt pocket and twisted it in Sam's face. "It was way more than half, and I'd tell you where to stick this," he said, "but I'd rather smoke it instead. Open that fuckin' window if your little girlie lungs can't take it."

Sam frowned and cranked the handle.

Mick pushed the lighter in and said, "Who am I flying with?"

"Pete Gaides and Buddy Reid. You'll be in 816PA and bringing the rest of the crew along with you; thirty of us, forty flight attendants, and a few mechanics too."

The lighter popped. Mick reached for it and asked, "When's Gerhard coming over?"

"He isn't. He'll be tied up with our airplanes' refit in Wichita. Besides that, he told me Hirsch has plans for some kind of upgrade for the airline. Says he wants to tap into this deregulation thing that's coming. Wants Gerhard to focus on that."

Mick blew a plume of smoke out the window and said, "*Upgrade?* Upgrade to *what?*"

"Something that passes for a real airline, I guess."

"What is he fuckin' nuts? Hasn't anyone told Manny *real* airlines lose *real* money?"

"Nuts? No … Manny's just a rich guy with a new toy. Probably sees himself dining at the Wings Club while Jimmy's kneecapping the competition in the cloakroom."

"Yeah, Manny covers all the angles. But look, if they go straight, I'm out of here right behind you, and you and I won't be alone."

"Trust me. Two weeks of flying empty airplanes around on a schedule will put paid to that delusion. They'll be back in the charter business, pronto."

Mick glanced in the mirror to check for traffic, then pulled into the westbound lane to pass an RV. As he merged right, he asked, "What's the plan going over there? Same as Reggie?"

"Yeah, same thing. But rather than going nonstop, I'm sticking to the coast until Gander. I don't trust that airplane. If it's hiding anything more serious than what I've seen, I want a chance to uncover it before going feet wet."

Mick mulled that over a moment and said, "I like it. Lot of options for diverting if something goes tits-up. I'll talk it over with my guys and see what they want to do."

"Sure. But don't forget Brad," Sam warned. "Now that he's taking over, he'll be weighing in heavily on your decision."

Mick scowled. "Oh, yeah? Well, fuck him," he snarled. "Let Captain Shithead fly it, then."

"No," Sam said firmly. "I want you in the seat. Pete's been hanging out in Alaska for the last two contracts and needs to get current. Besides that, Brad's got to set up the schedule for the hajj, the crew pairings, and all the rest. It's best for him to work that out with everyone present. You let Pete fly, and let Brad handle the logistics."

"What's the deal with him, anyway? Is he all set with the FAA, got their stamp of approval?"

"Yeah, he's done," Sam replied. "But it could have been you, you know. You or Dan or even Philippe would have been a better choice."

Mick looked at him like he was nuts. "Thanks, but no thanks, ol' buddy. I've had enough FAA supervision for one career."

"Well, then Brad's the new sheriff after I leave. What a bunch of knuckleheads you guys are."

"I heard he was with Pan Am before coming here. You ever hear that?"

"That's true. A friend of mine is a chief pilot with them in New York. We ran into one another a couple of years ago in Aguadilla, back when we had that travel club contract, remember?"

"Yeah. Sweet deal that was, wasn't it?"

"Yep, it was, and my Pan Am buddy was there on a diversion one night. I ran into him in the bar. He'd seen Stone getting into an elevator in his uniform and asked me how he was working out. When I told him Brad was a good stick but couldn't get along with anyone, my buddy told me he was the chief who fired him. He told me it was one of the toughest things he ever had to do. Although Brad had accumulated more than a dozen lousy probation reports from captains—some of them running two pages long—he sensed something suspicious about it and started digging deeper. But when he did, he was stopped by the VP of flight, who told him they didn't want Brad staying on with Pan Am. Apparently, Brad had uncovered a senior captain who owned and operated a brothel with underage girls in Santo Domingo. My buddy had no idea how Brad came across that information, but Brad had reported the guy and the company wanted it all to go away on the q.t. They retired the captain early and shitcanned Brad instead. Problem solved, no muss, no fuss, and since Brad was on probation, there were no residuals to deal with after it."

"Well, no wonder he's hardwired to the fuck-you position. I'd be too after getting hosed like that. And all those probation reports were fake?"

"No, not fake. My buddy said they were real but should have been corrected with counseling first. He said Brad didn't deserve to be fired. He was trying to do the right thing, but he got caught up in the wrong battle at the wrong time."

Mick glanced at him and raised a brow. "Sounds like somebody else I know. Remember what I said about Boy Scouts, Sam. No good deed goes unpunished."

• • •

When they arrived at Hangar Four, Mick pulled up to the curb and Sam got out. He took his suitcase and kitbag from the back of the car and leaned in through the passenger window. "Have a good trip," he said. "And give us a call on 123.45 when you're airborne. We'll be monitoring."

"Will do, and hey! Good luck with Jack. Everyone says he'll be a good fit with the crew, and Bobby and Joe gave him a thumbs-up."

Sam looked perplexed. "I thought you didn't know much about him?"

Mick smiled. "Small world," he said. "Even when we're out of it, we're in."

Sam returned his smile. "Call us when you're on your way," he said.

"Roger that, Skip. See you on the other side."

Sam patted the roof, then turned and grabbed his bags.

# THIRTY-FOUR

*Miami International Airport, October 26, 1978*

Jack was waiting for Sam in the hangar's office. When he arrived, they removed the charts and flight planning tools they needed from their kit bags, then Sam called the Miami Flight Service Station for a weather briefing. The briefer told him that a large high-pressure system was dominating the East Coast with clear skies across the region. In Miami, the temperature was 83 degrees and the wind northeast at seventeen knots, gusting to twenty-five. Gander was reporting partly cloudy conditions with a southwest wind at twenty-two knots and a temperature of 5 degrees Celsius. The forecast was for good weather to continue throughout the day and evening. When the briefing was complete, Sam taught Jack how to calculate the DC-8's best altitude for the flight. Working together, they determined the ground speed, fuel remaining, and the ETA for each of the charted waypoints along their route. With the flight plan complete, Jack called the Flight Service Station to file it, and Sam ordered the fuel they needed from Consolidated Services.

• • •

At 3:06 p.m., they were holding short of the runway. Outside, an orange windsock was horizontal to the ground and swinging back and forth wickedly. Jack gave it a glance as they awaited takeoff clearance and anxiously anticipated the conditions. Everything would turn on his performance today, and the wind wasn't helping.

"Douglas Four-Papa-Alpha, Runway 9, position and hold," the controller said.

"Position and hold, Four-Papa-Alpha," Jack replied. He looked to the right to ensure the final approach course was clear, and Sam taxied onto the runway as Bobby Mumford completed the Before Takeoff Check.

Sam turned onto the centerline, parked the brakes, and looked at Jack. "Your airplane," he said and smiled.

Jack straightened in his seat, took the controls, and was immediately struck by the difference in feel between the airplane and the simulator. Although the simulator had been thrilling and doubtlessly matched the airplane's performance and handling characteristics, it was no match for its visuals and sensations: the altimeter vibrators clicking loudly, the jets whistling, the howl from the pressurization system, the musty scent of its long unused ducts. He felt the pulse of the engines telegraphed through the throttles—each of them as powerful as a railroad locomotive—as he silently rehearsed the profile to ten thousand feet. Jack would depend on memory and his scant simulator training to overcome his anxiety and the distractions. The runway loomed ahead.

"Douglas Four-Papa-Alpha," the tower controller said, "wind, three-five-zero to zero-seven-zero at eighteen gust twenty-five. Fly runway heading. Maintain two thousand feet. Cleared for takeoff."

Sam replied to the clearance and reset the altitude alert from five thousand to two thousand. The alert warned the crew with a loud *ding* and a light whenever the airplane was approaching or leaving an assigned altitude. He looked across the cockpit at Jack and said, "Alright, so remember what I told you. Hold aileron into that crosswind *all* the way through the rotation and until we're airborne or the left wing will drop suddenly. Too much of that and we risk striking that number one engine on the runway. Also, that two thousand-foot restriction is going to come up fast, so be ready for it."

Jack gave him an anxious glance and a nod.

Sam reached up, turned on the landing lights, guarded the controls, and said, "Okay, let's go."

"Takeoff check complete," Bobby announced. "Ten bucks says he forgets the gear."

Jack looked half-back and snapped, "You're on."

He girded himself and was advancing the throttles when he felt Bobby's hand beneath his forcing them up aggressively. With the engines roaring, Bobby said loudly, "Power's set, 98 percent!" The airplane rumbled and shook and jerked in the wind but remained anchored in position. Jack looked about, anxious and confused.

Sam tapped the parking brake lever. "Brakes!" he said.

*Shit!* Jack lifted his feet to the tops of the rudder pedals and pressed down to release them. The airplane suddenly shot forward, and Jack was thrown back in his seat, the pedals now out of reach. He stretched to regain control, but in that moment lost it, veereing toward the side of the runway, and Sam had to assist in getting it back on centerline.

Jack regained control, but now the humiliating *thump, thump, thump, thump, thump* of the centerline lights resonated through the cockpit as the nosewheel tires hit every one of them. Jack's confidence in his rudder control was too tenuous to risk steering off them.

"Eighty knots," Sam announced.

Jack glimpsed his airspeed reactively but saw nothing. The mind-blowing acceleration of the jet, the g-force, and the demands of steering it in the gusty wind commanded his full attention. The takeoff profile he'd memorized was only a blur in his mind as the runway stripes raced toward him, the wheels rumbled, the air conditioning howled, the throttles vibrated, and the radio crackled with calls to other aircraft. *Simulator, my ass*, he thought, his eyes wide.

Moments later, Sam pushed his hand off the throttles and said, "V1!"

Jack gripped the yoke with both hands.

"Rotate!" Sam commanded.

Jack drew back at the cadence Sam taught him. The nose began to rise as his heart raced, the main wheels still rumbling along the pavement, the airplane still veering with the gusts, and Jack still fighting for control. He pushed the right rudder more firmly, and then Sam prompted him to use more aileron. A moment later, "V2!" Sam said, and an instant after that, "Plus ten."

The airplane left the pavement, and the left wing dropped sharply. Sam prompted him to use more aileron. "Keep it coming now," he instructed calmly. "Hold a 20-degree deck angle, keep her climbing. V2 plus ten—don't accelerate."

The DC-8 raced skyward. Jack gently released the cross controls, and the airplane crabbed into the wind.

"Douglas Four-Papa-Alpha," the radio crackled, "contact departure control on 125.5."

As Sam replied to the clearance and switched radios, the altitude alert *dinged* loudly and the warning light was lit. "One to go!" Bobby warned.

Jack eyed the vertical speed indicator with alarm. The airplane was climbing at a terrifying rate, 3,500 feet per minute, and with less than 1,000 feet to their assigned altitude, he'd blow right through it! He pulled the throttles back hard and was thrown forward as the airplane slowed dramatically. He lowered the nose in response just as he would do in any other airplane, and the jet's climb instantly ceased.

Out of the corner of his eye, he saw Sam shake his head and felt his hand pushing the throttles back up, the jet accelerating. "No, no," he said. "Stay on profile. Keep the power up, reduce the rate of climb with pitch, accelerate to two hundred knots, and clean up. Once you're clean, set your rate of climb with pitch and maintain airspeed with power." He put his mic to his mouth and said, "Miami departure, Four-Papa-Alpha with you, climbing to two."

"Roger, Four-Papa-Alpha, Miami departure, sir, left turn heading three-six-zero, climb and maintain one-zero-thousand, crossing traffic at two o'clock and three thousand feet."

Sam replied to the clearance and pointed at the Eastern 727 above them and to the right. He reset the altitude alert to ten thousand.

Jack glanced up, saw the 727, and rolled into the turn. He trimmed the nose down into the increasing airspeed. At two hundred knots, he called, "Flaps up. Climb power."

Bobby set the throttles, and Jack rolled out on the north heading. It was the first time since releasing the brakes that Jack felt caught up. Until now, he'd felt like he did as a kid when his crazy Irish uncle threw him atop a stallion bareback and slapped it on the ass. The horse reared and bolted, Jack clinging desperately to its mane, no more in control than a fly clinging to its back.

He took the opportunity to make inputs in pitch and roll to gain a better feel for the jet's response. Although the controls were much heavier than anything he'd ever flown before, he secretly smiled at the smoothness, stability, and precision they provided. It would take far longer to get a handle on the DC-8 than he'd ever imagined, but he'd relish every minute of it.

It was only then in the midst of things settling down that he realized how noisy the cockpit had become. It was much louder than he remembered from the maintenance flight. He looked about the panel, puzzled. There were no warning lights; there was nothing out of order. He looked across the cockpit at Sam, but Sam had his gaze fixed toward the west on the developed coast of Florida and the Everglades beyond it.

Sneaking a glance aft, Jack saw Bobby facing forward, his arms folded and an inscrutable grin on his face. Looking across at Sam again, Jack shouted artlessly, "I don't remember it being this noisy."

Sam turned around, smiled, and pointed at the gear handle.

"Ah, *SHIT!*" Jack hissed. Gesturing with his left hand, he said, "Positive rate. Gear up!"

Sam reached for the handle and pulled it up. Bobby let out a gale of laughter as the gear doors closed and the noise returned to normal. He put out his hand and said, "Ten bucks, kiddo. Cash; no credit."

"Fine," Jack grumbled, and he reached for his wallet.

As they climbed through eight thousand feet the controller said, "Douglas Four-Papa-Alpha, climb and maintain one-six thousand."

Sam replied and reset the altitude alert.

Leaving ten thousand feet, Jack trimmed the nose down and accelerated to three hundred knots, the normal climb speed at low altitude.

Beyond the windshield, they had a panoramic view of the Earth and sky, with the east coast of Florida stretched out below them and only a thin stratus deck above. Passing twelve thousand feet, the airplane climbed into the base of the clouds and then burst out the top, the cloud deck falling swiftly beneath them. Inside, only the hiss of the wind and whine of the engines disturbed the ethereal quality of the flight.

"Douglas Four-Papa-Alpha," the controller said, "climb and maintain Flight Level two-four-zero, and contact Miami Center now on 133.9."

Sam replied, reset the altitude alert, and checked in with the Miami Air Traffic Control Center. After clipping his mic, he returned the airport and departure charts he'd removed from his Jeppesen binder, snapped it closed, and returned it to his kitbag. He looked at Jack and said, "You've got that Mona Lisa smile."

"I'm sure I do," Jack admitted. "Do you ever grow out of it?"

"No … you don't," Sam said. "Once bewitched by a jet, you're hooked."

Bobby leaned forward and tapped Sam's arm. "We've just got a low oil pressure light on number three."

Sam's grin vanished, and he turned to look at the bright yellow light on Bobby's panel and then the engine gauges too. His eyes narrowed as he studied them. "Thirty psi and the temperature and quantity are good," he said. "Probably just the light, huh?"

Bobby agreed and said, "I'll keep an eye on it. If it's anything more, we'll know soon enough."

"Right. But if we have to shut it down anytime soon, we're headed back." Then looking at Jack, Sam said, "Monitor ATC, and I'll try and get hold of the other guys, let them know what's going on."

Sam turned on his overhead speaker, set the volume control, and picked up his mic. "Douglas Eight-One-Six-Papa-Alpha, this is Four-Papa-Alpha, over."

After waiting a moment and getting no reply, he tried again. "Eight-One-Six-Papa-Alpha, this is Four-Papa-Alpha, you up, Mick?"

There was no response. Sam clipped his mic and said, "They're probably not off yet. We'll try again in a little while."

Ten minutes later, Jack leveled the airplane at thirty-seven thousand feet and Sam showed him how to engage the autopilot, turn on the altitude hold, and use the manual control knob. They were flying the high-altitude route to the Carolina Beach NDB, but the autopilot didn't have the capability to track non-directional radio beacons automatically, so the course had to be maintained by hand steering the airplane with or without the autopilot. Hand flying was much more fatiguing, so the autopilot was always the preferred choice.

In cruise flight, the cockpit crew's workload was significantly reduced. Their primary tasks involved monitoring the airplane's navigation, flight and systems performance, and fuel consumption. Other than routine frequency changes as they traversed the boundaries of air traffic control centers, they were able to devote a portion of their time to Jack's training.

After critiquing his performance during the takeoff and initial climb and offering techniques and suggestions on how to improve, Sam began to review the long-range navigation and overwater communication procedures they would be using during the flight across the Atlantic later that evening.

Discussing the Loran unit on the pedestal panel, Sam explained that it received long-range, low-frequency radio signals from ground-based stations positioned around the Atlantic coastlines east and west. The signals the Loran received were indicated as waves on a small oscilloscope on the Loran's control panel. By aligning the two electronic waves on the screen, the pilots could determine the airplane's position by reading the time-differential numbers on the dials and matching those numbers to the corresponding numbered lines on a chart. The airplane's position was where the two lines on the chart intersected. Although the Loran system enabled the pilots to determine the airplane's position with reasonable accuracy, it did not have the means to plot or display a track from one fix to the next. For that purpose, two Doppler computer systems were installed.

The Doppler determined drift, groundspeed, and distance along the specific track that the pilots had programmed in the device. By coupling the Doppler to the autopilot via its NAV function, the autopilot flew the desired track. An odometer on the Doppler counted down the miles to the next fix and indicated the miles to go with three drums: hundreds, tens, and ones.

Sam then explained how the two independent Dopplers and one Loran were used together to fly an assigned track across the Atlantic. As the airplane approached a navigation fix, the pilots set the course and distance to the next fix in the Doppler. As the airplane flew along that course, the Doppler determined if the airplane was drifting left or right and signaled the autopilot to make corrections to bring the airplane back on track. When the distance in the Doppler odometer indicated zero, the airplane was at the fix and the pilots confirmed that position with the Loran. If the Loran indicated they were off course, the pilots adjusted the Doppler to correct the error for the next segment of the flight. Two Doppler computers were installed in the airplane so their performance could be compared continuously and any discrepancy resolved before the airplane had strayed too far from its course. Together, the Loran and Doppler systems satisfied the international minimum navigation performance standards requirement for a North Atlantic crossing at jet altitudes.

As Sam continued his instruction, Mick's voice came booming over the loudspeaker. "Eight-Oh-Four-Papa-Alpha, this is Eight-One-Six-Papa-Alpha, do you read?"

Sam grabbed his mic and replied, "Eight-Oh-Four-Papa-Alpha, we read you, Mick, go ahead."

"Hey, Sam, we just leveled off. How you guys doing?"

"We're eighty south of Carolina Beach and monitoring a low oil pressure light on number three. Looks like it's just a sensor because there's no other indication of a failure yet, but we'll need to keep an eye on it. How about you?"

"So far, no problems on our end. But listen, after looking at that line of weather bisecting the Tracks, we decided to skip the dogleg to Gander and go directly to Shannon. Looks like it could be a rough one between Gander and Shannon tonight."

"Yeah," Sam said. "We saw that too. But with the oil pressure issue, I'm glad we're sticking to the coast."

"Yeah, makes sense. Okay, Skip, if anything changes, give us a shout; we ought to be in range for at least a little longer."

"Will do, Mick. You guys have a safe trip, and unless that number three goes tits-up and leaves us stuck someplace, we'll see you in the morning. Figure we ought to get in about the same time you do, give or take a little."

"Roger that, Sam. You guys have a good one too, and we'll catch you up on the other side. Eight-One-Six-Papa-Alpha, out."

At 5:12 p.m. they were approaching Boston's airspace. Sam had an open plotting chart of the North Atlantic spread out between them and was briefing Jack on the use of high frequency radios for long-distance position reporting over the Atlantic. After he finished with the communications procedures, he put away the chart, opened his Jeppesen manual, and explained the emergency procedures for leaving an assigned track over the North Atlantic. As Sam was talking, Bobby leaned forward, tapped him on the bicep, and pointed to the Doppler's amber SENSITIVITY light illuminated on the panel.

"It came on a moment ago," Bobby said.

Sam grimaced and reached for the offending unit. He switched it from ON to STANDBY.

The radio crackled. "Douglas Four-Papa-Alpha, contact Boston Center now on 128.5."

Sam replied, switched frequencies, and checked in with Boston. When he was done, he looked at Bobby and said, "Reset the breaker. Maybe that'll fix it."

Bobby found the circuit breaker for the Doppler unit and pulled it out. After waiting a couple of minutes, he reset it.

Sam switched the Doppler back on, and the SENSITIVITY light illuminated again.

"One more time?" Bobby asked, a brow raised.

Sam thought it over for a moment and shook his head. "Nah ... screw it," he said. "We'll replace it with a spare when we get to Gander."

Bobby's face fell.

Sam gave him a sharp look and said, "What?" Then it dawned on him, and with his brows raised, he said, "Oh ... oh, shit. Don't tell me—"

"No can do, GI."

"And why the hell not?"

"Because all the spare electronics are on Mick's airplane."

Sam's face turned crimson. "*All* of them?" he snapped. "Are you serious?"

Bobby shrugged. "It was Stone's decision. He said with all the trouble this airplane's been having, he wanted everything loaded on the other two in case we didn't make it over there on time."

"Ah, for Christ's sake, Bobby! And you didn't call him on that?"

Bobby threw up his hands. "Hey," he said. "I told Gerhard I didn't agree with it, but he told me to take it up with Brad."

"And you did—of course."

Bobby looked at him like he was nuts. "Stone? *Fuck* him!" he blustered.

"Ah, *shit*, Bobby. For God's sake!"

"So, call Mick back and ask him to divert to Gander."

Sam winced. "No. I'm not doing that ... Screw it. We'll pull and reset the box when we get in and hope that does the trick. If not, we'll pray for good Loran coverage and get by with the one Doppler that's operating. I'm not dragging the entire crew to Gander just for this."

"Works for me," Bobby agreed. He gave Jack's shoulder a push. "What say you?"

Jack shrugged. "I'm with you guys," he said boldly. "Sounds like a plan to me."

With the matter of the Doppler settled, Sam returned to briefing Jack. Twenty minutes later, ATC called and said, "Douglas Four-Papa-Alpha, descend and maintain Flight Level 350 and fly a heading three-zero-zero for traffic at one o'clock."

Sam pointed to the contrail coming their way, read back the clearance, and reset the altitude alert.

Jack turned off the autopilot's altitude hold and eased the nose down with the manual control knob to begin the descent.

At 5:56 p.m. with the airplane level at thirty-five thousand feet, Boston Center called and said, "Four-Papa-Alpha, cleared direct Yarmouth and contact Moncton Center now on 127.2."

# THIRTY-FIVE

*The sky over Cabot Straight, October 26, 1978*

They were 160 miles southwest of Gander when Moncton Center called and cleared them to begin a descent to ten thousand feet when ready. Sam replied to the clearance, and reset the altitude alert, and Jack calculated a descent point.

Bobby put the frequency for the Automatic Terminal Information Service in the number two radio and copied the Gander weather and runway in use on a landing data card. After calculating the airplane's landing weight, he determined the flap extension and final approach speeds, wrote them on the card, and then pivoted in his seat and handed it to Sam.

As Sam tuned up the map light over his head and studied the card, Bobby studied him with a wary gaze. "Tough break," he said with a leading inflection. "All the way up here for nothing."

Sam made a face, shrugged, and tossed the card on top of the radar screen. "The wind's 240 degrees at 19 gusting to 25," he said to Jack. "They're doing visuals to three-one, the ILS is out of service. Runway two-two is closed for maintenance."

Jack turned up his map light and studied the Jeppesen airport diagram clipped to his yoke. Runway numbers conformed to the magnetic heading of the runway, so Runway 31 pointed in the direction of 310 degrees, 70 degrees to the right of the wind direction. That meant there would be a strong and gusty crosswind for the landing. Feeling let down—but relieved—he looked across at Sam and said, "So, this one will be yours then?"

Sam raised a brow. "No. Why?" he asked. "You don't feel up to it?"

Jack looked surprised. "What? *No!*" he said emphatically. "Yes, I want it. I just didn't think—"

Bobby had been listening to the conversation with his head between them, and his jaw dropped. He looked at Sam and deadpanned, "Tell me you're kidding."

"Do I look like I am?" Sam replied irritably.

"Ah, c'mon, Sam! An eight-thousand-foot runway with a blackhole approach, a gusty crosswind, and his first landing in this thing? Are you nuts?"

Jack knew that by *blackhole approach*, Bobby was referring to a landing at night on a runway without any electronic guidance or nearby visual features for depth perception. It would be akin to landing on the ocean at night, with only a tiny rectangle of white lights to determine the airplane's height and distance from an ink-black surface.

Sam turned up his map light again and took another glimpse at the airport diagram. "Actually, it's closer to nine thousand feet," he said. He dimmed the light.

"Ah, bullshit," Bobby protested. "If he panics and jumps on those binders before the anti-skid spools up, he'll blow a tire and we'll be here all fuckin' night swapping it out with a spare. Why can't we wait for better conditions?"

Jack said, "Hey, Sam … look. I mean, if you want to take it, I certainly understand."

Sam shook his head. "No. The landing's yours," he said with finality. "We came up here to get it done, and we're getting it done. Now go ahead and brief it."

Bobby scowled, rolled his eyes, and turned his seat to face his panel.

With an equal mix of eager anticipation and dread, Jack turned up his map light and studied the airport diagram. Given the night, the crosswind, and the turbulence, the landing would severely test his inchoate skill with the DC-8.

He cleared his throat and began the briefing: "This will be a visual approach to Runway 31 at Gander," he said. "The airport elevation is 496 feet, and the highest obstacle in the area is 1,000 feet, ten miles southwest of the airfield. The runway length is 8,900 feet. If we have to go-around,

I'll fly runway heading and follow the tower's instructions." He looked across at Sam. "Anything else?"

Sam shook his head, and pointing at the DME indicator, he said, "No, but we're coming up on 120 miles; it's time to start down."

Jack nodded, reached for the autopilot controls, and flipped the switch. "Autopilot's off," he announced. He tickled the stab trim forward and eased the airplane into a hand-flown descent.

Sam advised Moncton Center that they had begun their descent and then reached for the landing data card. He turned up his map light and, reading aloud from the card, called out the speeds for the flap settings, V-ref, and go-around EPRs for the engines. As he called them out, Sam and Jack set the bugs marking them on their airspeed indicators and the engine gauges.

When they were finished, Bobby said, "Descent Check: cabin signs?"

"On," Sam said, glancing up at the switch.

"Windshield heat?"

"On."

"Anti-fogging?"

"Not required."

"N1 bugs?"

"One point nine eight for the go-around ... set and checked," Sam said, pointing to the gauges.

"Airspeed bugs?"

"Set, checked ... both sides."

"Set and checked," Jack followed.

"Radio instrument switches?"

"Radio ... twice," Sam said, glancing at his and Jack's panels.

"Crash-net and galley secured," Bobby said. "Descent Check complete."

A crescent moon glimmered across the lakes and bays of the Newfoundland landscape, and only a few pale clouds dotted the cold, crystalline sky. The air was smooth, and the airplane stable as they descended through eighteen thousand feet.

Sam called out, "Transition altitude," and both Jack and Sam reset their altimeters from 29.92 to the airfield pressure of 30.12. Sam reached across his shoulder for his harness straps and buckled them to his seatbelt. Jack did the same.

Approaching ten thousand feet, Moncton Air Traffic Control called and handed them off to Gander Approach. Sam switched frequencies and checked in. "Gander, Douglas Four-Papa-Alpha with you out of eleven for ten, Information Oscar."

"Roger, Four-Papa-Alpha, Information Oscar is current, Altimeter 30.12. You're cleared to descend to six thousand feet and right turn now heading one-one-zero for vectors for a visual approach to runway three-one."

Jack pulled the throttles to idle, slowed the airplane to 250 knots, and continued the descent. But while passing through seven thousand feet, a sharp jolt of turbulence slammed the jet, and the further they descended, the worse and more constant the turbulence became. The cockpit furnishings creaked against the strain, and the crew were thrown into their seats or against their seatbelts. Cold coffee sloshed about in their Styrofoam cups. Bobby took them and tossed them into a plastic-lined trash bag beneath the forward jumpseat. "Approach check: altimeters?" he said loudly.

"30.12. Set and crosschecked," Sam replied.

"Set and crosschecked," Jack followed.

"Thrust reverse hydraulic shutoff?"

"Open and checked," Sam answered.

"Ignition override?"

"All engines."

"Fuel panel, set ... approach Check complete," Bobby announced.

As they approached six thousand feet, Jack leveled off, but he was too late in reducing the descent rate, and they busted through the altitude by two hundred feet. Jack corrected, overshot it going high, and then felt Sam prompting him on the controls.

"Lead more," Sam instructed calmly. "One hundred twenty tons of swept-wing jet is a *lot* more than anything you've ever flown before, so anticipate and stay ahead of it." With his hands beneath Jack's on the throttles, Sam pushed them forward. "Come in earlier on the power too," he suggested. "Lead by fifteen knots on the airspeed and one hundred feet on the altitude. As you get a better feel for the airplane, you'll tighten that up, but for now, that's a good place to start."

Jack nodded.

The radio crackled. "Douglas Four-Papa-Alpha, the airport now at eleven o'clock and two-zero miles, descend and maintain four thousand feet."

Sam replied and reset the altitude alert.

Jack drew the throttles to idle and began to descend and slow to two hundredknots. As he approached four thousand feet, he increased pitch and advanced the power to twenty-five hundred pounds on the fuel flow indicators as Sam had instructed in the simulator. The airspeed came steady at two hundred knots and the altitude level at four thousand feet.

"There. Like that," said Sam. "Nailed it, see?"

Jack smiled. It felt good to do well. His pride bristled whenever Sam needed to correct him.

"Douglas Four-Papa-Alpha, heading zero-six-zero degrees," the controller said. "The airport's now ten o'clock and one-five miles, sir. Call it in sight."

Sam searched ahead for the airport, spotted the green and white flashing beacon at the left side of his windshield, and pointing to it, he said, "There it is."

Jack looked at where Sam was pointing and saw the beacon too. It was isolated in a large area of black, with no lights or distinguishing features anywhere near it. The runway itself was not in sight. "Got it," he acknowledged.

"Douglas Four-Papa-Alpha, turn left heading now three-six-zero."

"Three-six-zero, Four-Papa-Alpha," Sam replied. Looking toward the airfield and relying on his previous experience flying into Gander, he told

Jack, "He's bringing you in a little tight." Gesturing with his right hand, he said, "I'll call the visual. Meantime go ahead and widen the base a bit to give yourself some more room. That southwest wind is howling up here, and you'll need a wider turn to final or you'll blow right through it."

"I still don't see the runway," Jack warned. "I'll slow down. Flaps 10."

Sam set the flap handle, and it clicked into place. "Good call," he said. The airplane slowed to 160 knots. "Flaps 20," Jack said.

Watching the airport beacon passing quickly from right to left across the windshield, Sam lifted his mic and said, "Four-Papa-Alpha, airport's in sight, request visual for three-one and have the tower turn up the runway lights, please."

"Roger, Four-Papa-Alpha, the airport ten o'clock and thirteen miles, you're number one, sir. Cleared visual approach Runway 31, contact tower now on 118.1 and advise them of your request."

"Descend to three and cleared the visual," Sam said. "Tower 118.1."

Sam switched radios and said, "Gander, Four-Papa-Alpha with you on a modified left base for three-one. Turn the lights up, please."

"Roger, Four-Papa-Alpha, you're in sight, sir. Cleared to land Runway 31, wind 240 variable 260 at 18 gusting to 23. Here come the lights."

"Cleared to land," Sam said. He turned on all the airplane's landing lights.

The runway lights suddenly flared brilliantly. They were in the middle of a large ink-black area southeast of the beacon and terminal lights. From their distance, the nine-thousand-foot runway appeared only a short, thin rectangle. It seemed like an impossibly small target from the perspective of the cockpit. The airplane was bouncing and weaving in the rough air. Jack's gut tightened. His pulse was racing.

Watching the runway approach, Sam said, "We're still too tight … Let's continue to configure. Ready for this?" he asked, reaching for the gear handle.

Gesturing with his left hand, Jack said, "Gear down."

Sam put the handle down. The gear doors opened with a loud blast of wind noise, and the nose gear thumped into place.

"Final Check: gear?" Bobby yelled.

Pointing to the lights above the gear handle, Sam said, "Down; three green." He shifted his gaze back to the runway. "Okay, here it comes," he warned, referring to the final approach course.

Jack rolled the airplane aggressively to intercept the extended centerline. "Flaps 30," he said.

Sam lifted the flap handle and put it in place.

The drag came on fast. Jack advanced the throttles as the airplane slowed and he tightened the turn to final.

Sam prompted Jack to use more power. "Three thousand pounds across the board now," he advised, referring to the four fuel flow indicators. He lifted his mic and said, "Four-Papa-Alpha, runway in sight, sir. You can lower the lights and thanks for the help." Turning the lights up was useful at night for locating the runway at a distance in clear weather, but once on final, they were too bright for landing.

"Roger, sir, they're coming down and you're cleared to land. Wind now 230 variable 260 at nineteen, gust to twenty-six."

Jack lined the airplane up on final. The runway was at an oblique right angle in the windshield as he crabbed into the crosswind to maintain their track across the ground. Added to the unsettling sight picture were the gusts that caused the airplane to balloon above or fall below the glide path. Jack could see this happening when the runway lights moved below the nose, indicating they were too high, or rose above it, indicating they were too low. He jockeyed the pitch, power, and heading to stay on glide path, on speed, and on track as they descended.

"Good, looking good now," Sam said. "On glide path, Ref plus 30. Pull it back a bit ... Plus 20 is plenty."

Descending through two thousand feet, there was another hard jolt and the left wing dropped sharply. Jack countered with right aileron and rudder and the left wing rose, but the nose swung left. Jack rolled in with left aileron and rudder, to counter it as he would in any airplane, but then the right wing rose and the nose swung right. His eyes widened and his pulse quickened. He was losing control! He rolled left aileron to correct it and—

"No, no, no!" Sam interjected. Prompting him with the yoke, he said, "You're overcontrolling; you're setting up a pilot-induced oscillation. Make smaller corrections, and remember, swept wing airplanes are subject to Dutch roll. The yaw damper's worthless if you're overriding it with the rudder. Like we did in the simulator, give her the reins, keep off the rudder, and let the yaw damper do its job."

*Simulator, my ass*, Jack thought. The simulator was a device, insentient and bloodless as a brick, but the airplane was a dragon. The jets were its fire, the turbulence the beat of its wings, the persistent bobbing and weaving of its giant head its menace. He straightened in his seat and set his jaw, his eyes shifting quickly between the night-black runway and his instruments. His concentration hadn't been this intense since racing the Suzuki at Bridgehampton—but the stakes now were much higher.

They were descending through 1,500 feet. "Flaps ... wing slots?" Bobby challenged.

"Set; 30, light out," Sam said, touching the handle and pointing to the flap gauge.

"Final Check's complete. Oil pressure on number three's still holding."

Sam gave him a thumbs-up but kept his eyes on the runway coming up fast. He sat up and guarded the controls. Without shifting his gaze, he instructed Jack, "As you begin your flare, take out the crab with a forward slip same as you did in the DC-3. Once she's lined up on the centerline, begin the power reduction but *nice and easy*. That slip will create a lot of drag—much more than you're used to. Pull off the power too fast and she'll drop out from underneath us like a load of bricks."

"Got it," Jack said with a nod, although he was irritated by the instruction. He needed Sam to shut up and let him get on with it. He'd get this; he had this. It was just a matter of feel, just a matter of getting it and doing it—and he was doing it, goddamn it!

"Oh, and one last thing," Sam added.

Jack shot him a pained look.

"Stay off the brakes until I call one hundred knots, understand?"

Jack groaned. "Sure. Got it."

Bobby leaned forward and drilled a finger into his shoulder. "Say it, goddamn it," he snarled into his ear. "I want to hear you *say* it!"

Jack yanked his shoulder away. "Yeah, got it, Bobby! *BACK OFF!*" he barked.

Bobby huffed, shot Sam a flinty glance, and sat back with his arms folded. The runway was one mile ahead, the airplane bouncing hard and angled into the wind. Thirty seconds later, it crossed the threshold, the huge numbers 3 1 glistening in its landing lights.

Jack pressed the right rudder, rolled in left aileron, and drew back on the yoke to begin his flare but the airplane—the dragon—paid no heed. It barreled toward the runway as if it had a mind of its own. Jack's ass tightened reactively against the impact, but just before they hit, the airplane leveled off in a gust of wind and sailed over the surface like a windblown leaf. The runway lights streamed past them at an alarming speed, and the red end lights beckoned ahead. *Go-around … go-around!* his pilot's brain screamed, and he started to push up the throttles. But then, in that same instant, the gust suddenly subsided, the airplane stabilized, and the sight picture was perfect.

As the last of the threshold markings raced beneath them, Jack eased the throttles closed and the DC-8 settled gently toward the runway. With the nosewheel above the centerline, the tires of the left main bogie slid slickly on the pavement. An instant later, the tires of the right main bogie were rolling along the runway too, and with a whine and a *thunk*, the spoiler handle flew back and hit its stop. The main gear struts compressed heavily, and the airplane squatted on the ground.

Jack continued fighting to stay on the centerline. As he eased the nosewheel to the pavement, he felt Sam take hold of his left hand and direct it to the reverse levers on the forward end of the throttles. Jack pulled them up sharply and the engines thundered as the airplane slowed.

"Hundred knots," Sam said over the roar.

Jack moved his feet up on the rudder pedals and began gently applying the brakes.

"Eighty knots," Sam announced. He forced Jack's hand down on the reverse levers. The clamshell doors behind the engines closed, and the cockpit was quieted.

"Sixty knots," Sam said. "Okay, I've got the airplane."

Jack relinquished the controls and fell back in his seat like a sack of seeds. He blew out his cheeks as Sam took control of the brakes and steering tiller to steer the airplane by the nosewheel alone.

"Four-Papa-Alpha, taxi via Bravo. Contact ground control now on 121.9," the tower controller said.

The only thing Jack heard was his pulse thumping in his ears. He wiped his sweaty palms on his slacks, his hands quivering.

"Four-Papa-Alpha, do you copy?"

"Yeah, tell him we're turning off here," Sam said.

Jack fumbled for his mic and switched frequencies. "Ground, Douglas Four-Papa-Alpha clear on Bravo," he said.

"Roger, Four-Papa-Alpha, taxi via Bravo to the ramp."

"Taxi via Bravo, Four-Papa-Alpha."

Sam cleared the runway, taxied a short distance, and brought the airplane to a stop. He parked the brakes, reached for the flap lever, and moved it to the up position.

Jack looked at him, puzzled, and said, "He cleared us all the way in."

Sam ignored him and looked at Bobby. "So, what do you think of *that*, you ol' cuss?" he asked. "What do you have to say now?"

Bobby made a face. "I'd say, the After Landing Check's complete," he grumbled.

Sam gave him a slap on the arm. "C'mon, you son-of-a-bitch, admit it," he said with a wry grin. "Admit it … and give Jack his ten bucks back."

"Ah, for crissake," Bobby growled. He looked at Jack, grabbed and shook his shoulder roughly, and said, "Good job. In the zone, slick as a baby's ass, and—most importantly—all our tires intact … *But*—a bet's a bet."

"And worth every penny." Jack sighed. "Phew."

# THIRTY-SIX

*Gander, Newfoundland, October 26, 1978*

S am aligned the DC-8 with a parking spot on the ramp, and a ground man marshaled him to a stop. As Sam set the brakes, the airplane was connected to electric and air carts. Sam shut down the engines and called for the parking checklist.

When the checklist was complete, Bobby got up from his seat and opened the forward entry door. Backlit by the glare of the ramp lights, a Canadian customs officer entered the cabin with a cold blast of maritime air. He was in a blue overcoat and cap and shouted to be heard above the noise of the wind and equipment outside. "Evening," he said with vapored breath. "Welcome to Gander, *eh!*"

Bobby stepped back as the officer entered, winced at the cold, and handed him an envelope with their paperwork and passports. The officer tucked it under his arm and poked his head into the cockpit. Smiling broadly, he said, "Evening, Captain. The station agent's office is to your right as you enter the terminal. The Flight Service Station is down the hall to the left."

Sam returned his smile and said, "Yes, sir, thank you."

The officer went to the galley to process their paperwork, and Jack looked across at Sam. "That's the most cheerful customs guy I've ever met," he chuckled.

"Yeah. I wish more of them would move to Miami."

The officer returned from the galley, handed Sam the envelope, and bid them goodnight and a safe flight.

Bobby pulled a flight jacket out of his suitcase to do the walkaround, and Sam pulled one out of his as well. Jack put on a light sweatshirt he'd bought in Miami, the only warm garment he'd brought with him for the hajj.

Sam and Jack ramped down the stairs with their kitbags. Sam gave him a sideways glance and asked loudly, "Is that all you brought for the cold?"

Jack's shoulders and face were scrunched against the chilly wind. "I figured we were headed to the tropics," he replied. "Never occurred to me I might need something more." He looked about the ramp and said, "Looks like we're the only ones here."

Sam glanced around, too, and said, "Back in the piston engine days, this place was the launchpad for the North Atlantic. Nowadays, if we hadn't wanted to stay along the coast and get you another landing, we wouldn't have stopped here either."

They entered the terminal through a small vestibule. Inside the building, the enameled block walls and the tiled floors reminded Jack of the Air Logistics office, his college dormitory, and his Army barracks at Fort Myer, Virginia. There was a plastic scent of paint, and the click of their heels echoed as they walked down the hall. They passed the station agent's office, a large wire glass window exposing the agent at his desk, dressed in a flannel shirt and cardigan even though the heat in the building was stifling as the steam radiators pumped it out at full tilt. Jack got the sense they were either on or off, and off was not an option after September.

"We'll take care of our flight planning first," Sam said, "then stop back here on the way out to pay the landing and parking fees, and order fuel."

The Flight Service Station was also behind a large wire glass window, and when Sam opened the door, they were greeted by the loud clatter of teletype machines and the peal of a telephone. The room had the tattered patina of a WWII squadron office, the walls covered in huge maps of eastern Canada, the North Atlantic, and Western Europe. Pale blue delineated the oceans and bays, dun and green the land areas, and white the Arctic regions. The principal airways—denoted in magenta—crisscrossed the charts, and a large compass rose in blue was aligned with magnetic north. On the wall to the right were the weather maps: the 500, 300, and 200 millibar charts, the winds aloft, and the surface and significant weather depictions for the high seas. Below the weather charts, long sheets of yellow telex paper hung on clipboards below signs that indicated their purpose: the TAFs or METARs, which reported the current and forecast weather for hundreds of airfields around the North Atlantic, as well as the SIGMETs, AIRMETs, and NOTAMs that pilots needed for flight planning.

With a half-dozen teletypes clicking madly and the pealing phone, the atmosphere was charged with an air of urgency and high adventure. Jack felt a secret thrill. Soon, he'd be traversing the Atlantic as a copilot in a DC-8. Coupled with his successful first takeoff and superb landing in challenging conditions, his spirits were soaring.

A heavyset man in a flannel shirt, suspenders, and khakis was on the phone and bent over his desk with the receiver wedged between his cheek and shoulder. He was reading aloud from a clipboard as Sam and Jack entered the room. He looked up and threw them a wave, then returned to his call. When he finished, he hung up the phone and came over to the counter where Sam and Jack were waiting. They were looking across the room at the weather charts posted on the opposite wall. "Evening, gents," the briefer said cheerfully. "You fellas bring in that diesel-eight?"

"That's us," Sam said with a smile.

"So, where you headed?"

"Shannon," Sam said. "Just a quick turnaround here; fuel up and go." Then, pointing at the North Atlantic surface depiction posted on the wall to his right, his eyes narrowed and he asked, "That low still deepening?"

The briefer turned to look at the chart. "Yes," he said, "and right across the tracks tonight. She's a monster, *eh?* Been buggering us for the last two days, but it's finally on the move. No way to get around it on the tracks tonight though, I'm afraid."

Sam nodded and continued to study the chart.

"I'll put together an eastbound folder for you, Captain," the briefer said. "Back in a moment."

Sam smiled and said, "That'd be great. Thanks."

The briefer walked toward his desk, and Sam said to Jack, "How about some coffee?"

"Sure."

Sam pulled some change from his pocket and said, "I buy; you fly?"

"Sure."

"There's an iron kitchen down the hall to the right. It's all they've got here, but it'll do."

"Black or cream?"

"Straight up," Sam replied.

By the time Jack returned with two steaming cups of coffee, Sam had the airplane's performance manual and other tools they'd need for flight planning laid out on the counter.

Jack handed him a cup of black and said, "I was wondering about dispatch. How do we get around not having a dispatch office? Don't we need one according to the FARs?"

Sam nodded, took a sip of coffee, and set his cup on the counter. Reaching for his airway manual, he opened it to a cardstock page behind a divider. Rotating the manual for Jack to see, Sam pointed to it and said, "We use these guys, International Air Services in Chicago. But we only do that when we're flying revenue and are required to have flight following. Ferrying under FAR Part 91, we save the expense and do it without it."

Jack took a sip and studied the page. At the top was the company's name and phone number and, beneath that, a Mercator projection of the globe with HF radio frequencies according to the geographical region.

Sam closed the binder as the briefer returned with an international document folder he'd prepared for them. He put the folder on the counter, opened it, and pulled out a copy of the surface weather depiction. "Here's that trough," the briefer said. "It's centered about 55 north, 35 west." Tracing the frontal boundaries with his finger, he indicated a warm front running east toward the Hebrides, and a cold front extending south into the mid-Atlantic.

As Sam looked it over, the briefer sifted through long sheets of teletype reports and located the Terminal Aerodrome Forecast for Shannon. He underlined it and passed it to Sam. The report read:

EINN 211615Z 0000 21010KTS 2000 –SH BKN020 OVC030 PROB 40 0715
V21035015KT 0300 RABR.

The briefer found the TAFs for Dublin, Ireland, and Manchester, England, and underlined them too. As he passed the sheet of paper to Sam, he said, "Dublin's marginal as an alternate, but Manchester's reliable if Shannon and Dublin go below minimums." Finding the TAF for Keflavik, Iceland, he underlined it and said, "Keflavik will be deteriorating as the low moves north and east, so if you need a good emergency alternate en route, then Gander or Goose Bay, Labrador, are better choices."

Sam studied the reports and then handed them to Jack.

"And where are the tracks relative to the weather?" Sam asked.

The briefer turned and went to his desk. He came back with a clear plastic sheet and laid it atop the surface depiction. The North Atlantic Tracks changed every night in accordance with the wind and weather conditions, and the briefer had grease-penciled that night's tracks onto the plastic sheet. When he overlaid the sheet on the weather chart, it was easy to see the tracks in relation to the low and its fronts.

A phone on the briefer's desk began to ring. "Let me take that while you're busy with this," he said.

Sam nodded and, without looking up, said, "Sure. Go ahead."

Speaking to Jack, Sam pointed at the track furthest south and said, "This one designated Whiskey looks best, but none of them are ideal." He pushed the weather depiction and track displays aside and reached for the stack of papers in the document folder. Sam found the 250-millibar winds aloft chart and pulled it from the cluster of other pages. He studied the isobars with an unquiet gaze and began tapping his finger on a sharp bend in the jet stream that bisected their route.

He started to say something to Jack about it when the briefer called out and interrupted him. Seated in his chair, his right hand cupped over the phone, the briefer said, "Captain, I've got the Coast Guard on the line here. They're running down an emergency locator signal and need a briefing. If you fellas have what you need for now, I'll—"

Sam waved him off. "Yeah, yeah, go ahead," he said. "Take care of them. We're all set."

The briefer threw him a wave and continued with his call.

Sam took the last sip of coffee, winced at the bitterness, and tossed the cup in the trash. He turned his back to the counter and folded his arms. While staring at the floor, he said, "Okay, look … while he's busy, there's something we need to talk about."

Jack's brow was knitted. "What's that?" he asked.

"We're not legal for the North Atlantic Tracks unless Bobby can get that other Doppler working."

"What are the odds he does?"

Sam gave him a sideways glance and answered with a shrug.

"But you said we could go with just one Doppler. You said that would be our Plan B."

"I said we could do that if the weather cooperated—but clearly, it's not. Beyond that, what I didn't tell you is that we're only legal to fly the tracks with one Doppler if the other one fails *after* the coast-out point, not before it. Additionally, we're only legal to do that if we're assured of Loran reception for the entire distance across the tracks. Lightning interferes with Loran reception, and from the looks of that surface depiction, there'll be a lot of lightning along that cold front tonight."

Jack paused to give it a thought and then asked, "What about getting the Doppler repaired here, or waiting for the weather to improve?"

"There's no time for either. Even if there's a radio shop on the airfield,

I don't want to mention the problem unless we're certain they can fix it quickly, and that's not assured. It's not worth the risk. Besides, once we get across the pond, we won't need a second Doppler again until we come home. As for the weather? You heard what the briefer said. That low's making a slow crawl east, and it could be days waiting for it to clear. The problem is we need two airplanes in Indonesia to begin the hajj by Monday morning, and we'll need all three in Colombo to ensure at least two are up and ready for service. Besides all that, we have other options. They're just not very good."

"What are those?"

Sam turned around and opened the North Atlantic Plotting Chart he'd taken from his kitbag. He spread it flat on the counter. "There are three ways of getting across the North Atlantic and avoiding the tracks, and I'll trace them from best to worst," he said. Using his finger to indicate the other flight paths, he explained, "The first choice would be to fly beneath the tracks at 29,000 feet or lower; the second choice would be to fly the old Blue Spruce Route here." He indicated a course that connected Gander, Greenland, Iceland, and Ireland. "The third choice is flying a course well south of the tracks here."

Jack shrugged. "They all look good to me," he said matter-of-factly.

"But in fact, they're not," Sam corrected him. "Although flying beneath the tracks would normally be the best option, that won't work tonight because of the weather. Any altitude below 29,000 feet will put us in the thick of it for turbulence and ice and lock us down there for the full distance across the pond. And while flying north or south around the tracks is a possibility, both routes will greatly extend our flight time and distance from a good alternate. Given that oil pressure warning on number three and the lousy forecast for Keflavik, neither of those are good options either."

Jack looked puzzled and said, "Okay, so what's the plan?"

Sam eyed him warily and said, "I'm leaving that choice to you: we can fly the tracks with one Doppler and hope for the best regarding Loran reception, or … you can jump ship and go home. I'll get Gerhard up here tomorrow to complete the flight to Colombo. At most, that would delay us a day, and while I'd like to avoid that, it's better than any other alternative."

Jack recoiled. He looked at Sam like he was nuts. "*What?*" he exclaimed. "*Quit?* Go home? Sam … are you serious? Why would I do that?"

"To avoid ruining your chances for Air Logistics if we get violated for a gross navigation error."

Jack looked vexed. "A what?" he asked. "Gross navigation error? I've never heard of that before."

"That's because you haven't flown the North Atlantic Track system. The tracks are unique. They have their own special rules called the North Atlantic Minimum Navigation Standards, or MNPS for short. The high density of traffic across the tracks and the lack of a means for monitoring their separation requires that every flight navigate with greater than usual precision. Any deviation from course by more than twenty-five miles results in a violation for the crew. Typically, when a deviation does occur, the crew is not aware of it until their flight is picked up on radar at the coast-in point—and by then it's too late to correct it. And don't forget: there are 1,800 miles of open ocean between Gander and the Irish coast. By navigating the track we're assigned with only one Doppler and no Loran, it'll take a lot more than an E6-B and a wind forecast to hit a twenty-five mile target accurately at the other end. My point is that there's no room for error, Jack, and I want you to be aware of that in making your decision about continuing on tonight."

Jack acknowledged what Sam had told him with a nod and then fixed his gaze across the room as he made a decision. Sam was right. A violation of that order would wreck any hope of securing a career with a reputable airline. Kegan had warned him to "fly safe," a pilot's euphemism for "don't fuck up." On the other hand, what hope did he have of a reputable airline, anyway? At least at Jetstream, Jack had a good job flying for an international airline operating heavy jets and for industry-competitive pay. Leave Jetstream now and Jack may never find anything else to replace it.

A teletype began to clatter loudly, and the briefer got up to read the message. As he walked to the machine, he looked across the room at Sam and said, "Is everything okay, Captain? Do you need anything else?"

Sam gave him a desultory wave. "Nah. We're all set," he replied. "Thanks."

The briefer waved in return and continued toward the teletype.

Sam looked at Jack. "So, what's it going to be?" he asked. "Shannon or home?"

Jack blinked and turned to look at him.

Sam said, "If you choose to go home, I'll give you cash to cover the cost of your travel and pay you in full for what you've earned so far. After I speak to Gerhard, I'll call Jake, give you a rave review, and square it all with him. You'll go back with some DC-8 training and flight time, your license intact, and a great career in your future. There's no need to put that at risk, Jack, and this won't be the only time you do if you continue on with us. Take my advice and move on. I'd planned on telling you this when we got to Shannon anyway, but it makes even more sense now."

Jack made his decision. He cleared his throat and spoke deliberately. "I appreciate the advice and concern," he said. "But if you understood what drove me to Miami in the first place, Sam—the flight event that compelled me to make a move—you'd understand why I don't want to quit this without something better in hand. Believe me, I understand the risks because I had to risk even more flying freight in DC-3s on a nightly basis, and I did it for a fraction of the income and the quality of the job I've got here. So, all things considered, I choose to go to Shannon. You and the other guys had your reasons for making this company your home. Please respect my reasons for doing the same."

Sam had fixed his gaze on the plotting chart as he listened to what Jack was saying. He paused a moment longer, nodded, and then, with an exasperated flip of his hand, conceded, "Okay … Fine. Your life, your career—your call." He pointed to the ICAO flight plan form on the counter. "Pass that to me, and pray Bobby's got it fixed."

# THIRTY-SEVEN

*Gander, Newfoundland, October 26, 1978*

They stopped at the station agent's office to order fuel and pay the landing and service fees. Sam had calculated they'd need 104,000 pounds of fuel for the crossing with an abundant reserve for any weather deviations, diversions, or other problems they might encounter. The airplane burned 10 percent of any additional fuel it bore just carrying the additional weight of that fuel in flight, so Sam ordered enough to be conservative in his planning but no more.

As the agent reached for his radio and called the fueler, Sam opened the zipper on a leather clutch bag he'd been carrying. Jack eyed the bundle of cash inside and let out a low whistle.

"Ten thousand bucks in this," Sam revealed, "and another thirty thousand in my suitcase."

"Why so much cash?"

"Because nothing moves the mountain to Mohammed like greenbacks in the Middle East."

The agent came to the counter, and Sam handed him the company credit card he'd taken from the purse. When he returned, he gave Sam the card and receipt. Sam gave it a cursory glance and let out a quiet groan.

The agent reached below the counter and put two pizza boxes and a paper grocery bag on top. "Your flight engineer radioed and had me place the order," he said with a smile. "They just brought it over. Still nice and hot."

"How much?" Sam asked and opened the clutch.

"$23.50 Canadian," the agent said.

Sam handed him a US twenty and a ten. "Keep the change," he said.

He looked at Jack and explained, "Bobby makes sure we've got provisions on these trips ... and I make sure we've got antacids."

. . .

They scrunched their shoulders and leaned into the wind as they walked toward the airplane from the terminal. Sam led Jack up the mobile stairs and burst into the doorway. "Jesus, it's cold," he exclaimed. "Glad you got the heat up!" he said to Bobby, who was leaning against the bulkhead by the galley. He looked glum.

Sam's eyes narrowed. "What?" he asked.

"Don't get comfortable," Bobby grumbled. "There's something you need to see."

Sam recoiled. "What *now?*" he asked.

Bobby zippered his jacket and sunk his hands in his pockets. "C'mon," he said, passing by Sam toward the stairs.

Sam dropped his kitbag and followed him. Jack put the pizza boxes and grocery bag in the galley and watched them head out the door.

When they got to the ramp, Bobby led Sam to the number two engine, and grimacing, he pointed to fuel dripping from the engine's cowl. The drops that weren't sheared away by the wind formed a small puddle on the pavement.

Sam winced, hitched up his slacks, and squatted to get a better view. He checked his watch and timed the leak.

Standing up, he looked at Bobby and said, "Twenty-six drops per minute. *Goddamn* it, I thought that was fixed!"

"I opened it up for a look but couldn't find the source. Probably the same thing it was in Miami—but look, there's good news and bad news," he said. "The bad news is we've got a leak; the good news is that it's minor and it quits when I turn off the pumps, so it's easily isolated."

"But it was still leaking after we shut it down."

"I spotted it on the walk-around. I figured it had formed before the pressure bled off. I went back up, turned on the pumps, and came back down. It was dripping like it is now, so I left them on for you to see."

"Turn them off," said Sam. "I want to see how long it takes to stop."

Bobby jogged up the stairs. As he stepped inside the cockpit, Jack looked up at him from the copilot's seat. "What's going on?" he asked with a worried expression.

Bobby shook his head, switched off the pumps, and turned toward the stairs without saying anything.

Jack followed him to the forward entry door and watched from there, his shoulders scrunched, his hands buried in his pockets.

By the time Bobby returned to Sam's side, the leak had begun to subside. "See?" he said with a hopeful air. "Just like I said it would. We can isolate it if we have to."

Sam made a face. "So, that's your plan for isolating it—shutting down the pumps and killing the *engine*, Bobby? That's your plan?" Sam asked with a sharp incredulity.

Bobby looked at his feet and shrugged like a five-year-old caught with his hand in the cookie jar.

Sam smirked. "Right," he said with a sardonic grin. "And what about the Doppler? Any luck with that?"

"No. I reseated the boxes in the panel and radio compartment a couple of times, but the sensitivity light comes back on after a minute or two. It's shot. It needs to be replaced."

"*Shit,*" Sam hissed.

"Hey, it's not like we haven't seen worse," Bobby assured him. "We can work with it, Sam. No reason to get stuck here. We'll figure out a Plan B."

Sam rounded on him and pointed at Bobby's chest. "We're already *on* Plan B," he snapped. "The goddamn Doppler and that low oil pressure light on number three … *remember?*"

Bobby threw a dismissive wave. "So what?" he huffed. "There's nothing here we haven't dealt with before, and you know that."

"Captain!" a man shouted. They turned to see a guy rounding the nose cone. Backlit by the ramp lights, he was a silhouette in coveralls and a knit cap, his breath trailing him like a steam locomotive.

Sam pulled his hand from his jacket and raised it.

"Ah, Captain," the man said. "I'm the ramp chief. I just want to let you fellas know that we're about to have a shift change. Unless you plan on leaving soon, it could be a little while before we've got a crew together to get you going."

"Ah, for fuck-sakes," Bobby blurted. Looking at Sam, he snapped, "See what I mean about this fuckin' place? Goddamn it!"

Sam gave him sharp look, then turned toward the ramp supervisor. "Thanks, Chief," he said politely. "I appreciate the heads-up. Unfortunately, we've got a maintenance issue. If you can give us a few more minutes, I'll let you know, okay?"

"Sure, Captain, sure," he answered. With his thumb pointing over his shoulder at a white construction trailer across the ramp, he said, "I'll be in the line shack with the crew. Just give a knock if you decide to go, and we'll come right over."

Sam smiled. "Will do, and thanks, Chief … Great job. We appreciate it."

The chief threw him a wave and left.

Sam returned his hands to his pockets, turned his back on Bobby, and examined the puddle of fuel with a brooding gaze. It wasn't just the operational risks that weighed on his decision but the cost to everyone if the contracted lift was breached in any way. No pilgrim could be left behind. At a minimum, all three airplanes would be needed to succeed. Canceling and attempting the needed repairs in Gander could put everything in jeopardy. The pressure to continue despite the risks was manifold, but even that wasn't what he feared most. His greatest fear was Jack. He regretted taking him along.

He was still staring at the puddle blankly when Bobby shouted, "Sam!" from behind.

He didn't respond.

"SAM!" Bobby yelled.

Sam turned his head slowly. He looked at Bobby with that same sad gaze, the icy wind buffeting his slacks.

"*Jesus*," Bobby complained. "It's fuckin' freezin' out here. C'mon, let's go!"

Sam blinked and looked up at the airplane, where Jack was standing in the doorway watching them. Sam signaled him to come down.

Jack launched down the stairs. As he came close, Sam pointed to the puddle.

"I saw you guys looking at that," Jack said. "I thought they had it fixed."

"Well, obviously they didn't," Sam replied with a sarcastic edge in his tone.

"Our DC-3s leaked that much in oil every time we shut them down," Jack offered.

"Yes. But you were never more than half an hour away from a runway. Tonight we'll be a lot further than that. Now throw in the failed Doppler, the unreliable Loran, the weather out there, and the low oil pressure indication on number three, and you'd say what if you were captain?"

Jack looked at Bobby. "What do you think?"

"Take her to Shannon, goddamn it. Everything we need is there including good local support. Here, we've got no spares, no tools, no hangar to work in, and if we turn it over to outside maintenance, we might as well pack up and go home. Every panel those guys open will expose a problem like a termite-riddled house. Besides that, they haven't got spares either. We either fix this shit-box piece by piece as we move along or park it now and walk away," he said. "Write it up *here* … and we're finished!"

Jack looked at Sam. "I'm with Bobby," he declared. "That leak probably began at engine start in Miami, yet our fuel burn matched the flight plan, so it's not severe. And if it was going to get worse, it would have done that by now. Anyway, I say start the engine, run it up, and check it again. If the leak is no different, we go."

"And the oil pressure's holding up fine," Bobby added. "There's no problem with the oil pressure, Sam."

"And the Doppler's a separate problem," Jack piled on. "The fuel leak's different."

Sam was staring into the distance as he listened and mulled it over.

Bobby gave Jack a look and rolled his eyes. His patience exhausted, he turned to Sam and roared, "*C'MON*, goddamn it! Let's go, Sam! Let's get the hell out of here before that crew has their shift change, and we're stuck in this godforsaken icebox any longer!"

Sam shifted his gaze to the leaking fuel and remained silent as he came to a decision.

"It's your choice, Sam," Bobby grumbled. "Leave here with what we've got and fix this thing in bits as we move along—or call Gerhard and tell him to bring everyone home. This hajj is a bust."

Sam closed his eyes, digested that a moment, then slowly turned and regarded Bobby with a flinty gaze. "*Fine!*" he said, pointing at him. "Get up there, start it, and run it up. If the leak's no worse, we go—but if it is, we stay. Now *do it*, goddamn it! Both of you!" he barked with a sweep of his arm. It was as if he was swatting them away.

Jack and Bobby turned toward the airplane and bolted up the stairs.

Sam scowled as he regarded the engine. He sunk his hands in his pockets and braced himself against the wind. If he'd had any idea what poor condition these airplanes were in, he never would have agreed to bring Jack along. He already had one young man's ghost haunting him, and he couldn't afford another. "No good deed goes unpunished," Mick had warned him, and sadly he was right. First Tommy and now Jack; first, one young man's life and now another's career. And then that other good deed Sam had suffered for all these years, yet another occasion when his good intentions resulted in his crucifixion.

The memory of it came flooding back.

It was a hot and hazy August afternoon in '66, the sky clear above a few scattered clouds, a dense white haze below them. The Trans Meridian DC-8 was in the procedure turn for an approach into Calverton with Sam in the forward jumpseat and on edge. A glint of sunlight reflected off the glareshield.

It was Larry Schaff's second attempt to pass his upgrade to captain. If he failed the test, Larry would be terminated as a pilot for TMA. Because of the stakes, Sam was assigned to supervise the check ride for the company, and an Air Line Pilots Association representative was there to observe as well. Charlie Simpson was the check airman conducting the ride, and Kenny Abramson the flight engineer.

Like Sam, Charlie had a good heart and he empathized with Larry's plight. Not only was Larry's career on the line at that moment, but his wife was in hospice and near death. The emotional stress of it all couldn't have been higher, and like everyone else in the flight department, Sam and Charlie believed Larry should have been allowed to continue as a copilot until his wife had passed and at least some of the stress was resolved. But the company would have none of it; instead, its corporate and budget-conscious VP of flight insisted that Larry complete his upgrade on schedule. No exceptions allowed.

Yet, despite the stress, he'd been doing well, and Sam was at ease until Larry busted the Minimum Descent Altitude on the second approach. By FAA standards, that was a fatal mistake and the check ride should have been ended immediately. But this time—given the stakes and the circumstances—Charlie glanced back at Sam during the go-around as if silently asking for a second opinion. Sam blinked … and then gave him a nod. The check ride continued.

But it wasn't only Larry's circumstances that affected Sam's decision. Truly, Sam believed that raw flying skill was not the only quality important in a captain. Just as important as a captain's control of the airplane was his control of himself. How would he react to an error? Would he get past it, or would he unwind in a graveyard spiral of lost confidence and command? Better a flying fault exposed, corrected, and debriefed than a perfectly flown check ride that masked an insidious problem.

The follow-up approach Charlie planned was a good setup, an even tougher test of Larry's flying skill, and a test of his ability to recover from a mistake under duress. It was a VOR procedure with a lot of step-down altitudes and a long final while level at the MDA. On top of that, Charlie added a simulated flap malfunction to complicate the procedure—but Larry performed well. His systems knowledge, checklist execution, preparation for the approach, and flying all met the FAA's and the company's high standards. His leadership of the cockpit remained composed, and throughout the approach, he was on course, on speed, and on altitude.

Sam felt vindicated by his decision, and during the go-around, Charlie glanced back and gave him a discreet thumbs-up. Sam smiled, did the same, and let out a sigh of relief.

The last approach of the ride was a two-engine ILS to Runway 14. Both engines on the left side of the airplane were at idle power to simulate their failure. Sam remembered passing the outer marker, the monotone signal in his headset, *dah-dah-dah-dah*, the small blue light flashing on the instrument panel. Everything was going well, and the ride was nearly over. The descent continued uneventfully, and Sam remembered the runway becoming visible through the haze, the sound of the middle marker passing, *dit-dah-dit-dah-dit-dah* ... and then nothing.

That was it; that was Sam's last memory of the event.

Three days later, he woke up in a body cast in the hospital and learned that he and Larry were the only survivors. The other men had been killed on impact.

The NTSB concluded the crash was caused by pilot error, but bird damage was a contributing factor. And although Sam had never accepted their conclusion, had no reason to believe either Larry or Charlie were at fault, the truth was that it was Sam who'd given Larry a second chance.

Had Sam not done that, they would have returned to JFK with Charlie flying, and the accident would have never occurred.

Sam's reverie was broken by the sound of the number two engine beginning to turn. Its turbines whined, and there was a low *thump* as the fuel ignited, the whistle of its exhaust splitting the air as the RPM stabilized. Soon after, Jack looked out from the captain's seat, his left hand in the okay sign.

Sam gave him a nod, and Bobby brought up the throttle. Sam held his ears as the engine roared. He stared intensely at the point of the leak.

Jack was right. The leak was slight, with the frequency and number of drops appearing few.

Sam watched for another minute, then looked up at the cockpit and signaled with his hand across his throat to cut the engine off.

The power came back, and the engine was shut down. Sam walked closer to examine it. The leak was slowing, a few lingering drops accumulating on the bottom of the cowl and shearing off in the wind.

Bobby opened the forward entry door. Sam looked at him and gave him a thumbs-up, then signaled that he was going to the line shack to get the crew.

Bobby let out a loud rebel yell, punched the air, and went back inside.

# THIRTY-EIGHT

*The sky over the Western Atlantic, October 26, 1978*

As Jack leveled the airplane at 37,000 feet, the moon was bright overhead, the autumn sky cloudless, and the airplane running well. Sam was on the number one VHF radio copying their oceanic clearance from Gander, and Bobby copied the clearance with him to ensure they'd made no mistake. They'd been cleared via track Whiskey—the North Atlantic Track they'd requested in their flight plan.

At 10:34 p.m. in Gander and 2:04 a.m. in Shannon, the odometer read 0 1 0, and the Doppler's amber ten-mile alert light illuminated. It indicated they were approaching their waypoint at 50W50N, or fifty degrees west longitude and fifty degrees north latitude. From that point on, while over the high seas and beyond the range of radar, they were required to report their position every ten degrees of longitude. Every ten degrees of longitude was separated by about 370 nautical miles, and their speed over the water was planned at 480 knots while cruising at .78 Mach. Like his fuel planning, Sam had filed for a cruise speed conservatively to allow for the low oil pressure indication on engine number three and the possibility of having to shut it down.

When the Doppler read 0 0 0, they were at 50W50N. Sam hacked the clock on his instrument panel and confirmed the Doppler shifted to Stage B, the course they'd plotted to their next fix. Sam jotted down the arrival time at the fix adjacent to the planned time on the flight plan and handed the clipboard to Bobby to tally the fuel. The difference in actual versus estimated time of arrival and the difference in actual fuel versus estimated fuel determined the reliability of the plan. If their planning was off, they'd have time to make any necessary adjustments to the flight before the situation became critical.

When Bobby had finished, he handed the clipboard back to Sam. Using the actual time of arrival and fuel remaining, Sam calculated the time and fuel they should arrive with at the next fix, 52N40W. When he was finished, he tossed the clipboard on top of the glareshield and said with a sigh of relief, "A minute ahead, and six hundred pounds up on the gas. Looking good, so far."

Jack looked across at him and said, "So, either that fuel leak has fixed itself or it isn't that bad."

Sam reached for the plotting chart they'd used in Gander and took it from his kitbag. "Not likely it's fixed itself," he said, "but luckily not getting any worse either." After opening the chart, Sam pointed to the various ATC sectors and explained to Jack the procedures they would use to report their position.

"To begin," he said, "the North Atlantic is divided into two communication and air traffic control sectors. There's Gander Control on the west side of 30W and Shanwick Control on the east. We'll report our position to a radio operator who then relays that position to an air traffic controller at a separate location. We'll use the high frequency radio for communication because of its long-range capability. But beware," Sam warned as he reached for the HF controls on the overhead panel. "The frequencies are always congested and noisy with static ... Watch."

Sam turned up the volume of the radio, and a loud hiss of static came from the cockpit loudspeakers. Moments later, the Gander Radio operator's voice warbled in a tinny crackle. "Icelandic Seven-Sixty-Five, roger," he said, "cleared to deviate twenty miles south of course, report back on course by three-zero west, over."

But before the Icelandic flight had a chance to reply, a pilot with a thick Italian accent broke in. "Gander Radio, Gander Radio," he said. "Alitalia Three-Nine-Four position on eight-eight, over."

"Alitalia, stand by, please, stand by. Icelandic, go ahead with your readback, over."

A pilot with a British accent broke in. "Gander Radio, Gander Radio, Laker Six-Oh-Seven, requesting deviation, over."

"Roger, Laker, stand by, please, stand by! Everyone calling Gander, stand by! Icelandic, continue with your read-back, over."

"See what I mean?" Sam said with his wry grin.

"Yeah. Chaos. Got to be aggressive to get in, huh?"

"It's a knack," Sam replied. "You'll pick it up. For now, grab your mic and give it a shot."

Jack reached for the clipboard, held the microphone to his mouth, and waited. The instant Gander Control had finished with the Icelandic flight, he squeezed the button, jammed the frequency, and spoke as if he was mentally impaired. "Gander Radio—Gander Radio—this is—Douglas Eight-Oh-Four-Papa-Alpha—position on eight-eight, over."

They heard only static in response.

Sam looked annoyed. "What the hell was *that?*" he asked.

"Gander Radio, Gander Radio," a pilot with a Spanish accent broke in. "Iberia Four-Nine-Three, position, over."

"Iberia flight calling Gander, say again."

"Technique I used in Vietnam," Jack said sheepishly. "When Charlie's crawling up your ass and you need a fire mission fast and everyone's screaming for the same thing, I'd just crunch the mic and jam the works until I got an answer."

Sam gave him a look and frowned.

"Ohhhh-kaaay," Jack said. "I'll, uh … I'll try something else."

"Like patience?" Sam asked.

Jack smiled.

After Gander read back Iberia's report, Jack immediately keyed the mic and called again. On this attempt, he got through.

"Roger, Douglas Eight-Oh-Four-Papa-Alpha, go ahead with your position, over."

Jack said, "Roger, roger, sir," and, reading from the flight plan, he continued, "Position. Douglas Eight-Oh-Four-Papa-Alpha. Five-zero-north, five-zero-west at zero-two-zero-six, flight level three-seven-zero. Estimating, five-two-north, four-zero-west at zero-two-five-four. Next, five-three-north, three-zero-west, over."

Gander acknowledged Jack's report and asked for the DC-8's SELCAL code. The constant traffic and static on the HF were torture to listen to, so the selective calling mechanism allowed the crew to turn down the HF volume while still staying in contact with ATC.

Jack read the code over the HF. "Bravo-Delta-Echo-Lima," he said.

"Roger, sir," Gander replied. "Stand by for SELCAL, Bravo-Delta-Echo-Lima."

A moment later, a two-tone chime like a doorbell sounded in the cockpit, and Jack confirmed receipt of the alert.

"Okay, good job," Sam said. "Now let's confirm the Doppler's not in error by plotting our position with the Loran."

He reached down and rotated the gain control on the Loran clockwise. While Sam waited for the instrument to warm up, he unfolded the plotting chart further and pointed out the Loran radio stations that covered their route. After dialing the numbers from the chart into the Loran receiver, two white trace lines became visible on its oscilloscope screen. Sam adjusted the controls to overlap the slave and master signals that were being broadcast, then jotted down the numbers from the instrument on his notepad and applied them to the plotting chart to obtain their fix. He drew a tiny triangle on the chart to indicate their position, and it was very close to track Whiskey that they'd plotted in Gander.

Jack looked at the chart and asked, "How close is that, actually?"

"Within a few miles, give or take," Sam answered. "But, like I said, reception depends on the weather. In clear skies like we're in now, the Loran will put us within a couple of miles of our actual position. But that lightning could knock it out altogether."

Jack nodded.

After stowing the chart in his kitbag, Sam took the flight plan and showed Jack how to set the Doppler up for the next leg of the flight, the leg that would follow the one they were on.

As Jack leaned forward and adjusted the dials, Sam read out the course and mileage they'd calculated to the next fix. When they were done, they sat back in their seats and Sam said, "So that's it, essentially. When the mileage on the odometer ticks down to zero, we'll note the time and fuel, and ensure the unit shifts to Mode B and the autopilot tracks the outbound course we just entered. Once the airplane's tracking properly, we'll confirm our position with the Loran and then make whatever adjustments to the Doppler's course and mileage numbers are necessary."

"What if we had both Dopplers working? What if they didn't agree?"

"Good question, but a knotty problem," Sam answered. "We'll need both working to unravel it, so let's hold that lesson for another day."

Jack nodded.

. . .

Half an hour later, with the hiss of the wind, the smooth ride, and the warm glow of the instrument lights, Jack felt the first pull of fatigue. He looked across the cockpit where Sam was rubbing his eyes and then back at Bobby, who had his head down on his chest, his eyes closed, and his hands limp in his lap. Jack was reminded of Ed that night in the DC-3. It seemed like eons ago.

Suddenly, a spectral blue halo flickered up and into the ionosphere. It caught Jack's attention, and he leaned forward for a better view. A moment later, there was another burst of ghostly blue light, and then another, and another … and then a pause. Jack looked at Sam and said, "Looks like that weather is starting to appear."

Sam opened his eyes and cleared his throat. He reached for the weather radar. He turned it from STANDBY to ON, and a moment later the antennae began to sweep back and forth, a pale green line illuminating the screen. An eerie glow lit Sam's face as he adjusted the radar's range to 180 miles and then the antenna's angle of tilt and the gain control. After several more sweeps, there were still no echoes from the thunderstorms firing far in the distance, and Sam sat back in his seat.

"That stuff's further out than I expected," he said. "That front must be moving faster than the forecast … Not good. If it's picking up steam, it'll be even nastier."

Bobby opened his eyes and said, "If it's going to get ugly, we probably ought to get that chow going now, huh?"

Sam looked back at him and nodded. "Sure," he said.

Bobby slid his seat back and disconnected his seatbelt. The buckle hit the cockpit floor with a loud *clunk*. He stood up, yawned, and announced, "Tank to engine," and started to leave the cockpit.

Sam rubbed his arms as if he was cold. "Hey, before you go, throw another log on the fire." With a suspicious countenance, he added, "And what's in that grocery bag? Anything besides those Newfie grease-steaks you like so much?"

Bobby fiddled with the temperature control and asked, "Like what?"

"Like a salad, maybe, or a BLT … maybe some soup?" Sam asked hopefully.

Bobby made a face. "They don't eat that kind of shit up here," he declared. "It's cheesesteak, pizza, walrus, or cod, and I don't eat fish."

"Walrus is an animal."

"Yeah, I know. That's what they made your cheesesteak out of … smartass."

Sam groaned. "Jesus. Alright," he said. "Cheesesteak and coffee for me."

"As you wish, my liege," Bobby replied sarcastically. Looking at Jack, he asked, "And for you, fine sir?"

"Pizza works for me," Jack answered with a smile.

Bobby said, "Damn straight," and with his thumb pointed at Sam added, "Never mind ol' fussy guts over there. These are the best pizzas and cheesesteaks anywhere in the world outside Philly. Trust me."

Sam scoffed. "*Newfoundland* cheesesteak and pizza? Sure."

"Ah, bullshit!" Bobby snapped with wounded pride. "How many times have I told you that little grease-ball who owns that grill is from Queens ... not Gander!" He looked at Jack. "Probably up here in one of them witness protection deals or something. But who cares? The mafia's loss is Gander's gain. Best damn grub we'll see 'til we get home."

Sam threw him a dismissive wave. "Whatever," he said.

Bobby turned and left the cockpit in a huff. When he was out of ear-shot, Jack chuckled, looked across at Sam, and said, "Takes his catering duties seriously, does he?"

"Oh, *yeah*," Sam moaned. "And unless you tell him how much you *love* that shitty pizza, he'll be sulking for the rest of the night."

Fifteen minutes passed uneventfully, and Sam looked back into the cabin through the open cockpit door. "Where the hell did Bobby get off too, anyway?" he asked as if to himself. Looking at Jack, he said, "I'm getting hungry, even for that walrus cheesesteak. How about you?"

"Yeah, me too. You think he's still mad?" Jack asked.

Sam smiled. "Nah," he said. "Bobby's a crusty ol' coot and it takes a little time to get used to him, but he's a great guy and an extraordinary engineer. Got a lot of heart. You'll see. Don't mind his gruffness going into Gander."

Jack shrugged. "I don't," he said. "Hell, if I were him, I wouldn't want to be in Gander changing tires on a cold, dark night either."

"Yes, but it's sometimes unavoidable with the anti-skid units in these early airplanes. They're reliable at lower speeds, but jump on the brakes too hard above 100 knots, and flat spotting and tire failures are not un-common."

"I'll remember that," Jack said. "So, how long has Bobby been working here?"

"Oh, a bit longer than me. He started out as a crop duster, and he owned and operated one of the largest outfits in South Carolina. He'd built the business up from a single airplane. Bobby's not only a hell of a mechanic but a hell of a good pilot too."

"Does he still own the business?"

"No, he sold long ago."

"But he's a pilot, you said. Then why's he here as an engineer?"

"Ernie Gann wrote *Fate Is the Hunter*, and fate came hunting for Bobby on a summer day in 1957. He lost his license soon after it."

Jack's brow furrowed. "How's that?" he asked.

"He was spraying a bean field in a Beech 18 and—"

"Wait! Whoa," Jack interrupted. "A *Beech 18*? That's an awful big airplane for dusting, isn't it?"

"Big fields," Sam replied. "Anyway, Bobby was approaching the end of a row with a highway and power lines dead ahead. As he closed in, he reached down for the spray lever to shut it off but found it wouldn't budge. He jiggled it a bit more, but it was still stuck. He glanced down quickly to see what was wrong, and by the time he looked up, it was too late. He had to either go through the power lines or go under them."

"Holy shit."

"Yeah, well, let me tell you from having flown with them, those duster boys may be a bunch of chaw-chewing shit-kickers, but *man* can they fly. No one better. So, Bobby just eases her down 'til the prop tips were clipping the bean tops and figures he'll go under the lines, easy-cheesy. But just then, he also sees this black convertible tooling down that highway with no change in their bearing."

Jack recoiled. "Oh, shit! Oh, my God!"

"Yeah," Sam said. "And it gets worse. Because as it turns out, the driver was this cute little *thang* in her daddy's new Ford, 'Lucille' cranking on the AM, and baby girl's oblivious until Bobby goes roaring overhead, prop tips whirring inches above her windshield."

Jack raised a brow.

"Yep … She panics, runs into a ditch, Daddy's little girl and new car soaked in Bobby's bug sauce."

"Ugh. *DDT?*"

"Probably. But other than wet panties and a fumigated Ford, there was no harm to either the kid or the car—except Daddy didn't see it that way. Turns out he was a big donor to Senator Strom Thurmond, and Uncle Strom took care of everything. He had the CAA pull Bobby's ticket, and that's the last time he flew as a pilot."

"Damn."

"Hey, the working guy always gets it in the ass. But Bobby's the son of a tenant farmer, and those folks are nothing if not resilient. So, he hangs up his flying goggles, picks up his wrenches, and within a year he's got that dusting operation ticking along like clockwork. He had a fleet of Stearmans, some N3Ns, and two of those Beeches. He was doing great and raking in the money until a friend came along one day and told him what a great job he had flying for Capital Airways: the sharp uniform, the time off, the money, the travel—the *flight attendants*—and that was all it took. Bobby wanted in. He leaves his dusting operation in the hands of his manager and goes to a flight engineer's school in Tulsa, Oklahoma. A couple of months later, he signs on with Malayan Airways flying Connies and sells the dusting business."

"And that's how he wound up here?"

"Yes, but after a stint at Southern Air Transport first."

"SAT, your old outfit? The one the CIA took over?"

"Yes and no. The CIA dropped the SAT certificate and morphed the company into Air America. The company Bobby went to work for bought SAT's certificate, but they were entirely new. In any case, they went belly-up a few years later, and that's when Bobby came to Pan Tropic. He got here a year or two before I came on."

"So, no Air America for either of you guys. I always imagined myself flying for them."

"No," Sam said. "But hold that thought." He turned around and studied the engineer's panel. "Hang on," he said as he unbuckled and got up. Leaning toward the panel, he reached for a switch. "I'm opening the CSD oil cooler on number four," he said. "Remind me to tell him when he gets back in case I forget."

"Sure. Everything okay?"

"Yeah, fine," Sam said. "But that CSD's carrying a little extra load. Probably the ovens in the galley causing it."

As Sam buckled back in, Jack said, "So, Bobby sold his dusting outfit to work for a non-sched like this. If that's the case, then why am I so different for wanting to stay on here, Sam? I mean, I like a sharp uniform, time off, good pay ... and flight attendants too?" He smiled at him with a Cheshire grin.

"The difference is you have a future and Bobby not only wanted to get back to flying but was also in the midst of another divorce and had to sell the business as part of the settlement."

"From what he told me, it sounds like he's had a lot of them."

"Marriage is a hobby for him, and Bobby's had a bunch of them. Four or five, at least. But then those are only the official ones. There's been some common-law breakups too. Bobby loves the ladies, no doubt about it."

"I noticed he has a thing for Maggie. I mean, at the bar that first night we met. He's old enough to be her dad, isn't he?"

"You know Maggie's a lesbian, right?"

Jack flinched. "A *what?*" he exclaimed. "No!" he said, looking bemused. "I didn't know. I mean ... I've never met any. I didn't know they looked like that—"

Sam rolled his eyes.

Jack cleared his throat. "Sam, I'm sorry," he said. "It just caught me by surprise ... But how is it Bobby doesn't know, either?"

"Oh, he knows, and Maggie's made it clear she wouldn't be interested in him even if she wasn't, but Bobby doesn't care. He just loves women ... *all* women. Fat ones, skinny ones, black, white, Asian, married or unmarried, lesbians, hell … a pregnant Mongolian testicle eater, for all I know—it doesn't matter. You just never know who will catch his fancy. Problem is he doesn't just *love* every woman he meets—he also *marries* them, and that's what gets him into trouble."

A man's gravelly voice boomed over the loudspeaker, the call coming in on the air-to-air frequency. "TWA Three-Forty-Two, fifty west at three-seven-oh. Looking for a ride report ahead."

Sam picked up his mic. "Tee-way calling for a ride report, this is Douglas Four-Papa-Alpha, two hundred west of forty west, three-seven-oh … Just some occasional light chop, sir."

"Roger, sir, thanks. Getting any returns from that weather ahead?"

Sam glanced at the radar. "Negative. Nothing yet," he answered.

"Roger, appreciate the report. Mind giving us a shout when you guys start painting that weather?"

"Yes, sir, will do."

"Roger, roger, thanks … TWA standing by."

Sam clipped his mic and then turned to look at the CSD oil temperature gauge again. The needle was returning to the green arc. Sam looked back into the cabin. "There's that son-of-a-gun," he said. "Still dickin' around in the galley. How long does it take to heat up pizza?"

"Want me to go back and get him?" Jack asked.

"Nah … He loves fussing with that stuff. He'll be back up here soon enough."

Sam faced forward, and moments later they heard a loud crash, metal trays hitting the floor, and a lot of loud swearing.

Sam looked at Jack. "Or maybe not." He smiled.

"By the way," Jack said. "Speaking of jobs and career choices, you promised you'd tell me about Cuba, the Bay of Pigs, and all of that, remember?"

Sam let out a sigh. "Okay," he relented. "But I'll keep it short. As it was, SAT had two C-46s at the time, one they owned and one they leased.

But it was a hit-and-miss operation from the start, and the company was never far from bankruptcy. The four acres of airport property they owned were worth more than anything else they had, including the airplanes and all the spares. In August 1960, I was in the office preparing for a freight charter to San Juan when three guys in fedoras walked in with suitcases full of cash—307,506 dollars and ten cents, exactly. As it turned out, that was the current value of all the company's shares, and the owners gladly took the offer to buy them out and ran. As for the rest of us, we had no idea who our new employer was until a few days later when some more C-46s arrived and then a day or two after that, a bunch of B-26 Marauders with hard points and machine guns, the airplanes fresh from an Air Guard unit somewhere up north, their markings blacked out. It was our first clue we weren't just civilians anymore. Eight months later, we were in the midst of the Bay of Pigs assault when JFK suddenly got cold feet and pulled the plug. They ordered us to get the 2506 brigade out of there before Fidel overran them, and we did the best we could—but a lot of those poor bastards got left behind. That's what Ramón—the barman at the hotel—was referring to. Ramón was with the brigade and lost a lot of friends. Anyway, after the Bay of Pigs, I'd had enough of that kind of adventure and decided to grow up and get a real job … Like this one." He smiled.

"So, who'd you fly for after the CIA?"

Sam scoffed. "I took anything I could find," he said. "I flew old Huff-Daland dusters for an outfit in Georgia for a while, and in between that, airshows in a 450 Stearman I'd rebuilt from surplus parts. Like my dad, I also fished a bit, but there's no money in that either. Then in the winter of '61, I got a call from Trans Meridian. A war buddy was a captain for them, and he told me they were at the beginning of a big expansion, military contracts especially. He said I'd make captain in no time and he'd give me a recommendation. I jumped on the offer, and as for the rest? Well … I think you know, yes?"

Jack nodded sadly.

There was a commotion in the doorway, and both of them turned to look up at Bobby as he stumbled into the cockpit with two steaming trays of food. "Hot, hot, hot!" he exclaimed as he squeezed past the engineer's seat, a tray in each hand.

Sam pulled two plasticized checklists from the copilot's seat pocket, put one on his lap, and handed the other to Jack. He turned and reached for a tray. "What took so long?" he asked gruffly.

"Sorry," Bobby apologized. "Had to make a pit stop first."

Sam winced.

Bobby looked insulted. "Hey! Don't worry about it," he huffed. "I washed my hands."

Sam groaned as he put the tray on his lap and a napkin in his collar. "By the way, that number four CSD's been running a little hot. I opened the cooling door."

Bobby glanced at his panel. "Looks okay now," he said. He toggled the door closed. Looking at Sam, he added, "I'm going back to get mine. Anyone need anything else?"

Sam studied his meal. "Yes … Pepto-Bismol," he wisecracked.

Bobby made a face and left to get his tray.

# THIRTY-NINE

*The sky over the Western Atlantic, October 26, 1978*

By the time they finished their meal, the airplane was approaching the next fix and the ten-mile alert on the Doppler illuminated.

"Coming up on forty west," Jack said.

When the odometer rolled down to 0 0 0, Sam hacked his clock, jotted down the time, 02:52Z, and passed the clipboard to Bobby to tally the fuel.

Bobby passed it back to Sam, who looked at it and said, "Two minutes ahead and up five hundred pounds. We're lookin' good." He smiled.

He took his E6-B from his shirt pocket, calculated the ETA and fuel estimate for the next fix, and passed the clipboard to Jack. "Alright," he said. "Time for more fun with the HF."

Jack turned up the volume on his cockpit speaker, waited for an opportunity, and passed his report to Gander. Gander read back the report and told them to contact Shanwick Control on frequency 6860 when they passed 30W.

As Jack clipped his mic, Sam leaned forward to adjust the radar. After three sweeps of the antenna, there were still no echoes. He slid his seat back, unbuckled, and said, "I'm going back to hit the head and stretch my legs a bit." He looked across at Jack. "Grab your oxygen mask and at least keep it handy."

Jack pulled his mask down from the quick-release mechanism above and behind his seat. When only one pilot was at the controls and the airplane was above 25,000 feet, the pilot flying was required to wear the mask to ensure he remained conscious in the event of a sudden loss of cabin pressure. Because of the discomfort of wearing it, however, most pilots disregarded the requirement and kept the mask on their lap.

As Sam slipped behind Bobby, he tapped him on the shoulder. Bobby looked up, and Sam gave a nod toward Jack. Bobby got the message and nodded in return. He'd keep a close eye on everything while Sam was gone.

After Sam had left, Jack said, "You're right about that pizza. It was actually pretty good."

"Glad you liked it," Bobby said. "But Sam's one of those health-food nuts, always trying to eat right—whatever the fuck that means. As far as I'm concerned, the only thing unhealthy about eating is *not* eating, and we had enough of that in my family during the Depression."

"He polished off that sandwich pretty quick, so I guess he was alright with it."

"Sam's too much of a gentleman to complain."

"I've noticed the gentleman part," Jack acknowledged.

"Sam's pretty special around here," Bobby said. "It'll be hard when he's gone for good. Without Sam Laney, this outfit will come apart like a cheap watch."

Jack turned around and looked at him with his eyes narrowed. "How so?" he asked.

"This isn't an airline, slick; it's just a loose formation of parts. The only thing holding it together on the road is Sam, and you'll see that soon enough—the twenty-hour duty days that run three, sometimes four days a week for weeks on end, everyone getting tired and testy and curing it with booze on our days off. Whooo-*eee*. Without someone who has the right touch, the right personality, someone everyone respects to keep everybody in line … there's not much hope."

"Why not Halder? He seems like a tough, hold-it-together type."

Bobby scoffed. "*Gerhard?* Nah," he said. "It's a people thing. Gerhard's an operations guy: airplanes, maintenance, scheduling, routings, budgets, and the nuts and bolts of an operation are his specialty. But people? Hell, Gerhard's as much a Type A asshole as the rest of us. And look, authority doesn't come with a badge around here and tough alone doesn't cut it. We're all tough, so tough isn't the answer. To run an outfit like this on the road, you need a lot more than just tough, and that's Sam Laney. He gets people problems fixed before Gerhard has to deal with it. And believe me, no one wants that. Because Gerhard has only one way of fixing people problems, and that's a ticket home."

"And you're saying not Stone either?"

Bobby shrugged. "Brad's smart and a damn good pilot," he said. "No one questions that. But the people thing? Jesus. You were there in the bar. You saw it yourself."

"But Sam grabbed him first."

"Because Brad was pushing his buttons. You understand what that was about, right?"

"Joe told me. He said they disagree about upgrading Larry Schaff."

"Yeah. Big difference of opinion about that. But that's not the problem. The problem with Brad is that he's trying to turn this company into a mini-version of Pan Am, and it'll never be Pan Am, or anything like them, because that's not the work we do here—nor is it the work any of us want to do. That's why Sam's so important. He gets that, and Brad never has. Doing everything by the book like Pan Am would kill this airline overnight. You can't run a hajj doing it by the book, like you're seeing right now. And you'll be seeing more of it in the weeks ahead. But the moment Sam steps into it, the bullshit gets left on the table and we're back to being one big happy, fucked-up family again. It's pure magic."

"Buddy Reid told me a lot of things changed when Hirsch took over. He said they instituted some rules regarding the personal relationships, that sort of thing."

Bobby laughed and said, "Buddy of all people. Who do you think they made the rules for? But yeah. There's rules, but only if it becomes a problem. Same with the booze. Don't let it affect your work, don't let it affect the mission in any way, and it'll never be an issue."

"I see."

"Exactly. Work hard, play hard, but get the job done. Beyond that, the only rule here is: if it works, it rules. Period. Point is, we're not Pan Am, and never will—"

The cockpit chime sounded, and Bobby picked up the receiver. "You rang, my liege?"

Sam said, "Hey, I'm in the back and both these door seals are shot. The squealing's so loud I can barely hear myself think. We've also got a barrier strap hanging outside the left one, or what's left of it anyway. Make a note for the log when we get in."

"Did you try pulling it in?"

"As much as I could, but there's still a piece of it out there slapping itself to death. It'll need to be replaced."

"Got it."

"Okay. On my way back," Sam said, and he hung up.

As Bobby returned the receiver to its hook, there was a flash of distant lightning ahead, the first distinctly white flash they'd seen.

Jack reached for the radar and adjusted the tilt down. With the next sweep of the antennae, a thin but clear row of echoes glowed in a green line across the top of the screen.

There was another white flash.

Jack picked up his mic to call the TWA flight that had asked for a report on the storms. But then the airplane suddenly began to rise, and he dropped the mic to his lap with the oxygen mask. It felt as if some massive beast was rising from the depths below them and lifting them on its back. The altimeter needles were moving up, and the autopilot was fighting the change, the control column moving forward to hold the altitude while the stab trim moved forward too.

There was something sinister in its aspect, like a rattlesnake beginning to coil, and Jack straightened himself in his seat and put his hands on the yoke. His eyes darted about the panel, searching for a clue. He'd never felt anything like this as a pilot; he'd never felt anything like it in his bones.

A shout came from the cabin, but it was unintelligible. The airplane was now sinking, sinking, sinking as if being driven down by an implacable force.

"Autopilot *off!*" Bobby commanded. "Do it *now!*" He reached up and turned the engines' ignition on.

Without thinking, Jack pressed the button on the yoke, and the autopilot clicked off. An instant later, they slammed into a vicious high-frequency chop like they were speeding over a washboard, and a timpani-like drum roll shot through the airframe, the instruments a blur. A series of violent jolts followed, driving them into their seats and throwing them against their seatbelts, Jack's oxygen mask and microphone flying up and smashing into his face. The rumble through the airframe was deafening, the shocks and sounds of it as if the wings were about to come off. The clipboard on the glareshield flew aft and crashed into the pedestal panel. The left wing dropped sharply, the nose pitched up, and the airplane yawed right. Jack jabbed the right aileron down, his right foot instinctively on the rudder to bring the wings level, but although the right wing went down, the nose yawed left!

"*NO! NO! NO!*" Bobby bellowed. "OFF THE FUCKIN' RUDDER! AILERON ONLY! CHECK THE RISING WING!" he yelled and frantically fumbled for the autopilot servo lever. The clipboard had jammed against it.

Jack pulled his feet from the rudder pedals and remembered Dutch roll and what Sam had taught him about recovery from it in the simulator. He snapped the left aileron down, and when the wings came level, he quickly centered the yoke. When the airplane rolled left, he snapped the right aileron down, and as the wings came level, he quickly centered the yoke. The airplane began to stabilize, and then the turbulence ended as abruptly as it began, the air on the other side disconcertingly smooth.

Jack continued controlling the Dutch roll as Sam had taught him until Bobby got the clipboard cleared and the yaw damper reinstated. The airplane stabilized completely within moments.

He blew out his cheeks. His pulse raced as he pushed up the power and began the climb back to 37,000 feet. They had descended more than two thousand.

Sam stumbled through the cockpit doorway, a hand on his head. He launched into his seat and said, "Okay, okay … Good job." He sighed. "Thank God … You got it."

Bobby looked at the matted blood on Sam's head and hand and said, "Christ, you're bleeding like a stuck pig. I'm going back for the first aid kit."

"No!" Sam snapped. "Forget it; I'm fine. Stay here!" he ordered.

"Forget it, my ass," Bobby growled. "We need you alive. I'm going for the kit." He turned and left for the cabin.

Jack leveled the airplane at 37,000 feet and turned on the autopilot. Sam picked up his mic and called the TWA flight to advise them of the severe turbulence.

Bobby returned with the first aid kit and put it on his desk. As Sam called Gander to report the severe CAT, Bobby opened the white metal box and took out the items he needed. He dampened a sterile pad with alcohol and said, "This is going to hurt."

He applied the bandage, and Sam winced in pain. Bobby continued fussing over him like a mother to a child. As he applied and replaced more bandages, the bleeding slowed. "What'd you hit?" Bobby asked as he worked. "Anything I have to go back and fix after I fix you?"

"A seat frame on the floor. I kissed it goodbye on my way to the ceiling."

"I don't understand where that came from," Jack said. "The ride's been so smooth. There's nothing to cause it. And why that Dutch roll?"

"East of forty west," Sam said. "The 250 millibar chart in Gander. I saw a sharp hook in the jet stream, and that's always a potential for strong turbulence. I meant to note it on our flight plan, but then the briefer interrupted and I let it slip. My fault," he said, disgusted with himself. "Too old to remember shit … *goddamn it*," he grumbled.

Bobby answered Jack's question as he continued to fuss over Sam.

"When you turn the autopilot off with the button on the yoke, you turn off all three servos, including the yaw damper," he reminded Jack. "The next time, either turn off the autopilot with the paddle switch only or don't forget to reinstate the yaw damper if you use the button on the yoke."

Jack glanced back at him and nodded sheepishly. "Yeah. I remember that now," he said. "It was a question Brad asked me during the oral. I'm sorry it didn't stick."

"Hey, we survived," Sam added. "Good job … all things considered."

Bobby finished drying the wound, put a fresh pad on top, then took Sam's right hand and made him keep pressure on the bandage. "Hold it there," he demanded.

Sam rolled his eyes.

Bobby cleaned his hands and asked, "Who wants fresh coffee?"

Sam said, "I'll take one, and double bag it. This night ain't half-over."

"Me too," Jack added. Pointing at the radar, he said, "That line of storms looks pretty solid."

# FORTY

Bobby returned with two steaming cups of coffee. He passed one to Jack and the other to Sam. "I did a quick check of the cabin," he said. "Thankfully, that thick skull of yours didn't do any critical damage." Sam gave him a look and reached for his cup.

Bobby sat down and buckled in, and as he took a sip of coffee, he studied the tabulated data beneath the clear plexiglass top on his desk. "We're good for three-nine-oh if you're interested," he said.

Sam was fiddling with the radar and watching the pattern of echoes from the storms ahead. "Nah," he said, speaking over his shoulder, "but thanks. I doubt we'll be able to top this stuff even at that altitude. We might as well stay put, and speaking of that, what's our buffet margin here?"

The airplane's tolerance for turbulence was determined by its weight, speed, and altitude but reduced to a single number for easy reference. Bobby looked at the data on his tabletop and replied, "We're good. Better than one point five."

Jack eyed the radar and asked Sam, "Where do you plan on going through?"

"I've been watching this spot here," Sam said, pointing at an area of the line to the south where the echoes were thinner.

Jack leaned forward, pointed to a break in the line further south, and asked, "Why not here instead?"

"Because that's at least ten miles further south of track than they'll clear us."

"Why won't they clear us for wherever we need to go?"

"Because there's no radar separation out here and doubtless everyone else is looking at that same spot you are. There's no way to provide and monitor adequate separation if everyone heads there randomly. Limiting the distance off course maintains a safe order. Gander will approve up to twenty miles for a deviation, and that's it."

"But what if we need more?" Jack insisted. "I mean, if it's a question of safety, right?"

Sam sat back in his seat. "Sure, if it was truly a question of safety, we could declare an emergency. But we're not going to do that because the risk of penetrating that line where I suggested doesn't rise to that level of risk. It'll be rough, but likely less than we just experienced. Besides, if everyone declared an emergency every time a little weather got in the way, there'd be no way to get everyone across out here. The number of flights would have to be reduced dramatically, and that's not happening. I mean, look," he said, "there's never any harm in asking for more, but twenty miles is all they'll approve. Here. Watch."

He reached for the HF controls, turned up the volume, and made a request from Gander for a deviation "up to three-zero miles south of track."

Gander replied, "Douglas Eight-Oh-Four-Papa-Alpha, stand by, sir, I'll call you back."

As they waited for the call, the line of weather drew closer and the lightning continuous. The ferocity of the flashes reminded Jack of the Arc Light missions in Vietnam, the nightly B-52 strikes west of Hue. He recalled the thunderous rumbling, the ground trembling, the plywood walls in their bunker flexing with the change in atmospheric pressure. He secretly shuddered, and then the SELCAL chimed and he jumped, startled.

Sam reached for his mic and replied, "Gander Radio, this is Douglas Eight-Oh-Four-Papa-Alpha responding to SELCAL, over."

"Roger, Eight-Oh-Four-Papa-Alpha. Gander Control clears Douglas Eight-Oh-Four-Papa-Alpha to deviate up to two-zero miles south of course. Be back on course no later than three-zero west longitude. Read back, please."

Sam gave Jack an I-told-you-so look and replied to Gander, "Roger,

roger, sir. Douglas Eight-Oh-Four-Papa-Alpha cleared to deviate up to two-zero miles south of course. Be back on course no later than three-zero west, over."

The Gander operator acknowledged the readback. Sam turned down the HF volume and clipped his mic before reaching for the radar and switching to the contour mode. After two sweeps of the antennae, he pointed at the screen and said, "Okay, so Plan B. See this area here?"

The area of the line Sam was pointing to looked like a slice of green Swiss cheese peppered with black spots.

"What are these?" Jack asked, pointing to the spots.

"Those show up in contour mode," Sam answered. He switched the radar from contour mode to normal mode and then back to demonstrate what he'd just said. In contour mode, the black holes were present, and in the normal mode, there was only green. "In contour mode, the black spots indicate the areas of heaviest precipitation and greatest turbulence," Sam explained. Then, pointing to a small area of green between two large black holes, he continued, "Turn south and head for here. We'll shoot for that green patch between those holes and hope for the best."

Bobby let out a snort. "That won't hold up worth a shit," he said. "But if that's the best we've got, I'm going back to take a leak before it gets any worse. Any final requests while I'm back there?"

Sam shook his head, and Jack said, "No, I'm good, Bobby. Thanks."

"Tank to engine," Bobby said as he unbuckled and got up.

Jack used the autopilot to turn the airplane south and toward the area Sam had pointed to. "You think Bobby's right?" he asked.

"Look outside," Sam said. Leaning forward, he pointed in the direction of the storms. "See there? The lightning's only on either side of that area in the middle, which supports the radar's return. Will it close up? Maybe. But it's still the best shot we've got."

Jack grimaced, looked at Sam, and said, "Looks pretty small."

Sam held up his hands and replied with a shrug.

When Bobby returned, the line of weather was eighty miles east of them. He plopped into his seat, fastened his belt, and asked Sam, "Ready for the heat?"

Sam glanced up at the anti-icing panel and said, "Sure. Go ahead."

Bobby flipped on the ignition switch and then turned on the engine anti-ice switches one at a time.

Twenty miles from the storms, they entered a layer of thin stratus clouds and a light chop, the first taste of the turbulence to come. Sam straightened in his seat, cinched his seatbelt, and adjusted the rudder pedals in preparation. "Okay," he said. "I'll take it from here."

Jack sat back, feeling disappointed but relieved at not having to fly this challenge, at least not yet.

The chop soon increased from light to moderate, and the airplane jostled and was knocked about. The ice crystals in the clouds created a deafening hiss. Then a ball of St. Elmo's fire suddenly blossomed around the nose cone, a sphere of spectral blue and white light that wavered and danced hauntingly ahead of them. Tiny bolts of electricity twitched and licked demonically at the windshields, and the crew had to shout to be heard.

Sam reached for the cockpit light controls. "Watch your eyes," he yelled. He turned on the storm lights. Jack winced as a brilliant fluorescent glare flooded the cockpit and reflected off the back of the windshield. The reflection blocked his view ahead, giving Jack an eerie sense of isolation from the maelstrom they were fast approaching. It was as if he was in a barrel and about to go over Niagara Falls.

Sam switched the radar from contour to normal mode, checked the screen, and then switched back to contour. Ten miles from the storms, the green area between the holes they'd seen earlier had turned black, just as Bobby had predicted. "Told you so," he said smugly, sitting back with his arms folded.

Sam ignored him, clasped the yoke, and turned the autopilot off with the paddle switch. "Autopilot's off," he announced. He pointed to the radar and commanded, "Take that out of contour and adjust the tilt ten degrees down."

As Jack manipulated the controls, the airplane was thrown down hard and then back up repeatedly, making control of the radar almost impossible. He looked at Sam and asked, "Why not leave it in contour?"

"Because airplanes have been lost when crews confused contoured weather with clear air. Contour's useful only for choosing a path before going into the weather, not once you're in it."

Jack nodded, switched the radar to normal mode, and then glanced across the cockpit at Sam. Although earnestly engaged with the flying, Sam appeared poised. Amidst the cacophony and chaos—the cockpit furnishings rattling, the airframe rumbling like an empty drum, the hiss of the ice crystals, and the lightning flashing furiously—Sam appeared as at ease as a man whittling a stick on his porch. Despite the turbulence and Sam's fingertip touch on the yoke, Jack noted that the airplane barely deviated from their altitude and course. It was the most amazing display of skill and aplomb in a pilot he'd ever seen. He discreetly turned around to look at Bobby to see if he was seeing this too.

But Bobby had his eyes locked on the electrical panel, where the generator bus power lights flickered skittishly.

The erratic voltages caused by the St. Elmo's fire were setting the generators on edge. If the eerie ball of electricity suddenly dispersed with its usual thud and blinding flash, it could take them out of service in an instant. The airplane would be on battery power alone, and if Bobby was unable to restore the power, there'd be precious few instruments and lights for Sam to continue flying with. They'd have only enough time on battery power to descend through the storms and ditch in the ocean.

Bobby glared at the flickering lights and threatened them beneath his breath. "Don't even think about it," he hissed.

Five miles from the weather, the stratus deck suddenly thinned and then disappeared and the St. Elmo's faded too, as if even St. Elmo demurred at the gates of hell. Sam turned off the storm lights, giving them a clear view of what they were headed into: a roiling black-gray mass of clouds backlit by explosive lightning, the tops of the storms towering miles above them, the bottoms miles below.

"Alright," Sam said. "Show time." He switched the storm lights back on, and moments later, they slammed into the maelstrom, the airplane brutally bashed about. The roar of the supercooled rain smashing into the airframe and windshield made all communication impossible. Jack attempted to adjust the radar, but he couldn't keep his hand on the dials.

"Don't bother," Sam yelled as loudly as he could. "It's attenuating; it's worthless!"

Lightning blasted through the storm lights with blinding ferocity, and the rumble of thunder could be heard over the cacophony of the rain.

Six minutes after they'd crashed into the storms, they burst out of them on the other side. It was as if they'd punched through a wall in hell and into the halls of heaven.

Sam turned off the storm lights.

All around them, the sky was crystal clear. The air was smooth as velvet, the moon beaming with a beatific glow. Thousands of feet below them, an endless sea of stratocumulus clouds lit by the moon extended to the horizon. Stars sparkled in the firmament. Only the soothing hiss of the wind filled the cockpit.

Jack sighed, then looked right and behind. "Jesus," he said. "It looks like that's a solid line all the way to the equator."

As Jack was looking south, Sam was looking above them to the north at a contrail he'd noticed. He leaned forward to study it for a moment.

"Number four generator's been dicey, but it's holding now," Bobby said. "I'm going to take it offline and reset it."

Sam turned to look at him and said, "Okay. I'll wait 'til you're done to put the autopilot back on."

Switches clicked quickly, and Bobby said, "Okay, we're good. Go ahead." He reached up and turned off the anti-ice and engine ignition.

Sam turned on the autopilot and handed the airplane over to Jack. As Jack took control, Sam reached for the Loran and said, "Now, let's see if we still have reception on the east side of that weather."

When the screen lit up, Sam attempted to adjust the receiver, but static made the trace lines invisible. He frowned and returned the Loran to standby mode. "Oh, well," he groaned. "So much for that idea."

"So, what do we do now?" Jack asked.

"Plan B," Sam said.

"What's that?"

"Watch." After a glance at the Doppler's odometer, Sam picked up his mic and, transmitting on the air-to-air frequency, said, "Aircraft approximately seventy west of thirty west at three-nine-oh on Whiskey, this is Douglas Eight-Oh-Four-Papa-Alpha, over."

There was a pause, and then a pilot with a Cornish accent answered. "Eight-Oh-Four-Papa-Alpha, this is Speedbird Six-Ninety-Six. We're fifty-three west of thirty west at three-nine-oh on Whiskey, so that may be us, sir. How can we help?"

Sam smiled and gave Jack a thumbs-up. "Roger, roger," he replied. "Appreciate the call back, sir. You guys have INS, is that correct?"

"Yes, sir, we do. Do you need a wind readout?"

"Yes, sir, that would be wonderful, thanks!"

"Roger, wind at three-nine-oh is two-eight-zero diagonal six-seven, temperature minus eight, over."

"Roger, we appreciate that, and are you guys coasting in at MALOT?"

"Ah," the Brit said, his tone implying he understood the underlying question. "That's affirmative, sir … You *too?*"

"Roger, sir, that's affirmative. Thanks again, and we appreciate the help."

"Cheers, and safe flight. Let us know if you need anything more."

"Wilco. Eight-Oh-Four-Papa-Alpha, out."

Sam clipped his mic. Pointing up at the contrail he'd noticed earlier, he said, "That's them."

Jack leaned forward and looked up. He saw a dark line above and to the north of them. It was backlit by the moon and tracing the sky from east to west. He sat back. "How can you be certain it's theirs?" he asked, looking skeptical.

"I can't," Sam admitted. "But British Airways has inertial navigation systems in their 747s, and those things are spot on. Given our deviation south for the weather, that well-defined contrail to the north of us, and the Doppler's near agreement on our longitude, it's the best we've got—so I'll take it."

"So, what now?"

"Come twenty degrees left and intercept their track. Once we're underneath and tracking it, I'll adjust the Doppler to fly that course and viola—we'll be back on Whiskey."

Jack looked less sure but used the manual control knob to intercept the contrail's course. A few minutes later with the contrail immediately above them, Jack banked the airplane to the right and followed it on a heading of 112°.

After ten minutes of tracking the contrail manually, Sam set up the Doppler and Jack switched the autopilot's heading control to DOP. He looked across at Sam and asked, "Why didn't you mention this as a possibility in Gander when we were discussing the risks of going with just one Doppler?"

"Because I told you what the alternatives were. I told you we could go around the tracks or beneath them and why we wouldn't do that, and you told me you were fine with that. The fact that following a contrail was a possibility was nothing we could rely on, so I didn't mention it at the time."

"Alright, I get that. But since we're through that line of weather now, why not descend to 29,000 feet or lower to avoid the tracks altogether?"

"Because of the higher fuel burn at the lower altitude, the icing in that stratus deck below us, the fact that we've got a good, mid-point fix on Whiskey, and finally because we won't need to deviate off Whiskey for weather again."

Jack looked down at his hands and considered what Sam had just told him.

"Look," Sam continued, "if you stay on here, this won't be the only occasion when you're in a position like this. We're not Pan Am or even Air Logistics for that matter. We don't have the luxury of writing up a problem in the logbook and leaving it for maintenance, crew schedule, and a gate agent to resolve. At an airline like ours, *every* problem on the road is *our* problem, and we pride ourselves not only on our ability to fly well but to get the job done come what may. Now, either you've got the chops for that or you don't. You assured me in Gander that you do, and now's your chance to prove it. Everyone's brave before the shooting starts, Jack. If this kind of flying isn't for you, just say so and we'll descend to two-nine-zero."

Jack bristled at the implication. With his eyes narrowed, he looked at Sam and said, "I asked you in Gander to respect my reasons for wanting to stay on here, and I meant it. What I'm asking you now is if there are any other things we can do to avoid an off-track violation at MALOT?"

Sam pointed at him and said, "Find the North Atlantic Orientation chart in your Jepps. Read the notes in the panels. Everything you need to know is there. I'd planned to mention that anyway. It might as well be now."

Jack's brows went up. "So you're saying there is something more we can do?"

"What I'm saying is, *no,* there is not, and for all the reasons I've just given you—and more … Now read!"

Jack turned for his kitbag and pulled out the stack of high-altitude charts he'd bound with a rubber band in Miami. He put them in his lap and began sifting through them, searching for the orientation chart Sam had mentioned.

Bobby rolled his eyes, pushed his seat back, and unbuckled his belt. "I'm getting a refresh on the coffee. Anyone else?"

Sam looked back and smiled. "Absolutely," he said.

Bobby returned his smile with an icy glance, then turned to Jack, who was sorting through his charts. "How about you, kiddo? Need a little caffeine boost after that lecture?"

Jack looked over his shoulder and with a wry grin said, "Yeah. Please."

Bobby turned to leave but then paused to check the fuel panel to ensure it was tank to engine. The tank to engine configuration was the simplest and most reliable way to feed fuel to the engines and the way flight engineers left it anytime they were going to be away from the cockpit. But when Bobby's eyes fell on the gauges, they went wide when they landed on the one for the number two main tank.

He plopped back into his seat, put his index finger on the gauge, and groaned. "Okay, Houston, I believe we have a problem here."

Recognizing Jack Swigert's immortal words from Apollo 13, Sam spun around, his gaze following Bobby's finger to the gauge.

"Down fifteen hundred pounds," Bobby said. "Looks like that leak's gotten worse."

Sam grimaced. "Shit," he grumbled. "How long has that been going on?"

"Not long," Bobby answered. "But whatever went wrong probably went wrong punching through that line. I told Gerhard we should've had that heat exchanger replaced, but he said no time for that and settled for the repair. All that rock 'n' rolling was probably enough to undo it."

Sam sighed. "Yeah … and not to mention the CAT we hit earlier … God*damn* it!" He looked at the other gauges and did a quick tally of the remaining fuel. Coming to a decision, he blew out his cheeks and said, "Alright. Give me the highest altitude we can sustain at Mach .78 on three engines and this weight. If we have to shut the engine down, I'd rather be at that altitude than scrambling on the HF for a clearance when we need it."

Bobby nodded and reached for the performance manual in his kitbag. He pulled out the binder, flipped through the pages, and found the Three Engine Cruise data. "So, at 220,000 pounds," he said, pausing as his finger searched the page of tabulated information. "Looks like 31,000 feet is a solid bet … and 33,000 a maybe. Both would be at max continuous power and 450 knots true airspeed … give or take." He closed the book with a slap of finality and put it back in his kitbag.

Sam said to Jack, "When we report 30W, request flight level three-one-oh."

Jack balked. "That'll put us in that stratus deck and we'll lose sight of the contrail. Why not wait as long as we can to keep it in view?"

"Because that would require declaring an emergency if we have to get down quickly, and that could open a can of worms in Shannon. We'll have problems enough when we get there. I'm not piling on any more. Period."

"Then why not go down just a little further to 29,000 feet and get below MNPS airspace?"

"Because if that stratus deck begins to break up at the top, the odds of seeing that contrail are better at 31,000 than 29,000, so higher makes more sense."

Jack nodded and looked away to signal his ambivalence to Sam's reasoning. Sam took note of the body language and said, "Okay, fair enough, Jack. But don't forget it was you and Bobby-socks here who wanted to fly with that leak tonight. Just be glad we didn't wind up sitting in a raft. *Capeesh?*"

Bobby scoffed and waved him off. "Fuck that," he chortled. "Better a raft than Gander."

Sam made a face and said, "How about that coffee?"

Bobby yawned, got up, and stretched. "Tank to engine," he grumbled. "Three cups of wake-up on the way."

# FORTY-ONE

The ten-mile alert on the Doppler illuminated, and Sam and Jack confirmed the outbound course. When they reached the fix at 53N 30W, Sam hacked his clock, logged the time, and passed the clipboard to Bobby to tally the fuel.

Bobby recorded it and groaned. "Down thirty-six hundred pounds," he said as he passed the clipboard back to Sam. "Looks like that leak's getting worse."

Sam examined the fuel gauge. He grimaced and ran his hand through his hair. "Yeah. You're right," he said with a sigh. "But go back and take a look. The beacon will give you enough light to see a vapor trail if there is one. I'd like confirmation it's the engine and not the tank before shutting it down."

Bobby nodded and left.

Sam finished the calculations for their ETA at the next fix, passed the clipboard to Jack, and then retuned and triggered the HF to 6860 for Shanwick Control. A loud bleating sound came through the loudspeakers as the HF retuned. When it ended and was replaced by loud static, Sam looked at Jack and said, "When you check in, request descent to three-one-oh."

Jack made the position report with the request for 31,000 feet. Shanwick acknowledged his report and told him to stand by with his request for lower.

Shortly after, Bobby bounded through the door and threw himself into his seat, breathless. "Yeah, it's the engine," he confirmed. "It's leaking like a dam burst. You want the checklist?"

"No, not yet," Sam said. "Let's give Shanwick a little longer. I don't want to declare an emergency and pull the trigger unless we have to."

"Goddamn, Sam … I don't know. We're losing a *lot* of gas."

"Yeah, but so far we've lost only what I padded in Gander. We've still got enough for Manchester with a twelve-thousand-pound reserve, so let's give it a few more minutes."

When the SELCAL chimed, Jack had his headphones on and was copying something on his scratch pad. He raised a finger to signal to Sam that he was busy, and Sam picked up his mic and responded to the SELCAL.

Shanwick cleared them for a descent to 31,000 feet. Sam read back the clearance, reset the altitude alert, and used the autopilot to begin the descent.

As they descended through 35,000 feet, Jack took off his earphones and said, "Sorry about that. I was getting the VOLMET from Shannon on the other HF."

Sam looked surprised. "Outstanding!" he said. "So, how are we doing?"

"Shannon's six hundred over in drizzle and light rain, visibility one mile, wind two-six-zero at twelve. Manchester's twelve hundred over and six."

"Damn good work, Jack," Sam complimented him. "Where'd you find the VOLMET information, on the orientation chart?"

"Yes," Jack answered. "But I also found the requirement to consult with air traffic control if we experience a loss of navigation capability. And so far, we haven't complied."

"And what would that do for us if we did?"

"Get us off the hook for a gross nav error?"

"Is that what it says?"

Jack balked. "Well, uh … it doesn't. But isn't that implied?"

"Not to me it isn't," Sam answered bluntly. "By the way, your airplane," he said, handing control over to Jack.

Jack assumed control with the autopilot and continued the descent, and Sam continued with an explanation. "Look," he said, "here's how this works: if we're off course by more than twenty-five miles when we're picked up on radar near MALOT, the controller will file a report. That report will then be filed with the FAA, and an investigation will be initiated by the Miami Flight Standards District Office to determine whether or not we declared minimum nav equipment. So, all things considered, unless we have no idea where we are—and we *do*—I'm not exposing us, and the company, to unnecessary scrutiny."

"Fair enough," Jack replied. "But then how about we give the Loran another try?"

Sam shrugged. "By all means. Try as often as you like," he said. "But in my experience, the sort of interference we're experiencing tonight won't end until that weather does."

Descending through 33,000 feet, they entered the tops of the stratus deck that had been below them and were enveloped in a vaporous black gloom that cut off visibility everywhere.

Jack leveled the airplane at 31,000 feet, turned on the altitude hold, and advanced the throttles to hold their speed at .78 Mach.

Sam looked back at Bobby, who was waiting with the emergency checklist in hand. "Alright. Let's do it," he said.

"Engine fire shutdown checklist," Bobby declared. "Number two throttle … idle."

"Number two, confirmed?" Sam asked.

"Yeah, number two, confirmed."

Sam pulled the throttle closed, the gear horn blared, and Bobby cut it off.

The airplane yawed left as the left inboard engine lost thrust, and the autopilot turned the yoke right to counteract it. Bobby reached forward and set the other three throttles for max continuous power at 87% N1 RPM.

Jack leveled the yoke with the rudder trim as Sam had instructed him to do during their simulator period, and then Sam looked at Bobby and said, "Continue."

"Number two fuel shutoff lever … off."

Sam put his hand on the lever and asked, "Confirmed?"

"Yeah … confirmed."

Sam pulled the lever out and shut down the engine. Warning lights began to flash on the panels, but Sam and Bobby pushed the light caps to cancel them.

"Number Two fire handle to fuel, air, hydraulics … off."

Sam reached up for the handle on the overhead panel. Bobby confirmed it was correct, and Sam pulled it out and pushed it into its detent.

"That completes phase one," Bobby said. "You want phase two?"

"No, not yet. Go back and inspect the engine first. Ensure the vapor trail has stopped."

Bobby unbuckled and bolted from his seat.

As they waited for Bobby to return, Jack reached for the Loran and moved the knob from SBY to ON. The screen lit up and the trace lines were visible now, but just barely, and after several attempts to get them to align, Jack gave up. He returned the Loran to SBY and conceded to Sam, "I see what you mean."

Bobby came through the doorway and said, "We're good. That got it." He took his seat and buckled in. Sam and Bobby completed phase two of the checklist, and the flight continued to their next fix at 53N 20W without further event.

· · ·

At 04:34Z they crossed the fix at 53N 20W, and Sam reported their position. Shanwick instructed them to contact Shannon Area Control at MALOT, their coast-in point on track Whiskey.

Sam set the VHF communication and navigation radios up for their arrival to Shannon from MALOT. He tuned the nav radios for Shannon VOR and set 096° for the inbound course on his Pictorial Deviation Indicator. Jack did the same. Then Sam went on to explain that the first indication of VHF navigation reception would be detected by the VHF

DME. After the DME sensed a signal, the next instrument to do so would likely be the two needles on the radio magnetic indicator. Soon after that, the PDI would come alive. But because of the 200 NM range of VHF nav reception, none of those instruments would be of any use to determine their position with certainty before Shanwick picked them up on radar at MALOT. And only then would they know if the Doppler had kept them within twenty-five miles of course—or not.

The flight time from 53N 20W to MALOT was planned at twenty-five minutes. The air remained smooth, the radio silent, and the cockpit a warm and softly lit cocoon immersed in the gloom. Sam was nodding in and out as he battled the need for sleep, while Bobby had surrendered. He was snoring loudly, his hands limp in his lap.

Meanwhile, Jack was wide awake, staring at his instruments and anxiously toying with a pencil. The three drums on the VHF DME were locked on 0 0 0, the RMI needles spinning mindlessly around the compass rose beneath them, and the PDI needle pegged against the right side of the display. The further the Doppler odometer rolled down, the faster Jack twisted his pencil and the more he squirmed in his seat. "Your life, your career—your call," Sam had warned him in Gander. "Fly safe" was how Kegan had put it.

Their words rang in his ears.

· · ·

At 04:52Z, the inky black of night morphed into the leaden gray of an Irish morning as the wan light of dawn appeared.

The ten-mile alert on the Doppler suddenly illuminated. Jack swallowed, looked across at Sam, and quietly said, "We're coming up on MALOT."

Sam gave a snort, opened his eyes, and looked about dazed. He cleared his throat, unclipped his mic, and put it in his lap at the ready.

Bobby woke with a start, blinked, and gave a cursory glance at his panel. He blew his nose loudly into a handkerchief, and then turned and reached up for anti-ice switches on the overhead panel. "You want these for the descent?" he asked Sam.

Sam looked up at the switches and nodded.

"You want an updated FOD?" Bobby asked.

"Nah," Sam muttered. "We'll get in."

The VHF DME drums suddenly began to spin, and Jack sat up in his seat. He shifted his gaze to the RMI, but the needles were still revolving.

The Doppler rolled down to 0 0 0, the amber light went out, and the autopilot banked left to intercept the inbound course they'd set for Shannon.

Sam picked up his mic and said with a cheerful tone, "Good morning, Shannon, Douglas Eight-Oh-Four-Papa-Alpha is with you passing MALOT at three-one-oh, squawking two-zero-zero-zero."

A controller with a heavy Irish brogue boomed in reply. "Roger, Captain, and good morning to you, sir. Squawk zero-seven-one-eight, over."

Sam reached down and reset the transponder to 0 7 1 8.

The drums on the DME suddenly spun, tumbled, and froze on 2 8 9 for a moment and then began spinning again. A moment later, they paused on 2 2 6 for a second and then began spinning and spinning again.

Jack fixed his gaze on the RMI needles. Their revolving had suddenly stopped, and like two bird dogs picking up a scent, they began oscillating back and forth across the top of the instrument.

His fingers worried the pencil; his eyes darted between the DME, the RMI, and the PDI as he awaited a verdict.

The PDI needle began twitching nervously, then shot across the instrument, bounced off the right side of the display, and pegged against the left.

The DME stopped spinning. It tumbled, shuddered, and froze on 2 1 8. A moment later it spun, tumbled, shuddered, and froze on 2 0 9 …

Tumble, shudder, freeze, 2 0 5 …

Shudder, freeze, 2 0 2 …

2 0 1 …

2 0 0 …

1 9 9 …

Jack could feel his heart beating in his chest, and a cold sweat broke out on the back of his neck. Any moment they'd get the call.

Bobby cleared his throat loudly, and Jack jumped, startled and angered by it. "Looks like we're starting to pick up some ice," Bobby said to Sam. "You want wing heat too?"

Sam pulled his penlight from his shirt pocket and directed the beam outside at the glaze of rime ice building along the windshield's seal. He nodded and threw a wave at the overhead panel.

Bobby turned the wing heat on and said, "We've still got six hundred pounds of fuel in the number two main. If you want it, we'd better use it or move it now. We might not get it all in the descent."

Sam answered with a nod and a yawn.

"I'll move it to number three main," Bobby said. He clapped Jack hard on the shoulder, making him flinch. "Balance her up good for you," he said as he shook his shoulder. "Set you up for a good landing."

1 8 5 …

1 8 4 …

The radio boomed. "Douglas Four-Papa-Alpha, I'm not receiving your transponder, sir. Squawk ident, please."

Sam pressed the ident button.

Jack twisted the pencil round and round, his gaze transfixed on the PDI.

1 7 8 …

1 7 7 …

"Douglas Four-Papa-Alpha, I am still not receiving your transponder, sir, if you have another one, please switch to that."

Sam reached down and recycled the same transponder he was using from ON to SBY and back to ON. It was the best he could do. The second transponder was inoperative and hadn't been repaired before they left Miami.

"Douglas Four-Papa-Alpha, negative transponder, sir. Stand by … "

1 7 0 …

1 6 9 …

The RMI needles suddenly stopped oscillating and locked up near the top of the instrument. A moment later, the PDI needle bounced full scale from left to right before locking up a dot and a half left of course.

Jack closed his eyes. They were off course. It only remained to know by how much. *Your life, your career … your call*, he thought. *Dear God, please …*

1 6 2 …

1 6 1 …

"Douglas Eight-Oh-Four-Papa-Alpha, ident for me, over."

Sam reached down lazily and pressed the ident button again.

1 5 7 …

1 5 6 …

"Douglas Four-Papa-Alpha, roger, sir, sorry about that. The problem was on our end. You're radar contact now sixteen miles northeast of MA-LOT. You're cleared present position direct Shannon VOR. When ready, descend and maintain flight level one-one-zero, over."

Jack's brows shot up and his jaw dropped. He slowly turned to look across at Sam, dumbstruck.

Sam replied calmly to the clearance, spun the altitude alert to eleven thousand, and clipped his mic.

"*Sixteen miles!*" Jack exclaimed. "Did you hear that?" he asked, beaming. He tossed his pencil in the air, collapsed into his seat, and blew out his cheeks.

Bobby exploded in a belly laugh.

Jack looked back at him, puzzled. "What?" he asked, his brow knit.

Bobby grabbed his earlobe and gave it a shake. "Had your panties in a bunch back there, didn't you, little sis? Figured your ass was on its way to Kilmainham Prison, some IRA chief's new colleen?" He howled in a gale of laughter. "Flying crooked Celtic style, eh? *Ah-oooooh!*"

Jack made a face and flipped him the bird. He looked across at Sam and snapped, "You guys knew all along, didn't you? You played me!"

Sam couldn't contain his smile. "Sorry," he said with a chuckle. "This ain't our first rodeo, cowboy … We were never that far off course."

Jack's jaw was set, his eyes shooting ice picks at Sam while Bobby tousled his hair. "You're too much, Jackeroo," he guffawed, sitting back and wiping his eyes with his sleeves. "Best fun I've had in years."

"Alright … alright, enough fun," Sam said. "Pull up the ATIS for me, Bobby. Let's see what we've got."

• • •

"Information Delta," Bobby said as he passed the landing data card forward. "Four hundred overcast and one mile in drizzle, rain; temperature's nine Celsius, dew point six, wind two-zero-zero at eight knots. ILS Runway 24 in use."

Sam gazed at the card and tossed it onto the radar screen. "This will be your approach and landing," he said to Jack. "Pull the plate from your manual, and I'll brief it."

"Even with an engine out?"

"You'd need an engine-out approach to complete your qualification anyway, so why fake it when we don't have to?"

"Makes sense to me," Jack replied. He turned and reached for his Jepp manual.

They continued their descent into the gloom, completed the approach briefing, and set their instruments for landing.

Forty miles from the airport, Shannon Control handed them off to Shannon Approach Control. When Sam switched frequencies and checked in, the controller cleared them to descend to five thousand feet.

Fifteen miles from the airfield, the controller said, "Douglas Eight-Oh-Four-Papa-Alpha, turn right heading zero-six-zero, descend and maintain four thousand."

Sam replied, and Jack pulled the throttles to idle to begin slowing for the approach. At 200 knots and level at four thousand feet, he called for flaps ten.

"Eight-Oh-Four-Papa-Alpha, left turn now heading three-three-zero."

Soon after, the controller said, "Eight-Oh-Four-Papa-Alpha, left now two-seven-zero. Maintain four thousand feet. Intercept the localizer for Runway 24, and you are cleared for the approach. Contact tower now on 119.6."

Sam read back the clearance, and Jack banked the airplane to intercept the final approach course. But halfway through the turn, he felt Sam prompting him with the yoke to increase the rate of turn. "With that dead engine on the left side, you'll need to roll more aggressively," he said. "Also, use some rudder with an engine out; don't depend on the yaw damper for everything."

Jack intercepted the localizer. When the glide slope indicated one dot high, he called for the gear down. When the gear indicated it was down and locked, Bobby called out the last items on the checklist.

As they descended through seven hundred feet, Jack caught brief glimpses of rolling green fields and stone fences as tiny drops of rain raced across the windshield in a gray and misty morning.

At five hundred feet, the sequenced approach lights came into view, the starburst of their beams diffracted through the rain-streaked glass.

At fifty feet, with his left hand on the throttles, his right hand on the yoke, and Sam guarding the controls, they crossed the runway threshold. Jack drew the power to idle, and the airplane sank more quickly than it had before. He pulled the yoke back sharply, and the airplane flared for the runway. He pressed the left rudder to stay on the centerline, and an instant later, he felt the main gear touch down almost imperceptibly. As he lowered the nosewheel to the runway, he drew the thrust levers into reverse. The engines roared, and the airplane rumbled as it slowed. At one hundred knots, Jack cautiously applied the brakes.

At sixty knots, Sam said, "Okay, I've got the airplane … Outstanding job."

As they exited the runway to the taxiway, Bobby grabbed Jack's shoulder and gave it a shake. "Nice, job, Jackeroo … nice job, indeed."

Jack hadn't felt such a sense of thrill and achievement since he'd first soloed.

*Part Three*

# DESCENT

# FORTY-TWO

*Shannon, Ireland, October 27, 1978*

S am was in the galley with the customs officer and Bobby at his panel completing the logbook entries. Jack stood inside the forward entry-way and gazed across the ramp as he waited for them to complete their tasks. They'd parked the airplane near the cargo terminal and adjacent to 816PA, their sister ship that had arrived an hour before.

The dreary morning and light breeze washed over Jack as he watched the activity at the airfield. A score of diminutive trucks and tugs zipped about the ramp and terminal with a fancied urgency—as if anything in Ireland ever abided by a schedule. He smiled. This was how he remembered Ireland from his boyhood visits, the gloomy weather, the human scale of things. He was first here when Sputnik orbited the earth in 1957, and now he'd returned as a man, as an international jet airline pilot, who'd just flown the Atlantic. Jack had arrived; a dream realized. He hadn't felt so grateful for his good fortune since leaving Vietnam alive and in one piece, nor had he ever felt so full of anticipation for what was ahead.

Sam and the customs officer came to the door, and Jack stepped aside to let them pass. As they walked down the stairs, Sam raised his arm and waved to a man Jack didn't recognize. He was approaching from their sistership and dressed in a green nylon flight jacket, jeans, and western boots. He smiled and returned Sam's wave.

At the base of the stairs, the customs officer left for the terminal and Sam greeted the other man. They chatted a bit before Sam turned and waved at Jack to come down. As Jack came near, Sam said to him, "Jack, this is Mick Salyer, one of our other captains and a very good friend."

Jack smiled and offered his hand. "Captain Salyer," he said. "I heard you on the radio coming up from Miami. Pleased to meet you, sir."

"Mick," he said, smiling and shaking Jack's hand.

Suddenly, Bobby was at the top of the stairs and booming. "Well, hey there, Mickey-dickey," he bellowed. "How was your flight? Ours sucked!"

Mick looked up and shouted, "Bobby-sox! Damn, I thought you'd died and gone to Gander."

Bobby gave him the finger and tramped down the stairs on arthritic knees. When he got to the ramp, he dropped his bags like sacks of bricks and put his hands on his hips. "Jesus, what a night."

Mick shrugged. "We did alright. Got a few issues to deal with but, from what Sam tells me, nothing like this thing," he said, jutting his chin toward their airplane.

Bobby looked back at it and said, "Yeah, issues . . . *Lots* of fucking issues."

Mick said to Sam, "Anyway, just so you know, Captain Shithead's already throwing his weight around. He says every gripe we've got with this pair of dogs has to get fixed here in Shannon. He says any problems we leave with and can't fix ourselves will have to be handled in Singapore, so better take care of them now."

Sam looked down at the ramp and nodded. "Brad's right," he said. "The problem is we don't have the time. It's Friday morning, and we need to have at least two airplanes in Indonesia by Tuesday morning for the first lift."

"So, how do you want to play it?" Mick asked.

"I've been thinking about it since thirty west," Sam answered. Pointing his thumb over his shoulder at the airplane, he said, "We'll start by grounding this one until everything's been repaired, and properly this time. Meantime, we'll put the full effort into fixing whatever yours needs and get everyone on the way southbound as soon as possible. Reggie's got the other airplane ready to go in Colombo, so that'll give us the two we absolutely need to get started. Bobby, Larry, and I will stay behind with this one and get Aer Lingus on it. Once I'm satisfied it's squared away, we'll be on our way to join you. With any luck, it won't take more than a few days."

Hearing Sam's decision, Jack felt crushed. He turned and looked aside in despair. He'd expected a delay while they got the airplane repaired, but he hadn't anticipated this. If Sam intended to replace Jack with Larry Schaff, then he assumed it was also Sam's intention to send Jack home. Whatever hope he'd had of staying on had just been dashed.

As the other men continued their banter, Jack remained silent and detached.

"Well, that sounds like a plan to me," he heard Bobby say. "Now, let's get out of here. I'm ready for a beer—or five, at least." He laughed.

"Make it one," Sam said dryly. "We need our mechanics and engineers back out here ASAP. Take a break for breakfast, and then get a crew together to work. Agreed?"

"Anyone ever tell you you're a pain in the ass?" Bobby snapped.

"Yes, you, in fact … and quite often."

Bobby scoffed and reached for his bags.

"Oh … one more thing," Mick said to Sam. "When the girls heard we'd be delayed for maintenance, they decided they're not hanging around. Charlotte said she'd organize a charter bus to Dublin to kill the time there."

Sam looked incredulous. "*What?*" he said. "Is she nuts? That's at least a couple of hours from here. No, no … no way," he insisted with a wave of his hand. "Everyone stays put. You'll launch the minute your airplane's fixed. I'm not sending out a search party for the crew."

"That's what Captain Shithead told her," Mick chimed in. "But Charlotte figures Captain Daddy will overrule him. Just letting you know, Skipper, before you get sandbagged walking in the door."

"I'm getting my key and going to my room," Sam said. "Tell her Brad's right. Everyone stays put. Period."

"Fuck this!" Bobby growled. "C'mon, I'm thirsty."

Mick pointed toward the freight terminal and said, "This way, girls. Our chariot awaits."

. . .

Jack squeezed into the back seat of the hotel's VW van and stared glumly out the window as they motored the short distance to the hotel. The Bunratty House was only a few miles from the airport, and as they arrived at the circular driveway, Jack shifted his gaze toward the quaint, two-story Irish inn, ivied, and set back from a country road.

When the driver stopped at the entrance, Mick got out and went inside ahead of the other three men, who collected their bags from the back of the van. As Sam signed them in and got their keys, Bobby pointed toward the pub room doors and said to Jack, "Get mine for me and meet me in there."

Jack eyed the stacks of crew bags piled against the wall outside the pub room's double oak doors and nodded.

Bobby grabbed his bags and bolted toward the pub; his arthritic knees had been miraculously cured. Mick looked at Jack and said, "See you inside?"

Jack put on a smile and replied with a nod.

Sam turned to give them their keys, and noting Bobby's departure, he handed two keys to Jack. "I'm in 114, you're in 116, and Bobby's 119. You'll see he gets it, yes?"

Jack took the keys sullenly and answered with a nod.

Sam noted his despair and started to say something before deciding he was too weary to get into it now. As he reached for his bags, he said, "Okay, I'm off. Tell the others I had to make some calls and we'll catch up later."

As Sam stepped toward the hallway and his room, Jack's disappointment exploded in indignation. "Sam!" he shouted.

Sam stopped, looked down, then turned back to him with a bleary gaze.

"What about me?" Jack asked. "With the airplane grounded and your plan to replace me with Larry, what happens to me?"

"I won't know until I talk to Gerhard," Sam answered flatly. "Crew manning is his decision, not mine." He turned and continued toward his room.

Jack watched him until he disappeared, then reached for his bags and trudged toward the pub. He dumped them outside among the pile of others.

He opened the doors, stepped inside, and paused at the entrance.

It was a traditional Irish pub with plastered walls cracked and mottled with age, a low beamed ceiling, and a blackened bar with a patina from timeless use. Across from that was the dining area with wood furnishings and a hearth glowing with embers. The room was packed with crew, and mixing with their cheerful banter was a trace of turf smoke and the tantalizing aroma of the breakfast being served: rashers, bangers, eggs, and slices of thick white toast heavily buttered.

Pilots and flight engineers dominated the bar, pints of ale in hand, while the flight attendants clustered in the dining area. Two harried waitresses scurried to and from the kitchen with plates of food, and Jack watched as the girls assisted the waitresses in distributing the plates and cleaning or organizing the tables. He admired them, these men and women without airs or a sense of superiority. Mission hackers, Joe had called them. A job needed doing, and they rolled up their sleeves and got right to it, no hesitation, no desire to be recognized or served. Jack had found a home among them—if only he were able to keep it.

He looked about the room hoping to see Joe—who better to commiserate with?—but Joe was nowhere in sight. He did find Bobby, though, standing at the bar among a group of other pilots and engineers. Jack started toward him, and as he approached with his room key in hand, Bobby caught sight of him and waved him closer.

Jack handed him his key, and Bobby threw his arm around Jack's shoulder and pulled him in tight. "Here he is!" he said loudly. "Jackeroo with the golden hands." He looked at him, smiled, and said, "I've been telling these guys how you saved our asses tonight, kiddo. Been telling them what a fine addition to our little flying club you'll be."

Jack blushed as the other men broke into a refrain of "For He's a Jolly Good Fellow." The girls were looking their way and rolling their eyes.

Mick Salyer came to Jack's side bearing a pint and pressed it into Jack's hand. "Try this," he said. "Nothing at home can match it."

Jack took a sip and his eyebrows went up. "Wow," he said, holding out the glass and admiring the reddish-brown color. "This is amazing."

"They make it locally," Mick explained. "Fresh from the brewery to the tap. Cheers," he said, clinking glasses with Jack. "So, Sam's doing his usual slam-clicker, is he?" Mick continued. "Leaving his crew to fill in for him at the debrief, huh?"

"He said he needed to make some calls."

"Yeah, to his wife, first and foremost, and then Gerhard. Sam's a Boy Scout through and through. But you've probably got that figured by now."

Jack coughed. "Oh! I've, uh … I've sensed that. I get the feeling he's trying to save me from me, if that makes sense."

"Bet on it," Mick said. "We've known one another since we were kids. There's a back story to Sam, tragic, and he's been wearing it all his life like the chains on Marley's ghost. I'll fill you in when we fly together, but make no mistake. Sam's a very good man, probably too good for his own benefit, and he just can't stop trying to save us all from ourselves. Me above all, and look how much of a failure that's been," he said with a laugh.

"You mean the training accident at TMA?"

"No, but that too, actually. What I'm talking about happened long before that. It was when we were kids."

"Oh—"

"Anyway, Sam told me you're doing a bang-up job. He says you're a shoo-in with Air Logistics, is that right?"

Jack shrugged self-consciously. "He seems to think so."

"But he says you want to stay on here. Is that right?"

Jack took a sip and wiped the foam from his lips. "Yes," he said. "Air Logistics is a great company, but I think I'm a better fit here, and I don't want to leave unless I have something clearly better in the bag."

"Makes perfect sense to me. Did Sam tell you he's retiring at the end of this gig?"

"Yes … or I've been told, anyway."

"He won't be the only one leaving soon," Mick said. "Most of the captains here are pushing sixty, and beyond that—if things go as planned—this airline's in for big changes, changes that most of us don't care to stick around for."

"Plans?" Jack asked. "Plans for what?"

"Not sure, but given all the money they're sinking into refitting our airplanes, we're guessing more travel club contracts, corporate junkets, political campaigns, and the sort of thing Manny has connections with. All that domestic shit we can't stand. But Manny and Freddie Laker are neighbors at their places in the Bahamas, and Freddie's fame and success with his airline has whetted Manny's appetite for the sport. That's why he jumped in and rescued Pan Tropic."

"How do you know that?"

"Freddie's yacht captain is a friend of mine from the Keys. He fills me in, stuff he picks up on the side." Mick smiled. "Anyway, they think this deregulation thing that's coming will be a free-for-all, and my buddy says Manny never shies from a fight. He says if Manny wants to be in the airline business, he'll be in it to the hilt. If I'm right about all this, the company will be needing new captains and soon. Go with Air Logistics and you won't see the left seat until you're damn near my age. Progression there is glacially slow, and that company is hidebound to its traditions. It'll be a wonder if they'll even survive."

"That's a good point."

"Damn right. So, have you spoken to Gerhard about it? If you want to stay on, make sure you do. I mean, Sam's like a brother to me and I'd never betray him, but it's your life and career, Jack, not Sam's."

"I know, and he's told me that too. But with his plans to ground the airplane and replace me with Larry Schaff, there's no point in keeping me on. I'm sure Gerhard will agree."

Mick shook his head. "No," he said. "Talk to Gerhard, tell him how you feel. If you want to stay on, my bet is he'll be happy to have you."

"Really?"

Mick downed what was left of his pint, planted the glass on the bar, and stifled a belch. He glanced at his watch. "Alright," he said. "I'm outta here. Long day ahead later and I got to hit the sack." He looked at Jack, smiled, and added, "Make sure he knows you want to stay. It'll make a difference."

"I will," Jack said. "But how?"

"Give him a call," Mick said, as if a call from Ireland took nothing more than a few quarters and a pay phone.

He threw Jack a wave and started for the door, and it was as if a secret signal had gone up. Suddenly, the entire crew began getting up and leaving like a flock of migrating geese taking to wing.

Jack paused and watched them go, feeling no impulse to join them. Despite Mick's kind words and assurances, it seemed more likely that Jack would soon be flying home rather than flying the hajj, so why not linger and enjoy these final moments as an international jet airline pilot? He leaned back against the bar, finished his beer, and was considering having another when his eyes met the gaze of the sultry auburn he'd met in Miami. It was the night of the briefing in the bar, and he struggled to remember her name. She was shuffling toward the doors of the pub and arm in arm with the brunette he'd also met that night, the snickering, insulting bitch who came to Auburn's side and laughed at Jack when he told them he was a pilot.

And then it came to him. Eddie! She'd said her name was Eddie, and later, Sam had introduced her too. *One drop-dead gorgeous Eddie*, he reflected. How could he have forgotten that?

She returned his gaze with a coquettish smile and a wink. Jack smiled too and raised his glass as if in a toast.

Brunette caught them flirting. She scowled at Jack, then yanked Eddie to her side. Eddie turned on her, gave her a stormy look, yanked back, and broke free. They appeared to exchange words but remained side by side as they continued toward the exit.

Jack watched them and was aroused by a carnal curiosity. And then, just before the exit, Eddie suddenly turned and snuck another glance at him over her shoulder. He smiled and tipped his glass toward her. She smiled in return and gave her hair a shake before continuing toward the door.

He looked down and into his glass, chuckled, and gave the beer a swirl. *So, they're a thing,* he thought. *Lovers, that explains it. Except Eddie's a switch-hitter, and it drives Brunette nuts. Ugh. Poor girl,* he mused. *Talk about tough relationships.*

He took a final sip, then wheeled around and put his glass on the bar.

"Would you like another, love?" the pretty barmaid asked, her captivating blue eyes sparking in the lights, jet-black tresses tumbling over her shoulders.

"Oh, uh, I would, actually … but I can't," he added with a note of regret. "I have a long day coming up. I ought to turn in."

She smiled. "Ah, well then," she said. "Sure, we look forward to having you back. Have a safe flight home, love, or wherever you're off to."

"I will," he said sadly. "Off to Philly in the land of wherever."

# FORTY-THREE

*Shannon, Ireland, October 27, 1978*

The hallway was silent as a tomb, and as Jack passed Sam's room, he eyed the Do Not Disturb tag hanging from the knob.

Jack's was the room adjacent to Sam's, and when he got to his door, he slipped the key into the lock, turned the knob, and gave the door a gentle push.

The room was barely lit though the drapes were wide open, the gloomy morning providing little ambient light. Jack put down his bags and walked to the nightstand to turn on the lamp. It gave the room a warm and soothing glow, and he was pleased as he looked around. The décor was in the Irish tradition, with an iron bed, a thick white quilt on the mattress, and an upholstered slipper chair in the corner. He placed his suitcase on a stand at the base of the bed and opened it to retrieve his shaving kit.

He got undressed, hung his slacks and shirt in the closet, and folded his sweatshirt, which he left on the chair. The bed was a double with large, soft pillows. He tested the mattress with his hand, and it felt heaven-sent. He'd plunge into it and sleep until he was called to go home.

The bathroom fixtures were heavy white porcelain, the floor tiled in a vintage gray and white pattern, and the faucets aged brass. Across from the tub, a thick cotton towel was hanging on a heated rack, and above that was a small window with cotton drapes. He wondered how old the inn was. It looked like something from another era, a time of Pan Am Clippers and Irish coffee served on arrival, a time when air travel was still elegant and gracious, a time before jets and Holiday Inns.

The faucets squeaked as Jack opened them, and as he waited for the water to steam, he separated the drapes with a finger to peer outside. Raindrops were dripping down the glass, and he watched a man pedaling a bicycle along a narrow lane, unhurried by the downpour. It brought back other images of Ireland he remembered from his boyhood, the walks he'd taken with his grandfather over verdant fields with stone fences and sheep grazing, his grandfather with a blackthorn walking stick in one hand and rosary beads in the other. A stream burbled alongside, watercress dancing in the flow. He smiled as he remembered it, those walks, the beauty and serenity, the gentle piety of a man he so dearly loved.

Steam was rising as Jack pulled the stopper to begin the shower. The water was near scalding as he stepped into it. He turned his back to the stream and closed his eyes as it pelted away the grime of the night.

When he was finished, he dried himself with the towel, put it around his waist, and secured it with a tuck. He wiped the steam from the mirror and ran his fingers through his hair before flipping off the light and leaving.

Feeling as down, defeated, and drained as he could remember, he drew the heavy drapes closed listlessly and was pulling down the bedclothes when he heard a soft knock on a door.

He looked at it, bemused.

The knock came softly again.

He cinched the tuck tighter and padded across the carpet to see who it was. A hotel clerk with a message, his flight home already booked?

He checked the peephole, saw no one, and then disconnected the chain lock. He turned the knob and stood aside to hide his state of undress as he opened the door. But suddenly he felt himself pushed from the other side, and he stepped back in surprise.

She slipped between the narrow opening of the door and frame as easily as a railbird through reeds and was inside in a flash. With her hands behind her back, she pushed the door closed with a quiet click, then smiled and gave him an approving once-over.

"*Eddie?*" he exclaimed. He was thoroughly baffled. "I, uh … I don't—"

She put a finger to his lips, her liquorish gaze holding his as she teased her finger in s-turns down his throat, to his chest and abs, and then inserted it between the linen and his skin.

His blood ran hot and his breath quickened as she worked her finger around his waist toward the towel's tuck. "Charlotte said you're a queer," she cooed in a silky drawl as she continued holding his gaze. "And I said, 'Oh *no*, sugar … *No*, he is *not!*'"

She teased the tuck, her impish eyes locked on his, and with a firm flick, it opened and the towel flaked to the floor in a heap.

She looked down—paused and smiled at his arousal—and looked up. "I win," she giggled.

His right hand shot from his side, and he grabbed her by the nape of the neck. He pushed her against the wall and parted her legs, her short, pleated skirt rising. He forced his tongue into her mouth, and she stiffened against the violence; it wasn't what she'd expected.

He sensed her fear and softened his grip and moved his mouth to her neck and caressed it gently. His left hand slipped beneath her cashmere sweater and found her breast, her nipple.

She moaned softly and then threw herself into it wholesale, twining her arms around his neck, her tongue probing, throwing her legs up and around his waist as they kissed, and kissed madly.

He wheeled her around, carried her to the bed, and tossed her onto the mattress. She squealed with delight, her hair flying in folds around her.

He dropped to his knees and reached beneath her skirt to remove her panties, but there were none. She sat up and, in one seamless move, stripped off her cashmere and flung it across the room. He was spellbound at the sight of her breasts, round and firm and high … no tan lines.

He sank his head into her cleavage and caressed her, her skin growing moist, overwhelmed by the beat of her heart, her quickening breath, her hands moving his head to her nipple …

He forced her back onto the bed, pulled off her ballet slippers, and tossed them recklessly over his shoulder. He kissed her feet and began drawing his tongue along her leg to her inner thigh, and slowly, pain-fully slowly, he drew it toward her center. Her fist was in her mouth and her eyes tight in anticipation. She gasped when it arrived, hot, wet, and softly firm.

He stayed there teasing and provoking her, her passion rising like a flooding tide swirling and filling her until she peaked. With her hands gripping the sheets, her back arched, her legs stiffened, and her mouth wide open in a silent scream, she convulsed in a violent shudder and a strangled gasp before collapsing onto the bed, breathless. She rolled on her side and locked her ankles, her breath coming fast and hot. He pulled gently at her legs to open them and start again, but she waved him off, pleading, "*Stop ... stop ... stop!*" between labored breaths. "*Not yet!*"

He smiled and relented. He slid up alongside her, and they spooned as she settled, his arm across her and embracing her breasts, his face nuzzled into the back of her neck, her hair cascading over him.

They stayed like that awhile, the only sound the pattering of the rain on the glass.

Then she rolled around and looked into his eyes, put her hand on his cheek. He took it in his hands and kissed it, his tongue working between her fingers, and then began sliding to the floor again. She stopped him and pulled him back. She nipped him on the neck and it stung. Then she put her tongue in his ear and reached for him and fondled him until he could bear it no longer, and sensing this, she stopped.

He groaned and looked at her as if to ask, *But why?*

She smiled, put her hands on his shoulders, and forced him back onto the bed. She rose and pinned him there with her left hand and reached for him with the other. She mounted him, taking him sharply, and gasping as she did.

With her eyes closed, her head thrown back and her hair in wild disorder, she began riding him at a slow and steady rhythm, the only sound her soft and steady breathing. But soon her tenor picked up and her passion became louder and louder until the violence and volume of her lovemaking was unhinged.

With every thrust, the bedsprings squeaked and the headboard clobbered the wall with a loud *thump*. Harder and harder she rode him and louder and louder she became until finally, with a wall, thudding jolt and an ear-rending yelp, she convulsed and collapsed on his chest, again breathless.

He held her gently as her breath returned and her heart slowed, her head on his chest, Jack smoothing her hair.

They stayed that way awhile, the rain drumming against the glass as sleep began overtaking them.

Then wordlessly, she rose and gazed into his eyes, and he smiled up at her. She gave him a peck on the lips, then lowered herself to the floor. When her knees reached the carpet, she clasped his hands and drew him up to standing.

She took him in her mouth, and he caught his breath, her rhythm slow and even, her tongue flicking, teasing. Soon, the tremor that began in his leg became a seizure in his loins that spread upward through his chest and neck, throttling him. Gripped in spasm, his head thrown back, he released with a primal groan, and his legs went out from beneath him. He fell to the bed like a man shot dead, but a dead man panting.

She slid alongside him and nuzzled her face in the side of his neck as he settled.

They lay there together, Eddie at his back, her arm across his chest, Jack clinging to it as sleep came on strongly. But she caught herself in time, forced herself awake, kissed him softly, and got up.

She began searching for her sweater, her slippers, and the skirt that he'd pulled off and thrown across the room at some point in the melee. She found a slipper on the carpet and the skirt behind the chair in the corner. Jack was up on an elbow, aroused again and watching her as she shimmied into it.

"They're sending me home," he let out dryly. "At least I won't have a problem with the rules."

Eddie stopped her search for the other slipper, narrowed her eyes, and turned to look at him. "Who told you that?"

"About the rules?" he asked.

She made a face. "Don't be ridiculous. I mean about being sent home."

"It's been the plan all along."

She rolled her eyes and continued her search.

Jack thought of Sam in the adjacent room trying to sleep or on the phone to his wife or Halder, with the bed pounding the wall in the background and Eddie yelping like a wild thing being whipped.

She found the missing slipper by the door, pulled it on, and then the sweater nearby. She shook out her hair, turned to look at him, and smiled. "So, you think because you broke the rules they're going to send you home?"

"Broken airplane, broken rules …what difference does it make?"

She giggled. "You're so cute."

"Easy for you to say."

She gave him a look and told him, "You're a very clever and fetching young man, Jack Dolan … but a bit naïve. Has anyone told you that old joke about the Pan Tropic pilot, the preacher, and the doctor?"

"No. But we're Jetstream, not Pan Tropic."

"You're ruining my joke."

"Sorry."

"So, a Pan Tropic pilot, a preacher, and a doctor go duck hunting and—being that boys love to brag on their dogs—the preacher says, 'Watch what mine can do.' A duck flies by, he shoots it, his dog retrieves it, gives it a blessing, and buries it. The doctor says, 'Well, that's pretty amazing, but watch what mine can do.' A duck flies by, he shoots it, his dog retrieves it, gives it CPR, and the duck flies away! They turned and, looking smug, said to the pilot, 'So, what about *yours*, flyboy?'"

"The pilot shrugs and says, 'Watch this.' A duck flies by, he shoots it, his dog retrieves it, eats the duck, fucks the other two dogs, and takes three days off on a layover."

Jack grinned.

"Welcome to Pan Tropic, baby doll. Now you listen up, and your lover's going to give you *all* the rules you need to prosper here: first, I *will* see you later because you're not going anywhere we're not going; and second, you *will* keep that magic tongue and joystick of yours where they belong. Now those are the only rules you need, sugar. Over and *out*," she said, fixing her gaze on him.

He nodded. "Deal."

She made a kissy face, put a finger to her lips, then opened the door. She checked the hall and then slipped out and vanished as quickly as she'd appeared.

Jack dropped onto the bed, stared at the ceiling, and smiled as he relived every moment with her.

He yawned, reached for the lamp to turn it off, then rolled over and buried himself in the covers, her intoxicating scent lingering on the pillows.

Fuck the rules. He was leaving with a bang; he chuckled.

He'd pick up the pieces in Philly.

# FORTY-FOUR

*Shannon, Ireland, October 27, 1978*

H e woke, blinked, and stared bleary-eyed into the dark.

There was a knock on the door, impatient hammering.

He wiped his eyes and turned to look at the clock on the nightstand: 08:23.

Another knock, this time harder, louder.

He wiped his face and then remembered. She was back! She said she would! An erection stirred as he threw back the covers. He nearly tripped on the towel as he stumbled toward the door, smiling with anticipation. He was in full bloom; he was ready!

He opened the door while standing to the side to hide his condition, expecting her to push the door back to enter the room, but this time there was no push. He peeked around the edge, bare-chested, his hair disheveled, and his eyes like two piss holes in the snow.

His lascivious grin vanished along with his erection. *Oh, shit,* he thought. *Sam!*

He slammed the door closed, a shot of panic running through him. "Uh, just … just a minute," he croaked. "I … uh, I need a moment." He stumbled toward the closet.

"Get dressed," Sam barked through the closed door. "Get yourself together. We need to talk."

Jack ran his fingers through his hair. *Shit. Here it comes,* he thought. *My fait accompli: death by ticket to Philly.*

He pulled on his slacks and grabbed his sweatshirt off the chair. He went to the nightstand, turned on the lamp, and then wobbled back to the door.

He opened it partway. Sam pushed it open further and brushed past him. He grimaced as he sidestepped the towel and surveyed the room. The bed looked like it had been bombed.

Jack followed his gaze. "Sam. Look … about last night—"

Sam made a face, turned on him, and said, "Last *night?* No, Jack. This—*this,*" he said, gesturing around the room, "*this* was this morning."

Jack looked at the drapes and the darkness surrounding them. He pointed to the clock. "It's only 8:30," he said.

"At night!" Sam snapped. "You've been asleep all day, damn it! Wake up and get it together."

Jack looked even more confused.

"Things have changed," Sam continued. "You need to clean up, pack up, and get yourself to the airport … You're leaving, *now!*"

Jack nodded and, with a dejected frown, replied, "Yeah … I already knew. You've been making that clear since I started. What time's my flight?"

"As soon as you get there."

Jack pointed at him, angered. "Enough with the fucking games, Sam. Where am I going? New York, Miami? What airline and where?"

"Colombo, goddamn it! You're replacing the copilot in Colombo. He's got some personal problems," Sam added regretfully. "He's being sent home."

Now Jack was really puzzled. "*What?*" he exclaimed. "What are you talking about? How long? How long until he comes back?"

"He's not," Sam said. "He has a problem with alcohol, and it can't be fixed. This was his last chance; it's not working."

Jack was dumbstruck.

"Get moving," Sam snapped at him. "The airplane and the entire crew are out there waiting for you. It's taken all day to get this worked out, but it's done. I just got off the phone with Gerhard. Telegrams and calls have been going back and forth from Miami to Colombo and here all day. You're hired. You got the job; you got what you want."

"*Full time?*"

"Am I speaking Chinese?" Sam asked impatiently.

Jack bristled at the sarcasm but let it pass. "Okay … okay," he said. "Jesus, I … I mean, it's just not at all what I was expecting. I'm sorry about his situation, but—"

"But it works for you," Sam said, finishing the sentence with an edge in his tone. "Fine, but save the celebration for later. They're waiting for you and an overflight clearance downline. Once they've got both, you're leaving."

Jack began turning in circles, searching for his shaving kit. "Okay, okay!" he said. "I'm on it … I'm going!"

"Put your uniform on or whatever you have of one. The cockpit crew on ferries across the Middle East are always in uniform. It helps with access to airport facilities."

"What? *Flying?* I'm flying the entire crew?"

"We need to complete your line qualification as soon as possible. You'll be flying with Brad and Joe Bartolini."

"*Brad?*" he said with a look of dread.

"Get used to it. He'll be your chief pilot when I'm gone. Besides that, though Brad can be difficult, he's a damn good pilot. Learn to make it work. All of you'd better." He turned and started for the door. "I'm going back out there to help in any way I can. Get moving—"

"Sam!"

He stopped with his hand on the knob and looked back with a weary gaze.

"About this morning," Jack said awkwardly, "I … I mean, the rules. I figured I was finished, anyway. It was just one of those things and—"

"Eddie makes her own rules."

"Wait. *Eddie?* You know it was *Eddie?*"

"*Everyone* knows, for Christ's sake," Sam grumbled. "The entire hotel knows. It's not like you two made any effort to be discreet."

Jack blushed and looked aside.

"She's complicated, Jack."

He gave Sam a sideways glance. "I know. I've seen that."

"Not the half of it," Sam corrected him. "Do you know she's got a pharmacy doctorate from ULM?"

"No … but then why would I?"

"Can you picture her in a lab coat behind a counter in Houma all her life?"

"No."

"Neither could she."

Jack acknowledged it with a nod.

"Eddie's an icon here, Jack. If it becomes a problem, it'll be a *big* problem for you, not her, understand?"

"Yes, sir … I'll take care of it."

Sam held his gaze for emphasis. "Be certain you do," he warned. Then he opened the door and left.

When the door closed, Jack broke into a wide grin. He jumped up and punched the air. He did a little jig around the room as he searched for his shaving kit. He found it, stripped off his clothes, and hit the shower.

Once finished, he dried quickly, dressed, and threw together his things. He left the room wearing his white airline uniform shirt, epaulets, black dress slacks, and the black oxfords he wore for his interview at Air Logistics. His sweatshirt was his only outer garment.

He approached the front desk at a fast walk, his bags in hand. The clerk—a middle-aged woman in a floral shift and gray cardigan—looked up at him and smiled. "Yes, love?" she said.

"I need a ride to the airport," Jack told her. "As soon as possible, please."

She turned and spoke toward an adjoining room. "Nolin!" she yelled. "There's another of them pilot fellas here; he needs a lift to the airport."

"Ah, *Jaysus*," came Nolin's indignant reply. "The feckin' airport *again?* I just sat down w'me cup o' tea. Tell 'em to go to the car … I'll be out in a wee bit."

She looked cross. "Ah, here—up with y'now!" she scolded. "You're not to be keeping him waitin'!" Holding up some mail, she added, "And drop these at the post on your way back."

"Aye," he groaned. "And put a broom up me arse to give the floor a sweep on the way out too, will I yea?"

She clucked and looked at Jack with a professional smile. "He'll be right with you, love," she said. "Do you have your key?"

"Oh … yes!" Jack put down his bags, fumbled for it in his pocket, and handed it to her.

She looked at the number and said with a sly grin, "Nolin, he's 116!"

Nolin was at the door in an instant and staring at Jack as if he was an apparition.

Jack said, "Uh … Ready when you are."

"Oh! Right, yea!" Nolin replied. "Well, we're off then," he said as he darted past the clerk.

She held up the mail. "The post, Nolin … the *post*," she reminded him.

・ ・ ・

Rain was coming down in buckets, the wipers on the VW clapping uselessly, the musty scent of Nolin's wool sport coat salting the air. He pulled to the curb at the freight terminal, parked the brake, and jumped out to get Jack's bags from the back.

Jack took out his wallet for a tip, and seeing this, Nolin waved his hand to stop. "Ah, *Jaysus*, no," he said. "They'll make that room a feckin' shrine, Our Lady o' the Ride!" He laughed. "They'll be keepin' me in whiskey and the black stuff when I tell 'em I knew ya."

Jack laughed too and tipped him anyway.

Inside the cargo terminal, he stared dolefully across the ramp. The airplane was at least three hundred yards away, the cabin lights on, the forward entry door mostly closed against the deluge. As he tried to figure out a way to get there without getting soaked, a driver with a tug pulled alongside him and came to a stop. "You need a lift?" he asked cheerfully.

"Sure do," Jack yelled over the thunder of the rain. "It's that DC-8 over there." He pointed toward the airplane. It was one of four jets parked on the ramp along with a Lockheed Electra.

"It's feckin' lashin'," the driver replied. "Do you not have a coat?"

"No."

Reaching for a soiled tarp on the passenger seat, the driver handed it to Jack and said, "Here, throw this over ya."

Jack tossed his bags behind the seat. He pulled the tarp over his head and shoulders, looking like an old woman clutching a shawl.

The driver took off, the rain pummeling the windshield. When they arrived at the mobile stairs, Jack gave him a thumbs-up, sprang out, and tossed the tarp in the back. He grabbed his bags and bolted up the stairway. As he got to the landing, Joe opened the door and Jack flew in.

The moment he stepped into the brightly lit entryway, he was greeted with an explosion of applause, cheers, and whistles as if he were a celebrity arriving at an event. He looked into the cabin and smiled self-consciously.

Joe grabbed the bags from his hands. "Here, give me these," he said. "Sam and Brad are in the forward galley. Go back … They want to talk."

Jack looked alarmed. "What now?" he asked.

"Not *you*, y'putz … something else; don't worry about it," Joe said. "Now go … *go!*" he insisted, jutting his jaw toward the galley.

• • •

Sam and Brad were having a conversation when Jack arrived.

They broke it off and Brad looked at him. "We have an issue," he said. "We're ready to go, but our overflight permission for Syrian airspace has been denied. It was all arranged and paid for, but there's been a screwup somewhere and they've rescinded it."

"What does that mean?" Jack asked.

"It means we're either stuck here until it's resolved, or we leave without it and hope it's approved by the time we get to Syrian airspace. It's not the first time we've run into this sort of thing. Sometimes it's just the bureaucracy, and sometimes it's these Third World shitholes leveraging us for more money. Anyway, Gerhard's working on it at his end, and we're deciding what to do."

"Can we get ATC clearance without it?"

"Sure. ATC doesn't care. It's a Syrian matter."

"And what if they don't give it to us?" Jack asked. "Can't we avoid it by going around Syria altogether?"

"Not in any practical way," Brad answered. "The same problem comes up everywhere else in that region. Some countries are friendly to the US and its air carriers and some aren't, so we might as well deal with the one we've settled on. The good news is, it's only a fifteen-minute run through the Damascus FIR and we might be able to bullshit our way through it. We've done it elsewhere before, and Sam and I think it's worth a shot."

"And if that fails, then what?"

"Then we divert to Cyprus or Crete to wait it out or come up with a Plan B. But in that case, it would have been much less expensive to just stay here."

Jack picked at a nail and was silent for a moment as he considered the options. With a glance at Sam, he said, "I mean, if you're asking me, I say let's go. It isn't broke until it's broke, and if there's a chance it'll come through in time, let's do it and figure it out as we go along. If getting to Indonesia on time for the contract is the priority, then closing any distance we can makes the most sense, right?"

Sam looked at Brad. "See what I've been telling you?"

Brad gave him a nod and said to Jack, "That's what we're figuring too. Now let's see how everyone else feels about it."

Brad stepped out of the galley and into the aisle. "Okay, guys, listen up," he said loudly. "We've got another issue here, and I need a show of hands."

The crew went silent and looked up at him from their seats. They were scattered through the cabin and dressed in civvies, sweats and tracksuits, comfort clothing for the ferry.

"As most of you know," Brad continued, "we commonly need overflight permission from countries that control the airspace we fly through. Third World countries like Syria often treat these rights like a tollbooth and charge high fees to pass through them. Tonight, we have to fly through a small portion of Syrian airspace. Unfortunately, though we paid for and received overflight permission from the Syrians, for some reason that permission is now being denied. So here's the choice, and I need a vote: Option A, we take off and either get permission to fly across Syria in time or bamboozle our way across it if we don't; or Option B, we sit here waiting for the permission to come through. The problem with Option B is that we're already pushing it on the schedule, and if we don't keep moving, we could wind up in breach of contract at the start of it. That would be very expensive for everyone given the terms of the deal Manny negotiated. Anyway, with all of that in mind, all those in favor of Option A, please raise your hands."

Everyone's hand went up except for one of the new girls sitting at the back of the cabin. "Okay, that'll work," Brad said. He tamped down his arms for them to lower theirs. Pointing to the dissenting young woman, he said, "I'm sorry, miss, we haven't met. Please stand up and tell me your name."

She was a pretty redhead with wideset blue eyes, porcelain skin, and a sprinkle of freckles across her nose that gave her the aspect of a child. She was wearing a black turtleneck and jeans, and when she stood up to speak, her eyes flicked anxiously around the crewmembers seated ahead of her.

She cleared her throat and was wringing her hands. "Jessica," she said. "Jess … Jess McCormick."

"Welcome aboard, Jess," he said. "So, tell me what's on your mind?"

"Captain, I—"

"Brad," he interjected. "Just Brad, please. But go ahead."

She glanced down anxiously at the swarthy, green-eyed brunette in the adjoining seat as if looking for support. The brunette was looking up at her and scowling.

"It's what you said about Syria," Jess continued. "I mean … wasn't it Syria or something like Syria where that airline pilot was shot and killed last year?"

"You're referring to the Lufthansa captain who was murdered during a hijacking last October, is that correct?" Brad answered. His dark piercing gaze, his angularity, and his five o'clock shadow lent to his imperious air.

Her eyes began welling with tears. "Yes … yes, I guess that's it," she said.

"That was in Yemen, Jess. We won't be flying near there tonight. But you're right, the Middle East is a dangerous place, and you're wise to be aware of that. I'm impressed by your memory of that event."

She nodded and wiped a tear away with her hand. "I mean … if we don't have to go without permission, I don't think we should."

Brad looked back at Sam. Sam knew intuitively what he was asking and gave him a nod.

Brad looked at Jess and said, "The other possibility is that you remain here with Sam's crew and come down with them when their airplane is repaired. The only problem with that solution is that you may be faced with the same problem we're having now. It's a natural part of what we do, Jess. It's not uncommon for small, unknown airlines like ours to run into this sort of thing. It's happened before, and it will happen again. I know it can be nerve-wracking when you're new, but it's something to which you'll become accustomed as your experience grows."

"Would that be okay?" she asked tentatively. "I mean … staying behind? I won't be fired?"

Brad appeared taken aback. "*Fired?* No … no, of course not," he said. "But please gather your things and come forward quickly. Sam will be leaving for the hotel, and you can return with him."

Her tears continued as she collected her bags and began walking up the aisle. The brunette stood up and joined her, but without bags.

"I'm so sorry," Jess said with a sniffle as she approached Brad. "I'm sorry ... I'm not brave—"

Brad's eyes flashed, and he raised a finger to her in a threatening manner. "Don't!" he scolded. "Don't ever say that!"

His tone was so sharp she recoiled and then more tears came.

Sam stepped closer and said, "What Brad's saying is that you are brave, Jess. You're brave because you have the courage to speak your mind even when everyone else disagrees." He smiled at her. "Don't say you're not brave because you may be the bravest one of all."

"Yes, that's what I meant," Brad said. "Sometimes I ... well, anyway." He looked across the other crewmembers and said loudly, "Jessica thinks she isn't brave because she has sensible concerns about going without an overflight permit. Everyone who thinks Jessica isn't brave, raise your hands."

No hands went up.

"Now, everyone who thinks Jess is brave for speaking her mind, raise your—"

The crew erupted in cheers, whistles, and applause.

Jess turned around and smiled broadly at them.

Brunette gave her a shove from behind. "See?" she taunted her. "What'd I tell you? You're not a wimp after all ... you *wimp!*"

Jess turned on her and made a nasty face. Brunette made a face back, then extended her hand toward Brad. "Martha," she said audaciously.

They shook. "Nice to meet you, Martha," Brad said. "Are you guys buddies?"

"Yes. We were hired together. We're interns at Mr. Hirsch's accounting office." She looked at Jess and gave her another shove. "Stay," she said. "I told you there's nothing to be afraid of."

Brad glared at her. "Why don't we let Jess decide that herself?"

"No ... no, it's okay," Jess replied. "I'm okay. What you said, that this has happened before, it makes sense, I guess. That there's a plan and this happens sometimes. We're not going without a plan, right?"

"Yes, a plan ... *of sorts,*" Brad said inscrutably.

She nodded and wiped an eye. "I'll go," she said. "I mean, I'd like to go if it's still okay?"

"Of course!" Brad said. He looked over his shoulder and gave Sam a nod.

Sam zipped up his jacket, held a newspaper to the top of his head, and bolted for the door.

Jess turned around to go back to her seat, and Martha helped with one of her bags.

"Ladies!" Brad said to their backs.

They stopped and turned around.

"Have you ever been in the cockpit during flight?"

Martha's eyes widened. "NO!" she exclaimed. "Can we? Both of us?"

"Of course," Brad said, gesturing toward the front. "Please."

Joe had been watching what was happening, and as the girls followed Brad forward, he moved to the forward entryway. "Right this way, kids," he said as the girls got close. "C'mon in and I'll get you squared away. Just leave the bags by that forward closet there, and I'll take care of 'em for you."

Martha entered the cockpit first with Jess behind her, the two of them looking over the array of instruments and controls.

Jack was in the copilot's seat preparing for the flight. He turned and offered his hand to Martha. "Hi, I'm Jack," he said with a smile. "I'm new here too!" he added.

"Martha," she said with knowing eyes and a puckish grin. "Yes, I know ... I've heard."

Jack blinked and shifted his gaze to Jess. He put on a smile. "Jack," he said. Jessica gave him a thin smile and averted her gaze.

Joe helped the girls get settled in the jump seats. Martha took the forward, Jess the aft. Joe briefed them on the use of the seat belts and shoulder harnesses, as well as the use of their oxygen masks and the evacuation procedures. When he finished, he took his seat and Brad came into the cockpit and took his. "So, you guys work for Hirsch Enterprises?" he asked as he buckled in.

"We're accounting majors," Martha answered. "My dad talked me into it, but it's so boring," she said, her eyes at half-mast, her shoulders slumped.

Jessica spoke up. "Stop saying that, Marty! You keep telling everyone that. It's not boring; it's interesting, actually, and no business, not even this one, can run without it."

Marty rolled her eyes. "Jess plans on becoming a CPA. I plan on throwing myself off the roof," she deadpanned.

Brad was adjusting the rudder pedals. "So, how'd you guys find this?" he asked.

Marty said, "We saw the posting on the company bulletin board in the breakroom. We interviewed with Mr. Caffaretti, Maggie Dunn, and Grace Burke. Maggie and Grace are so cool. They've been *everywhere*, and we thought, why not, it'll be a hoot, a real adventure. My dad blew a gasket, though … Jess's too."

Brad sat back, reached for his shoulder harness straps, and said, "Okay, guys, from this point on until we reach a safe altitude, we avoid all distractions, including any questions or nonessential chatter until I give the all clear. Once I do, you're free to ask anything you like."

Marty scrunched her shoulders. "This is so exciting!" she gushed. "Thank you so much for letting us do this!"

Dianne, the flight attendant working that leg, came to the cockpit. "Cabin's ready," she announced. "Anyone need anything before I close up?"

Brad looked over his shoulder and gave her a smile and a thumbs-up. She nodded and closed the door.

Brad turned to Jack and Joe, gave them a takeoff briefing, then called for the Before Starting Engines Checklist. At the completion of the checklist, he picked up his mic. "Cockpit to ground," he said.

The groundman's voice crackled from the overhead speaker. "Roger, Captain, brakes parked; you're cleared to start, sir."

Brad reset the parking brake and replied, "Brakes are parked; cleared to start."

Joe said, "Pressure's good; thirty PSI."

Brad reached for the engine start buttons on the overhead panel. "Okay, guys," he announced. "Here we go—turning number three."

# FORTY-FIVE

*The sky over the Celtic Sea, October 27, 1978*

At 10:32 p.m. local time they were climbing through eleven thousand feet with Jack flying the airplane. Brad turned off the no smoking sign and seat belt signs, and a moment later the cockpit chime sounded. He picked up the black telephone-like receiver at the back of the pedestal panel and said, "Hey."

"Sam told me Casanova's probably starved since he hasn't eaten since last night," Dianne said. "I've got chicken, beef, or pasta, and plenty of everything if you guys want to eat too."

Brad looked at Jack and Joe. "She's got meals. You guys hungry?"

"YES!" Jack said eagerly. "Absolutely."

Joe shrugged. "What's she got?"

"Chicken, beef, or pasta."

"I'll take beef and the usual to drink," Joe replied.

Brad pointed the receiver at Jack.

"Oh, um … beef too," he said. "Beef and a Coke would be great."

Brad put the receiver to his ear. "A beef and the usual for Joe, a beef and a Coke for Jack, and I'll just take a coffee with cream. Let me see what the girls want."

"Got it. But break time's over for the ladies," Dianne said. "Tell them to come back; it's time for more training. We've got a dead passenger in the aft lav, another with a heart attack in the offing, and the other lav plugged and in need of mucking out."

"Gotcha," Brad replied. He hung up the receiver, turned to the girls, and said, "Sorry, guys. We have meals coming up, and Dianne says she needs you back there to continue training."

Marty unbuckled and said, "This has been wonderful. When we're done, can we come back?"

"Sure," Brad said, "but Jack and I have some training to do as well, so how about I give you a call when we begin descent for Kuwait? Until then, there won't be much to see, anyway."

Looking out the windshield as she got out of her seat, Marty asked, "Where are we right now?"

"We're over the Celtic Sea and heading toward Land's End, England. From there we'll continue southeast over France, crossing Nice and then continuing south along the west coast of Italy over the Tyrrhenian Sea. From there we'll proceed across Crete and Cyprus in the Med and then over Beirut, Lebanon, and from there—*hopefully*—across Syria toward Saudi Arabia. From there we'll make a dogleg northeast into Kuwait for our arrival about six and a half hours from now."

Marty smiled and said, "This is amazing. I'm so happy we're doing this and not sitting in that *fuc* … er … stuffy office back in Miami." She looked back at Jess. "Aren't you?"

Jess smiled modestly. "I am," she said. "And thank you for all your help earlier, Brad. I'm sorry if I was—"

"Stop!" Brad said, waving his finger. "Asking questions is a duty in this business. It's never something to apologize for."

"Thank you."

Brad returned her smile.

The girls left and closed the door behind them. Brad looked at Joe and asked, "How long do you think she'll last?"

"Who? The little redhead? She'll be on her way home with Walt."

"Who's Walt?" Jack asked.

The radio crackled. "Douglas Eight-One-Six-Papa-Alpha, contact London Control now on one-three-two-point-six."

Brad replied, set the frequency in the radio, and said, "London, this is Eight-One-Six-Papa-Alpha with you climbing through flight level one-nine-zero for two-five-zero, over."

"Roger, Eight-One-Six-Papa-Alpha, London Control, you're radar contact, sir, climb and maintain flight level three-nine-zero."

Brad replied to the clearance, reset the altitude alert, and clipped his mic in its holder. Joe leaned forward and trimmed the throttles to maintain climb power.

Jack continued flying and said, "So, who's Walt?"

Brad said, "The copilot you're replacing."

"Oh."

Changing the subject, Brad said, "Let's talk about your takeoff and departure profile. Overall, I thought everything looked good. My only suggestion is that you slow your rotation rate a bit. The pace you're using is technically correct, but that assumes a balanced field condition and that we know our actual takeoff weight precisely. In fact, all the airports we'll be using have long runways except for Medan, so we'll have runway to spare and no obstacles to clear to anywhere we're flying besides Medan. Also, while flying passengers, we'll never know our actual weight with any precision, especially on the back half of the pilgrimage. You'll see why when the time comes, but for now, using a slower rotation with a higher speed at liftoff will provide a buffer if the actual weight's a lot more than we planned. And if it's not, the performance penalty we've incurred will be minimal and an acceptable tradeoff under the circumstances."

"Makes sense," Jack replied, feeling mildly unsettled. The Brad Stone he was flying with wasn't the man he'd expected, the man he'd dreaded when Sam told him who he'd be flying with. Somehow, something had changed, and Jack didn't know how to read it. Although quick to let his guard down and quick to look past slights, there were times in the past when Jack had been too quick. He wouldn't do it yet. He'd stay guarded with Brad until he sorted it out. Sam wasn't gone yet, and if there was any trouble with Brad, Jack would take it up with Sam.

"Did you pick up a copy of that book I recommended, *Aerodynamics for Naval Aviators?*" Brad asked.

"I did, and I've been reading it thoroughly."

"Great. So, let's move on to the airplane's flight characteristics and performance." From there, Brad continued into a detailed survey of jet aircraft aerodynamics including a discussion of critical Mach number, shock wave formation, shock-induced separation, force divergence, the advantages and disadvantages of sweepback, and so forth. Their discussion continued through their meals, and even a second and third meal for Jack.

He found Brad's knowledge impressive, and by the end of his dissertation, Jack had begun to consider the pejoratives hurled at Brad by his colleagues to be unfair. It occurred to him that Brad's unpopularity may be due less to a grating personality than to his image: gaunt, dark, and humorless, the caricature of a sniping little tyrant at a motor vehicle bureau rather than a coolheaded captain of an intercontinental jet. But if that was all there was to it, then Jack could take him in stride; indeed, he could even sympathize. He was warming to Brad. Jack hoped it would last.

· · ·

An hour and fifty minutes into their flight, they were passing over Nice. Brad pressed the call button and asked Dianne to get one of the captains to come forward and take his seat while he used the lavatory.

A few minutes later, Mick arrived and traded places with Brad. As Brad left the cockpit, Mick buckled in and said to Jack with a smile, "You look like you've settled right in over there. How's it going?"

"It's going good."

"Captain Dipshit treating you okay?"

Jack flinched. The insult took him aback, but he decided upon a diplomatic approach with Mick. "To be honest," he answered, "Brad's been great. Though, to be equally honest, I'm pleasantly surprised. I was prepared for the Brad in Miami."

Joe said, "Bullshit. He's just doing his best Sam impression. Everybody said he tried the same thing when he started out in Karachi, but it didn't last."

Mick looked at Joe and, with a nod toward Jack, asked, "Have you discussed any of this with him?"

"A bit," Joe replied. "I told him Brad was a good stick, but he needs some personality lessons."

Mick scoffed. "Nah, it's more than that," he said to Jack. "We don't have time to get into it now because he'll be back any minute, but we'll talk about it more when we fly together. The problem with Brad is that he's pushing for changes here that no one wants. It puts him at odds with everyone."

"You mentioned that this morning," Jack said. "And Bobby did too. Domestic flying that nobody likes, that sort of thing?"

"Yeah, that … but more."

"Like what, specifically?"

"Like specifically is exactly the problem. Specifically doesn't work here. There is no one-size-fits-all solution, no fixed set of rules to govern what we do. Flexibility and thinking on your feet are everything here, and our survival depends on it. But Brad can't get it out of his head that we're not Pan Am or any other airline like them. We're not a scheduled carrier and the sort of regimentation, structure, routine, and rules that work well at those airlines won't cut it here. But that hasn't stopped Brad from pounding square pegs into round holes, and that's where he's at odds with the rest of us. He's relentless. He won't quit. But then, neither will we, so it's a constant state of war."

The cockpit door opened. As Brad walked in, Mick and Jack suddenly went silent.

As if Brad sensed that they'd been talking about him, he paused next to Joe. Looking at the engineer's panel, he broke the awkward silence by saying, "She's running like clockwork tonight. Looks like we've got most of the bugs worked out. I hope Sam and Bobby have the same luck with theirs."

Mick unbuckled and got up. "Let's hope so," he grumbled. "That airplane's a shit-box. Nothing less than a complete overhaul will straighten it out."

Brad sat in the aft jumpseat so Mick could pass. "Thanks," he said, looking up at Mick as he slipped by.

"Sure," Mick replied. "Anytime."

The radio crackled. "Douglas Eight-One-Six-Papa-Alpha," the Marseille controller said. "Contact Roma now on one-three-four-point-eight."

"I got it," Jack said. He reached for his mic and replied, "Roma, this is Douglas Eight-One-Six-Papa-Alpha level at three-nine-oh."

"Douglas Eight-One-Six-Papa-Alpha, you are radar contact. Cleared on course Upper Mike seven-two-eight, VENTO, maintain flight level three-nine-zero."

As Jack read back the clearance, Brad climbed into his seat and buckled in. He looked across at Jack and said, "You need to head back?"

"Yeah, I think I will."

Jack unbuckled, got up, opened the door, and stepped into the cabin. The lights were set low, and most of the crew were sleeping, though a few were reading and a handful of others stood in the aisle or aft galleys and chatted quietly. He paused for a moment and glanced around in a search of Eddie. He felt a twinge of anxiety. How would she react to him in public? He'd had no prior sexual experience with such a profoundly self-assured woman, not to mention one so beautiful.

He spotted her seated in mid-cabin. She was in an aisle seat and appeared to be reading. Charlotte was across the aisle from her, stretched out on the three coach seats, asleep.

Eddie didn't look up. He paused for a moment longer in the hope that she'd see him and react, but she didn't. He opened the door and entered the lav.

Meanwhile, in the cockpit, Brad looked at Joe and said, "While Sam and I were talking in the galley, he asked me to speak to Jack about Eddie.

He said there wasn't time to get into it all back at the hotel and he wants me to fill him in before we get to Colombo since Sam won't be there. But now, on further thought, I'm thinking since you and Jack seem pretty close, would you mind discussing it with him instead of me?"

Joe gave him a look and blew out his cheeks. He hesitated for a moment but accepted. "Okay," he said. "Maybe I'll bring him on the walkaround or somethin' in Kuwait, just the two of us. I'll see what I can do. What the fuck is wrong with her, anyway?"

Brad scoffed. "You're asking me?"

"I'm askin' anyone."

"Who knows? But I appreciate it, Joe. I wouldn't know where to start."

"Neither do I. But I'll take care of it."

Jack left the lav and chanced another glance at Eddie. This time she was looking up as if she'd been expecting him. Their eyes connected and he smiled at her warmly. But she appeared to be looking right through him, not a wink, not a smile, not something, *anything* in return.

Eddie was older than Jack by more than a few years, and he'd figured it was only a fling from the start, his first and only fling since his boss's wife at the bike shop. But that was going nowhere before it even began, and with Eddie, it was different. She'd said as much, and now her chilly indifference to him stung. It occurred to him that he wasn't cut out for flings. Was that unmanly? The thought unnerved him.

He reached for the cockpit door, and when he opened it, he found Joe seated sidesaddle on the aft jumpseat and the engineer's seat pulled back, blocking access to the pilots' seats. Jack looked at him, puzzled. "My turn," Joe said. "Plunk your ass down there, kiddo," he told him, gesturing at the engineer's panel. "Let's see how much you remember."

The distraction was welcome. Joe's timing had been perfect; Jack's thoughts about Eddie were quickly subsumed by the airplane's systems. He became completely absorbed as Joe had him set and reset the generators, balance and transfer fuel, make changes to the pressurization and air conditioning controls, manipulate the hydraulics, and review system limitations and emergency procedures.

An hour later at 04:19 local time, they were approaching Crete, and Brad had Jack return to the copilot's seat. After he'd buckled in, Brad pushed the call button for Dianne and asked her to come to the cockpit.

"You rang," she said with a smile as she came through the door.

"How are those new girls doing?" Brad asked. "Got that dead body taken care of, the heart attack healed, and the lav mucked out?"

"Oh, yeah," she said with a roll of her eyes. "Of course, Philippe volunteered to be the dead guy again. He was slumped over sitting on the toilet when Marty opened the door, his pants down around his ankles, and, so … well, now there's *that*," she said with a flip of her hand. "Marty and Philippe. Ugh."

Brad winced and said, "Perhaps you should mention Joyce to her."

"Joyce, as in Joyce from the property management office? The Joyce you sent home from Karachi after that ugly scene with Anna?"

"That Joyce, yes."

"No. But if you want something said, I'd mention it to Maggie. Marty's a pepper pot, and there's no one better at dealing with pepper pots than Maggie."

"Good plan," Brad agreed. "I'll get her on it when we get there. Now, look, on another matter, if Dan is awake back there, ask him to come up, please. Tell him I've got a question for him."

"Hang on, I'll check," Dianne said. She opened the door and left.

Joe looked at Brad and asked, "What's up?"

"I've got an idea I want to run by him. A Plan B if we don't get our overflight permission in time."

"Can't wait to hear it," Joe groaned.

A few minutes later, the cockpit door opened and Dan Petersen, the captain and former Tuskegee Airman, walked in. "Hey!" he said with a giant smile. "What's up, guys?"

Brad swung around to look at him. "Got a favor to ask, Daniel," he said.

Joe slid his seat into his panel, allowing Dan to step closer. "Sure," Dan said as he sat down sidesaddle on the forward jumpseat. "Shoot."

"Someone told me that you flew for Aramco after the war, is that right?"

"Yeah, for ten years. But then I met my wife in Morocco and we came home to New York. Got picked up by Pan Tropic not long after that, the only airline that would hire me with my tan. Been here ever since."

"Do you speak any Arabic?"

Dan pursed his lips and shrugged. "Sure, a little, I guess. But that was a long time ago, Brad. Why ask?"

"Like how little?"

"Like how I spoke a little French in Paris after the war. G.I. French. You know—enough to get laid."

"Gerhard told me you do some acting too. Is that right?"

"*What?* No," Dan said with a laugh. "I mean … I help my wife with her lines, for her gigs on Broadway when she's rehearsing."

"But that's something, right?"

Dan made a face. "Yeah, sure, Brad. They're putting me up for a Tony. What's this all about, anyway?"

Brad pulled an index card from his map holder and handed it to him. "Take a look at this," he said. "It's a transliteration of Arabic script, you know, Arabic spelled out so it can be read in English. If you can read it and you can act a little, I need you to be an Imam traveling with our pilgrims on the hajj."

Dan looked at him like he was nuts but took the card and studied it. He moved his lips as he attempted to decipher what he read.

*Allo, Marhaba … Allo.*

*Isma' ya hatha, khidmat al mola haq min khidmatak. Nahin fi rahlat al Hajj, wa la yumkinak hitijazna. Nahin fi khidmat Allah al rahim wa! Allah akbar!*

*Hadha ma yumlih imlayna alshare!*

"So, what do you think?" Brad asked.

Dan shook his head and attempted to give the card back to Brad, but Brad waved it away.

"No," Dan said emphatically. "I mean ... I can make out a little of it. But read it like I'm an Imam? No way. Where did you get this?"

"My roommate in college is from Lebanon. He's a doctor in Detroit these days, but he was in Miami for a conference a few years ago. We got together while he was there, and I was telling him about all the trouble we'd had during that Mali hajj we'd just flown. Remember that one? All the overflight issues and other things. What a pain in the ass, right?"

"Yeah. So, what's your point?"

"I asked my buddy if he had any ideas on how to get a pass through the system. You know, talk-the-talk with the locals, something we could use when they're throwing roadblocks at us. He gave me that," he said, pointing at the card. "He wrote it on a cocktail napkin, and I typed it onto that index card. I've kept it in my kitbag ever since."

"Did he tell you what it says?"

"He did, but I don't remember. He said it could work but warned me not to fuck around. He said it was *big* medicine and to go all in if I used it. Speak it like you believe it—or else!"

Dan frowned and looked at the card. "Why's it broken into three separate paragraphs?"

"My buddy said to read the first line and when they answer, respond with that longer passage. And then, if they say anything more, just read that last line and walk away. He made a point of that. Walk away and whatever you do, *don't* say anything more."

"Jesus. You're serious."

"I wouldn't mention Jesus."

Dan gave him a look and said, "We're flying from Ireland, a Catholic country, and I'm supposed to be an Imam? How many pubs did we have to empty to fill the airplane, Brad? Do you think that might occur to them?"

Brad gave him a sheepish shrug.

"So, Arabic with a *lilt*, is that it?" Dan continued.

Another shrug.

Dan threw the card at him. "You're fucking crazy! *That's* your Plan B?"

Joe said, "C'mon, Dan, you said you could speak at least a little of that Arab talk. Hash it out. Give us a hint. I want to know what it says."

Dan looked at him and deadpanned, "*Combien pour votre sœr?*"

Joe recoiled. "That's *Arabic?*"

"No, Joe. It's French."

"What's it mean?"

"It means, how much for your sister?"

Joe's jaw dropped. "*What?* Oh, shit!" he exclaimed. "You can't say that! You'll get us killed!"

"Exactly!" Dan exclaimed. "And for all I know, that's exactly what's on that card." He grabbed it from Brad and shoved it in front of Joe's face. "Look at it, goddamn it! Does it look like anything more than gibberish to you? I know it's got something to do with Allah and the hajj, any idiot can see that. But there's something more to it," he said, eyeing the card with a pained expression. "Something … *demanding* … something … *insulting*." He looked at Brad. "You *really* want to do this?"

"It's all we've got. Unless someone's got a better idea, we'll have to divert or find some other way around the Middle East—and it'll have to be a very long way around at that."

"How much time do we have?" Dan asked. "How long until the Damascus FIR?"

Jack reached for the clipboard and ran his finger down the page. "Damascus at 03:39 Zulu," he said.

Brad glanced at his watch. "A little less than an hour and a half from now."

Dan got up from the seat, his expression grim and the card in his hand. "Alright, I'll see what I can do, but don't count on it," he said. "My wife practices in front of a mirror. I'll lock myself in a lav. I'll let you know if I have any luck."

"Okay, thanks, Dan," Brad said to his back as he left. "And, hey! Ask Dianne to come back up. Tell her I need her help too."

Dan answered him with a nod, then continued out the door. As he walked aft, he passed Dianne outside the forward galley, standing and filing her nails. She looked up at him as he went by. "What's going on?" she asked.

Dan flashed the index card at her. "Brad's got this cockamamie idea on how to get across Syria without clearance," he said. "I'm going back to try and figure it out. Oh … and he asked for you. Apparently, you're being drafted into this looney bin too."

She shrugged and put her file in her apron. "Sure," she said. "I'm always a fool for a caper."

She entered the cockpit saying, "Dan said you wanted me."

Brad looked over his shoulder and said, "Dianne, yes. I've got a favor to ask." Pointing to his black uniform cap hanging by a clip on the aft bulkhead, he asked, "You mind grabbing that and covering the fabric portion of it with gauze from the first aid kit? Or even paper towels if that works better. Anything white to hide the black fabric on the cover."

Dianne looked at the cap and then at Brad, puzzled. "Hide the black? Why?"

"I need it to look like a 'white hat,' a Pan Am pilot's cap to match the livery on the airplane. I'll fill everyone in if we go through with it. For now, let them sleep."

She reached for the cap and examined it. "Sure. I'll see what I can do."

"Great!"

As she turned and left, Jack looked across at Brad and said, "Okay. Explain."

Joe rotated in his seat and leaned forward, and with his forearms on his thighs and his face toward Jack's, he said, "Oh … let me." With his thumb pointed at Brad, he began, "Captain Hotshot here thinks we might get intercepted with this fuckin' little ploy he's cooked up, and having that hat on is supposed to save our asses. Ain't that right?" he snapped at Brad, wagging his finger at him. "You're gonna give me a fuckin' heart attack here! Are you nuts?"

Brad bristled and said, "What's painted on the side of the airplane, Joe?"

"Right. But does this flying garbage truck look like any Pan Am airplane you ever seen?"

"It'll be early dawn as we're going through there. There'll be very little light. You think some Syrian fighter jockey's going to notice the paint doesn't shine?"

"You're gonna get us shot down, Brad. You're gonna get us fuckin' killed if you play this game. This isn't the follies, pal. These people over here? They don't fuck around."

"No, they don't, but they won't shoot, and here's why. No matter who we are, if they do shoot us down, that's the last dollar they'll ever see in overflight money. No one would come near Syria for another hundred years, so no one's shooting us down, Joe. Besides that, how'd you like to be the poor bastard who has to wake up Assad for permission to shoot down a Pan Am jet that's about to leave their airspace? No way. No one's shooting us down."

Joe threw up his hands. "You're fuckin' nuts!" he exclaimed. "Thank God, Dan will never go along with it. He's got more sense than that. And neither will anyone else, for that matter! No one's going to agree to this."

Jack had been watching them in silence, his eyes shifting between them. Brad noted his look of dismay and said, "Speak up. What's on your mind?"

"I agree with Joe's concerns, but I'm okay with the plan so long as we're prepared to do a one-eighty and get out of there if they refuse entry," Jack said. "If that's the plan, then let's give it a try. If not, then I'm with Joe."

"Believe me, if they refuse us entry after we've tried this thing, we'll divert. But if Dan says he's game, I'm not going to give up without at least an attempt. We owe it to ourselves, our company, and our passengers on the hajj to press on if possible. Everything turns on keeping the contract on schedule, and getting stymied here could blow it." He reached for the clipboard on the glareshield and studied it for a moment. "Cyprus, in forty minutes," he said, tossing it down. "We'll get Dan up here and make a decision when we reach Cyprus. No point in arguing about it now."

Joe started to say something, but Brad cut him off by showing him the back of his hand. "Wait for Dan," he ordered. "We'll see what Dan says, then put it to a vote. It's a crew decision. It won't be mine alone."

# FORTY-SIX

*The sky over the western Mediterranean Sea, October 28, 1978*

It was 5:19 a.m. and morning twilight cleaved the eastern horizon with a line of sumptuous pastels that alchemized upward from vermilion to aquamarine and then indigo. Above the DC-8, stars twinkled brightly, and below it were the lights of Cyprus, the island still in the dark as the airplane raced eastward through air as smooth as velvet.

Brad glanced at his watch. It had been four hours and fifty minutes since they'd taken off from Shannon. He reached for the flight attendant call button on the overhead panel and pressed it twice.

Dianne answered. "You rang?"

"Is Dan still locked in the lav?"

"Yup. He went back there with specific instructions not to bug him. He's in there yelling like a nut in a New York subway. You want me to go back and get him?"

"Yes, please. Tell him we're over Cyprus with fifteen minutes until the boundary for Beirut. I want to know if he thinks this thing's a go or not."

"I'll ask and call you back," Dianne replied.

A short while later, the chime sounded and Brad answered. "Hey."

"Dan says it's a go. Make the PA and don't bother him again—'goddamn it'—until it's showtime."

"Got it. And hey, bring the cabin lights up slowly. I need everybody awake. I'm going to ask for another show of hands. When everyone's awake, let me know."

"I will. And I've got your hat if you want it."

"Great! Bring it up. Thanks, love."

A few minutes later, the cockpit door opened and Dianne walked in with Brad's hat. As she handed it to him, she said, "Still a couple of sleepyheads back there, but mostly they're up, grumpy, and crowding the galleys for coffee."

Brad smiled as he examined her work on the hat. "Oh my God, Dianne," he complimented her. "You're a genius! It's perfect!"

She shrugged. "Bandage gauze, medical tape, and toilet paper. Just don't wear it in the rain. Why do you need it, anyway?"

"Likely I won't," he replied. "But it's a little insurance just in case." He looked at her and said, "I'll make a PA and explain what's going on. Anyone who's still concerned can come up and we'll discuss it."

Dianne gave another shrug, nodded, then turned and left.

Brad switched his mic selector to PA. "Okay, guys," he announced. "Sorry to disturb you, but we're passing over Cyprus with another forty minutes until we reach the Syrian boundary. Unfortunately, we still have no word from the company regarding our overflight permission, but Dan and I have been working on a plan we think might work. As I mentioned earlier, the distance across Syrian airspace is very short, a tad under a hundred miles or about ten to fifteen minutes of flight time. What we've got planned is a bit of soft-shoe and sleight of hand to befuddle Syrian ATC long enough to get us across their airspace. If they buy it, great. But if not, we'll have to turn around and divert someplace to sort things out. I'll keep you posted on where we're headed if we do. Anyhow, that's the plan. Please give Dianne a show of hands for all who agree."

In the cabin, everyone's hands went up except the mobs gathered around the fore and aft galleys for coffee, who cared about nothing else. Dianne rang the cockpit and told Brad the results.

Brad returned his mic to its clip. He looked at Joe and Jack and said, "We're good. They're all in."

Joe's eyebrows went up, and he asked, "Soft-shoe? Sleight of hand, Brad? That's what you call this? Let me tell you from my experience flying for the Air Guard around here, you push this too nutty scheme too far and the only diversion we'll be making is a smokin' hole in the ground. You understand that, yes?"

Brad bristled but before he could speak, Jack broke in. "The plan is to do all this in Beirut's airspace, Joe, to get approval there before entering Damascus," he said. "Syria isn't going to shoot us down over Lebanon."

"No," Joe replied. "But *fuhgeddaboudit!* Nothin' works as planned over here, know what I'm sayin'?" He looked at Brad and, with a finger raised in his face, warned, "Be *ready!*"

"So, what is it you want to do, Joe?" Brad asked him. "You want to divert now? Where do you have in mind? You want to spend the rest of the day sitting in this airplane as we figure out another way to get to Colombo without blowing the contract or flying across some other Middle Eastern shithole or goddamn warzone? If you've got a better idea, Joe, go ahead … I'm all ears!"

Joe snorted and threw up his hand. He rotated his seat to face his panel and turned his back on Brad.

After a moment, Brad reached for his shoulder. "Look," he said. "I understand your concern, and I'm not discounting it. But we've paid for our passage across Syria, and whether this is a shakedown or just some bureaucratic snafu on their part, it's bullshit! I say let's at least give this thing a try. If it doesn't work, we'll turn around and figure it out from there. If we weren't so pressed for time—"

Joe threw up his hand. "Fine!" he said, cutting him off. "I just don't trust these trigger-happy sons-o'-bitches. It's like that kid said, what's her name—Jess … smart girl, that one." He put his finger to his head like a gun. "You fuck with me? *Bang.* Bullet in the head, wise guy."

· · ·

At 5:22 a.m. local time, the radio crackled. "Douglas Eight-One-Six-Papa-Alpha, Nicosia Control, you're approaching KUKLA intersection. Contact Beirut control now on frequency one-three-one-decimal-eight, over."

Brad replied to the clearance and switched frequencies. "Good morning, Beirut," he said. "Douglas Eight-One-Six-Papa-Alpha is with you at flight level three-nine-zero, estimating KUKLA at oh-three-two-five Zulu, and squawking zero-seven-five-two, over."

"Douglas Eight-One-Six-Papa-Alpha, Beirut Control. You are radar contact, cleared on course Beirut, maintain flight level three-nine-zero, over."

Brad read back the clearance, then reached for the call button and chimed Dianne. "Hey, it's me," he said when she answered. "Tell Dan it's showtime; we need him up here now."

A few minutes later, Dan entered the cockpit smiling and waving the index card like a kid coming home with all As. "I got it!" he exclaimed. "I can do it!"

"You figured it out?" Joe asked. "What's it say?"

Dan looked at him like he was nuts. "No, of course not. But it doesn't matter!" he gloated. "Here, let me show you." He straightened and threw out his arm like a Shakespearian actor about to let loose a soliloquy. "*Allo! Marhaba ... Allo!*" he bellowed in a stentorian roar.

Brad cut him off. "No, wait, wait!"

Dan looked at him. "Why?" he asked, crestfallen.

"We don't have time," Brad said. "All that matters is you think you can do it, yes?"

"Yeah," Dan said. "But you gotta see this! I've got a great schtick! Watch!" he pleaded.

"No!" Brad insisted. "Surprise me. There's something I forgot, and I've got to make another PA before they hand us off to Damascus in just a few minutes."

Brad switched to PA and said, "One more thing, guys. Please gather $20,000 of every captain's traveling money and bury it in the usual places, the raft linings or down the lavs if you have to. If we're forced to land and pay to get out of there, I want the damage limited."

. . .

At 5:29 a.m. local time, they were crossing the city of Beirut when the radio crackled. "Douglas Eight-One-Six-Papa-Alpha, Beirut."

Brad reached for his mic. "Roger, sir, Eight-One-Six-Papa-Alpha, go ahead."

"Douglas Eight-One-Six-Papa-Alpha, Damascus is refusing to accept the handoff. When ready, I have holding instructions for you."

"No way!" Dan exclaimed. "Don't take it, Brad! It'll screw up everything. Ask them if we can switch over to Damascus now. Tell them we need to work it out with them. Whatever you do, don't accept that holding clearance!"

"Good plan," Brad agreed. He lifted his mic and said, "Roger, sir, Eight-One-Six-Papa-Alpha copy regarding the handoff. Our company has advised us of a problem involving our call sign, and that may be the issue. Requesting permission to switch frequencies to Damascus now so we may work out the problem with them directly."

"Roger, Douglas Eight-One-Six-Papa-Alpha, contact Damascus now on one-two-seven-decimal-seven. If they will not accept the handoff, return to me on this frequency, over."

"Roger, sir, and thank you for your assistance," Brad said. He quickly changed frequencies.

"Stall!" Dan said. "Don't call them yet! What's the fix at the Damascus boundary?"

"QATAN," Jack answered. "It's twenty-four DME from Damascus, and we're thirty-five miles from there right now, so we've got only eleven miles to go."

"Which gets us eleven miles closer to the Jordanian boundary," Brad said. "Dan's right. We'll wait until they call us first."

Joe put his face in his hands and shook his head.

The mileage on the DME rolled down, and as the others watched it anxiously, Joe's eyes were fixed on the sky ahead of them.

Suddenly, the radio crackled and a man with a heavy Arab accent said tersely, "Douglas Eight-One-Six-Papa-Alpha, this is Damascus, do you read?"

Brad fingered the mic but didn't answer.

When the DME indicated 0 2 4, the radio crackled again. "Douglas Eight-One-Six-Papa-Alpha, this is Damascus control," the man said angrily. "If you read, squawk ident! Douglas Eight-One-Six-Papa-Alpha, you are entering Damascus airspace without clearance. You are to remain clear of Damascus control, do you understand? Remain clear! Do you read?"

"Bingo. We're there," Jack said.

Brad cleared his throat and put his mic to his lips. "Damascus control," he said with an affected nonchalance. "This is Pan Am Five-Three-Three with you passing QATAN at oh-three-three-five Zulu, flight level three-nine-zero, squawking zero-seven-five-two, over."

"Aircraft calling Damascus, say again?"

"Roger, sir, this is Pan Am Five-Three-Three squawking zero-seven-five-two passing QATAN. We're estimating ZALAF at zero-three-four-six Zulu, flight level three-nine-zero, over."

"Aircraft calling Damascus, I do not have a Pan Am. I have a Douglas Eight-One-Six-Papa-Alpha. Are you Douglas Eight-One-Six-Papa-Alpha? I do not have a Pan Am."

"Roger, sir, there seems to be a mix-up. Our company called us and explained what happened. We're a charter flight flying the hajj and somehow the call signs were confused. We are Pan Am flight Five-Three-Three, and I am squawking ident, sir. I apologize for the confusion."

"Negative, negative, Pan Am. You do not have clearance to enter Damascus control. You are in Damascus airspace without clearance. You must remain clear of Damascus, do you read?"

Brad tapped the throttles and looked back at Joe. "Push 'em up," he said. "Put her on the barber pole and keep her there, one knot under the clacker. Haul ass—NOW!"

"We're inside QATAN by sixteen miles," Jack announced. "Seventy-four miles to ZALAF, the Jordanian boundary. If we're turning around, we'd damn well better do it now."

"Pan Am calling Damascus! You must land Damascus! I have clearance to Damascus when ready to copy! Do you read, over? You must land Damascus!"

Brad lifted his mic and said calmly, "Ah, roger, Damascus, that's a negative, sir. Our company has directed us to continue to Kuwait for refueling. We are flying the hajj and cannot be delayed. Our company has not authorized a landing at Damascus, do you read?"

"Negative, negative, NEGATIVE!" the controller screamed. "You do not have clearance for Damascus airspace. You must land Damascus, you must land Damascus, do you understand?"

"Ah, roger, sir, stand by," Brad replied calmly. "We are in the process of getting clearance from our company. Be advised, they are very upset. We are flying the hajj and cannot be delayed, do you understand?"

Silence.

"Shit," Dan muttered. He leaned down and searched the sky ahead.

*CLACK, CLACK, CLACK, CLACK, CLACK, CLACK, CLACK . . .*

It was the overspeed warning clacking loudly, and they all jumped. Joe reached forward and eased the throttles back slightly. The warning ceased.

"Right there," Brad said breathlessly. "Just keep her right on the edge, Joe."

The cockpit door opened. "What the hell's going on?" Mick demanded.

Brad threw up his hand. "Not now!" he yelled. "Stand by, everybody, stand by, goddamn it!"

Dan pointed out the windshield. "Oh *shit!*" he said. "Here they come!"

Two silver streaks shot by them like missiles blasting past from nose to tail.

"Fuckin' MiGs," Joe said, his hands on his temples as he watched them go by. "MiG 21s. Not good ... oh, *Jesus* ... I told you, not good!"

"MiGs! MiGs! MiGs!" a man shouted from the cabin, and then people were piled up at the cockpit door and in the forward entryway.

Brad switched to PA and picked up his mic. "Alright, guys, alright. Looks like we've got company. Everyone, and I mean everyone, get the hell away from the windows. I want everyone standing in the aisle. No one near the windows!"

Everyone moved to the aisle.

Brad switched to the radio and said, "Roger Damascus, this is Pan Am Five-Three-Three, it appears we are being intercepted, sir. Be advised this is scaring our passengers and we will have to report this incident to our company. Do you read?"

"Pan Am Five-Three-Three, this is Damascus. You must land Damascus. You must land Damascus! You must follow our aircraft. You must follow our aircraft, do you understand?"

"How far to ZALAF?" Brad asked anxiously as he searched the sky for the MiGs.

Jack eyed the DME. "Forty-two miles," he said.

"MiG nine o'clock!" a man shouted from the cabin. "Left side! Coming up on our left side!"

"Gimme my hat!" Brad yelled.

Joe handed it to him and Brad put it on. He picked up his mic. "Damascus Control, this is Pan Am Five-Three-Three. We have your aircraft in sight and will follow his instructions. But please be advised I have someone onboard who would like to talk to you before we proceed to Damascus, do you read?"

"Pan Am Five-Three-Three, you must follow our aircraft, do you understand?"

"Oh, shit! Here he is," Dan said. "Look at those fucking missiles!"

Brad turned and saw the MiG in close formation with them off the left wing. He smiled and waved as if it was a fire truck passing in a parade. The pilot of the MiG was clearly in view, his helmet and mask visible. He didn't return the wave. Brad stared at him with a rictus grin and hissed, "Alright, Dan, it's up to you. God help us ... Break a leg."

Dan reached for the speakers above the pilots' heads and turned the volume up full. He grabbed the microphone from the jumpseat audio panel and switched it to the transmitter.

He cleared his throat, stood erect, and let it fly. "*Allo?*" he said loudly, the speakers squealing with feedback. "*Allo? Marhaba … Allo!*"

Silence.

"*Allo? Marhaba … Allo?*" Dan repeated.

Jack and Joe were looking up at him, astonished.

"*Marhaba sidi,*" the controller replied, "*na'am anna isma'ak. Tufadal bi ir'salak.*"

"What'd he say?" Joe asked. "What'd he say?"

"Who the *fuck* knows?" Dan said, leaning down, his eyes locked on the MiG.

"Just read the next line," Brad hissed through clenched teeth as he continued to wave at the MiG. "Don't wait. Just read the next fuckin' line, and read it like you fuckin' mean it, Dan."

Dan stood erect and read from the card. With his arm waving like a madman, he yelled, "*Isma' ya hatha khidmat al mola haqmin khidmatak. Nahin fi rahlat al Hajj, wa la yumkinak hitijazna. Nahin fi khidmat Allah al Rahim wa Allahuh akbar!*"

Silence.

"What's he doing?" Dan asked. "I can't see him standing up. I can't see!"

"Nothing," Brad hissed. "He's still there, still watching us like a hawk."

Suddenly, the radio crackled, "*Yajab 'ahlak al habut fi Damashq ow sanaqum b'isqat al tahira, hal hatha wadih? Ahwul.*"

"What'd he say?" Joe asked anxiously.

"Goddamn it! I don't know!" Dan said. "But he sounds pissed off. What now, Brad, what now?"

"Where's the other MiG?" Jack asked. "There were two of them."

"They're Russian-trained," Joe said. "That means he's three to five miles behind us on our six, missiles armed and ready to fire."

"Just read the last line and walk away," Brad said. "Say it with conviction, Dan, and don't screw around!"

"What if it doesn't make sense against what he said?" Dan asked. "They'll figure out it's a ruse. We're dead!"

"Just read it, goddamn it!" Brad hissed. "My buddy warned me—stick to the script!"

Dan took a breath, put the mic to his lips, and threw himself into the part again. He punched the air and, with his middle finger raised, yelled into his mic, "*Hadha ma yumlih imlayna alshare!*"

Silence followed. The MiG was still fixed in position.

"How far?" Brad asked, his eyes locked on the fighter.

"Close," Jack said. "Ten miles."

"What's happening, Brad?" Mick shouted from the cabin. "What the fuck's going on?"

The radio crackled. "Pan Am Five-Three-Three, do you read?" the controller asked.

"Ah, yes, sir," Brad replied. "Pan Am Five-Three-Three, we read you. Go ahead, over."

"Roger, Captain, Damascus clears Pan Am Five-Three-Three on course ZALAF. Maintain flight level three-nine-zero. Squawk zero-seven-five-two and contact Amman control at ZALAF on one-two-four-decimal-seven … *Allahuh akbar!*"

Brad turned and looked up at Dan in awe. "Holy shit," he said. "Holy shit! You did it! It worked!"

"Answer him," Dan snapped. "Ask him if we can switch to Amman now."

"No, no," Brad said. "I want it to look like we're not in any rush." He lifted his mic, "Roger, roger, cleared on course, maintain three-nine-oh and contact Amman at ZALAF. Thank you for your assistance this morning, sir, we appreciate your help and apologize for the confusion. *Allahuh akbar!* God is truly great!"

Jack pointed to the MiG and asked, "If they cleared us on course, why's he still there?"

"Escorting us to the door," Joe answered.

Jack glanced at the DME and said, "Three miles to ZALAF."

The MiG pilot suddenly gave Brad a crisp salute, and Brad saluted in return. The MiG snapped left and peeled away to the west. It was gone from view in an instant.

"He's gone!" one of the girls shouted from the cabin. "He's *GONE!* He's *GONE!*"

The crew erupted in cheers, applause, and whistles. Dan wheeled around and waved his arms to silence them.

Brad switched frequencies. "Amman control, this is Douglas Eight-One-Six-Papa-Alpha with you at ZALAF, flight level three-nine-zero, squawking zero-seven-five-two, over."

"Douglas Eight-One-Six-Papa-Alpha, Amman, you are radar contact three miles east of ZALAF, cleared on course, maintain three-nine-zero. I have two call signs, Captain, Eight-One-Six-Papa-Alpha and Pan Am Five-Three-Three, which one is correct?"

"The correct one is Eight-One-Six-Papa-Alpha, sir," Brad replied. "We apologize for the confusion."

"Douglas Eight-One-Six-Papa-Alpha, you are cleared on course."

Brad switched to PA. "Okay, guys! *We're clear!*" he exclaimed. "We're in Jordan's airspace!"

Cheers and whistles erupted again, and Dan was pulled into the cabin like a conquering hero. Dianne pushed her way through the others and into the cockpit. She grabbed Brad's hat from his head, threw it into the jumpseat, and gave his hair a tousle.

Jack beamed.

Moments later, Aretha Franklin's "Respect" was rocking the cabin through the loudspeakers, the girls dancing in the aisle. One of them came into the cockpit, grabbed Joe's arm, and pulled him from his seat. He danced with her in the forward entryway, doing his version of the twist.

Brad looked back, and Joe rolled his eyes and smiled.

Looking at Jack, Brad said somberly, "Churchill said there's nothing more thrilling than being shot at—and missed."

Jack blew out his cheeks. "Believe me, I know."

"Never again," Brad said. "Joe was right. That was a massive miscalculation."

# FORTY-SEVEN

Their approach and landing at Kuwait had been uneventful, and the DC-8's refueling and turnaround for their continued journey to Colombo were completed quickly. They'd departed Kuwait at 9:15 a.m. on that Saturday morning, and at 4:35 p.m. the airplane was level at 39,000 feet and crossing the Lakshadweep Islands, four hundred miles northeast of Sri Lanka. They had little more than an hour remaining of their flight.

With the sky sunny and clear and only a light chop gently jostling the jet, a familial placidity had overcome the cockpit and cabin. As Jack monitored the flight instruments, Brad was reclined in his seat with a clipboard on his lap, and Joe was logging performance information from his gauges. Back in the cabin, the crew was lounging, and a few of the girls were doing dancer's stretches in the aisle.

The spreadsheet Brad was creating was for crew pairings during the hajj. Every morning, two flights would depart Colombo: one for Medan, Indonesia, and the other for Jakarta. Flying time to Jakarta was an hour longer than Medan, so once they departed Colombo, the flights would be separated for the day. Upon their return to Colombo with pilgrims, they'd refuel the airplane and have a crew change. By early afternoon, they'd depart for Jeddah and arrive back in Colombo by 2:00 the following morning. Each crew would have one day off after flying, and each day one of the three airplanes would remain in Colombo for maintenance.

It was a simple enough schedule to build but complicated by the need to rotate crew pairings to avoid personal conflicts. Friction was inevitable on extended contracts like this one, and mixing the crews and routes helped mitigate that problem. Putting together a functional schedule was the first step in avoiding trouble, and with Sam retiring soon, that task now fell to Brad. Sam was a genius at resolving personal conflicts, Brad not as much. Brad was keenly aware of this, particularly after his experience managing the operation solo during Sam's absence in Karachi.

As Brad and Joe were quietly occupied, Jack was relaxed too, his eyes glancing at the instruments but his mind wandering until once again it was back to the previous morning with Eddie. Eddie slipping into his room, dropping his towel, her legs around his waist as they kissed passionately, the scent of her hair, the image of her lying on the bed …

Brad cleared his throat and said gruffly, "Given any thought to starting down?"

Startled from his reverie, Jack shifted his gaze to the Doppler's odometer and saw 0 9 0. "Oh, shit," he muttered before looking at Brad in alarm. "Yes. Sorry. We need lower … *now!*"

Brad put his clipboard aside and reached for his mic. "Chennai Control," he said, "Douglas Eight-One-Six-Papa-Alpha requesting descent."

The Indian controller cleared them to flight level 130 and then handed them off to another sector. As Brad changed frequencies, Jack flipped off the autopilot's altitude hold, pitched the nose down abruptly, and yanked the throttles to idle. The gear horn blared, and their ears popped at the sudden loss of pressure in the cabin.

"Hey!" Joe griped. "Gimme a heads-up before you do that!"

Brad gave Jack a sharp look, spun the altitude alert down to seventeen thousand feet, and checked in with the next sector. The controller responded by saying, "Douglas Eight-One-Six-Papa-Alpha, descend and maintain flight level zero-nine-zero and report leaving two-nine-zero."

Brad read back the clearance, and then, pointing at Jack, he said, "Don't *ever* push the nose down like that again before making sure the cabin's prepared, understand? This isn't a freighter," he scolded. "Keep the people in back in mind at all times."

"Sorry," Jack said. "I wasn't thinking."

Brad pointed at him again and snapped, "Bullshit! You've been thinking plenty, but about something other than flying this airplane. Bear in mind that when you've got the controls and the captain's occupied, you're the captain. Clear?" He reached up and snapped on the seatbelt and no smoking signs and then signaled Dianne.

When she answered, he said, "Hey, sorry about that. Everybody okay?"

"Yes," she said. "But good thing no one's wearing a skirt."

Brad grinned and said, "Yeah … won't happen again. Anyway, landing in about twenty-five minutes. Oh, and hey. Tell Marty and Jess I'm sorry I forgot to invite them up for the landing in Kuwait, but they're welcome to come up now if they like."

"I'll let them know," she said.

Brad hung up the receiver, and then, eyeing the towering cumulus on the horizon, he reached forward, turned on the radar, and adjusted the distance and angle of tilt. "Hopefully we get in before that weather gets any worse," he said as he studied the screen. So far, there were no returns.

Moments after Jack started the dive, the flight deck was transformed from a state of placid equilibrium to high-strung chaos: the altimeter needles spinning down, the airspeed needle winding up to the airplane's limit, the wind a deafening howl. Joe had to shout to be heard with the checklist. "Descent Check: Cabin signs?" he said.

"On," said Brad, glancing at the switches.

"Windshield heat?"

"On."

"Anti-fogging …"

Joe completed the checklist, and a few minutes later, Dianne called back. "Jess is on her way," she said, "but Philippe and Marty are getting very cozy and she said she'd pass … He's such a dick."

Brad sighed. "Okay. Whatever," he said, shaking his head as he hung up the receiver.

Joe reached forward, tossed the landing data card on top of the pedestal panel, and said, "Weather's twelve hundred over and two, thunderstorms, light rain, wind zero-eight-zero at seventeen, ILS 04 in use."

Brad picked up the card, gave it a glance, and passed it to Jack. "Your approach, your brief," he said.

Jack removed the approach plate for ILS Runway 04 from his Jepp binder and studied it for a moment before beginning his briefing. Bandaranaike International Airport was on the west coast of Sri Lanka and close to the shore. Their approach to the airfield would be straight in to the runway from across the sea with only a short distance across land. Jack was pleased to see the runway was more than ten thousand feet long. Other than any weather they might encounter, this approach and landing would be the easiest so far.

Brad called the controller and reported leaving 29,000 feet. The controller cleared them to continue the descent to nine thousand feet. Brad replied to the clearance and reset the altitude alert.

Soon after, Jessica entered the cockpit and paused. She was taken aback by the roar of the wind, the nose of the airplane pointed down, and the sense of disorder in the cockpit. It had been nothing like this on her last visit. Brad looked back over his shoulder, pointed at the forward jumpseat, and shouted, "Make yourself comfortable. Joe will give you a hand. We're landing in about twenty minutes."

Jess took the seat and began buckling in without assistance, adroitly assembling from memory the tangle of belts and shoulder harnesses that were hanging around it. Joe watched her, impressed. When she was done, she leaned toward him and asked with a shrewd curiosity, "Is everything okay? It's so much noisier than before."

Joe cocked his head toward Jack and said, "Champ forgot to start the descent on time, and now he's got his pecker in a vice trying to catch up. The lower we get, the denser the air, the noisier it gets going this fast."

"Is that dangerous?"

"Only to his pecker," Joe said with an impish grin.

She giggled and then made a little pout.

Jack overheard them and chanced a look back. She gave him a polite smile and a little wave. Their eyes locked for a moment, hers captivating blue with flecks of silver, her red hair radiant in the tropic afternoon light. She was much prettier than he recalled from the previous morning. He had to force himself to break his gaze from hers and return to his instruments.

"How'd you like them MiGs?" Joe asked her.

She brightened and leaned toward him. "Oh my God," she said. "You know, at first, I was terrified. Especially when I saw the bombs under the wing. But then, when it was happening, I suddenly realized I felt more engaged than frightened. It was an amazing sensation, feeling terrified and thrilled all at once. I've never experienced anything quite like it. Did you feel the same?"

"Missiles," Joe corrected her. "They were missiles, not bombs."

"I'm not sure I'd know the difference," she said. "Anyway, I can't wait to tell everyone back home that we got intercepted by MiGs! Do you think it'll happen again?"

Joe's jaw dropped. "I give up," he sighed.

Brad looked across at Jack and asked loudly, "So how're we doing?"

"Still too high," he shouted, eyeing the altimeter and then the DME from Colombo.

"Did you have a chance to use the ejectors with Sam?"

Jack shook his head. "No," he yelled. "I started down on time."

"What's the airspeed limit for extending the ejectors?"

"Three hundred ninety knots," Jack answered. "We're only doing 340, so we're good."

Brad reached for the overhead panel and toggled the switch for the inboard ejectors to extend. As the cowling cones that carried the clamshell devices behind the engines moved into position, the airplane rumbled and slowed further.

"Now, pull up the number two and three reverse levers, and leave them at idle," Brad said.

"This fast?" Jack asked.

"That's how Douglas built this thing. Boeing's solution to added drag is speed brakes. Douglas went for engine reversing. It's noisy and disconcerting as hell, but it works remarkably well. Go ahead and give it a try or you'll never get down in time."

Jack reached for the levers and drew them up. A roar bellowed from the engines, and the airplane rumbled and shook like a platform next to a passing train.

"Now pitch down to maintain max speed at .85 Mach and then the barber pole at the crossover. Watch what happens to the descent rate," Brad instructed.

Jack edged the autopilot pitch knob forward to accelerate to the airplane's .85 Mach limit while using the autopilot, and the descent rate quickly doubled. "I see," he said. "But man, it feels like it's coming apart."

"Yeah," Brad said, "and that's using only the inboards. Next time we'll do it with all four. Remember, it's not only calculating a top of descent point that matters but the ground speed too. We've picked up forty knots of tailwind over the last hour, and it's eating your lunch right now. That's the price of not keeping your mind on your flying, understand?"

Jack nodded ruefully.

They were thirty miles from the airport and descending through fifteen thousand feet when Brad adjusted the radar again. Areas of green were showing up at the top of the screen and near where the airport would be. Brad sat back and said, "The dates of the hajj change every year according to the lunar calendar. This year it's during the second inter-monsoon season down here, which means frequent periods of strong winds and rain. Just our luck." He groaned.

Moments later, the cockpit door opened and Eddie stepped in. Brad turned and looked back over his shoulder. She'd changed out of her gym wear and into a pair of hip-hugging Palazzos and an olive ribbed bra top that left little to the imagination.

"Mind if I join the party?" she drawled with a presumptuous air.

Jack flinched at the sound of her voice but resisted the urge to look back. *What the hell's this?* he wondered anxiously.

"Yeah, sure," Brad said. "But Jess stays in the forward jumpseat; you take the aft."

Eddie answered him with a roll of her eyes and a flippant wave. She settled into the aft jumpseat without a word.

The radio crackled, "Douglas Eight-One-Six-Papa-Alpha, descend to five thousand feet and contact Colombo approach control now on one-two-four-decimal-eight."

Brad responded and set five thousand feet in the altitude alert. "Keep the speed up and the descent going," he said to Jack. "Once we're level, leave the ejectors out and the engines in reverse to slow quickly."

Jack responded with a nod.

"Colombo approach," Brad said into his mic, "this is Douglas Eight-One-Six-Papa-Alpha leaving zero-nine-zero for five thousand feet. Requesting to continue the descent. We've got Oscar."

"Douglas Eight-One-Six-Papa-Alpha, altimeter 30.09. Descend and maintain three thousand feet, expect vectors for the ILS Runway 4."

Brad responded before resetting the altitude alert and his altimeter, and Jack did the same.

"Approach check: altimeters?" Joe yelled.

"Set and crosschecked," Brad replied.

"Set and crosschecked," Jack said, too.

As Joe continued the checklist, the altitude alert chimed, and the light came on.

"One to go!" Brad warned.

The airplane was still plummeting down, and with the distractions of the altimeter adjustment and the checklist, Jack had lost track of their altitude. The alert came as a shock. At the rate they were descending, they'd bust right through three thousand feet—an FAA violation for certain.

Jack started to pull back on the autopilot control knob to reduce their descent rate, but Brad pushed his hand off of it. "Too late for that!" he yelled. "Manual control, goddamn it! And remember, we've got people in back—not boxes!"

Jessica winced at Brad's reproach and felt embarrassed for Jack.

They were twenty-five miles from the airfield when Jack disconnected the autopilot and applied as much pressure to the yoke as caution allowed, but still, the g-force came on strong. It was yet another humiliating mistake that everyone could feel. When the airplane came level, they were at 2,600 feet and well beyond the accepted margin of error, but the controller said nothing, and Jack assumed they'd gotten away with it. He brought the airplane back to three thousand feet, his heart racing and his pride badly wounded. Self-confidence was everything in this business, and Jack's had been dealt a serious blow.

Once level and with the engines still in reverse, the airspeed fell off fast, and Brad had to remind him, "Watch your speed!"

Jack eyed the airspeed indicator, the needle passing 200 knots, and he threw his left hand behind the throttles and tried to advance them. But the two inboard levers stubbornly refused to budge.

"You're still in reverse," Brad corrected him.

"Shit!" Jack hissed. He shoved the reverse levers down and pushed the throttles up as the airspeed slowed below 190 knots.

Jess leaned toward Joe's ear and discreetly asked, "Are we still okay? It feels like things are getting worse."

Joe was sitting back and regarding the scene with the bemused look of a man watching a house burn down across the street. He gave a shrug. "Yeah," he said, "but he's getting behind-er and behind-er, and if he doesn't get caught up soon, Brad will have to take over. That's a big no-no in this business. Pride is everything."

"He must feel bad," she said.

Joe scoffed and waved her off. "Pilots got big heads," he said with a laugh. "Never hurts to deflate them a little now and then."

The radio crackled, "Douglas Eight-One-Six-Papa-Alpha, left turn zero-seven-zero, vectors to the ILS Runway 4."

Brad replied, and Jack looked at Joe and said, "Coming back."

Joe silenced the gear horn as Jack pulled the throttles to idle. They were fifteen miles from the runway at three thousand feet but now too fast. Jack called for "flaps ten," and Brad moved the flap handle to the detent. "What are the limitations for use of the ejectors beside the maximum airspeed?" he asked.

"No use with flaps."

"And?"

"Uh, right," Jack grumbled. "And no use on approach."

"Bingo," Brad said. He reached up and toggled the ejectors to retract.

"Douglas Eight-One-Six-Papa-Alpha, you're cleared to intercept the localizer and cleared for the approach. Contact the tower now on one-one-eight-decimal-three."

Brad switched frequencies and said, "Colombo tower, Douglas Eight-One-Six-Papa-Alpha with you on final for zero-four."

"Eight-One-Six-Papa-Alpha, Colombo, you are cleared to land runway four, wind zero-nine-zero at twelve."

"Cleared to land," Brad replied.

The localizer needle began moving across the instrument, and Jack banked the airplane to the left to intercept the final approach course. At ten miles from the runway, the glide slope needle was one dot above center and Jack said, "Gear down."

Brad reached for the gear handle. The nose gear doors opened with a loud *whoosh,* and the strut thumped into place. The airspeed began to drop off further, and Jack called, "Flaps twenty."

As Brad set the flap handle, lightning suddenly flashed through the clouds. Brad reached for the radar and put it in contour mode, but the blobs they were approaching remained solid green.

"Flaps thirty," Jack said, and rain began pounding the windshield.

Brad positioned the flap lever and said, "That weather doesn't look too strong, so keep it coming."

"Final Check: gear?" Joe asked.

"Down; three green," Brad replied, testing the handle and pointing to the lights.

"Flaps … wing slots?"

Another brilliant flash, the rain becoming heavier and turbulence now jostling the airplane.

"Set; thirty; light out," Brad said, touching the handle and pointing to the flap gauge.

"Final checks complete," Joe said.

"Douglas Eight-One-Six-Papa-Alpha, cleared to land, be advised wind now zero-nine-zero variable zero-three-zero at eighteen gusting twenty-two, over."

Brad clicked his mic twice and let that suffice for a response. They were passing through one thousand-three hundred feet, the rain surging, the turbulence increasing, the lightning flashing more frequently.

At one thousand feet, Brad straightened in his seat, guarded the controls and said, "One thousand, sink nine, on speed." He glimpsed the radar. "Keep her coming."

Moments later, the approach lights came into view through the rain-streaked windshield, the airplane angled right and into the crosswind.

Jack cinched his gut and straightened in his seat, his concentration intense. Jessica's eyes were wide and staring straight ahead.

They crossed the runway threshold, and Jack took out the crab. The airplane suddenly dropped like a brick and an instant later smashed into the runway with a bone-jarring crash. Jack was shocked and stunned by the violence of the impact. As the airplane ricocheted off the runway and back into the air, he fought instinctively to keep the nose up as the main gear slammed into the asphalt again. By the third impact, he released the back pressure on the yoke, and the nosewheel hit the ground with a loud and embarrassing bang. The ground spoilers deployed, and the airplane was planted to the pavement as if the hand of God was pressing down on it from above.

Loud hoots, whistles, laughter, and the staccato of applause burst from the cabin.

The white centerline stripes were zipping past as Jack lifted his feet on the pedals and began to apply the brakes.

"NO BRAKES!" Joe yelled. "Hundred knots," he reminded Jack.

Jack dropped his heels to the floor, and Brad grabbed his hand, moving it to the reverse levers. He swore at himself silently and pulled up on the four reverse levers. The engines roared as the airplane slowed.

"Eighty knots," Brad said, putting his hand over Jack's and forcing the reverse levers closed. "Sixty knots," he said before taking the controls. "Okay ... I've got the airplane."

Jack released the yoke, fell back in his seat, and had never felt so humiliated in his life. What had he not seen this time that he'd seen so well before?

"Douglas Eight-One-Six-Papa-Alpha, taxi via echo four and contact ground control on one-two-one-point-seven."

Jack was oblivious to the call.

"Eight-One-Six-Papa-Alpha, Colombo."

"Tell him wilco," Brad said. "Tell him we'll clear on echo four and go over to ground."

Jack's fingers quivered as he tuned the ground control frequency. He reached for his mic and checked in with the controller, who cleared them to the ramp.

As they taxied in and the laughter abated, Eddie shattered the silence with a gale of laughter. "Well ... we're here!" she cackled. "Nice of you boys to DROP in!"

Jack closed his eyes and imagined his fingers wrapped around her throat.

Brad raised a hand to silence her.

Jessica was frozen and staring straight ahead.

# FORTY-EIGHT

*Colombo, Sri Lanka, October 28, 1978*

B rad was guided to a spot on the ramp that was adjacent to the airplane's sistership, 823PA. The ground crew attached the electric cart, Jack shut down the engines, and Brad called for the parking checklist. It was 5:47 p.m. local time.

When the checklist was complete, Joe tucked it into the copilot's seat pocket, got up, and left the cockpit to open the forward entry door. The tension in the cockpit was palpable. Jessica and Eddie quietly unbuckled, got up, and returned to the cabin without a word.

Joe disconnected the emergency slide and waited. When he heard a slap on the door's exterior, he lifted the handle and threw the door open. A blast of steamy air scented with rotting vegetation and a whiff of raw sewage rushed in. Reggie Bennington—the captain who'd flown the lead airplane and crew to Colombo—was standing on the landing of the stairs with a Sri Lankan station agent. With his arms wide and a beaming smile, Reggie yelled, "Welcome to Colombo, guys!"

The agent stepped around him and entered the airplane. Looking back into the cabin, and with a Sinhala lilt to his fluent English, he said, "Ladies and gentlemen, please! When you are ready, meet me outside. Once we are all together, I will guide you to the terminal for crew customs and immigration inspection. Thank you very much."

The crew was disembarking and assembling on the ramp as Joe grabbed his flashlight and left the cockpit. Brad snapped his kitbag closed, looked across at Jack, and said, "Okay. So, tell me what went wrong?"

"With the descent or the landing?"

"Is there a difference?"

Jack made a face. "No. There's not," he admitted. "I got behind and stayed that way. I was never stabilized. I was behind the airplane all the way until touchdown."

"One crash and two touchdowns, to be exact."

"Thank you for reminding me."

"And what could you have done to prevent it?"

"Slowed down, configured earlier, descended faster with greater drag, or simply requested a three-sixty or two to buy some time and space rather than continuing straight in."

"Were those the best options?"

"No. The best option would have been starting down on time and not getting behind."

"Exactly. Because even though getting behind in any airplane is a primary cause of accidents, heavy jets are particularly unforgiving of that mistake. Situational awareness, staying ahead of the airplane, and maintaining a stable flight path in every phase of flight are our top priorities, Jack. Keep all of that at the front of your mind from now on."

"I will," Jack said, feeling chastened.

Brad got up. "I'm catching up with the others," he said as he reached for his kitbag. "But sit tight. Joe wants a word with you too."

Jack looked puzzled. "*Joe?*" he said.

"Yeah, he's doing his post flight. He'll be right back."

Brad left the cockpit, grabbed his suitcase from the forward closet, and walked down the stairs to join the crew assembling near the airplane.

Jack got up and sat sidesaddle on the forward jumpseat and licked his wounds. He felt embarrassed and let down by his performance. He'd failed basic airmanship and done it in front of them all. The humiliation was all he could bear. Brad was right to dress him down. It wouldn't happen again.

He looked toward the cockpit door as he heard Joe enter the airplane. Joe pulled the earplugs from his ears as he entered the cockpit and put his flashlight in his kitbag. He turned to Jack and met him with an even gaze. "I'll get right to it," he said with a frown. "She's married, you putz."

Jack looked confused and said, "Okay. So what?"

Joe glowered. "So *WHAT?* That's all you got to say?"

"Yeah, so what?" Jack repeated. "She's a pretty girl, obviously smart, and planning to become a CPA. Seems like a catch to me, so why wouldn't she be married?"

Joe's eyebrows went up. "Not *Jessica*, you moron … *EDDIE!* It's Eddie I'm talkin' about!"

Jack recoiled and, looking even more puzzled, asked, "Wait … You're saying what?"

"She's married, you idiot. And not just married, but married to Jimmy Caffaretti, Manny's Odd Job, the guy with the …" He gestured at the back of his head. "You know, the ponytail thing. I know those types of goombahs back home, and you don't want to fuck around with them, understand? They know one way of fixing problems, pal, and it ain't pretty."

Jack's jaw dropped. "Oh, no … *please*," he muttered.

"Oh, *yes* … please."

Jack blew out his cheeks and ran his fingers through his hair. "She never mentioned that," he grumbled. "There's no ring. It never occurred to me to ask … Why would I? Plus there wasn't time—"

"Well, now there is, and now you know, so get your head out of your ass."

Jack looked at him. "But the other one, her girlfriend," he said defensively. "What's that all about?"

"Charlotte? How the hell do I know? But here's the thing, champ. Some men like that kind of thing, know what I'm sayin'? But you … *YOU?*" Joe exclaimed, pointing at him. "You think he's going to think the same thing about *you?* Good luck with that, you schmuck."

"Sam said she was complicated," Jack muttered. "I figured it was just the girl thing."

"And that ain't complicated enough for you? *Fuhgeddaboudit!*" Joe barked. Pointing at him again, he said, "If you're smart, you'll keep it in your pants and stay away from her, know what I'm sayin'? You give up now while there's still time before we go home and maybe it all goes away, *capeesh?*"

Jack looked glum. "Yeah. *Capeesh*," he replied.

"Alright. Enough, already. Let's lock this thing up and get the hell out of here. They're waiting for us, and I'm ready for a hot shower and a clean bed."

• • •

The twenty-six-mile bus ride to the hotel was an hour and fifty-minute stop-and-go trundle through the poorest and most densely populated place Jack had ever seen. Da Nang and Saigon were no match for Colombo's ramshackle structures, noisome clouds of diesel and moped smoke, bleating horns, and mass of humanity who crossed and clogged the streets. Jack felt both daunted and thrilled by it. He'd seen scenes of Calcutta, but to experience anything like it firsthand was another matter. The crew was silent as they took it in. Hope that the hotel would offer refuge from what they were witnessing had quickly faded. They assumed it would be another Bamako.

But by the time they'd crossed the short, castle-like bridge from the city to the hotel, night had overtaken the day and the crew looked at the Mount Lavinia's great white edifice in shock. Outside its softly lit balustrades and cannonades and great wooden doors, doormen were in spotless white tunics and pith helmets awaiting their arrival.

Originally constructed as a governor's home during Sri Lanka's days as British-ruled Ceylon, it was modeled on a classic colonial villa and set atop a steep mount west of the city. Protected by the ocean on three sides and a deep railway ravine on the other, no sea-locked English castle was more secure from the hoi polloi beyond its ramparts than the Mount Lavinia.

The crew let out a collective sigh of relief.

• • •

Jack entered his room—with its parqueted floors and lacquered furnishings—put down his bags, and pulled open the drapes. He gazed west through the night across the Arabian Sea and smiled. There was no other job, no other place on earth he cared to be.

After showering and a brief nap, he woke, dressed in shorts and a T-shirt, and left the room for a beer. He stopped by the poolside bar populated by well-heeled guests speaking French or German and ordered a pint of the local Three Coins lager. He took a sip, admired the taste and color, then ambled toward the balustrade past the pool on the patio. Some of the other crewmembers were out there, too, gathered here and there in small groups of three or four.

He stopped at the edge and looked down to a steep rock bluff that dropped straight into the sea. Not a place for drinking, he decided. Shifting his gaze across the sea, he took in the air as rich and warm as his beer. It was Saturday night, and the entire crew was off until Tuesday morning. He fantasized about Eddie making another pass. He dreaded—and dreamed—that she would.

"Jack!" a man called out. "Jack … over here!"

He turned to look to his left. In the shadows past the pool lights, a man was reclined on a lounge chair that had been directed toward the sea. He held a pint in his left hand and raised his right hand to wave.

Jack strolled toward him. As he got closer, the man offered his hand but made no attempt to get up. "Pete Gaides," he said with a smile. "I'm one of the copilots. Sorry we haven't had a chance to meet."

He was a robust forty-ish guy with a confident air. He was unshaven, broad-shouldered, and strongly built in a tattered white polo, cutoffs, and Topsiders. His mahogany hair was uncombed and tousled by the breeze.

"Pleased to meet you, Pete," Jack said as they shook. "I don't remember seeing you at the briefing in Miami."

"Nah … I never go to those things," he replied.

Jack leaned back against the balustrade and, with a glance down at the rocks, said with an anxious laugh, "Not a great place for drinking. Given the age of this place, I'm sure it's seen its share of the 'white man's burden'—alcohol—while falling to their fate."

Pete laughed too. "Yeah, that's quite a drop," he said. Shifting his pint to his right hand, he held it up and offered Jack a toast. "So, hey, cheers," he said. "Glad to see you were able to stay on."

They clinked glasses and Jack said, "Yeah, until this morning I figured they were sending me home. If they had, I'd have nothing to go back to."

"I heard you've got a shot at Air Logistics."

"Maybe. The chief pilot told me if I got a couple of hundred hours of DC-8 time, they'd give me another look. He didn't say anything about just a few takeoffs and landings."

"I heard that too. Sam looking after you, was he, sending you on your way?"

Jack answered with a nod and a shrug before changing the subject. "How about you? Have you ever interviewed with them?"

"Me? No," Pete replied. "I was with Eastern."

Pete's announcement came as another unwelcome surprise. Was everyone here fired? Was every pilot a refugee from some fuck up at a world-class airline? He secretly cringed and was loathe to ask.

Sensing what Jack was thinking, Pete answered the question without being asked. "Nope, not fired," he said. "I just quit. I didn't go back after the last furlough," he continued. "It was the second layoff in nine years, and that was enough for me. My wife and I are from Idaho but always wanted to relocate to Alaska, so that's what we did. When Eastern recalled me, I told them *adios*. Doing another stint as a flight engineer on reserve and commuting to a crash pad in Queens or Miami was off the table."

"I can imagine. That would be a tough commute. Where in Alaska do you live?"

"Ketchikan. My wife's a doc, and I started a bush plane operation there. We run an air ambulance and guide service. I'm here only part-time."

Jack raised his brows and said, "I didn't know that part-time was an option."

"Usually it's not, but I come in handy as a ready reserve in cases like this, situations where there's back-to-back extended contracts. If one of the regular copilots needs to bow out, I'm usually able to take his place."

"What about for captains and engineers?"

"Nope. Copilots are considered ancillary here, and look, as you and I both know, there's always plenty of guys looking to build some heavy jet time and ready to do it on a moment's notice. They're a dime a dozen and easily qualified on the cheap. Captains, engineers, and mechanics are another matter. When they're called, they have to go. That's why I don't upgrade. I don't want it full-time."

"Then why bother with it at all?"

"Because the money's good and helps fill the coffers when business back home is slow. Plus, it keeps me in the game in case I ever need it again, and much as I love Alaska, what's not to like about what we're doing right now, right?"

Jack glanced toward the sea, the soft breeze washing over him. "Got that right," he agreed.

"Mick told me you want to stay on. He said you prefer this over Air Logistics."

Jack looked back at him and said, "It's an appealing alternative, particularly since the upgrade here could come decades sooner."

"Hey, tell me about it. It was the same at Eastern, and then every time you did upgrade, it would be back to the bottom of the seniority list again, years sitting on reserve followed by years of endless turnarounds, all-nighters, and all the other shit the senior guys passed on. I said fuck that."

There was a quiet interlude, Jack reflecting on what Pete had said, and then, deciding to tempt Pete's candor a bit further, he said, "If you don't mind, I'd like to ask you something as one not-so-attached-to-the-company-copilot to another."

"Go ahead. There's no secrets in this outfit."

Jack scoffed. "Oh, I'm not sure about that," he said. "But anyway, what are your thoughts about Brad and Sam, their differences in management style, and the future of the company?"

"Of course," Pete answered, "and that's a good question. But to start, you have to understand that Brad's been tasked with bringing the airline up to date, to bring it up to contemporary standards and put an end to the flying club antics that have existed here since it was started in 1948. Gerhard's keenly aware of that, and Sam too. But unlike those two, who have tried and were forced to give up under relentless resistance by everyone else, Brad doesn't give a shit about stepping on toes and pissing people off. The point is, like Brad or not, he's the future and the type of manager the airline will need to survive. If you're planning on staying here, then you should be rooting for him. As for Sam, you're asking me about Larry's upgrade, that thing between him and Brad, yes?"

"Yeah. I was there when they got into a scuffle at the bar in Miami. It was unsettling, to be honest."

"Well, I'm no psychiatrist, but my guess is Sam's upgrade of Larry is an attempt to purge his demons from that accident before he goes out the door. Gerhard and Brad have figured that out, too, but only Brad is willing to stand up and put a stop to it. Gerhard's a lot softer than he comes off, and he's more inclined to put off any decision about Larry until it can't be put off any longer, maybe hoping it somehow resolves itself, who knows? And though I've never flown with Larry, on that matter I'd trust Brad over Sam. I think the world of Sam, but from what I've heard about Larry from some of the other captains, Brad's judgment regarding his upgrade is likely the better call."

"Okay, so that makes sense. But then how does Brad's dodging through Syrian airspace without clearance increase our flight standards here or square with Brad wanting to do things by the book?"

"Raising standards doesn't mean always doing things by the book,"

Pete corrected. "It means not taking risks willy-nilly. It means using the industry's best policies and procedures to reduce the risk of error in routine operations. That can be as simple as using standardized procedures, callouts, and briefings, and not running the flight deck like a single-seat airplane and excluding your other crewmembers from making decisions. It means more training and staying up with current advances in safety, and—above all else—it means anybody at any time can speak up when they see something they don't agree with. As you just saw with that new girl in Shannon, Sam and Brad are *very* good at encouraging that because of their background—but they're in a class by themselves. Most of the other guys just blow you off and do what they please. At Eastern that was never the case. We were always doing it by the book, always flying on the straight and level. The Eastern Shuttle between New York, Boston, and D.C. several times a day? Hell, why wouldn't we be? But out *here?* Well, good luck with that. More often than not, the only way to get the job done is by pushing limits, and Brad understands that as well as anyone. This company's DNA is non-sched, Jack. We take jobs that no one else will. It's a lot like bush flying, which—from my crusty point of view—makes it so much more appealing than flying for Eastern ever was. Beyond the money, it's the reason we all stay on here. Once this kind of flying gets in your blood, it's hard to shake."

Jack gave him a glance and nodded in agreement.

Pete raised his pint and offered a toast. "So, here's to flying crooked," he said, "and may I never do another Boston–LaGuardia turnaround."

Jack smiled and clinked glasses. "Amen to that," he said. "Mine were Boston–Philly, and more often asleep than awake."

"I bet."

"I appreciate the insight and support, Pete. I got a chilly reception from the copilots Sam introduced me to in Miami. I figured they saw me as unwelcome competition for the left seat."

"Nah … that's not it," he said. "Like me, they either have no interest in upgrading or, like the guy you're replacing, the company was never going to give them the option. What you saw at the bar that night is a tight group of people who are suspicious of any newcomer. We're like a team of sled dogs. You don't get to be one of us until everyone's had a chance to sniff your ass."

Jack winced and then doubled over in laughter. He looked at Pete and said, "You're okay, Pete. We're a lot alike. Same time, same place tomorrow?"

"I'll be here," he said, smiling and raising his pint.

Jack bid him goodnight and left to order something to eat.

# FORTY-NINE

*Colombo, Sri Lanka, October 29, 1978*

On Sunday morning, October 29, Brad had asked Jack to assist him in completing the schedule for the hajj. Jack had felt honored to be asked and was pleased to help out. By Monday afternoon their work was done and the schedules distributed to the crew. With the task complete, Jack decided to take a walk along the beach south of the hotel, an opportunity for some exercise and a chance to explore Sri Lanka.

But after walking a short distance on the sand, he came upon a pile of dung of a type he vaguely recognized. Not far beyond that, he saw more and then even more until the piles speckled the beach above the waterline. The number and composition of them caused him mild alarm. Whatever their source, they were not from a small animal and certainly not from one living on a diet of grass and oats. He continued his walk but with furtive glances toward the thatched shacks and tumbledown structures created from scrap beneath the palms at the shoreward edge of the sand. If it were the residents' dogs responsible for the feces, he'd have to dart into the sea to avoid them if they attacked. But what then? Swim back?

He decided to turn around and return to the hotel. He was moving at a brisk pace when ahead of him and at some distance he saw a woman with long black hair and wearing a dark robe squatting on the sand. Her robe was hitched up behind her, and Jack froze—the mystery of the dung resolved.

She was staring back at him with a wary gaze, and he felt more saddened than relieved by his discovery. Respecting her dignity, he shifted his gaze across the sea and kept his distance until she was gone.

He returned to the hotel wondering what other unpleasant realities he'd find on a walk through the city and decided to forego that, too, at least for now. Swimming in the hotel's pool and navigating among tourists drifting about on floats with umbrella drinks would have to suffice for exercise. Life could be much worse. It certainly appeared to be for those impoverished people living along the southwest shore of Sri Lanka.

• • •

On Tuesday afternoon, October 31, Brad, Jack, and Joe boarded a van accompanied by Dianne, Sharron, Kerry, and Jessica for the ride to the airport. They would be the crew flying the first turnaround to Jeddah. The girls were dressed in their sky-blue uniform blouses with gold wings, navy blue slacks, and pumps. At Maggie's directive, they wore very little makeup, and their hair was modestly styled to accommodate the white hajibs the company had provided for them when they were on duty with pilgrims.

The airplane they'd be flying, 823PA, had departed Colombo early that morning for Medan, Indonesia. Mick Salyer, Pete Gaides, and Buddy Reid were flying the turnaround to Medan and back. Once they returned to Colombo, there would be a quick crew change and refueling, and then Brad and his crew would continue to Jeddah with a return to Colombo empty. It was a six-and-a-half-hour flight in each direction. The cockpit crew had a gruelingly long day of work ahead of them, while the girls would be able to sleep and relax on the return.

When they arrived at the airport, Brad and Jack went straight to the flight planning office beneath the tower. Dianne and her crew remained in the terminal with Joe, waiting for the airplane to arrive. Soon after, they watched the DC-8 rolling out on the runway, the engines roaring in reverse. As it was guided to a parking spot, Joe put his earplugs in and left the terminal with his kitbag and a small duffle for an overnight stay, should that be needed.

Mick brought the airplane to a stop, and an electric cart was plugged in. The engines were shut down, but immediately the captain's sliding window was opened and Mick leaned out. Looking at Joe, he sliced his hand across his throat and then signaled for him to come up.

"Ah, shit," Joe groaned. "Something's wrong. Not good." Whatever it was, he figured a long day was about to become longer.

A truck with mobile stairs pulled up to the airplane, and when Buddy opened the door, Joe charged up with his bags in hand and entered the jet. Over the howl of the electric cart, Buddy put his hand on Joe's shoulder and leaned toward his ear. "All the Freon's gone," he yelled, "so no A/C. It was already gone when we left this morning, which means the leak began sometime sooner. No time to fix it today, so you're stuck with it."

Joe leaned toward Buddy's ear and shouted, "What about a conditioned air cart?"

Buddy shook his head, pointed at an Icelandic DC-8 parked next to them, and said, "There's only one on the airfield, and Loftleider beat us to it. They've got pilgrims from Jakarta and aren't scheduled to leave until after we do."

Joe grimaced and walked around him and into the cockpit. Mick and Pete were packing up their kitbags, and upon hearing Joe enter, Mick turned around. "This thing's going to become a steam bath, and fast," he said. "You'll need to make the turn quick. You want me to wait to talk to Brad, or are you okay with it?"

"No, go ... go," Joe said. "The van's waiting out front. We'll deal with it."

"You'd better," Mick warned. "Have you checked out our people? I don't think there's anyone back there under age seventy."

Joe frowned and looked toward the cabin. One hundred eighty elderly men and women—some of the men in white robes—were staring back at him with anxious eyes. Seeing a man in an airline uniform standing by the galley, Joe looked at Mick and pointed over his shoulder. "Is he the charter's agent working the flight?" he asked.

"Yeah, the Merpati Airlines guy," Mick answered. "His name's Hassim and he's sharp. Tell Brad and the girls to make their announcements, and he'll repeat them in Indonesian. Other than the airplane problems, this looks like it's going to be the cleanest hajj we've ever done. Fingers crossed." Mick smiled.

"Okay, go … go," Joe insisted. "Meantime, I'll go back and open the doors, get some air through this thing."

As Mick and Pete got up, a yellow fuel truck pulled up to the airplane. Buddy stepped inside and said, "Brad and the girls are on the way."

Mick said to Joe, "Let Dianne know I called ahead for extra ice and water. Don't leave without it! You'll need it until you get to altitude. It was the same for us coming from Medan."

Mick tramped down the stairs with Pete and Buddy following behind. When they got to the ramp, Mick said to Brad, "Everything's running well but the A/C. Joe will explain."

Brad grimaced and said, "Okay, got it. We'll get it turned around quick. Climb and maintain 60° Fahrenheit, I guess."

Mick gave him a clap on the shoulder. "Have fun … Be safe," he said. "See you, tamale." Then he turned and waved for his crew to follow him to customs and immigration.

While Mick was briefing Brad on the ramp, Joe had opened the sliding windows in the cockpit, then went aft to open all the doors. The moment he did, the howl of the generator rushed inside along with a blast of steamy air and a plague of small black flies. They immediately spread through the cabin, buzzing around the people's faces, everyone swatting them away. It was misery set atop misery, but the pilgrims bore it all in silence with weary eyes and worried faces.

Brad and Jack boarded as Joe did his walkaround inspection. Jack paused to look back into the cabin. Speaking to Brad, he asked, "Why are some of them wearing white robes?"

"It's an Islamic ritual for the hajj. The robes are only worn by men. It's called Ihram, and the clothing represents a state of mind, a sort of state of grace, all their thoughts and actions directed to Allah."

"They're oddly quiet," Jack noticed.

"That's also a part of the hajj. There can be no complaining, no fighting, and no intimate relations, among other things, once they embark on the pilgrimage. Can you imagine an airplane full of New Yorkers bound for Miami and the same situation?"

Jack cringed and laughed. "I'm calling my lawyer!"

Dianne came forward and said, "It's already a sauna back here. Will we have time for a water service?"

"Sure, and keep at it until Joe goes back to secure the doors." Seeing the perspiration on her face, he added, "Will you guys be okay?"

Dianne blew out her cheeks and pulled at her hijab. "It is what it is," she replied.

"We'll be out of here as quickly as possible. Hang in there. By the time we climb out of ten thousand feet, it'll be cooling off markedly."

She answered with a nod and returned to the cabin.

Brad looked at Jack, who had taken his seat and was setting up his instruments. "Go ahead and call for clearance," he said.

Joe returned from his walkaround inspection and entered the cockpit. He grabbed the checklist and said, "Ready when you are."

Brad nodded, then reached forward and adjusted his rudder pedals.

"Here comes the clearance," Jack announced.

Brad switched his audio selector to radio number one and listened to the ATC clearance as Jack copied it on his scratch pad. At the end of the clearance, the controller added, "… Captain, be advised Jeddah Control has a just given all flights inbound to Jeddah a one-hour ground hold due to traffic. Your departure time is now scheduled for 09:35 Zulu, over."

Brad threw up his hands. "Son of a bitch," he grumbled. "When it rains, it pours." He reached for the call button and pushed it twice. Dianne came to the cockpit, and Brad looked back at her and said, "They've given us a one-hour delay on our departure for traffic at Jeddah."

She let out a long sigh. "The heat's bad enough, but the flies are even worse."

"Take turns going outside; get some relief under the wing in the shade. If we need more water and ice, let me know."

"We're okay for now," she said, "but we'll need more at this rate."

"I'll call for it," Brad told her. He looked at Jack and said, "Jeddah's the busiest airport in the world during the hajj, and they manage the traffic flow like they do at Chicago O'Hare. The only difference here is the heat and these goddamn flies," he added, swatting one from in front of his face.

"I'll go back and get us some water," Jack said. He took off his headset and got up.

Brad slapped the back of his neck and exclaimed, "Damn it!" Looking at his hand, he sighed, "Mosquitoes *too?*"

Jack went to the galley and paused to look back into the cabin. Not a word was being spoken, and everyone was still except the girls as they went back and forth from the galleys with plastic water bottles, cups of ice, and damp paper towels. He fixed his gaze on Jessica as she leaned across a row of pilgrims to distribute the water and ice. Their eyes met, she smiled modestly, and Jack was transfixed by the white hajib framing her face and tumbling softly across her shoulders. Rather than diminish her beauty, it enhanced it, and rather than minimizing her distinction as a woman, it greatened it. Her smile widened as if somehow she'd read his thoughts.

Embarrassed having been caught staring, he forced himself to shift his gaze. He retrieved three plastic bottles of water from the galley and returned to the cockpit.

. . .

At 2:05 p.m. local time, the tower called and released them to depart. Three hours later, they were nearly halfway to Jeddah, the cabin long since cooled and made comfortable by the dry, frigid air at that altitude.

Brad was doing a crossword puzzle and occasionally eyeing the instruments as he considered an answer. Jack was perusing the airplane's systems manual. Joe was gently nodding in and out, his chin on his chest, when suddenly a male soprano's voice trebled from the cabin.

Without taking his eyes off his puzzle, Brad said, "That's the *muezzin* calling them to afternoon prayer."

"You know a lot about the hajj," Jack said. "You've studied it?"

"Yes," Brad replied. "The Qur'an and Sunnah and Western works as well. The better informed we are, the better we do our job. Same as flying."

Jack listened to the prayer, spellbound by the ancient, haunting lyrics.

• • •

The remainder of the flight was uneventful, and the turnaround in Jeddah was accomplished quickly. They returned to Colombo and landed at 4:10 a.m. local time. The ride to the hotel was short, the roads devoid of cars and people.

The Freon system was repaired by the company's mechanics with spare parts bought from Air Logistics. It was restored to service the following day.

# FIFTY

*Mount Lavinia Hotel, November 1, 1978*

Jack slept until 3:15 that afternoon. After waking and washing, he put on a T-shirt and bathing suit. With his bare feet in sneakers, he left the room and walked out to the pool.

The afternoon was sunny and hot, the umbrella tables on the ocean side of the patio populated by a mix of crew and European tourists. The crowd was the same mix at the poolside bar where Jack stopped and ordered a freight dog's breakfast: a pint of Three Coins beer and a bowl of the hotel's spicy rice and curry.

The barman delivered Jack's pint in a tall plastic cup, and as he waited for the food to arrive, he leaned back against the bar and took a sip. He caught sight of Eddie at the far side of the pool. She was walking between the tables in her tiny bikini, laughing and stopping to chat with some of the girls, a drink in her hand.

As he watched her vacantly, his thoughts returned to a night long ago. It was 11 p.m. at the post-race party at a bar in Huntington, Long Island. Jack was nineteen, and Heather, twenty-five. Her husband, Jerry—the owner of the motorcycle shop where Jack worked as a mechanic—was pushing forty. Heather was a rakish brunette who'd been flirting with Jack since the start of the racing season. She'd assured him that her marriage to Jerry was "open," but Jack was wary of that, callow and credulous as he was.

He'd been putting Heather off until that night when his desperate desire to lose his virginity, his second-place finish at the race in Bridgehampton, and Heather's advances went to his head. He had left prudence on the bar—and Jerry in the men's room—as he and Heather slipped out the door.

Northern Boulevard was breathless that steamy August night, the streetlamps cloaked in haze as they roared past on his '63 Triumph bobber,

Heather clinging to him from the pillion pad, her squeals of delight loud behind him. Jack succeeded in losing his virginity on that sultry night—and then his job the following week.

It was one thing to make a mistake and learn from that lesson, but it was another thing to repeat it, and Jack would not. Married women, no matter how flirtatious and attractive, were off the table. Fortunately, it seemed Eddie was back to avoiding him and Jack had become invisible to her.

Goddamn Eddie.

He was taking another sip of beer when, "You're alive," he heard a woman say.

He looked to the right and couldn't contain his smile. She was wearing a blue floral one-piece that clung to her curves. Modest as they were—Jessica was petite in or out of clothing—she was striking. Her blue bathing suit matched her eyes, and the tiny red flowers patterning it blended beautifully with her hair.

"It's a well-honed habit," he replied with a laugh. "Daily death and resurrection is a way of life for freight pilots, and I'm quite good at it."

"Is that why you came here?" she asked artlessly. "To learn how to fly passengers?"

Jack chuckled. "No," he said. "There's no difference. People, boxes, lab rats, hand grenades … the airplanes fly the same."

Her eyes narrowed. "Then why here?" she asked. "How do pilots choose one airline over another?"

"It's more like airlines choose them. Pilots are a dime a dozen. It's the most competitive career in existence. Airlines have dozens upon dozens of highly qualified candidates for every position available, and on top of that, we've got a shelf life. If you're not hired by the time you're age thirty, you're passed over by most of them. Companies like this one are an exception."

"You don't look that old."

"I'm not. I'm twenty-six."

"That's what I figured—or younger, really. So, why do you do it?"

she asked. "If there's no predictable path to success, why take the chance?"

The barman came over to take her order. She smiled and pushed the two clear plastic cups she'd brought with her toward him. "Rum and Coke, and a pina colada," she said with a smile.

The barman smiled in return, shook his head, and left to mix her drinks.

Pleased by the chance to change the subject, Jack's eyes followed the barman, and he said, "Funny how cultures are so different, isn't it, shaking their heads to mean *yes*?"

"Oh, I know," she said with a laugh. "The first morning here, I ordered eggs, and when I took my first bite, I nearly died! The *curry!* Oh my God, the curry!"

"Me too," Jack agreed. "I like spicy, but *wow!* And when I called the waiter back and asked for not-so-hot, he shook his head, and I nearly flipped out! What the hell? He's telling me no?"

Her laughter trailed off. "So, back to what we were talking about, why? I'm curious, why do you do it? Is it the money, the adventure, the thrill, the travel … the MiGs?"

He pursed his lips, looked toward the pool, and paused before giving her an answer. "Actually, no," he said. "There's more. I mean, those things, too, but for every pilot I know, it's more than just that. It's the confluence of the machine and the environment. Airplanes and flying are like sailing ships to seamen, the China Tea Clippers, say, racing across an azure sea under full sail. Flying is beauty, adventure, skill, and so much more, but it's the machines that hold the greatest allure for most of us, and the most coveted machines for making a living are transport jets. They're pure magic," he said with a dreamy air. "A never-ending challenge to know and master."

"Like when to descend and how to land?" she deadpanned.

Jack reddened and his eyes narrowed. He turned and glowered at her.

She put her hands to her mouth to stifle her giggles, her eyes pinched and tearing. "I'm sorry," she said, shaking her head. "I'm so sorry … but I couldn't resist."

A thin smile creased his lips and then widened. "Oh … *you!*" he said, choking back a laugh. "*YOU!*" he repeated. "Little Miss Innocence with the cherub's face and cute little freckles? Oh, sure! But so, so … *MEAN!*"

She put down her hands and affected a pout. "That *was* mean," she admitted for a moment but then was immediately wracked by more giggles, her hands covering her mouth again.

He rolled his eyes and put his back to the bar. Try as he did to stifle it, her laughter was contagious and he joined her giggles.

She looked at him, and between laughs, she said, "I happen to be very sensitive about my freckles."

He pointed at her and said, "And I happen to be very sensitive about crashing!"

More giggles erupted. "I'm sorry," she said as she tried to contain them, wiping her eyes with her hands. "I can't help it. I'm the youngest of four kids and the only girl. My brothers were murderous, especially to me. I rarely left the dinner table not running to my room and crying with my dad yelling at them to stop."

Jack scoffed. "Well, you're certainly prepared for this outfit. Mean people like you are what this place is all about. You'd better be able to take as good as you give," he said, looking at her with a wry grin. "I've got the bruises to prove it."

She smiled and put her elbow on the tiled bar. Meeting his gaze, she raised her right hand and, with her pinky crooked, asked, "Friends?"

He smiled and raised his hand. "Friends," he said, hooking her pinky and giving it a shake. A shot of heat raced through him.

He let go, put his back to the bar, and shifted his gaze across the pool. Marty was glaring at him. "I think your other friend's mad that I'm keeping you here."

Jessica gave her a look and said, "Marty's mad about a lot of things. She'll get over it."

The barman came over with her drinks and Jack's bowl of curry. He put them on the bar, they thanked him, and Jessica reached for the drinks.

"Before you go," he said, "it's my turn."

She looked at him, puzzled. "For what?"

"For why here? For why now?"

She let go of the cups, shrugged, and said, "A change of pace, a break, that's all. That's what I told my dad. I told him it was Marty's idea, and for once I agreed with one of her hairbrained schemes."

"Are you happy you did?"

She looked down at the drinks and with a serious air said, "Yes. I am … But also scared."

"About the MiGs?"

"No," she said, looking at him, their eyes locked. "I'm scared I'm liking it … I'm scared I'm going to want to stay."

"I was watching you yesterday," he said. "But in a good way," he hastened to add. "Helping the people. You looked like an angel in that hijab, and the people were looking back at you the same. Do they have angels in Islam? I'll have to ask Brad."

"They're so old," she said with a heartfelt look. "I helped an old lady to and from the aft lav and showed her how to use it. She was so grateful, clutching my arm as we went back and forth, speaking to me in Indonesian—I had no idea what she was saying—but I felt like she was thanking me. I can't tell you how it made me feel. I've never done anything like this. Not that I haven't wanted to, but I've just never had the opportunity. My mom died when I was young, and my dad, with his business, and me and my brothers to raise, there was never anything more than work and school and growing up. But on the way back here last night, suddenly I was scared, and in a different way than before. I became scared when I realized this is what I really want to do. I don't want to work in an office. I want to do work like this."

He raised his eyebrows. "Me too," he said. "Not scared in my case, but wanting to stay here. I began to realize that not long after I started. You're not alone, Jess. We're not alone. I've learned that everyone here's the same. Once it's in your blood, you're hooked."

She closed her eyes and, with a nod, admitted, "I believe it. But it can't be. My family's depending on me. I have to go back."

They were quiet for a moment, a gentle breeze tousling their hair.

Breaking the spell, he looked at her and said, "I'm sorry for what I said about your freckles, and I don't really think you're mean. I mean … at least not *that* mean."

She looked at him and smiled. "And I'm sorry for what I said about your shitty landing … even though it was a *really* shitty landing."

Now he was the one giggling. "It really was," he said. "I was so embarrassed."

She reached for her drinks, started for the pool, and then stopped. She looked back across her shoulder and gave her hair a flip with her head. "Friends," she reminded him with a coy smile. "For *now*."

"For now," he repeated, his heart skipping.

• • •

He finished his curry and ordered another beer. Across the pool, the girls were playing a boombox, classic rock 'n' roll hits of the '60s and '70s, some of the girls dancing.

Jessica was reclined on a lounge, Marty in a lounge next to her, when a tourist in a Speedo walked up to her. He asked her something; she smiled and nodded and got up. They walked to the center of the patio to join the others dancing. "Runaround Sue" was on the box.

Jealousy gripped Jack as he watched her with the other man, and then slyly, subtly, as if she knew Jack was staring, she glanced at him, smiled, and raised her fist as she swung her hips. Her pinky was crooked.

He felt a stir in his chest.

Jessica could dance. Oh man, could she dance.

# FIFTY-ONE

*Jeddah, Saudi Arabia, November 3, 1978*

It was Friday at 5:05 p.m. local time. The inbound hajj was reaching its peak before the sacred rituals began on November 9, and the airport was jammed with airplanes and people.

Sam had arrived in Colombo from Shannon the previous Wednesday. He'd flown in with Larry Schaff and Bobby Mumford on 804PA, which had been fully repaired and restored to service. On Friday, he was flying with Jack and Buddy Reid. They'd arrived at Jeddah from Colombo with pilgrims from Jakarta.

Brad's airplane was parked on the ramp nearby, having arrived earlier with the pilgrims from Medan. All the flights that day had proceeded on schedule. The airline and airplanes were running well.

Sam shut down the engines and ran the parking checklist. He asked Jack to plan and file their return flight to Colombo without assistance. It was the first time that responsibility had been delegated solely to Jack, and it felt good; in fact, it felt *very* good. It meant Sam was ready to release him to fly as a fully qualified copilot and no more check airmen as babysitters. He was beaming as he walked to the airport's flight planning office with his kitbag and Sam's clutch bag in his hands.

Sam left the cockpit with the deplaning pilgrims. He walked over to Brad's airplane to have a word with Maggie. She'd been having problems with Philippe, Marty, and Anna, and was at her wits' end with all of them. She'd asked Sam for his intervention before she'd left the hotel with Brad's crew that morning. Sam told her they'd discuss it when they got to Jeddah if they had the chance.

When Sam arrived at the other airplane, Bobby Mumford was doing his preflight walkaround, and Sam threw him a wave before charging up the stairs. He found Maggie standing in the forward galley. "What's up, sweetie?" he asked with a smile.

She gave him a hug and said as she let go, "What's up is between Philippe's legs, as usual. We'll have another whore's melt on our hands like we did in Karachi if you don't put a stop to it, *da*. I asked Brad to handle it while you were in Shannon, but he said to wait for you. Philippe isn't one of Brad's favorites, either."

Sam winced. "I'll talk to him tomorrow. I agree it's got to stop. I'll tell him I'm notifying Gerhard if it doesn't."

"Aye, good … and while you're here," she said. "Brad's looking a bit knackered. I'd say he's got a bug of some kind, but he won't let me put me hand to his head to check for a fever. Talk to him, *da*. Maybe he shouldn't be flying?"

Sam agreed to speak to him and waited for Brad and Larry Schaff to return from the flight planning office. As the two of them entered the airplane, Sam took Brad by the arm and guided him back outside to the landing at the top of the stairs. He looked at Brad closely and said, "Maggie said it looks like you're getting sick. Are you okay?"

"Just adjusting," he replied. "I always get something like this when I first get to the tropics. I'll be alright. I'd rather get back than be stuck here until it clears."

"You're sure? Maggie's a nurse. Why not let her feel your temperature?"

"Don't be ridiculous. What if it's contagious?"

"Then we've all got it already, Brad. Now, c'mon. Let her check your temperature."

Brad shook his head. "No. I want to get out of here. The hotel will have a doc. I'd rather deal with it when we get back. Nothing I can do about it now, anyway."

Sam sighed. "Okay, suit yourself." Then, jutting his chin toward the cockpit to indicate he was asking about Larry, he added, "How's he doing?"

Brad made a face. "You know my concerns, Sam. I've seen nothing to change my mind about it. In the end, it's up to Gerhard. We'll let him make the call."

Sam acknowledged him with a nod.

Changing the subject, Brad asked, "How about Jack? Think he's ready?"

"Yes," Sam answered. "We'll release him for the line tomorrow if you agree."

Brad gave him a thumbs-up. "I owe him an apology," he admitted. "He's sharp. I shouldn't have put him through what I did. A year on the line as a copilot for seasoning and another year with left seat authority, and he'll be ready to upgrade. He'll make a great captain."

Sam clapped him on the shoulder and said, "I agree. Safe trip back, and if you need a few days off, I'll cover for you. We need everyone healthy and on deck. If Philippe doesn't change his ways, I may be sending him home."

"Better you than me," Brad said with a sardonic grin.

Sam smiled, threw him a wave, then jogged down the stairs.

• • •

At 2:10 a.m. local time, Sam was gazing blearily out the windshield, Jack looking just as blearily at the Doppler ticking down the miles, and Buddy ogling an old *Playboy*.

Suddenly, the number two VHF crackled loudly and startled them. "Pan Tropic Three-Eight-Eight … Pan Trop… Seven-Four … you up … over?"

Sam looked across at Jack. "That's Bobby," he said. "They're too far ahead of us for good reception." He picked up his mic and answered, "Go ahead, Bobby. We read you, but you're breaking up. Say again."

"Sam!" he replied. "Sam, we have … situation … over."

Buddy dropped his *Playboy* and rotated his seat to face forward. "Shit. That doesn't sound good," he groaned.

Sam straightened in his seat. "Say again, Bobby. What situation?"

"Brad's out of the seat," Bobby replied. "Maggie has him in the cabin … burning up."

432

Sam grimaced and said, "Put Maggie on, Bobby. Let me speak to Maggie."

Moments later, the radio crackled again. "Sam! It's Maggie … hear me?"

"You're breaking up, Maggie, but go ahead."

"Brad … dengue symptoms … high fever, vomit … swollen glands, confusion, sensitive to … him … cabin … trying … it down."

"Copy, Maggie, copy. Understand Brad's got a high fever, you think it might be dengue, is that correct, over?"

"Yes, possibly dengue … serious. Fever high … delirium … critical care."

"Copy, I copy. Please put Bobby or Larry back on."

A moment later, Bobby's voice came through. "Sam, it's Bobby … ahead."

"Where are you now, Bobby? Have you declared an emergency?"

"Roger, affirmative … two-hundred north … How far … you, how soon … over?"

"About an hour behind you, Bobby. Don't worry about us. Take care of Brad. Do you copy?"

"Roger, roger. Weather building, Sam, but Madras is just as bad … no choice. Tell Larry, no choice!"

"Understand Larry wants to divert to Madras, is that correct?"

"Madras, affirmative, but further away … weather same. Colombo sooner."

"Roger, I agree, Bobby. If the weather's the same, Colombo's the better choice if it's closer. Stay with Colombo, stay with Colombo, do you read?"

"Roger, but Larry says no. Please advise him, over."

"Stay with Colombo if the weather's the same and it's closer. Advise him I said stay with Colombo, over."

There was a pause and then, "Roger. Will proceed Colombo. Pan … Seven-Four-Six, out."

As Sam clipped his mic, Jack said, "I've heard of dengue fever. But I don't recall if it's contagious."

"No. It's vector driven. Mosquitoes," Sam said. He switched his transmitter to HF, turned up the volume, and lifted his mic. Using the company's call sign and their flight number, which they used only when in commercial service, he said, "Bombay, Bombay, Pan Tropic Three-Eight-Eight on one-six, over."

The ARINC radio operator replied with a lilting Indian accent, "Flight calling Bombay, say again, over."

"Bombay, Pan Tropic Three-Eight-Eight requesting current TAFs for Colombo and Madras, over."

"Roger, Pan Tropic. Stand by, Captain. I will call you back."

Sam clicked his mic twice to reply and turned down the volume on the HF.

"Is high fever always an outcome?" Jack asked. "What about those other symptoms?"

"No. Most often it's mild, but it can be serious and even life-threatening. We lost a flight attendant to dengue years ago in the Philippines. If it's dengue and Brad's got a fever high enough to cause confusion, he needs critical care."

The SELCAL chimed and Sam answered the call.

"Roger, Captain. Colombo is currently reporting six hundred broken, one-thousand-one-hundred overcast, one mile, rain, thunderstorms. Wind two-six-zero at one-five. Forecast is for the same until zero-five-zero-zero Zulu. Madras reporting, five-hundred broken, eight-hundred overcast, two miles, light rain, thunderstorms, wind three-four-zero at one-eight, and forecast is the same, over."

"Roger, roger. We copy, Bombay. Pan Tropic Three-Eight-Eight, out."

Sam clipped his mic and said to Buddy, "Push 'em up. Let's move it."

"But we've all had the vaccines," Jack said. "How did he get infected?"

Sam shook his head. "There's no vaccine for dengue."

"What about the quality of medical care in Colombo?" Jack worried. "Everything outside the hotel looks pretty rough. Have you been on the beach at all?"

"Yes. And I take it you have too?"

Jack nodded.

"That's life in some of the places we fly, Jack. Get used to it," Sam said bluntly. "Just be glad we're not in Mali."

. . .

An hour later they were three hundred miles from Colombo when the SELCAL chimed again. Sam looked puzzled, turned up the volume on the HF, and said, "Bombay, Bombay, this is Pan Tropic Three-Eight-Eight, responding to SELCAL, over."

"Roger, Pan Tropic Three-Eight-Eight. Captain, the Colombo airport is currently closed. When ready, I have holding instructions for you, over."

Sam looked at Jack and said, "They must have stopped on the runway to have Brad taken off. That's a good call. I hope it was Larry's." He sighed, lifted his mic, and said, "Roger, Bombay. Ready to copy holding instructions."

"Roger, Captain. Bombay clears Pan Tropic Three-Eight-Eight to hold at Trivandrum on Gulf Four-Six-Two, right hand turns, two-zero-mile legs. Be advised, Captain, that the Colombo airport is closed indefinitely. I do not have an expected further clearance time for you at this time, over."

Sam was unmoved. "That'll change as soon as the runway's clear," he said confidently to Jack. He lifted his mic, replied to the clearance, and asked to be updated the moment more information became available.

. . .

Fifty miles from Trivandrum VOR at the southeastern tip of India, Sam picked up his mic and said, "Madras Control, this is Pan Tropic Three-Eight-Eight approaching Trivandrum to enter holding. Requesting further information regarding the airport closure at Colombo, over."

"Pan Tropic Three-Eight-Eight," the controller replied. "We have no further information, Captain. The airport is closed. Say your intentions, over."

"Stand by," Sam answered. He turned and looked at the fuel gauges, and with his eyes narrowed, he did a quick calculation. Looking at Jack and Buddy, he said, "We'll start heading for Madras. If anything changes and we've got the fuel, we'll reroute to Colombo." He lifted his mic. "Madras, Pan Tropic Three-Eight-Eight, requesting change of destination to Madras, over."

"Roger, Captain. Stand by for clearance to Madras."

· · ·

At 10:40 a.m. local time, the airplane was parked on the ramp at Madras International Airport. The DC-8 was connected to electric and air carts to provide power and air conditioning. The crew had drawn the window shades down to fend off the blazing sun, and Sam set a two-hour-on, four-hour-off watch schedule for himself, Jack, and Buddy so they'd all have a chance to sleep while ensuring the cockpit radios were monitored for any change in Colombo's status. A flight plan had been filed for their return, and the airplane was fueled and ready to depart on a moment's notice.

Sam slept first. After he woke, he checked his watch and became increasingly on edge as the time passed and the airport remained closed. Colombo was a major connector and technical stop for flights from Indonesia during the hajj, and closing it for so long meant something had gone very wrong. He was pacing the cabin with his head down while Jack was on watch in the cockpit and killing the time by perusing Buddy's *Playboy*.

The SELCAL suddenly chimed and startled Jack. He dropped the magazine and picked up his mic to reply as Sam bolted for the cockpit.

"Pan Tropic Three-Eight-Eight," came the operator's reply. "Stand by for phone patch from Miami, over."

Sam burst in, grabbed the mic from the forward jumpseat audio panel, and switched the transmitter selector to HF. He looked at Jack and said, "I've got it."

A moment later, the radio crackled and in a warbling voice dappled by scratches and pops of static came, "Sam … Sam, it's Gerhard, do you read, over?"

Sam was standing as he answered. "Yes, Gerhard, we have you. Go ahead. We read you, over."

There was an anxious pause, Buddy and the girls piling close by the door to listen.

"Sam," Gerhard said, his voice cracking. "Sam, there has been an accident. Brad's airplane has gone down, do you read? There has been an accident, over."

There was a gasp from the girls, and Sam looked back angrily and waved at them to be quiet. Lifting his mic, he said, "We read you, Gerhard. Where was the accident and how severe?"

"On final approach to Colombo, Runway 22. It's bad … very bad," he repeated. "Rescue efforts were delayed by heavy rain and difficult terrain. The airplane went down one mile short of the runway in a coconut plantation. The tower reported seeing the airplane's landing lights through the clouds, but then a large fireball soon after. The rescue crew reported that it had been totally destroyed … Sam … They found some of the crew, but there are no survivors."

A loud cry came from one of the girls. The others had tears in their eyes as they tried to console her.

Sam paused as he digested this, his eyes closed, his head bowed, the other crewmembers looking at him in shock.

"Sam … Are you there?"

Sam's hands were shaking as he lifted his mic. "Yes, Gerhard. I copy. Besides the cockpit crew and Maggie, who were the other flight attendants?"

"Justine Creed, Sharron Bulette, and one of the new girls … Jessica McCormick, over."

At the sound of her name, Jack flinched. He turned to look out the side windshield, dumbstruck. He felt like he'd been shot.

Sam cleared his throat. With his eyes closed, he lifted his mic and said, "I … I copy that, Gerhard, I copy … dear God." He ran his fingers through his hair.

"The airport will reopen soon, Sam. Where are you now, over?"

"We're on the ramp at Madras. We're ready to leave as soon as they release us, over."

"Please do, Sam. I need you back in Colombo and keeping things moving as much as possible. In the meantime, Jimmy Caffaretti and one of Manny's lawyers will be leaving here tomorrow to assist you. I don't have to tell you what is coming both here and there, Sam. The Feds will be all over this. Also, please tell Jack I need him back here at the office as soon as possible to help me through the initial investigation and also with the families. Manny is planning a service for the crew late next week. I'd like Jack to meet arriving family members at the airport, over."

Jack was still staring out the windshield in shock. He wasn't listening.

Sam signed off and clipped his mic. He reached for Jack's shoulder and gripped it gently. "Did you hear that?" he asked. "Gerhard needs your help."

Jack turned to look up at him, his face flush, his eyes welling with tears. "She was my friend," he said, his voice cracking. "Her dad needs her home, Sam. She told me she needs to go home … she was scared she wouldn't go home."

# FIFTY-TWO

*Colombo, Sri Lanka, November 6, 1978*

I t was early Monday morning, and the mood of the crew at the hotel was somber in the wake of the crash. The hajj flights had resumed with the two airplanes that remained, but the prospects of completing the contract in full had greatly dimmed. The NTSB Go Team had been dispatched to Sri Lanka along with members of the FAA, who were scheduled to arrive early that afternoon. The crash site had been secured by the local authorities, and no one from the company had been allowed access, though Sam had tried.

Even more than the others in the crew, Jack's sentiments were dark. Beyond the loss of his friends—and the deep sense of grief he felt for Jessica—Jack grieved for himself. The uncertainty of his future with the company weighed heavily on him. He figured there was small hope Halder would pay for his return to Colombo even if the contract would be finished in full.

On Sunday, Sam told Jack he'd be traveling with him in the van to the airport. Jack was departing that morning for Amsterdam with a connection to Miami. Sam would be meeting the Feds at the airport after Jack departed to assist them as needed in the investigation. Jack was waiting for Sam in the lobby and was taken aback by his appearance when he arrived. Sam looked like he'd aged ten years, and any sense of grief Jack felt for himself disappeared. Of everyone in the crew, no one's loss was greater than Sam's. Maggie was like a daughter.

They boarded the van in silence and continued in silence as it trundled toward the airport, the roads teeming with vehicles and people. Jack was staring glumly out one side window and Sam just as glumly out the other, when suddenly he turned to Jack and said, "Brad told me in Jeddah that he owed you an apology."

Jack looked at him, puzzled.

"He regretted treating you as he did regarding the oral. He said you were sharp, that you'd make an outstanding captain, that you were ready to be released to fly the line—and I agreed."

Jack gave him a thin smile in return and acknowledged what Sam had told him with just a nod.

"Most of us here enjoy flying as both a vocation and an avocation, Jack, and I know that you do too. But to be honest, the very best pilots I've known draw a line between the two. When they come to work, they come with their vocation in mind and leave their avocation at home—and that was Brad. As much as any of us, Brad was aware that rules sometimes had to be bent or broken to make this kind of commercial flying a success. But unlike most of us, Brad took no pleasure in doing that. He did what he had to do and no more."

"Pete Gaides told me something similar," Jack replied.

"We start our career in one place, our passion for flying superseding everything else. But over time, we grow. Our passion for flying remains, but other things hold sway. We want a home, a family, time off for other pursuits, better pay, and—not the least as we age—a sound retirement plan, meaning the money. Bouncing around the world on crazy missions to exotic places has its appeal at twenty-six, but much less at fifty-six—at least for some of us."

A nod as Jack listened to him.

"I don't know where this will lead, Jack. But I'm finished—and now more than ever—when this is done. With Brad gone and Gerhard ready to leave as well, there's no one else to take over. It all turned on Brad."

"I understand."

"Stop by Air Logistics when you get back. Talk to Jake. I'll send him a telegram and give him my recommendation for you, and I'll mention what Brad told me as well. Consider it carefully before you come back here. Consider what I've told you."

With a wan smile, Jack said, "I will, Sam … I truly will. I know in my heart that's sound advice. Thank you for everything you've done for me. And I'm so sorry … so terribly, terribly sorry about Maggie. I can only imagine the pain."

Sam's eyes glistened with tears. He nodded and turned away.

• • •

Late Monday night, Jack was waiting in the terminal for his connection to Miami early the next morning. With time to kill, he used his credit card and a pay phone booth to place a call to Frank at their apartment in Delaware.

"Frank," Jack said when he answered on the fourth ring.

"Jack! Oh, *man!* So cool! Where are you? Are you in *Arabia?*"

"No, actually. I'm in Amsterdam on my way to Miami."

"Really? I thought you said you'd be in Arabia for a long time?"

"Yeah, well … long story. I'll fill you in when I can. But look," Jack said, cutting him off. "I'm on a pay phone, and these international calls are very expensive. I just wanted to check in and see how things are going. It's likely I'll be back there soon."

"*Here?* Oh, man, you know … same ol' shit, I guess. How about you? Have you gotten laid?"

Jack rolled his eyes. "Actually, I did," he deadpanned. "It was Lynda Carter from *Wonder Woman*. She was doing the hajj and decided to do me in the lav instead."

Frank sighed. "Get *out* of here!" he said. "*Really?*"

"These calls are expensive, Frank. How's my car doing? Everything okay? The money I gave you for rent is still good, we're square?"

"Yeah, no problem, man. But hey, sorry, guy. Your car got towed. The super said people were complaining. They said it looked like it was abandoned with that flat and all, so they towed it someplace for storage."

"Ah, *shit*, Frank!"

"Sorry, man. They grabbed it when I was at work."

"Did they say where they towed it?"

"No. But if you want, I'll find out."

"Please do. I'll check back with you soon and give you a number where I can be reached once I'm settled in Miami, okay?"

"Sure, no problem. And oh, hey … I saw that chick Amanda you used to date. Man, she's hot!"

"Glad to hear it. Why don't you ask her out?"

"You think so? *Really?*"

"Sure. If you enjoy sticking pins in your eyes, why not?"

"She's really hot, though."

"I've got to run, Frank. I'll check back with you soon. Take care, okay?"

As Jack reached to hang up the receiver, he heard Frank yell, "Wait, Jack! *WAIT!*"

Jack made a face and put the receiver back to his ear. "What now?" he asked impatiently.

"Sorry, man. I forgot to tell you. There's a letter here. I think it's from an airline."

Jack knitted his brow. "An *airline?* What airline?"

"I don't remember. But it's in the pile of mail I've been putting on your bed. Want me to get it?"

"If it's quick, Frank. These calls are crazy expensive," Jack replied testily.

He heard the receiver hit the floor with a *clunk*, and he winced.

A minute later, Frank was back. "I've got it; I found it," he said. "It's from American Airlines."

Jack scoffed. "Forget it," he said. "It's just another rejection. I get them all the time. Put it back. I'll read it when I get home."

"Okay, I just wanted you to know. Don't want you pissed off that I forgot to tell you something important."

There was silence as Jack closed his eyes. How much more bad news could he bear?

"Jack … Jack, are you there?"

"Yeah, I'm here. Screw it," he said. "Open and read the damn thing. What does it matter?"

The receiver hit the floor again with another *clunk*.

A moment later, Jack could hear the envelope being torn open in the background, and then a letter removed and unfolded. "Huh," he heard Frank mutter moments after that. "Actually … actually this is really …"

"*Frank!*" Jack said loudly into the receiver.

"… really cool," Frank continued.

"*FRANK!!*" Jack yelled.

Frank picked up the phone. "Oh, man, this is—"

"Read the letter, Frank!"

"Sure, man, sure … *geez*. Anyway, what it says at the top is: American Airlines, and under that October 6, 1978. And then it has your name and our address, and then under that—"

"Just read what *FUCKIN' MATTERS!*" Jack yelled at him.

"Hey! Don't be such an *asshole!*"

"Sorry. But please … *please*, Frank. You're killing me here."

"Alright, I'll skip to the chase: 'Dear Mr. Dolan, we are pleased to advise you that you have been selected for Phase I of our pilot selection process. Please call Pilot Recruitment at …'"

Jack's jaw dropped, and he fell back against the wall of the booth. When Frank was finished, Jack fumbled for a pen in his pocket.

His hands trembled as he wrote the number on the palm of his hand and then again on his wrist.

# EPILOGUE

J ack was pulling his bags out of his car when an air horn blasted nearby. There was another blast, Jack winced, and then three more in quick succession. Jack gave an irritated glance at the big yellow flatbed that had stopped in front of his VW.

Ignoring it, he reached back inside to grab his uniform cap, and the truck honked again.

"Hey, you schmuck!" he heard a familiar voice yell. "Get your head out of your ass!"

Jack straightened up and looked toward the cab. "Oh … my … *God*," he muttered and then beamed. A bald stocky guy in coveralls launched out of the truck's door and rushed toward him with his arms spread wide.

"*JACK!*" he shouted. "It's you! It's *you!* I knew it!"

Jack held his arms wide to greet him as they collided.

Joe nearly squeezed the breath out of him as he rocked him side to side. Then, holding Jack at arm's length, he exclaimed, "Well, look at you! Look … at … *you!* American Airlines! Well, ain't you somethin', kiddo!"

Jack returned his smile and said, "You too, Joe. You look terrific!" Then, pointing at the flatbed, where *JOEY's GARAGE* was emblazoned on the door in garish red letters, he asked, "And what's this?"

Joe glanced back. "I bought my uncle out of my pop's business that he screwed up after Pop retired. Fuckin' Italians—nothin's free, know what I'm sayin'?"

Jack laughed and asked, "So, what are you doing here?"

"I got the contract for the employee lot. Mostly flight attendants coming home from trips, dead batteries, flat tires, lockouts, that kind of thing. First time in my life pretty girls are always happy to see me!"

"Oh, I remember some pretty girls who were always happy to see you, Joe!"

He looked sad and shifted his gaze to the middle distance. "Yeah, yeah ... hard to think about, huh?"

"You saw the accident report?"

Joe looked at him like he was nuts. "Who? Me? No," he said. "The hell with that. Fuck the NTSB. What do they know?"

"They know a lot, Joe. They know that the GPWS had been deactivated, and Larry began the descent late and that he continued at a very high sink rate throughout the approach. They know from the CVR transcript that the required callouts for altitude and sink rate weren't made. On top of that, they know the approach lights were out of service and had been for months. And on top of that, they know it was at night, the crew badly fatigued, and thunderstorms blanketed the airport. On top of all *that*, they know the approach was poorly planned, poorly flown, and very rushed, likely due to Brad's pressing need for medical care. But in the end, you're right, Joe. It's what the NTSB didn't know and couldn't know that was the underlying cause of the crash. In the weeks I assisted him after the accident, Gerhard told me Larry was indecisive and didn't handle pressure well. Everyone who'd flown with him knew that, including you. You told me Brad was right about Larry; you told me Larry had issues."

Joe frowned, waved him off, and said, "Whatever. He was family and that comes first. What's done is done." Then, eyeing the wedding band on Jack's finger, he reached for his hand and changed the subject. "Talkin' about family," he said. "What's this?"

"Got hitched," Jack said. "We bought a house on Long Island."

"A flight attendant, huh?"

"No, actually ... a girl I met before I went to Miami. She works for Grumman in Bethpage. She's an aerospace engineer working on her doctorate, and you'll love this, Joe. She's building an airplane in our garage! Can you believe that?"

"*What?* No *fuckin'* way!" Joe exclaimed. "A girl building an airplane? How'd you pull that off, a *schlump* like you?"

Jack shrugged and said, "The Gary method. Works every time."

"The friggin' *who?*"

"Long story."

"So you got kids? She keeping you straight?"

Jack laughed. "Straight?" he asked. "Sure. She tells everyone she's my centerline, and I tell them I'm her wild blue yonder. How's that for a match?"

"It's good?"

"Yeah. Really good. No kids yet, but they'll be coming. She's an Italian girl and wants a mob ... er, a *tribe*, I should say."

"Good for her!" Joe said. "But look," he continued, "I got a girl waiting for a car to be fixed, and you probably have to sign in for your trip, right?"

Jack glanced at his watch and then towards the crew bus entering the parking lot. "Yeah, I have to go too," he admitted.

"Alright. I won't keep you. But hey," Joe said, a finger drilling into Jack's chest. "The little missus is going to want to meet yours, know what I'm sayin'? So no fuckin' around, kiddo. You call me, okay?" Joe reached into his pocket, pulled out a business card, and handed it to Jack. "Use this number," he said. "We got an answering service twenty-four hours a day. And look, you tell your little missus if she ever needs anything— *anything*—workshop-wise to get that airplane together, you come by the garage any Sunday. We'll open it up, take care of whatever she needs. My little missus will make us a pot of sauce, and we'll have a big cook-up when we're done! The girls can talk babies, and you and me can catch up."

Jack smiled and said, "I'd like that, Joe ... I'd like that a *lot*. And hey! Does the little missus have a name?"

Joe looked puzzled. "Of course," he said. "Her name's Angela." And then as it dawned on him, he steepled his hands and said, "But please— *PUH-LEASE*—whatever you do, don't call her Angie! It's Angela ... only *Angela!*" he insisted.

"Got it!" Jack said with a smile. "Angela or little missus it is."

Joe scowled. "That ain't funny!" he snapped. "Now what's yours?"

"Debbie," Jack answered. "Debbie Dolan, poor girl."

Joe turned toward his truck, stopped, and then turned half-back. Pointing at Jack, he demanded, "You call me!"

"I will. Promise."

Joe threw up his arms. "Ah, fuck it!" he exclaimed. "Gimme another hug first."

# ACKNOWLEDGMENTS

*Flying Crooked* was inspired by actual events that I experienced as a young commercial pilot intent on advancing my career in the mid-1970s. Special thanks to my sister-in-law, Elaine Vander Clute, for encouraging me to write this tale during a dinner conversation more than twenty years ago.

I am deeply indebted to my many friends and colleagues who endured my endless revisions. Special thanks to my wife, Jeanne, and my daughters, Kate and Alicia, for their encouragement to see it through as well as my sister and fellow aviator, Colleen Borgess. Also special thanks to my editors—Elaine Vander Clute and Carla Perch, and especially my copy editor, Hannah Morin at Upwork.com—for their sharp eyes, editing skill, and grammatical expertise. Further thanks are due to my many beta readers and avid fans of fiction who guided me in this journey: Jeanne Vander Clute, Kevin Cross, Candy Purcell, John Frost, Jim Hykes, and Paul Glennon.

Any mistakes in the manuscript are entirely my own.

I am also indebted to Stacy Beck, VP of Brands & Licensing at Pan American World Airways, LLC, for permission to use the images drawn from Pan Am DC-8-21 flight manuals.

There were many books I consulted in my research for the novel, but most importantly these:

Prados, John. *Safe for Democracy, The Secret Wars of the CIA.* Ivan R. Dee, 2006.

Mehmet Caner, Ergun. and Emir Fethi Caner, *Unveiling ISLAM.* Kregel, 2002.

Hammoudi, Abdellah. *A Season in Mecca,* Hill and Wang. 2005.

Emerick, Yahiya. *The Complete Idiot's Guide to Understanding Islam.* Alpha, 2004.

Finally, I am deeply grateful to Mr. Robert Graves for his poem *Flying Crooked*, not only for its inspiring title but for his delightful allegory to a life off the straight and level.